THE LAST
CENTURION

BAEN BOOKS by JOHN RINGO

The Last Centurion

Ghost
Kildar
Choosers of the Slain
Unto the Breach
A Deeper Blue

The Legacy of Aldenata Series
A Hymn Before Battle
Gust Front
When the Devil Dances
Hell's Faire
The Hero with Michael Z. Williamson
Cally's War with Julie Cochrane
Watch on the Rhine with Tom Kratman
Yellow Eyes with Tom Kratman
Sister Time with Julie Cochrane
Honor of the Clan with Julie Cochrane

There Will Be Dragons
Emerald Sea
Against the Tide
East of the Sun, West of the Moon

Princess of Wands

The Road to Damascus with Linda Evans

with David Weber:
March Upcountry
March to the Sea
March to the Stars
We Few

Into the Looking Glass
Vorpal Blade with Travis S. Taylor
Manxome Foe with Travis S. Taylor
Claws that Catch with Travis S. Taylor

Von Neumann's War with Travis S. Taylor

THE LAST CENTURION

JOHN RINGO

THE LAST CENTURION

A Baen Books Original

Baen Publishing Enterprises
P.O. Box 1403
Riverdale, NY 10471
www.baen.com

ISBN 10: 1-4165-5553-6
ISBN 13: 978-1-4165-5553-7

Cover art by Kurt Miller

First printing, August 2008

Distributed by Simon & Schuster
1230 Avenue of the Americas
New York, NY 10020

Library of Congress Cataloging-in-Publication Data

Ringo, John, 1963–
   The last centurion / John Ringo.
       p. cm.
   ISBN 1-4165-5553-6 (hc)
   1. Catastrophical, The—Fiction. 2. United States. Army—Officers—Fiction.
I. Title.

   PS3568.I577L37 2008
   813'.54—dc22

                                                        2008010836

10 9 8 7 6 5 4 3 2 1

Pages by Joy Freeman (www.pagesbyjoy.com)
Printed in the United States of America

—•—

To everyone who has ever felt
they were looking out over Hadrian's Wall
while Rome crumbled behind them.

—•—

BOOK ONE

In a Time of Suckage

— CHAPTER ONE —

Days of Wine and Song

Call me Bandit.

Okay, hopefully that's, like, the last time I'm going to make a literary reference. But you never know. Beware . . . bewaaare . . .

There's a bunch of these stories out there now that people are getting back on the Net. I figured, what the hell? I've got one, too. Sure, we all do. But, you know, what the hell?

People started calling it the Hell Times after some pundit was spouting about it on TV. I mean, The Great Depression was taken and they didn't have the Plague or the Freeze thrown on top. I know, it wasn't a plague and all you nitnoids are going to point out that it was some fucking flu virus and plague is bacterial infection and . . . Yeah. I know. Thank you. We ALL fucking know, all right? Christ, there are times you wished it had been targeted at nitnoids. Everybody calls it the Plague, okay? Get over yourself.

Anyway, people call it the Hell Times. I dunno, maybe I've got a better personal fix on hell than they do or maybe I don't. Personally, having been in combat and blown up and shot and seen people I care about blown up and shot and even people I *didn't* particularly care about blown up and shot and having visited a volcano once and thought about what it would be like to spend the rest of fucking *forever* in one, I don't call it the Hell Times. Bad as it was, seems to be an exaggeration. Me? I call it the Time of Suckage.

This is my sucky story about the time of suckage.

So there I was in Iran again, this is no shit... It was my fourth trip to the sandbox in my short years as a soldier. And it was a maximally fucked up tour even before the Time of Suckage. Look, you spend any time as a soldier and you get good chains of command and bad chains of command. Good jobs and bad jobs. You deal. It didn't help that the Prez was a whiny bitch who really wanted us out of there but couldn't figure out how to get reelected *and* stab us in the back. Equipment was short, training was crap, the muj knew all they had to do was hold their ground and we were eventually going to leave.

And boy did we. Not that it helped *them* much, huh? Heh, heh.

Seriously, I met some Iranians (and Iraqis and Afghans) that were pretty decent people. And I'm sorry as hell for what happened to the good people, most of them, that inhabited those countries. But... Ah, hell. I'm getting ahead of myself.

Way ahead.

Maybe I should talk about myself for a bit to give a little context. I was one of the very few remaining farm boys in the Army at the time. Seriously. I mean, most of my troops were from rural areas but that's not, exactly, the same thing as being a farm boy. I grew up on a family farm. Well, I grew up on one of the family farms owned by the Bandit Family Farm Company, LLC.

Wait? LLC? Family Farm? How do those two go together?

Like bacon and eggs, my friends, like bacon and eggs. Forget everything you've seen in a bad movie about family farms. If you're going to survive in *this* economy, you'd better know what the hell you're doing. And I'm not talking some hobby farm where the "farmer" is a construction contractor and has a couple of cows or a chicken house or twain that are some added income. (Or more often a tax write-off.) I'm talking about making *all* your income from farming.

And it's pretty good money if you do it right. Farmers are the richest single income group in the U.S. Were before the Time, during the Time and after. Sure, some of them lost their farms during the Time but damned few. (Except for the Big Grab but I'll get to that.) Smart farmers weren't saddled with killer debt when the Times hit. And, hell, people always got to eat. Sure, there were less mouths to feed but the government was always buying.

Anyway. Grew up on a farm in southern Minnesota near Blue Earth. It was one of nine the family owned in six counties in southern Minnesota. That one was right on two thousand acres, most of it tilled in time. Pretty much the standard rural upbringing. Went to school. (Yes, I *was* captain of the football team.) Played with my friends. Dated girls. (I'm straight for all you pining fags out there.) And did some chores. Yes, I've tossed haybales. But not all that many. Baling is time and labor intensive and thus unprofitable. Better to roll. Takes one guy with a tractor the same time to clear a field of rolls as it takes fifteen guys with bales. Do. The. Math.

Did I ever get up before dawn and milk cows using a bucket and a stool? No. The family owned two cow farms. Both were run by managers. At o dark thirty the cows would walk to the barn and into their stalls. Why? Because they had full udders. Full udders hurt. The cows learned quick that if they walked to the stall the hurt went away. Cows are very dumb (if not as dumb as sheep) but they *can* be trained.

A team of people (usually four) would then hook them up to the milking machines. They'd drink coffee while the cows were getting their udder dump, unhook them, and the cows and crew would then have their breakfast. After breakfast the cows got turned out and most of the crew went off to day jobs. The milk was stored in a steel vat until the truck came by to pick it up and take it to the processing plant. Manager, who was full time, handled that. In the evening, repeat.

Again. Do. The. Math. Forty cows (smaller farm). I milked one cow, once, by hand when my dad made me "familiarize" with it. It took me a good fifteen minutes. Figure an expert can do it in maybe five. Four guys, thirty minutes. Or one guy doing it all damned day. Sure, the equipment's a tad expensive (like a half a million dollars). It's amortized.

Then there's the whole . . . sepsis issue. Look, milking by hand you put *milk* into an *open bucket* in a *stall* that's occupied by a *cow*. Bessy is not, take it from this farm boy, a clean creature. Bessy's tail hangs down the same spot her poop (which is mostly liquid) comes out. Bessy walks in her poop. Flies surround Bessy like politicians at an all-you-can-steal lobbyist giveaway.

Milk is also a prime food for just about *anything*. Including bacteria.

We had no interest in being in the news as the evil farm corporation that killed x thousand customers from salmonella or some shit.

Doing it by hand spells "Going Out Of Business." We liked our farm(s). We wanted to keep being farmers. We did it the smart way.

That extended to everything. Look, combine harvesters are very expensive. The flip side is, the bigger they are the more expensive they get *but* the more economic they are. So bigger, in general, is better.

However, some of our fields were too small for the really big combines. And a combine only makes its money a couple of weeks out of the year. Harvesting is about it.

There are companies that do that shit. Since harvests, for really obvious reasons, don't happen everywhere all at once, they move around harvesting and planting. Most of the guys doing the actual work were from South Africa or Eastern Europe. (Mexicans never got in on that racket. Not sure why.)

We had a couple of small combines (price tag right at a quarter mil a pop) to do some of the smaller fields and cleanup. For the main harvesting, Dad would arrange, like a *year* in advance, to get the combine company to come in.

Farmers are planners. The Big Chill and the Big Grab really fucked with us but it was fucking with *everybody* so I'll get to that later. Adapt, react and overcome ain't just a Marine motto. Of course, the Time of Suckage proved that it just might be an exclusively *American* motto and at the time confined to a relatively small fraction. Insert sigh here.

So. Grew up on a farm. Maximum suckage once a year picking rocks. (Another essay.) Went to college (UM, Farmington) on a football scholarship. Got cut sophomore year.

Dad had a college fund for me but . . . Well, if I dipped into it for, you know, tuition and books it really cut into my discretionary income. The insurance for a twenty-year-old on a Mustang GT-175 is *not* cheap. And buying the ladies *nice* dinners tends to get you laid more than McDonalds dinners do. I did *not* want my discretionary income tapped.

ROTC was just sitting there. Most of my family had been Navy. (Don't laugh. I think most of the Navy is crewed by Midwesterners.) But there wasn't a Navy ROTC program. So I went Army.

Okay, yes, there was a war on. But, again, I did the math. Death rates in that war were pretty much on a par with death rates during previous peacetimes. Don't believe me? Check the figures yourself, I'm not going to hold your hand. But it's true. And death rates among combat forces were not significantly higher than in the *Navy*. Being at sea is an inherently dangerous process. Lots of people die from accidents. Most of the people dying in the *Army* were from accidents.

And ... Oh, hell. Yes, okay. I did have a "desire to serve in combat." Call me stupid. My life, my choice. I wanted to go over and fight. Look, I was twelve when those bastards hit the Twin Towers. I watched those clips over and over just like the rest of you. I knew I didn't want to cruise around on a ship. I wanted to fight. Insert appropriate lines from "Alice's Restaurant" here.

So I went ROTC. Got my degree and my brown bars the same day. Went off to Infantry Officer Basic Course. Which *sucked*. At the time it was my definition of suckage.

Got sent to the 3rd ID in Savannah. Which wasn't a bad place to be for a junior officer with a decent stipend from my shares in the corporation. All I had to do was put up with the bullshit aspects of the Army for six years, go get my Masters in Agronomy and I'd be manager on one of the satellite farms until Dad retired. I was shooting for the mixed crop farms near Hanska. The walleye fishing on Lake Hanska was great and we owned a couple of cottages over there. And since the Hanska manager was in charge of ensuring the upkeep of the cottages ...

And then we did our first deployment. And, oh, hell, I enjoyed it. Yes, I lost two troops to sniper fire, James Adamson and Litel Compson. They were good guys, both of them. Damned fine troops. I could talk about both of them all day.

But we were doing a tough job in a tough environment. Even with the support of the Iranian government, there were lots of people who really wanted the mullahs back in power. Not going to do an essay on that, this is about the Time of Suckage. We did our job and as a guy in charge of making sure that everything went right, well, for a first deployment I didn't do too bad. Farmers are planners; the CO and my platoon sergeant (Sergeant First Class Clovalle (pronounced "Clo-Vail") Freeman) didn't have to tell me about planning to prevent piss poor performance. And, hell, I always got along with people. I liked my troops and vice versa. Mostly. There's always a few assholes.

But for a first time deployment as a cherry LT I didn't do too bad. And my OER more or less said the same thing. (Actually, it sounded like I was fucking Napoleon but the decent ones always do. That got explained to me in detail.)

I was doing good work and doing it well. Frankly, that first deployment made me rethink the whole Hanska Plan.

Back we went to Savannah. I got promoted to 1LT and went off to Advanced Course. It sucked but not as bad as IOBC. Then I went to Ranger School and got a new appreciation for maximal suckage. (Edit by wife: The author of this is too humble to admit he got Distinguished Honor Graduate in Infantry Officer's Advanced Course and Honor Graduate in Ranger's School. He's an idiot but I love him.) Oh, sure, I like a challenge as much as the next over-testosteroned young idiot. But Ranger School wasn't a challenge in any way except staying awake. It was just suckage, day in and day out.

Oh, yeah, and I went to Jump School right after IOAC. Forgot about that until I remembered the maximally suck jumps in Ranger's School. Jump School, these days, just *tries* to suck.

When I got back we were getting ready for another deployment. I was too senior for a line platoon, it wasn't time to rotate the Mortar Platoon leader and I was too junior for XO. So I got stuck in battalion in the S-3 (Operations) shop.

There are jokes about Fobbits. Those are the guys who stay in the Forward Operations Base. Dude, all I'll say is that I'd much rather be out doing patrols than stuck in the fucking FOB. FOB duty is boring *and* stressful. There are more PTSD cases among Fobbits than line troops.

(Of course, most Fobbits are REMFs who wanted to avoid being shot at so they got a job that didn't involve shooting. There was one MI guy who had a nervous breakdown about once a week and had to go get "counseled" in a rear area. Smart guy, seemed to really want to do the job, just *did not* have the constitution for it. Can't even call him a coward, just . . . didn't have the constitution.)

Not being out where you could actually *do* something was the worst part. No, the worst part was constantly having to work with Fobbits. No, the worst part was the S-3 who was a dick and incompetent to boot. No, the worst part . . . Damn, there are *so* many worst parts. The tour was maximum suck. Hanska here I come.

Back at Savannah we're doing all the shit that soldiers do when they're not fighting. I'm still in the 3 shop (new S-3 thank God and Major Clark was a real mentor during this period, wish we'd had him in Afghanistan) and we're in charge of making sure everybody gets trained back up to standard. Look, sure, combat experience is important and there are things you learn in combat you can't learn anywhere else. But ... There are things you forget in combat, too. Things that you could have used. But guys build up a small skill-set that works to carry them through. Getting them to learn a couple *more* skills on top of that skill-set is a *good* thing.

Okay, and we had to fill in all the fucking check boxes of some Pentagon weenie who'd sort of heard there was a war on but needed to justify his existence by creating check boxes for us to fill. Yes, that's a lot of it.

And we had a big part in making sure all the equipment that had gotten fucked up on deployment got unfucked. That was mostly my stuff and Jesus there was a lot of stuff to unfuck. And find. And then admit had disappeared and do reams of paperwork explaining *why* it had disappeared. I'd say "in triplicate" but most of it was electronic. We had to *file* in triplicate, though. Thank *God* I had a clerk for that. Rusty was a fine guy for a Fobbit.

I'd done extra staff time. Either because of that or because the battalion commander liked my winsome good looks I got the battalion Scout Platoon. Honestly, with the way that we worked it wasn't much different from having a line platoon. But the battalion had started to use the Scouts as sort of an integral special operations unit. When there was a high value operation to perform (like capturing a particularly bad boy) and the fucking SEALs or Rangers or Delta or SF were otherwise busy sharpening their knives or taking pictures of themselves doing push-ups we got to kick the door.

It was a very hoowah fucking time for me. We went back to the Sandbox, this time to Iraq which was still having trouble over by Syria, and we got to kick a lot of doors. The "real" spec-ops guys were busy in Iran and Afghanistan. They didn't care that various Sunni countries (Cough! Cough! Saudi Arabia! Cough! Cough! Syria!) were still funneling weapons, money and personnel into Iraq. The news cameras were all in Iran so naturally that's where SOCOM went.

They didn't, per se, end up on the news. But I took a little tour of the Delta Compound one time, (Okay, okay, I was being recruited, I'll admit it) and there were some very interesting news articles pinned up in cases with small comments underneath like "Detachment One, Alpha Squadron."

Now, don't get me wrong. The SOCOM guys are good folk who do a hard job. But, come on, it's like anything else. When they're looking for a guy to promote or give a special (i.e. interesting) job, they're going to remember the guys who did their job very quietly but also did it well enough that they ended up, unmentioned, in the news. Take the capture of Mullah Rafaki. Sure, supposedly it was 4th ID that got him. Nope. It was really a team of SEALs. And those guys are still unable to pay for their bar tab, not to mention the platoon leader is getting fast-tracked to lieutenant commander.

The point being, CNN and company were in Iran. Iran was the happenin' spot. We were in a backwater in Iraq which was, to most of the world, a done deal.

The downside? Nobody knew we were still fighting in Iraq and you had to explain it over and over and over again. The upside? Dude, I was the *Scout Platoon Leader.* Platoon leaders are supposed to sit back and direct. I did that. Sure. Absolutely. That's where I got these damned scars from a door charge I (very stupidly) got too close to. But we still did the house and pulled the bad-guys. Who? Me do a door? No, Colonel, of *course* I didn't do the door.

Very hoowah time. Rule One (no drinking, "fraternization" or pornography) was still in effect. Nobody paid a damned bit of attention to it. I was still an officer. I practically fucking *lived* with my grunts. We ran together, fought together, drank together and . . . Okay, there was a degree of fraternization on that one trip up to Kirbil. With girls. Hookers. Let me make it clear that we were *not* fraternizing with each other.

Good days, good days.

And back to Savannah. And I made captain on the "short list" and I got a company. Bravo called "The Bandits." Six is the military designation for "commander." Ergo, I became Bandit Six and have used it as a handle any time I can get away with it since.

Now, taking over a company when you've never been an XO is a bit of an adjustment. I got my first "does not quite walk on water but can negotiate the top of mud" evaluation during my first eval period as CO. Deserved it. I was not succeeding in my primary tasks. Some personal issues but I was not succeeding.

I begged forgiveness and, even more, begged help. I'm not good at asking for advice. I'd gotten used to asking NCOs what they thought and then using it or not. But going to the battalion commander (Lieutenant Colonel Nick Richards, good guy) and admitting I was getting a bit lost in the swamps as a CO was hard.

He didn't kick my ass for it, though. He just gave suggestions. And they were very good suggestions. I got better very fast. (Getting over the personal issues helped. Okay, yeah, they involved a girl and no she did not get pregnant but thank God we also did not get married is all I'll say.)

The company considered me a bit rocky when we deployed but we sort of mutually got over that in the Rockpile. My performance was coming up even before deployment and, hell, I *like* deployments. I'd finally gotten over my tendency to (badly) micromanage the company. Just in time, too, because I was not going to be a Fobbit on deployment if I could help it. I did help it.

God forgive me for what I put my driver through, though. You see, I'd have at any time two or three things going on at once out in the boonies. In different areas. Most of the unit would travel fairly heavy, at least a platoon. I wanted to see all of it and especially when the shit was hitting the fan. So myself, my driver and two RTOs (actually, Bobby and Buddy were my bodyguards) would go raring off across a fairly questionable to hostile Kandahar Province countryside, mostly by ourselves. Occasionally this involved stopping and paying a visit to one of the local "friendlies." I put the quotes on it because you never knew until you pulled up (and sometimes not even then) if they were friendlies *today*.

Occasionally it involved attempts by unfriendlies to stop *us*.

Lord love my boys. They never seemed to tire of bailing the CO out of a firefight. Probably because they were trying to catch up. And they never seemed to tire, either, of being in the middle of a firefight and "Bandit Six" suddenly roaring in to jump in the fight. Days of wine and song.

(Wife's Edit: Sigh. "Attention to Orders. *Bandit Six* is hereby awarded the Distinguished Service Cross for conduct above and beyond the call of duty in actions in Kandahar Province, Afghanistan, on March 15th, 2017.

"While travelling to meet with local friendly tribal leaders, *Bandit Six* was informed that a small group of Special Operations personnel had been ambushed and were pinned down by local Taliban related forces. Without any regard to personal safety, *Bandit Six* immediately ventured to the area of combat and closed with the Taliban forces. His personal vehicle damaged by concentrated rocket propelled grenade fire which injured both his radio telephone operator and himself, *Bandit Six* exited the vehicle and engaged the enemy with his personal weapon. With the support of continued machine-gun fire from his damaged vehicle, directed by hand and arm signals, *Bandit Six* advanced upon the enemy ambush location and using concentrated fire, the expenditure of all of his personal store of grenades and person-to-person combat skills, *Bandit Six* turned the flank of the enemy position. During the process of the advance *Bandit Six* was wounded three times but continued to move forward expeditiously against the numerically superior Taliban forces until they retreated from their positions. Upon analysis of the combat the relieved special operations unit commander credited *Bandit Six* with over twenty (20) personal kills including more than six (6) due to knife and bayonet.

"Entered service in the Armed Forces from Minnesota." End Wife Edit. I swear, he drives me nuts sometimes.)

— CHAPTER TWO —

I Was and Am an Idiot

And then we were back in Savannah. About halfway through our "Stateside deployment" Colonel Richards left and we had a new BC.

Okay, here's the skinny. I can get along with just about anybody. I'm a very laid-back guy in most ways. It is rare that I deal with somebody that I just *cannot fucking stand* and the feeling is mutual.

Mitigating circumstances. It didn't help that the new BC was a long-term Fobbit. He'd never led so much as a platoon in the Sandbox and we were scheduled to go back to AOR Iran. Not only Iran but Fars Province, which was the center of the Resistance. It was going to be a very fucking hot deploy.

Here he was, knowing everyone was looking at him, like, "who the fuck are *you* to be leading this battalion in combat?" And there was Bandit Six grinning and spoiling for a fight.

The problem being my time was up as CO. Up or out, baby, up or out. They only give you so many days of wine and song in the Army and mine were about over. Oh, I wasn't up for the ultimate butt-fuck, being promoted to major (the one shittiest rank in the Army) and having my mandatory lobotomy performed. But I was looking at doing more staff time. Look, I can do staff work. But it doesn't mean I *like* doing it.

But there's staff work and there's staff work. Now, adjutant fucking sucks as a job. But it's a good position for a guy like me. It looks good on your military resume if you will. Assistant S-3. Better position for my interests and looks almost as good as Adjutant. Brigade S-3 (Air). These are good positions career-wise.

Fucker stuck me in S-4. I nearly threw a shit-fit. I probably should have. It looked like I was a fuck-up. *Nobody* goes from company command to S-4 unless they've fucked up. He might as well have sent me over to Protocol Office at Corps. No matter *what* my fucking OERs looked like, it was going to hang over my head for the rest of my career.

So I deployed to the Fars op as an S-4 weenie. The actual S-4 was a major and a total luzer. I mean with a capital L. Even getting ready for deployment, even on deployment, doing his job wasn't hard. Trust me, I did it. *He* sure as hell couldn't and *somebody* had to make sure the battalion had beans and bullets. (Not to mention batteries, water, fuel . . .) But it wasn't fucking hard.

That was sort of why I didn't throw a shit-fit. I threw myself on the grenade instead. The BC sweet talked me into the position. Manipulated me was more like it. "We're going over to Iran. The S-4, who I can't get rid of, is not going to do the job we need, the *battalion* needs. I need somebody there I can trust."

I hadn't realized what a back-stabbing prick the BC was at the time or I would have swallowed my care for the battalion, which was high, and told him to stick it. But I sucked it up and saluted and went to do the job.

Here's the thing. Remember what I said about that first OER. If your OERs don't make you seem like the reincarnation of Scipio Fucking Africanus it's a death knell to your career. Bad enough that I went from company commander to S-4. There are ways to write an OER for that position that make you seem like, at least, the Scipio Africanus of Supply Officers.

"During this period *Bandit Six* performed his duties in a manner which was fully acceptable . . . " is not one of them.

• But what do you do? Go screaming about "fully acceptable"? The fact was, I'd done my duties in way that was "fucking outstanding." I was doing the job of *my superior* the whole fucking time. It wasn't a hard job, but it also was well above my paygrade and in a field that was radically different from mine.

I knew my fucking career was toast if I didn't get some sort of positive movement after the deployment. I reconsidered the Delta offer. They could smell bullshit in an OER and I knew I had to wait until I was Captain Promotable to go Over the Wall.

Of course, Selection was maximum suckage and the training period took out almost everybody that made it through qual. But I figured I was the best fucking infantry captain in the Army. I could make it into Delta. Which would wipe out "commander to S-4" not to mention "fully acceptable."

Then I got an e-mail from my dad. When I'd been a Fobbit in the 3 shop I barely could keep up with home. I was working my ass off eighteen hours a day, seven days a week. As "assistant S-4" I'd considered starting a blog. God knew I had the time.

I don't know if you remember, I don't know if you realize it, but both bits of news hit the same week. Most people didn't notice the one my dad sent me for months. But it was reported the same week.

The article my dad sent me was from a British source. See, there was this solar physicist in Britain who had sort of gotten out of the solar physics field and entered the long-range forecasting field. Weather, that is. We all know, Lord God do we know, that all that baloney about "greenhouse gases" and "man-induced global warming" was so much horse shit. But back then it was all "global warming! CO2 will kill us all!" Man, we *wished* we'd had that sort of CO2, didn't we?

But the thing about this guy, don't recall his name, was that he did long-range weather forecasts based on solar activity. He'd studied the sun until he should have been blind and had figured out that just about everything related to the sort of weather farmers cared about came down to solar output. Forget CO2, it was all the sun. We all know that now. Most of you probably know who I'm talking about. Damn, why can't I remember his name?

Anyway, Dad sent me this article. It was complicated. I had to dredge up some long-stored memories from my "Weather and Agriculture" classes but I finally figured it out. Basically, the guy was being very cautious in saying that Our Friend the Sun had turned off.

Oh, not completely. But his predictions were way more cautious than normal and just fucking dismal for the next growing season. He even put a caveat in the end. I recall it to this day.

"Based upon these indicators, NYP (Next Year Predictions) indicate significant chance of severe cooling regimes."

Severe cooling regimes. That would be 2019. *Nobody* has to be reminded about 2019.

And then there was Dad's note at the end. "Investing heavily in triticale."

For all you non-farmers and non-*Star Trek* buffs, triticale is rye. See, there's a couple of things about rye. The first thing is that it's not exactly a big need crop. Wheat? Lots of markets for wheat. Ditto corn. (Maize to you Europeans and Canoe-Heads.) Soy? Always good markets for soy. Beans of various sorts. Peas. We grew it all, even seasonals like broccoli. All good markets.

Rye is a niche market. Not a bunch of people lining up for rye. (Didn't used to be back then. Less so now, too. Thank God we're past eating nothing but rye bread from the lines, huh?)

But the main thing about rye is that it grows fast and is cold hardy. Winter wheat's cold hardy but ... Oh, it's complicated. There's also only so much winter wheat market and it's touchier than rye in certain cold and wet conditions. Look, I'm a professional. Do not try this at home.

Bottomline? Dad trusted this guy enough to be prepared to take a *big* hit economically on the basis that that was going to be the only way to survive.

Farmers are planners.

I looked at it and shrugged. "How bad could it be?"

Well, we all know *that*, don't we? I thought I was a grown-up. What a fucking maroon. You're about to find out how much of a fucking maroon I was in those days. (Still am I'll admit. But at least now I know it.)

The next day was the Battalion Weekly Reorientation Exercise. It says a lot about our battalion commander that he couldn't call it a Battalion Command and Staff Meeting or even a Battalion Weekly Meeting.

I'd been an assistant S-3 and a company CO under previous battalion commanders. I knew the weekly staff meeting like the inside of my mouth. That was until this dickbreath came along. Weekly staff meetings, are, by and large, ritual dick-beating exercises. Everyone stands up and presents their action items for the previous week, completion function thereof and action items for the upcoming week, schedule thereof. They're actually necessary but God *damn* they're a pain.

My previous COs had been big on maximal info, minimal dick-beating.

Not so the new guy. If the previous meetings had been, say, a Catholic High Mass of dick-beating, this guy was full up Aztec Sun Day ritual dick-beating with a cast of thousands and everyone has to give up their still beating heart. The best and the bright-est were flayed and he wore their skin around for the next week. I thought when I was a CO I'd had a little micromanagement issue. I grew to understand a whole new term under this CO. One staff meeting the motherfucker took, I shit you not, *four hours* to "properly implement" issue of *bottled fucking water*. It was like he simply could not let it go. Look, you take the number of troops in a unit, add ten percent and send them that much fucking water. It's not rocket science.

At one point the Adjutant, the motherfucker who had my job and who had his office right outside the BC's so that he could slip in there from time to time and give the colonel a right nice sucking, suggested implementing issue based on individual body mass.

Body mass. He wanted his clerks to compile all the *weights* of the guys in the unit and issue water based on that. Potentially with each "aqueous packet" being detailed to individuals.

Dude, I'm a big lad. There was one of my troops when I had that platoon on the first deployment who was a fucking shrimp. Barely over minimum height and they had him on the weight control program to get his weight *up*. Drank about three times as much as me. I didn't get heat stroke, he didn't die of dihydro-genmonoxide poisoning.

Two bottles per head, four bottles per head, six bits a dollar. I don't give a rat's ass. Pass the fucking water out and let's be DONE.

Speaking of not being able to let it go.

The point is, what had been a two to three hour meeting now had to be scheduled for most of the fucking day. And I'm not talking about starting after 0900. I'm talking about from "cain see to cain't see."

It was late afternoon. We'd eaten MREs in the meeting for lunch. My tummy was rumbling. I wanted nothing more than to go back to my hooch, put in my iPod and wash this day out of my brain.

And it got up to the battalion surgeon's presentation.

The guy practically sprang to his feet. I'd noticed he looked as if he had to piss his pants all day long. Usually he sort of checked out like the rest of us. But he'd been practically bouncing in his chair, like, *all fucking day*. When the XO pointed to him he bounced up like a fucking land-mine. I actually tried to pay attention.

"We've got an important directive from the Chief of Staff," he said.

"The Med Branch chief of staff?" the CO asked.

"No, sir," the captain said. "It was sent *through* Med Branch *from* the Chief of Staff of the Army. The Chief of Staff's portion is two lines. I'd like to read it and then expand."

"Go," the colonel said pompously.

"'Indicators indicate significant outbreak of Human-to-Human transmission of H5N1 virus in China Operational Zone. Begin immediate Type Two immunization procedures for all DOD and affiliated personnel in your AOC upon receipt of vaccines. End.'"

H-Five-N-*Motherfucking*-One. I snorted and went back to sleeping with my eyes open.

Th-th-th-that's right, people. I got two months advanced warning of what was about to occur. With both the Great Cold and the motherfucking Plague. Two. Months.

And I went back to sleeping with my eyes open.

Okay, here's a few of the things going on here. Item the first: The Battalion Surgeon.

Now, the guy had a set of brass ones. I knew that, intellectually. We'd been over there long enough, and soaked up enough casualties, that he'd been out there with his teams keeping them alive. The line commanders thought he walked on water. If I'd been a line commander I probably would have thought he walked on water.

But.

The guy was just a geek. Look, I never beat up the geeks in school, not even when I was a kid, and I tried to stop it when I got to where people listened to me. But that didn't mean we were pals. Some of them thought we were *because* I stopped it. They were like the adjutant, I swear. Bottomline: I don't talk geek; they don't talk me. I can pick up most of what they say. I'm not stupid. I just don't get off on what they get off on.

And the battalion surgeon was the geek's geek. Rumpled uniform, glasses, pens sticking out any which way, that geek scrunch. Social skills? The guy couldn't get laid in a Bangkok brothel if he was holding a billion dollars in small bills. Balls the size of the great pyramids, total fucking Grade-A-Number-One geek.

He flapped his hands when he talked. I don't mean used his hands to talk. When he got excited, which was often if he wasn't cutting on somebody, he held both hands out bent inwards at chest height and flapped them like he was trying to take off.

Geek.

I tuned him out. It was that or grab his extremely good surgeon's hands and rip them off at the wrists. It drove me fucking nuts.

I did, however, check back in when he said "Experimental polycoat serum . . . "

Wait, what was that? Back up . . . retrieving voice file . . . processing . . .

"Wait," I said, sitting up. "They're not using us for guinea pigs *again*?"

"Yes, it is experimental . . ." the surgeon said.

"Oh, no," I replied. "No fucking way. Anybody recall the studies on the anthrax cases? I don't want to have Alzheimers at forty. Besides, most flu vaccines don't even *work*!"

"It's an order, Captain," the CO said, angrily. "And you *will* carry it out."

"May I explain, sir?" the PA asked.

Now, the physician's assistant was a captain, too, but he had all the right merit badges. He'd been a medic before going to the Dark Side and got his combat medic's badge. He spoke the language of the grunt. He was asking the CO but I knew he was asking me as well.

I let the CO nod. Hell, he thought it was his battalion, why not?

"Getting the Type Two polycoat immunization serum, if we *do* get it, is a very good thing, sir," Warrant Lomen said. "H5N1 is a slippery sucker if you don't mind my putting it that way. The standard serum attacks binding sites. H5N1 has been shown to have mutated binding proteins. What that means, sir, is that some variants of H5N1 may be resistant to the standard immunization. The Type Two is actually a broad-spectrum flu vaccine that detects flu protein coats across almost the full spectrum, possibly the entire spectrum, of flu viruses. Thus the mutated binding sites become unimportant. What that means is that we're more protected. Yes, it's experimental. I've seen the raw reports on it and they all look quite clean. I wish they'd fast-tracked it; as it is most civilians won't be getting it and that could mean significant public health issues."

("Significant public health issues" I'm putting that down for the classic, all time, there is nothing to top it, understatement of all time. I know I repeated all time. How many of you *dis*agree?)

"Bandit Six, I take it that resolves your issues?" the CO said.

"Mitigates, sir," I replied. "But it's going to be hell to sell to the troops. I still don't like it."

That's right people, we got the good stuff. We got it two months before the Great Outbreak. And I was *bitching* about it. I was *BITCHING* about it.

Fuck.

Fuck that person. Me I mean. The person I was then. The lame-brain fucking maroon I was then. That know-it-all, I can lick the world person. Even now, thinking back, I just want to fucking cry.

The only important part of the meeting, which I mostly still tuned out, continued when Bravo spoke up.

"Is there any supplementary information besides the Chief of Staff's order?"

Bravo had been one of my JOs and, thus, was a good guy. Otherwise he'd never have gotten a company. I did not let cock-ups get ahead. It also meant he was not one of the BC's ass-buddies like Alpha. But it was a germane question.

"There's a WHO bulletin indicating a possible human-to-human outbreak in Western China," the WO said. "But that's all we've got and it's currently unconfirmed. CDC has not issued a warning."

Look, I'm not sure who all is going to read this. So I'm probably going to be covering stuff that most of my readers know. Little kids (sorry about the language) might not be as up on it. Hell, maybe nobody will read it, but I feel like I need to include stuff that about anybody knows. Like the story of Jungbao and how people viewed flus in *those* days.

Hardly anybody knew much about the World Health Organization in those days. I sure as hell didn't give a rat's ass about them. The WHO was just another nongovernmental organization that occasionally got in the way of soldiers doing their jobs. I didn't see, didn't care about, the WHO reporters in foreign lands. Or that their job was to be soldiers on the front lines of the battle against disease. Disease was licked. That was most people's attitude. Sure, some people had gotten scared into a frenzy over this "bird flu" thing. But they were just the usual sort of "I'm afraid of everything" idiots. That's what most of us thought. You got the flu, you felt sick for a couple of days and you got better. Flu didn't kill anyone.

Hard to believe, now, I know. But that's how we thought. That's how *I* thought.

— CHAPTER THREE —

Three Sentences All Alike in Fuckedup'edness

That was the other part of my mostly going back to sleep. You see, I was (and am to a lesser extent) a skeptic. Global warming, resource depletion, all the rest of the mantra the left constantly used to scare us. It went in one ear and out the other. If somebody told me the sky was falling, I wouldn't look up.

This time I got hit in the head by a chunk of sky. But I wasn't the only one.

Here's what was really happening as we can see with blisteringly clear twenty-twenty hindsight.

In a town called Jungbao, a lot of people suddenly got sick. Really, really incredibly sick. Dying sick. There's all sorts of estimates. Jungbao is about the only place that people are starting to open up the mass graves to get a count. And what exactly happened might never be known. Currently, the best estimates I've found go like this:

A lot of people got sick. The local medical boss, who was a WHO reporter, contacted Beijing with his estimate that H5N1 had become human to human transmissible and had, possibly, become more lethal. He wanted to report it to the WHO. He was told to hold the fuck on.

Back then there were about a billion and a quarter Chinese under a government that was still officially Communist (more like fascist but that's another essay) and pretty repressive. China, for a lot of reasons (another essay) tended to be where major illnesses first broke out. And the Chinese government found this embarassing.

I know. The kids who grew up in this post-Plague chilly world think that I've got to be shitting. I'm not. The Chinese government was not up on telling the WHO that bird flu was now human transmissible and that a lot of people were dying of it in Jungbao.

So what did they do? Well, as far as anyone can tell, they sent in the Army. It had orders to cordon off the area and prevent anyone from leaving. They also sent in, slowly, more doctors and "began official examination of the nature of the events in the Jungbao area." That last is from a document found in one of the offices that the historians are starting to pick over. There's just so damned much and so few experts who speak Chinese to do it at this point that the record's barely starting to firm up. But that looks like what happened.

Well, here's the thing. If you don't directly know what bird flu is like when you get it, you've got somebody who has told you the tale. If you don't know, you're a kid. (Sorry about the language. That's how soldiers are.) Probably it's been described to you by your mom or step-mom who freaks out totally when your fever goes up a single point.

But these guys had never seen it. They sent in the Army, cordoned off the area, started rounding people up for examination. And the soldiers weren't vaccinated.

Seems like a no-brainer, right? Well, the Chinese, individually, are smart as whips. Before the flu and maybe more since, those that are still alive. But their fucking government at the time? Serious fucking idiots.

Call it denial. Most of the guys running the government were old. They didn't want to admit that bird flu was breaking out and things were going to change. They didn't want foreigners poking around in their country and examining the realities of Chinese peasant life. (Which sucked then and sucks more now.) They wanted things to stay the same.

So they sent in the soldiers, who weren't vaccinated. And they got sick. And the survivors or the sick but mobile, started fleeing the area. Including some of the soldiers (maybe all of them, we're not sure).

That was about the same time we got our warning order from the Chief of Staff.

Now, things generally don't work really fast in the military. I mean, if it's a combat op, it goes really fast. But things like world-wide distribution of immunizations? I figured it would take a year.

It wasn't all that long, but it was nearly three weeks before we got our shipment. By then, the WHO was on the scene in Western China and it was getting harder and harder for the Chinese government to cover up what was, and is, the biggest disease outbreak in the history of mankind. The news media still wasn't in the area but they were reporting second- and third-hand stories of mass deaths.

And we mostly blew it off. Why? Because "if it bleeds, it leads." The twenty-four-hour news cycle had gotten so competitive that even the most minor thing in those days, say a tornado in Kansas, which is about as "irregular" as blowing your nose, suddenly became the first sign of the End of Civilization! "Tornado in Kansas! THE WORLD IS COMING TO AN END!"

Call it the "Cry Wolf" syndrome. You all know the fable. Well, the news media had predicted so many ends of civilization they were about as well regarded in that area as a guy on a street corner holding a sign saying "The End Is Coming!" (Possibly a metaphor that won't work for the younger generation since, well, street people . . . Nuff said.)

Having said that, they also sort of soft-pedaled it. Basically, they were having a hard time believing the second- and third-hand reports. The only first-hand really good sources were the WHO guys who were having a hard enough time surviving much less talking to the news media. And the WHO brass were . . . well, brass. Top officials don't say things like "Look, people, this is the fucking end, okay? Flee to the hills! I'm out of here, you can stay here and die if you want!"

Honestly, the WHO might have had a chance if the Chinese had worked with them. Might. Maybe. Probably not but . . . Alternate histories.

Anyway, the news media was getting reports of "thousands dead." But they couldn't get camera crews into the area, or even guys with pencils and papers. People were streaming out of Western China but they had to avoid the roadblocks. Which meant they weren't exactly hunting up reporters; they were trying to stay away from the soldiers who were trying to stop them and get ahead of the Plague. (Good luck on that one, sucker. NOBODY got ahead of the Plague. We're only on *one fucking planet.*) A few of them went to reporters but when they said "everyone in my village is dead, thousands are dead..." Well, if you want to run a story like "thousands dead" you need one or two of a few things. You need someone you trust to eyeball it, like one of your own reporters. Or you need a government official to say it. If even the WHO had said it, people would have believed it. The WHO, though... Well, they were brass. They were getting sporadic reports from their hard-core and trustworthy guys that lots and lots and lots of people were dying.

From one of the few reports the WHO has made public:

"Entered village of Kai-Ching on 28th. Village abandoned. No live personnel save myself and driver. In one-hour period counted sixty-three bodies in early stages of decomposition. Found one large grave, unable to assess contents in any reasonable time. Primary site, Pou-Chin, not allowed access."

And there's another thing. So there's one village that's got sixty-three dead people in it. That's bad, don't get me wrong. But... It's not thousands dead. And even looking at a map, getting more and more reports, a hundred here, fifty there... It was hard for anyone to truly comprehend and say "This is the Big One." Actually, they *were* saying that, internally, but they didn't want to panic people.

The U.S. government has their own people for assessing this stuff. CDC and the USAMRIID (United States Army Medical Research Infectious Investigations Department) and Army Medical Resource and Materiel Command are tied into the WHO like arteries are tied to veins. Many of the WHO respondents were U.S. government personnel. And they were reporting back to the U.S. (This is, by the way, one of the reasons that the Chinese didn't like WHO. *Most* of the respondents were government workers from one country or another and *all* were considered spies.) The U.S. government was getting the same reports. But then you get to "what do we do about it?"

And thus we get to President Warrick.

Warrick, for all she was a micromanaging bitch, was like a lot of micromanagers. Making a firm decision and sticking with it was anathema. Thus the "I want to get out of Iran but can't figure out how." Now she had people telling her that bird flu was coming and the world was coming to an end. It was only the beginnings of her problems but we all know *that*.

Anyway, the DOD ordered immediate and required Type Two (fuck me, fuck me) immunizations. They had already stockpiled them. Logistics at the strategic level got suddenly very fucked up as they began using every plane in the inventory to move them to every detachment in the world. Priority parts? Forget it. Personnel? They wait. These were birds that had been blocked out *months* in advance and, thank God, suddenly every single block, EVERY SINGLE BLOCK became "serum distribution."

That is how to respond to a plague. The Chiefs of Staff ordered it, soft-pedaling it to their idiotic bosses and to the media (because that was the party line) because they saw the writing on the wall and weren't idiots like me.

President Warrick?

"Under Executive Order 423 I am hereby ordering a distribution of vaccines to local health officials. These vaccines will be available to anyone who feels it necessary to get a bird flu shot. My advisors recommend them primarily for the elderly and the young."

I'm rubbing my temples in remembered anger. It is as fresh now as it was ten years ago. Every time I see that pinched face on TV I want to vomit. If I was writing this by hand, I wouldn't be able to. My hands are shaking too bad in a *need* to kill that bitch.

Three sentences, all of them alike in totally absolute FUCKED UP'EDNESS!

I will take them one at a time.

"Under Executive Order 423 I am hereby ordering a distribution of vaccines to local health officials."

There were over three hundred million stockpiled doses of Type One and nearly a hundred million of Type Two. She specifically ordered Type Two to not be distributed because it had not completed human testing requirements.

Okay, you can give it to the soldiers but not to civilians. Civilians can and will sue. Soldiers cannot. Civilians comprised most of her voting block. And a bunch of her voters, as became obvious, were bug-shit nuts. She wasn't going to tell them to take the better stuff. Better to just go with the known quantity.

But that's not the real core of the fuckedupedness of this sentence. You see, what Executive Order 423 actually ordered was distribution to county health clinics. Only.

The lady was a big believer in socialized medicine. I know, I know, laugh. We all know, now, that that was a death sentence. We know a lot of things. Twenty-twenty hindsight. But she was a believer in it like the pope believes in God. It was Right and it was Just and it was The Only Way.

Under Executive Order 423 . . . hang on . . . I'm sorry, the memories, the hatred, the deaths . . . Fuck. I just have to keep stopping.

Where was I? Oh, first sentence.

Under Executive Order 423 the doses were sent to county health officials. Only.

Effectively, going back to the bottle of water thing, she did what I would have done if I was a complete and total fucking idiot. The federal government had a list of the address of every county health office in the country and a fair guess of how many people they potentially served. That is, if there were ninety thousand people in the county and one health office (common in those days) then they were good for ninety thousand of the total population of the U.S.

They then gave each office sort of a percentage and sent out THE WHOLE STOCKPILE OF VACCINE.

Well, not every bit. They kept a bit back, something like twenty million doses. Not that it helped in the long run. I think I read somewhere that they actually all went bad when Milwaukee had one of their long blackouts and the refrigerators shut down.

Let's make this perfectly clear. Then and even now most people could not tell you where their county health clinic is. Or if there's more than one. When people got sick, they went to their personal physician. Ditto immunizations and such. If they couldn't get an appointment they went to a Doc-In-The-Box. If it was bad, they went to the hospital. Not much has changed.

County Health offices did some reporting and mostly helped out the poor. The people working in them were, by and large, there because it was easy work, steady if low pay and there was a small amount of ego gratification. (And for some, petty power.) Thus the workers, the management, the whole structure tended to be one that was, shall we say, less than suited to crisis management. They went to the seminars and had classes and all the rest. But these were pencil pushers and stampers and people that gave a few shots a month. They were the health equivalent of Fobbits.

They weren't bad people. Don't get me wrong. They were, by and large, good people. Probably better morally than me.

They were the WRONG fucking people to expect to respond heroically to a plague.

These offices, which had limited cold storage space, were suddenly INUNDATED with boxes of serum that HAD to be refrigerated. And because the news media had been beating the drum of BIRD FLU they were, AT THE SAME TIME inundated with customers. At that point you got down to individual reactions. They were as diverse as the county health administrators. All I can do is give three examples. These are not "worst to best" in a grand sense, simply cases I've researched and categorized myself.

Worst: Orange County, California/L.A., CA. I choose this as the classic example of utter fucking stupidity but compounded by sheer volume.

Now, without any real warning they received, at their central warehouse, nearly sixteen *million* doses. They had cold storage for a bare million. The response of the county health manager (whose name I will not write. Ever.) was to have a meeting. While the doses that were not in cold storage sat in a trailer in hundred degree heat. They had been unloaded from reefers (refrigerated trailers) and placed in the only available storage, outside "CONEX" shipping containers. Unrefrigerated.

According to the minutes of the meeting, this was brought up, repeatedly, by the warehouse manager. The term "heated" and "raised voices" was used in the minutes.

The meeting went on for over six hours. *No* resolution was found. It didn't really matter. By the time adults stepped in, all the doses were useless.

They were *useless*. The protein chains they depended upon to do their work were destroyed by heat in less than the six hours it took to have the meeting. By the time a decision was made (days later) by the governor of California, it was *so* far too late it was insane.

There were, however, one million remaining doses. They were then rationed to those who "truly needed them." This included everyone in county government down to trash collectors. (Although those guys earned their doses later. Those that didn't desert.) And, of course, the head of county health.

There went fifteen million doses of serum.

Intermediate: St. Louis, MO.

Six million doses. Storage for three hundred thousand.

Upon receiving the shipment, the warehouse manager took one look at it and ordered the trucker to drop the reefer. When the trucker refused (it was a leased reefer) the manager explained that what was on there was vital medicines, they did not have storage and that if necessary he would have a cop *shoot* the trucker if he tried to drive away with the reefer.

(This was in a deposition, witness the truck driver, Morell Hermon, who asked for and received one of the shots while he was there. He stated that at the time he was angry at the decision because it caused him some personal grief and economic hardship, but wanted to thank the warehouse manager for being so farsighted. Alas, his boss was less so.)

Thus the six million doses were saved for the nonce.

The head of county health, however, chose to obey the letter of the Executive Order (big essay possible on constitutional issues there but we've had talking heads on that one for so many years I'm sick of it) and set up a distribution network for the County Health Branch offices. Would have been a decent one. If they hadn't gotten fucking *swamped*. Emergency services got their own distribution (more or less by walking in and saying "Give us vaccine. Now." at the warehouse), got the shots spread around to all emergency service personnel (and in some cases friends and family members according to more depositions) and eventually started raiding the warehouse to set up shot centers at firehouses, police stations, etc. They even hit a few schools before the Plague hit.

The county health centers?

There were only a few real riots. A riot being defined as ten or more people in a mass fight. Only one that really could call itself a riot when the Springfield Street county health office was burned to the ground. Total of six deaths. None of them health-workers, by the way. They were evacuated by the police when the situation went critical.

Figure six people in an office. There were nine offices. The population was over five million. Worse, they played by the letter of the law in distribution. Only one or two of them were "qualified" to give immunizations.

The lines were . . . astronomical. Truly ludicrous. People camping out for days. They still were when the Plague hit (also when the riots started) and the conditions were ripe for spread. The very people most determined to get vaccinated ... were some of the first to get infected.

Total distribution in the county? 138,000 doses. Some 60% by emergency services personnel who were not authorized to do so. Population? 5.2 million. Deaths? Who knows. Estimates are 2.8.

It's times like these that I'm glad granpappy taught me how to make a still and the *real* use in the world for potatoes.

You'll notice I didn't mention deaths in L.A. That's because, really, nobody knows. As of last census there is a population in Orange County, CA of five hundred thousand, mostly centered around the harbor area, Long Beach and Malibu. But H5N1, bad as it is, does NOT kill 90% of the population. Where are the rest of the former inhabitants? Well, there were significant death rates due to the Freeze (Californians were NOT prepared for the winters) and people just *moved*. Fled in the first wave of the Plague, moved out to try to find better climes (or better support structure) at the Freeze ... One of the census questions that was part of a statistical sample was "Were you a resident of your current living area prior to the events starting in 2019?" Nationwide the average was 82% "Yes." In L.A. County the average is 63% "No." L.A. County, effectively, depopulated and has been slowly filling back up. Hell, the weather there is still better than Blue Earth, trust me. If I thought it was fucking cold in Minnesota growing up ...

But I digress.

Best:

Everybody knows the answer: The Big Apple.

Damn if a Democrat mayor didn't hit it right on the fucking nosey. Admittedly, he had the example of Giuliani on 9/11. But he did what was right and damn the consequences.

Most people know the story but I'll tell it for those who are interested in my take or who have just terminally been out of the loop. (I've got a couple of friends who have just come out of hiding. There may be more.)

Upon receipt of the vaccines, the central distribution manager did the same thing as St. Louis. "Oh, no, you are NOT fucking taking the reefers away."

Peripheral note. The reefers were coming from the manufacturer, Winslow Pharmaceuticals, who was being paid to handle the distribution by the federal government. They'd also been paid to do the long-term stockpiling. Some people might have been following the investigations and trials surrounding the distribution. My take. The feds paid Winslow to pay truckers using temporary rented reefers to distribute the vaccine. Winslow followed their directives because that was what it was directed to do and was being paid to do. One of the Winslow logistics guys is on record (e-mail exchange with surgeon general's office) protesting the use of temporary reefers for the very reason of what happened in L.A. But that's what they were told and paid to do. Trying the CEO, etc, of Winslow was criminal in itself. The fact that no *federal* officials were tried makes it worse. The fuck-up was at the fed level, not Winslow.

County health looked at the Executive Order and started to do what was ordered: distribute only to county health offices. Mayor Cranslow stepped in and said "Not only no, but HELL no." His exact words from the minutes of the meeting were: "Just because you are told to commit suicide doesn't mean you have to stick the pistol in your mouth and pull the damned trigger."

Within two days, a distribution system was set up (under a former Army S-4 proving that all S-4s are not lame-brain dickbreaths). Each hospital, county health office, physicians' office (to include Doc-In-The-Boxes and even *psychiatrists and plastic surgeons*) and hospital was given an initial supply, amounting to forty percent of the on-hand at the warehouse and based on their best estimate of initial requests. Every emergency service person was vaccinated and called in on mandatory overtime. They even recruited fourth-year med students and set up street-level vaccination centers.

During this time there were repeated emergency broadcasts. A replication of one:

"There is a high probability that the New York area will soon experience cases of the Asian Bird Flu. Two times out of three, this disease will *kill* you. In no more than (started at three days) a distribution system will be in place so that *everyone* in the New York area can be vaccinated. If you *do* not get vaccinated, you have a two in three chance of dying. Even the stupidest gambler doesn't go for those odds. Do not try to get it now. Your city government is working as fast as it can to get the doses ready. When we're ready, it will be available at all county health offices as well as hospitals, fire stations and even your personal physician. Don't rush, there is still time. But *get* the shot. This has been Mayor Bill Cranslow. You pay me to make sure you stay alive. Let's both work on that."

In two days the system was in place. Then New Yorkers were told to get the shot and not panic.

Get the shot. Do not panic. There are no cases in the U.S. yet. But get the shot. And do not panic.

Get the shot. Do not panic.

Over and over again. Along with "let's work together on that."

And it worked. Everywhere there was a rush the first day. But the shots were everywhere and cops, firemen, meter maids, garbage collectors, were standing by to distribute more as stocks dwindled. The biggest bottleneck was the supply of syringes and peripherals. Syringe disposal boxes ran out the first day and never really caught up. New Yorkers reacted, adapted and overcame. They made them out of red-painted bleach bottles. New Yorkers took time off from work to go to their fire station. They went to their physician's offices. They went to hospitals.

Health care workers were overworked and often frustrated, but they dealt. And the broadcasts continued.

Schools. The H5N1 could be administered either with a syringe or with the less common air-gun. Pupils in schools were lined up and given their injections, airgun, mass production style by order of the mayor. There were some protests and threats of lawsuits. I'm not sure what happened with most of those. I suspect a lot of the protesting parents didn't get the shots themselves. For reasons that will become clear, later, there were and are a tremendous number of orphans in our great country. If you haven't taken one in, look up your local government foster care system and sign up. It's a lot easier these days than before the Plague and there are a hell of a lot more needy children. We've got four. What have *you* done for the world today?

Within two weeks the crush was over. Every New Yorker that was going to get immunized did get immunized. And they had spares. Not enough to help places like fucking L.A., but they had spares.

Mayor Cranslow, by the way, was reelected last year in a true landslide. His campaign slogan? "Let's work together." The bastard makes me question being a Republican sometimes. If, when, he runs for President he's got my vote. I'll work together with him by fucking God.

But let's get back to the Executive Order.

"These vaccines will be available to anyone who feels it necessary to get a bird flu shot."

Okay, here we go into some tedious but necessary shit. Spread prevention games theory.

The basic premise of infectious disease spread prevention is sort of like a game of Othello.

I need to explain Othello, don't I?

Sigh.

In Othello each player gets a bunch of rocks, colored black on one side and white on the other, and plays them on a board filled with indentations or squares. If there is a black rock on a square and a white rock on either side of the square, the black rock becomes white and vice versa and so on. Basically, you try to surround your opponent.

Spread prevention works the same way. Say that a person has the flu and they only see two other people a day, say in an office. (I know, impossible, but work with me here.) The infected person is the black rock. They can only infect the other two people around them. If both of them are immunized (and the immunization is good) and they wash their hands and . . . Look, work with me. If they can't get the flu, they can't pass it on. So whether the person who's infected lives or dies, it stops with him.

That's the *critically important thing* to mass immunization. You have to create enough white rocks that the black rocks can't flip them. They *can't get past them* to uninfected portions of the populace. The problem being, hardly anybody ever deals with only two people all the time. Think about your day. You deal with hundreds of people every day. Or at least dozens. And they deal with dozens and *they* deal with dozens.

That, as any school kid these days knows, is how disease spreads. To stop it, you have to cut off its ability to infect. If you find a "patient zero" fast enough, or a location zero at least, you can try to encircle it, what's called "ring immunization." Which was, sort of, what the Chinese tried. They just did it very badly.

Now, don't get me wrong, there were a lot of people (obviously from the above) who *wanted* to get immunized. Maybe, if the distribution hadn't been so cocked up, enough to stop the spread.

But probably not. Look, it's a complicated computer model but to stop a major spread you have to have 93% of a population (statistical) immunized. 93%. You can't get 93% of any population to *decide on the color of the sky.* The only way to truly stop a disease, butt cold, is mass, *forced* immunization. You've got to hit everybody you can get your stinking hands on if it means breaking down doors.

Let's take a look at our "optimum" example, NYC. NYC, good as it was, did not, not NOT act as a white rock. Why?

Illegal aliens, homeless, the criminal class, idiotic nature-loving vegans (sorry, highly redundant there), big-shot lawyers and stockbrokers who "didn't have the time for this crap . . . " None of them got immunized. And because flu doesn't actually have to infect someone to get passed (it can get passed through handshakes even if the person with it on their hands doesn't get it) you'd be surprised how fast a big-time lawyer can get it from a street-person. Street person to drug dealer, drug dealer to drug dealer's boss, boss to his lawyer. Doesn't have to be on their hands, can be on cash. Put in a waiter in the middle if it makes you feel better.

Robust diseases are slippery fuckers. They will *get* your ass if there's not that 93% of "white rocks" around you.

Fortunately, with the exception of illegal aliens the people in NYC who didn't get immunized are, sorry and being as callous as fuck, not worth the immunization. If you were too stupid to get it, stockbrokers and lawyers, you're better off out of this world. Criminals that were afraid they'd be arrested if they went to county health? Lessee, five days for violation of a restraining order or death. Hmmm . . . Homeless? There was even a program to go around offering it to them in their "habitual areas." Mostly by firefighters and cops which might have put some of them off. Hardly any got the shot. Why? Most homeless had mental health problems. (For you youngsters that grew up in the Post-Plague world they're what are called, again, bums.) There used to be a shit-pot full of them. I mean, like, dozens on any street in any major city. Hundreds of thousands of them. Most were too whacked to understand or believe about the flu. It was all a government plot. More alien mind control rays. Whatever.

Most of them died. World ends at six. Poorest hardest hit. Go figure.

And, sorry, given all the rest that died that tried, intelligently and aggressively, to live, don't got much for the homeless and the rest of those idiots. There's a reason I live in Blue Earth again. All the planning in the world doesn't help if you're not *allowed* to have the medicine that will save your life. The homeless in NYC, and the rest that decided "I don't trust it," "I don't have the time" . . . Got nothing fucking for them. Got *nothing*.

So there we have the stupidity of sentence two. If you're not going to mass immunize, you're not going to stop a disease. It worked with smallpox and polio. It might have worked with a bunch of other diseases, but we got weak. There's a program in the works right now to get started on slamming the door on everything possible, that is everything that transmits only through humans and domesticated animals. Don't know if it will ever work but it's worth a shot.

So, Warrick you pinch-faced lying incompetent bitch, let's take a look at sentence three.

"My advisors recommend them primarily for the elderly and the young."

What advisors? Her advisors for a situation like this were the National Science Advisor, the Director of the National Institute for Health (NIH), the Surgeon General, the Director of the Center for Disease Control and the Commander of USAMRIID.

All five have testified under oath at this point about the decision process, such as it was, leading to 423. Two, the National Science Director and the Surgeon General, took the Fifth. Fuckers. The other three, including the only two epidemiologists consulted, have, however, spoken at length.

The first meeting was called by the National Science Advisor and included, along with various hangers on, the Director of the CDC, the NSD, the Secretary of Homeland Security and the Surgeon General. At that meeting, the President announced that the vaccine was to be distributed immediately and that it should be available through county health services. And that it should be given to the young and old first.

Note: This was before any input from the advisors. This according to both the DCDC and the Secretary of Homeland Security.

The DCDC has stated that he demurred after it was clear that neither the NSD or the SG were going to. Why?

First, there was a plan already set up for vaccine distribution. Called, incredibly, the Emergency Vaccine Distribution Plan (incredibly because it actually made sense), it had been in place for years and regularly updated. It was a complicated distro but, effectively, it spread the vaccine through both military and emergency civilian channels to *all* healthcare providers. There were identification methods. Following initial distribution there was a forced immunization program as a sub-codicil nobody wanted to really use. It was cumbersome. Everyone knew it was cumbersone and that it would take at least a week to get the vaccine down to civilians. But it was designed to work. Might not have, but it was the Plan.

In the first three minutes of the meeting, the Prez had thrown the Plan right out the window. So much of sentence one and two. This is really about sentence three.

Bird Flu was strange. Most flus, the major deaths occurred in the old and the young. And, don't get me wrong, the bird flu killed off both groups.

But like the earlier Spanish Flu, bird flu was not a secondary killer, it was a primary. Secondary and primary . . . Sigh.

Most flus don't kill you. They just get you very sick and, notably, flood your lungs with fluids. Secondary viral and bacterial infections then get in those fluids and kill *some* people through pneumonia. Notably . . . the old and the young. Thus, the deaths are from secondary infections. Secondary killers.

There are very rare flus, though, which are primary killers. Death qua death, the Grim Reaper, Pushin' Up Daisies, occurs because specific portions of the brain (we don't need all of our brains, just ask Al Gore) die. There are various ways that those portions can die; anything that cuts off oxygen to them for long enough will do it. (Such as, say, having your head cut off.) But *something* has to kill them.

Besides all the usual stuff that bird flu did, it spread systemically. First there was the danger of pneumonia. But even if you survived that, it tended to hang on. Blood vessels are designed to keep fluids *in*. Infected vessels let the fluids out, they accumulate in lungs, in body cavities, kidneys fail, brain swells, pressure kills neurons, breathing stops, etc. If your immune system couldn't kill it, it got into the brain. Fluid builds up, pressure on brain causes dementia, then strokelike symptoms . . . And then, well, you quickly went mad and then died. Thus the pattern of get sick, seem to recover, relapse, die.

Worse, like the Spanish Flu and for reasons that are still being studied, it hit the "prime" population *harder*. That is, the young and old tended to get the pneumonia but if they shook *that* off (which if there was health care was normally possible with anti-biotics) they survived.

People in "prime ages" went through all that, (if they didn't die of pneumonia) felt better for a couple of days, relapsed and then died.

Mortality amongst prime population, 15–55, was *twenty percent higher* than among peripheral population, the young and the old.

So, let's see, in that one meeting the Prez ignored the Plan *and* chose the wrong group to focus on immunizing.

Don't get me wrong. I care for all living beings except slow drivers in the left-hand lane, terrorists and pedophiles. And I'd have loved to be able to save all those youngsters and old folks. Well . . . Sort of. The youngsters, certainly.

Face facts. I loved my dad and he wasn't even in the "old" category. But old people, retired people that wander around playing shuffleboard . . .

We were looking at *surviving*. Not prospering. Not becoming better. *Surviving*. The advisors knew how lethal H5N1 was. Destroy a certain percentage of any society and it crumbles. The models based on wars and previous famines and pestilence was twenty percent. At that point, the society devolves to survival level. (At least that was the model. We found out how robust some societies were and how weak others. But I'm getting ahead of myself.)

But of that twenty percent, *old people don't matter*. They're done. Even if they have the desire to rebuild, they don't have the strength or stamina. They're smart, they're wise, sure. (The good ones.) But they *can't rebuild a society*. They're the past. If you have to sacrifice any group in a survival situation, The. Old. Go. First. Cold survival logic is like that. Not nice, but survival logic isn't.

Sigh. "Women and children first" would have been the right call. Why? Because they matter. Children are the future of any society. Immunize the kids first? Hell, yeah. Forget that they're less susceptible. They're going to take care of the survivors in the survivor's old age. If they make it.

Children are important.

But . . .

Kids can't rebuild a society. I don't care what you've seen or read in a science fiction story, they just can't. They don't have the experience; they don't, yet, have the strength that is going to be needed. Most of them would, eventually, become of reproductive age. If they survived.

Look, mortality from H5N1 dropped with age to about seven then picked up again. Say that it was even more lethal than it was and killed off everyone in the middle.

You'd have a planet filled with oldsters and children.

Think they're going to get factories going again? That they can run farms?

Think again.

You'd better have that functional middle or the kids are going to starve and the oldsters are going to starve and die off and nobody's going to remember or care what the fuck the Mona Lisa was or why she was smiling like that. Kids growing up scavenging in the ruins. Read "A Boy and His Dog." But don't believe the end; there's nothing a teenage boy won't do for pussy.

Women? I'm just a sexist, right?

Not if you're looking at survival. Look, it's logic most people don't like but here it is:

Once upon a time the whole human population of the world got *wiped out* except about forty-four reproductive aged females. (Based on DNA data. Look it up.) How many males doesn't matter. As long as there was one, we're good. He'd be *busy* but we're good. Nobody knows or cares how many males were in that group that eventually grew to six billion and change. All that mattered were *forty-four females.*

Sad but true, women have babies. Males have more utility than just sperm, don't get me wrong. But when you're talking about something as tight as bird flu, women matter *much* more. "Reproductive age" women.

Everything that Warrick was, though, prevented her from even *thinking* about that. Warrick was the ball-buster's ball-buster. I am woman hear me roar. You'd think she'd have made sure the immunizations went to women first for that very reason, but she couldn't even survive *that* logic.

The worst part, the *absolute worst part*, was that even if the distro had worked it was going to be going to one group that wasn't going to be of use in the immediate aftermath and a group that wasn't of any true functionality at all.

So the Director of the CDC demurred. He was about the only male in the room, so he was ignored. So he pointed out that there were others that were missing from the meeting. Notably, the Commander of USAMRIID and NIH, both of whom were missing.

Another meeting was called. Both USAMRIID and NIH were in the more or less DC area so it assembled that evening. The second meeting, according to testimony from the DCDC, CUSAMRIID and the DNIH (three males in a meeting chaired by and filled with female ball-busters) was "acrimonious." Neither the National Science Advisor (a former patent lawyer) nor the Surgeon General (an MD specializing in "women's historical medicine" whatever the fuck that means) would disagree with the three actual, you know, specialists in fighting plagues. On the other hand, they also did not support them. And the President, from her vast store of experience trying to take the medical industry apart like a chicken, Knew that children and old farts were the Most Vulnerable and Had To Be Protected.

Well, yeah, gee. Nice sentiment. The only problem being that we weren't dealing with the common fucking COLD lady!

She also didn't listen to reason on the subject of the other two sentences. Go figure. Men had testicles and therefore were Wrong.

Just before WWI started the kaiser sent a message to the king of England, who was some sort of cousin, saying something like "War is now inevitable." He was still bargaining, but from the POV of "we're going to kick your ass unless you surrender now." But that's not really the point.

The point is, as of the end of that second meeting, a biological *disaster* in the U.S. was inevitable.

Most people in the U.S. don't realize how important getting the right President is. Sure, the Prez gets blamed for a lot of things that he or she can't control. The Prez does not control the stock market or the Federal Reserve. But the reality is that the Founding Fathers, having no real previous experience of democracy or a republic and having lived under a monarchy their whole fucking *lives*, created a temporary king to run the country. They were, at heart, monarchists. They just didn't like the current one and didn't want to make it hereditary. (Don't get me started on Bush, Warrick, Bush, Warrick. But from history it's a *very bad sign*.)

So every four years we elect a king. Since people like consistency, we tend to elect the same king as many times as we can get away with. (See previous paragraph.) And the king, especially in any sort of emergency, has a lot of power. They don't always, or even most of the time, have enough to fix things right away. But they've got *a lot* of power.

Including the power to totally screw things up.

Everybody in the room that had the power to change the President's idea of a fucking plan *also* worked for the bitch. Legally, they were *required* to follow her orders. They could argue, they could recommend but that was like talking to the Great Wall of China. She knew what was Right and what was Good and the people arguing against her had Dicks and they were Wrong.

For the kids reading this, this is a very important point. When you choose your king, forget most of the reasons you think you should vote for the king. Mostly, the king can't do much about the economy but ruin it. They can't make you richer or smarter (although they can manage the reverse). If you want one suggestion, think about all the contingencies under which that king (or queen in this case) may hold *your* lives in his or her hands. And choose wisely. About half the U.S. population chose unwisely. (48.2%. It was one of *those* elections.)

Quite a few of them died. *Every* person who voted for Warrick deserved it.

– CHAPTER FOUR –

They Always Forget the Emergency

Patient Zero, USA, was in Chicago. What the fuck?

Definitions. Patient Zero. The first detected case of a disease. Generally, that required lots of investigation as the disease was tracked back.

In this case, Ching Mao Pong was easy to find. Just follow the screaming.

But Chicago? What the fuck?

Most of the epidemiologists who were scattering out to try to stop things had headed for the West Coast. Why? Most immigration and movement from China came from that direction. And it wasn't just China anymore. H5N1 was breaking out all over Southeast Asia. Some of it being spread by bird movement but more from people movement. The Chinese had little tendrils all over Asia and people were following those tendrils trying to escape the Plague.

Outside of China the first reports, by a few minutes, were from Thailand. Then, within a day, every single country in Southeast Asia except Vietnam (which right up until it turned into a wasteland didn't admit any cases) reported cases.

All of them tried containment. But it was impossible to contain. None of them had the sort of health system that the U.S. did, they were physically connected to China, they had birds migrating from China that carried the Plague, none of which we had, and *we* couldn't contain it. (Maybe we could have. If, possibly. If wishes were fishes . . .)

41

There was the Plan. Called the Epidemiological Emergency Response Plan (with the unfortunate acronym EERP, which sounds like someone who has just had a very bad practical joke played on them); it had several parts. It probably wouldn't have worked because what every Emergency Plan leaves out is the fucking *emergency*.

Example: Hurricane Katrina. Okay, okay, most of the shit about it was urban legend. There were not tens of thousands of dead. There were no riots or rapes in the Superdome and people were neither starving nor "out of water." They were being *rationed*, which the fuckers that were complaining *thought* was starving, but that's not the same thing. But let's look at the evacuation Plan.

Okay, Nagin was a total fuck-up and never even tried to initiate it. He'd never looked at it, despite a fucking *hurricane* being headed for *his* city which, by the way, was *below sea level*. So calling him a fuck-up is insulting fuck-ups. But there was a Plan.

The Plan was to use school and city buses to evacuate all those who were "transportation challenged." Whether Nagin used it or not was sort of a moot point, though. People had forgotten little details. Such as, there was no emergency call list for the drivers.

In any group that does emergency response, from the military to cops and even including child services, there is a call list. Generally it's a call tree. Person at the top gets a call. He or she calls three people, then starts getting ready to head in. Those people call two or three people lower than them and start getting ready. Assuming more or less equal transportation distances, the bosses get to work first, which helps in most cases.

There was no such phone tree for bus drivers. So there was no real way for anyone to get ahold of them in an emergency.

Oops.

Drivers *had never been told* that they were supposed to drive people out in an emergency. So they weren't exactly sitting by the phone if there had been a phone tree. They had jobs and cars. They were packing to leave or already gone.

And that was the last point. The order to get out was sent out before any thought was given at all to the "transportation challenged" plan and even the evacuation order was more of a bow to reality; the roads out of New Orleans were packed (by among other things *the bus drivers*) when it was given.

People who develop emergency plans always seem to leave out the *emergency*.

But the EERP wasn't a bad Plan as such things went.

The first part was the Emergency Vaccination Distribution Plan. Spread the vaccine to health providers. At the same time, spread it to emergency services personnel and the military including National Guard. As time permits, go to nationwide forced immunization if it got that bad.

Simultaneous with that, call up all the National Guard and Reserves. Mobilize all active units to full combat status. If necessary, start a "staged redeployment" of the rest of the military world-wide.

Second step, shut down the country. It's called "zone quarantine." Close *all* the borders, not only between the U.S. and other countries but internally. Preferably, close it down to county level where possible. International travel shuts down first. Planes coming from other places are turned back. U.S. citizens and residents can enter the country but go into quarantine, not home. This would probably start before the first vaccine shipped. It was planned (there's that word again) to be total "primary" quarantine in three days. I think that's optimistic, but we'll give it that just for shits and giggles.

When, not if, you have outbreaks you start "ring immunization." That is, when you find someone who has the flu you ensure immunization status of everyone they've come into contact with or anyone they *could have* come into contact with. You do not ask for permission; unless they can prove they're immunized, you stick them with a damned needle whether they like it or not. You go through the whole neighborhood the person lives in, you go to the stores they've visited, you stick everyone at their workplace. You stick people that just sort of knew them in school or that they sort of remember from seeing across a bar.

There are leakers. Always. You find them and do the same thing, hopefully quicker. You broadcast that such and such a person had the flu and beg people to go to a doctor and get checked. And anyone who has been in contact with *those* people.

You hit that motherfucker with a full fucking court press.

You don't open up the borders, any of them, until you've killed the son of a bitch.

Fuck the economy. Fuck anything. Shut the fuck down until

your population is safe. They can't buy trinkets or gas or groceries if they're mostly dead.

Nothing. Else. Matters.

There were some plans for this we knew were going to work. 9/11 had proven we could ground aircraft at will. We'd called up the National Guard enough times to know exactly its predictable response rate. Deploying troops internally had been done enough that most units could do it in their sleep.

Distribution? Ring immunization? Zone quarantine? Nobody had tried it, ever, in a Western country. We'd never had to, not really.

As it turned out, we never did, not really. Oh, the words were spouted, but . . .

"Forced immunization is not an option."

That's not really what the bitch said. Look, Presidents get paid to, among other things, handle emergencies. And there are supposed to be emergency drills. Yes, it's a busy job and not every contingency can be covered. But mass epidemic *was* a scheduled drill. (Congressional Testimony On H5N1 Spiral Event.) One that the President was supposed to attend.

Seemed she was meeting with, irony of ironies, some Chinese businessmen the day the drill was scheduled. And despite being a lawyer, apparently never took the time to even RTFM (read the fucking *manual*).

So when the meeting finally came around where the Secretary of Homeland Security was explaining the full EERP, it went, apparently, something like this:

"Mass requisite innoculation program . . ."

"You mean forcing people to take the drugs?"

"Yes, Mrs. President."

"That is not an option."

Now, you can't go to *school* these days without a measles shot. And four or five more, some of which have some good clinical studies showing they are a. not very useful and b. very very fucking nasty. But unless you can prove, with a doctor's test, that you are allergic or something, you can't go to school without the shot.

But . . . well . . . politics.

Look, there are "freedom uber alles" wack-jobs on both sides of the political spectrum. There are the guys who feel very very strongly that the Constitution *entitles* them to owning an M-1

Abrams with full load. (Okay, okay, that *would* be me. Love and hate those fuckers depending on if I'm cranking one or killing one, done both . . .) And Don't Tread On Me and Pry My Gun From My Cold Dead Fingers. Also "If I don't want to take a fucking shot, I'm not going to take a fucking shot. And anybody who tries to give me that devil poison, or fluoride, is going to get blasted by my Mark-Four-One Blaster with Puring Optical Sights that I whack off on every single day! End the slavery that is government! With no government, things would be perfect!"

Blah, blah. Libertarians with a capital L and hand me that rifle, buddy. Ask one some time if their utopia has building inspectors. Or, you know, how much it looks like, say, Somalia. Or Detroit after the Plague.

Okay, that's the nuts. Let's take a look at the fruits.

"End the cycle of violence. Eating animals is murder." "A rat is a pig is a dog is a boy." "Don't poison your body with pesticides and hormones. My body, my choice . . . "

Guess which side contributed about 15% of Warrick's core supporters. Not to mention:

"The Southwestern U.S. was once Mexico's and shall be again!"

And I did mention Chinese businessmen?

Warrick had a whole team of people, working in the very crowded and space short for really important shit White House, that did nothing but monitor blogs. Oh, not the "Pry it from my cold dead hands" blogs; the other guys. In that, she was politically nearly as smart as her husband and a bit more techno-savvy. Her team of nerds were mostly *members* of the blogs and occasionally passed on juicy news, thus increasing the importance of their most crucial supporting blogs. But more importantly they kept the pulse of the fruits.

And the fruits were *not* going to be forced to accept innocu-lations. Some of them were screaming for them, others were explaining how a diet of honey and organic herbs would prevent *any* flu. AIDS in Africa, after all, was a plot by the free-market world to kill off the black-man, blah, blah . . .

"Forced immunization is not an option."

Ring immunization?

"Forced immunization is not an option."

So there goes ring immunization being any effect at all.

Then there was sealing the borders.

Look, I've worked at sealing borders. It ain't easy. You basically have to station people, in groups so they don't get overrun, at close and regular intervals. And you can't be nice to those who are attempting to cross. Not if you *really* want a sealed border. Part of the military plan for sealing the border with our southern neighbor included shoot-to-kill orders for runners. If they did not stop, they got shot. Ditto people attempting to cross internally. If the car or truck or whatever wasn't willing to stop, light them up.

"Force is not an option. Closing internal borders is not an option."

Okay, can we at least cut off international travel?

Actually . . . no. Persons who were from "affected" countries were to be quarantined, nicely and for no more than three days. "Affected" countries were countries which had declared *themselves* to be "widely and endemically infected" by H5N1.

Look, China, which is now about a quarter of its pre-Plague population and five countries and change in a fourteen-way internecine war, *never* declared themselves "widely and endemically infected."

We didn't cut off international travel. *Everyone else* cut off international travel from *us*.

Of course, by then it was too late. There were still planes flying to and from Hong Kong after it had basically ceased to function. They stopped because they couldn't be sure of getting refueled. And they were flying straight from Hong Kong, which was in direct contact with the Mainland, to LAX and San Francisco and Seattle. People would be held for a couple of days in isolation, board another plane and fly on. Some of them to Europe which cut off travel from *us* before we came close to shutting *down* from *anyone*.

Frankly, the only reason it didn't break out faster was people ignoring their orders. Sure, the guys sitting in the room with the Prez arguing till they were blue in the face had to send down suicidal orders. Didn't mean that the guys and gals in the field obeyed them.

Quarantine in L.A. was heavy until things started to break down in California. Ditto Seattle. Not so much in San Fransisco which is probably one of the reasons they got hit pretty quick. And hard. Lord forgive those fags, they got hit *hard*.

Then there were the big order breakers. People still have a hard time codifying the response. It depends on who's writing about it. "Pseudo-secessionists" is one term. "Knee-jerk reactionaries" was a term used at the time along with "racists" (never quite understood that one unless they were talking about Mexican immigrants), "fascists," etc. Big litany of "you're bad people."

Hawaii was the big winner in the "racist/fascist/reactionary" category. Okay, Hawaiians *are* racists. If you're not native Hawaiian there are laws saying you can't have certain jobs. There are Natives and there are "haoles." But, strangely enough, nobody was calling them that. In fact, despite their actions at the time, nobody was quite sure how to respond.

Lemme explain. The news media was filled with liberals. They might not like what the Hawaiians did but, hey, they're our little brown brothers! (Hawaiians, like Samoans and for similar reasons, tend to be motherfucking *big* little brown brothers. But it's pretty hard to get a liberal off their mental grooves.) Conservatives by and large thought they were about the only smart people in the nation and wished they were in Hawaii.

Basically, Hawaii cut itself off. No planes were permitted to land to do more than refuel or get fixed if they needed it. Then "hie-away with you! No fucking lei for your ass! Aloha!" Ditto boats from outside Hawaiian waters. They'd give them some food and fuel if they had it but then get the fuck out of here.

They shut down internal travel as well and required documentation of immunization. And the immunizations that got sent to them a. arrived slower than on the mainland and they could see the Prez's order was fucked up and b. were packed for air-travel so they kept for long enough for everyone to get the fucking clue.

Hawaii came through the whole damned thing with nothing but a major depression. Racist fuckers. *Smart* racist fuckers, I'll give you.

Then there were the ones that did get called racists and fascists and all the rest; the L states.

I put it that way because it wasn't exactly the states of the Confederacy. Tennessee was a border state in the War Against Slavery. And there were some that weren't near the Old South like Wyoming.

Why the L states?

Way back in the 2000 election a map came out of the vote

patterns. Back then we'd call it the "red and blue" states. Red states went for Bush, blue states went for Al "I Invented The Internet" Gore.

I always hated the "red/blue" divide. I'm military. Red forces are the bad guys. I'm not a bad guy and I'm a red stater.

But if you look at the map, it's a big fucking L for the red states. Southeast, then up through the midwest with a bit on either side in the southwest and northeast.

Fly-over country. The Dust Bowl. Hell, the Bible Belt.

Not all of them were "reactionary." Missouri followed the President's orders to the letter. See St. Louis.

Others, however, had a different opinion. I call it "disorganized civil disobedience." They waited for the Prez to announce the Plan, heard the New Plan and went "Oh, *hell* no!"

A lot of them got some or most of the immunization plan right. When reports from Mississippi started coming in of shipments of vaccine and nowhere to store them the word went down, from the governor, not the state director of Health, that they should store them anywhere. Get cops to help if necessary.

Short example. County Health in Jefferson County, Mississippi, got a bunch of styrofoam boxes from FedEx marked "Vital Medical Material: Refrigerate." They didn't require a truckload, fortunately for them.

The director of County Health, a nice old lady I caught on the news one time talking about her response, called the only store in town, Piggly Wiggly, and told them she had a *big* problem. Piggly Wiggly dumped out enough room in their storage room for all the boxes.

Atlanta? Screwed the pooch. Ditto Mobile, Birmingham, Chattanooga, Knoxville, Savannah . . . The list is long.

Small towns? Small counties? Small cities even? Better than 50% by current estimate "presented optimal or near optimal distribution response." They reacted, adapted and overcame.

Okay, call it "red/blue" if you wish. Red got it about 50% right. Blue? About 7%.

The response expanded from that. "Forced immunization is not an option." Yeah, right, tell it to the people of Mississippi, Texas, Georgia, South Carolina and Tennessee. There were areas where forced immunization *wasn't* an option, mostly the big cities, due to lack of vaccine. But the order went out and damn the President or the media wailers. School kids were immunized production line style in every state. Smart or not, those governors went for "children first" at the very least. Overtime paramedics, EMTs, cops, nurses, whoever had a clue about sticking a needle, visited work-places. It didn't last long; things went to hell too fast. But the order went out and the process started.

The President actually ordered the National Guard in those states to be used to *stop* the forced immunizations. Even when they were as a part of ring immunization responses. (CDC was just outside Atlanta and the guys and gals left there tried. *Lord* they tried . . .)

The term here wasn't really mutiny. Okay, it was mutiny. But by then things were going to hell in a handbasket and everyone knew it. Obeying the increasingly shrill bitch at 1600 was the last thing on anyone's mind.

That would be about early April. But that was more than a month after Patient Zero when the Prez finally ordered "staged redeployment" and I got left holding the shit end of the stick. And then there was the whole "Emergency Powers Act" fiasco.

Patient Zero was in Chicago.

Why Chicago you ask. Well, since plenty of people have answered and I obsess on questions like that these days I'll repeat.

Ching Mao Pong had been a peasant as a child. He grew up in central China and became one of the large class of "undocumented workers" who moved into the coastal areas as common laborers. Apparently at some point he convinced a Chinese smuggler, what is called a "snake-head," to get him to the U.S.

How Ching Mao Pong became infected is unsure. All that is known is that he was loaded by the snake-head, along with fifteen others, into a cargo container bound for the States. Its destination was Chicago where an accomplice snake-head would open it and let the immigrants out into the freedom of virtual slavery in the U.S. until they paid off the extortionate price of the transportation. There was sufficient food and water packed into the container to sustain all sixteen. (Twelve males and four females, by the way.) Don't ask about sanitary facilities.

How could a container of immigrant Chinese possibly make it to Chicago you ask?

Uh, ship to Seattle then Great Northern Railway to Chicago. Not that hard.

Oh, customs?

Containers were categorized several ways. At the low end were containers from sources that were both "unrecognized" and known drug smuggling areas/companies. If, say, a container entered the U.S. that was a. from Colombia, b. from a company that did not have special documentation with Customs and Immigration Service and c. did not have a pre-cleared seal on it, it was *five percent* likely to be checked.

That is, of containers coming from known drug source countries without any indication that they didn't contain drugs, only five out of a hundred actually got opened and inspected.

Oh, there were all sorts of special systems to examine them. Dogs might walk by, X-rays if they weren't something that might get damaged, neutrino systems were even in consideration.

But only five in a hundred from the *worst possible source* got opened and examined thoroughly.

Why?

Money. Time. Interference in commerce. Call it an iron triangle. Nobody wanted to spend the money on the (huge) number of inspectors that would be necessary to actually check, say, every dodgy container coming into the U.S., much less *every* container without slowing things down to a crawl. There were containers that never were supposed to get *opened* in the U.S. There were times when it was smarter and cheaper, if you were shipping something from, say China to France, to ship it via rail across the U.S. It got loaded on a ship in China, dumped off in L.A., put on a train, carried to Jacksonville and loaded on another ship for Nice.

There were a fuckload of containers coming from China in those days. Most of them *were* to addresses in the U.S. Hell, you couldn't go into a store and *not* buy *something* from China. Even the plastic your food was wrapped in came mostly from . . . China.

And China was not considered a threat source. Yes, people got smuggled but not, you know, drugs or bombs. Sometimes it was discovered after a "packet" was found that a highly trained bomb-sniffing dog had walked right past one of these snake-head containers and never even quivered. They were good dogs. They were looking for drugs or bombs. People *did not count*. Don't bark at People. Good dog.

A snake-head named Chan Twai opened the container when it

was dropped off at a rented warehouse. He later said that upon opening it he thought everyone in the container was dead. He knew what was happening in China. He ran, hoping he hadn't caught the Plague.

Ching Mao Pong, though, was alive. Apparently nearly insane but alive. He stumbled out of the container into a country about which he knew virtually nothing with no one he could speak to and nowhere to go.

He did what he'd done in China. He looked for food and work. According to his accounts he ate garbage and drank from bathrooms for two days. He saw people bumming for money from people and the police did not stop them. He bummed money and food and even cigarettes and he was not told to stop once by the police, which he found to be very nearly paradise. Truly America was the land of opportunity.

On the third day he found men that looked somewhat like him standing on a street corner. He was picked to go work on laying sod for a new building in the final stages of completion. He couldn't speak the language of any of the men he worked with but "working with your hands was working with your hands."

He knew he had been exposed to the Plague. He had gotten sick. He had nearly died. Most of the others in the compartment had died, two from when one of them went mad. But he survived, he recovered. He thought he was fine. He was feeling somewhat unwell when he finally found work but he had had little good food recently.

He collapsed while working on the job. The contractor who had hired him cursed, loaded Ching in his pickup truck, dropped him off at the emergency room and made himself scarce.

Ching was semicoherent when dropped off. He was directed to sit in a chair. There were more police and they apparently wanted him to stay. He sat. He collapsed again. The emergency room personnel, who were not masked and had not received their immunizations, put him on a gurney and moved him up the triage list.

The responding doctor saw a slightly emaciated Asian male in his mid thirties who was suffering from high temperature and disorientation. Initial exam determined he was suffering from, among other things, dehydration. He was given an IV. He went into spasms shortly afterwards and dropped into unconsciousness.

A Chinese-speaking nurse was called in when he regained consciousness. By then the possibility of bird flu was considered and Nurse Quan was in Cat Four dress. Ching was questioned closely. He was initially uncooperative until the nurse, who was an immigrant, called in a security guard and, unknown to the doctor or any of the others including the guard, warned that he would be sent to "reeducation" if he did not tell her everything she asked. He spilled his guts.

He went back into febrile disorientation a few hours later, slipped into a coma that night and died before dawn.

CDC, by that time, had over sixteen active quarantines on the West Coast. Specialists got on the still flying planes for Chicago and arrived just as Ching breathed his last. They attempted to get the Illinois and Chicago authorities to override the President's directive against forced immunization. Two problems. Chicago was one of the cities that had screwed up its receipt of vaccine and they weren't even willing to do forced immunizations with what they had.

But the news media got the news that a confirmed case had been detected in Chicago and Katy Bar the Door.

CHAPTER FIVE

When the Turbine Blows Up

Now we get to the subject of "trust." Trust, as a society, is something that most people understand poorly. Trust is vital for a society to function. It's not hard to explain, though. Trust means that if you loan your lawn mower to a neighbor, you've got a pretty good chance of getting it back. There's an implied contract. I let you use the lawn mower. You return it in pretty much the same condition you got it.

You don't loan it to your cousin who then uses it to cut his clients' yards. If you borrow it, you don't break it and give it back and then insist you didn't break it. You don't sell it. You give it back in pretty much the same condition you got it.

There are several different types of societal trust but they really boil down into two major groups. Familial and general. Familial is the society where if you loan your lawn mower to your cousin, he'll give it back. But if you loan it to your neighbor, who is not your cousin, you don't know if he'll give it back or not. So you don't loan it to your neighbor. You don't do anything for anyone if you can possibly help it. You don't trust the cop unless he's a cousin. You don't trust the banker unless he's a cousin.

If you've ever been overseas (or, hell, in certain areas in the U.S.) and had someone say "I have a cousin who . . . " then you're in a familial trust society.

Then there are general trust societies. The U.S. is, by and large, (and we'll get to Chicago, L.A. and Detroit in a second) a general trust society. In most segments of American society you could loan your lawn mower to your neighbor with a fair expectation of getting it back. If you didn't, you could take him to small claims court and the judge wasn't going to care about you or your neighbor, mostly, just about the merits of the case.

Trust is vital in a society. If societal trust is too low, people trust *no one*. Except, maybe, their cousins.

This brings us to "multiculturalism."

A study was done by a *very* liberal sociologist back in the mid-oughts. The study set out to prove that multicultural societies had higher levels of societal trust than monoculture societies. It seems a no-brainer that the reverse was the case, but at the time multiculturalism, along with a bunch of other urban myths, was the way of the world.

However, it *was* a no-brainer. The study proved the *exact opposite*. That is, the more diverse an area was in cultures, the less societal trust there was.

Look, humans don't trust "the other." The name every single primitive tribe gives for "other" translates as "enemy." Apache was the Hopi name for the Apache tribes and that's the exact translation: Enemy.

But it's more complex than that. Say you're from a general trust culture. A neighbor moves in next door who is from a familial trust culture. You offer the use of your lawn mower. It never comes back. You point that out and eventually learn that it's been used to cut about a hundred lawns. If you get it back, it's trashed.

The neighbor considers you a moron for loaning it to him in the first place. And he doesn't care if you think he's a dick. He doesn't trust *you* anyway. You're not family.

Actual real-world example I picked up on a forum. Group in one of the most pre-Plague diverse neighborhoods in the U.S. wanted to build a play-area for their kids in the local park. They'd established a "multicultural neighborhood committee" of "the entire rainbow." I got this from the liberal "general trust" side of the story. I'd have loved to have gotten it from the rest of the cultures. If they could stop laughing.

Anyway, this group of "let's all sing kumbaya" liberals got their little brown brothers together and proposed they all build a playground for their kids. There was a kinda run-down park in the neighborhood. Let's build swings so our children can all play together. Kumbaya.

There were, indeed, little brown brothers and yellow and black. But . . .

Well, it's kinda difficult to tell the difference between a Sikh and a Moslem unless you know one's turban looks cool and the other's looks like shit. (For general info, I can not only tell the difference between a Moslem and a Sikh, I can 90% of the time tell the difference between two tribes of Moslems. Yes, I may be a culturist SOB, but I'm a *very highly trained* one. *I* can tell the difference between a Moslem and a Sikh *and* talk about the history of conflict between the two groups.) And Sikhs and Moslems can barely bring themselves to spit on each other much less work side by side singing "Kumbaya." The liberals had, apparently, never noticed that the fucked-up-turban guys never went into the cool-turban guy's corner store.

The Hindus were willing to contribute some suggestions and a little money, but the *other* Hindus would have to do the work. What other Hindus? Oh, *those* people. And they would have to hand the money to the kumbaya guys both because handing it to the *other* Hindus would be defiling and because, of course, it would just disappear.

(At some point I need to talk about India. It is not the India today that it was in 2019.)

When they actually got to work, finally, there were some little black brothers helping. Then a different group of little black brothers turned out and sat on the sidelines shouting suggestions until the first group left. Then the "help" left as well. Christian animists might soil their hands for a community project but not if they're getting shit from Islamics. Sure, they're just two different tribes that lived right next to each other in Africa. Speaking of kumbaya. But they've also been slaughtering each other since before Stanley ever found Livingston smoking his bong.

Trust. If you lived in a mostly white-bread suburb before the Time of Suckage you just can't get it. But when trust breaks down enough in a society, nobody trusts *anyone*. Blacks don't trust black cops. Whites don't trust white cops. Nobody trusts their mayor, nobody trusts their boss. Nobody trusts *nobody*.

What the study found was that the *more* multicultural a society, the *lower* the societal trust. (The professor, by the way, *refused to accept his own results*. He sat on them for five years and even then spouted bullshit about "education" as the answer even though *that was covered in the study*.) The *only way to get generalized trust* is to blend the societies and erase the differences. Back in the 1800s an Italian wouldn't be bothered to spit on an Irishman unless he'd just stuck a knife in his back. These days the only way you can tell the difference in the U.S. is one has better food and the other better beer.

So why does this matter to Ching Mao? Doesn't, really, he was dead and never really cared. But it mattered, a lot, to the response in Chicago.

You see, by that time Chicago was a very multicultural area. Gone were the days of it being pure white-bread and kielbasa. Only recent immigrants, who didn't recognize the local white guys as being anything *like* Polish despite their names, spoke the Old Language. Where there had once been mostly assimilated German and Polish and Russian Jew and a smattering of Black communities there were now Serbian and Pakistani and "Persian" and Assyrian not to be confused with Syrian and Iraqi and Fusian who were *not* Manchu who were *not* Korean or anything like who were definitely *not* Cambodian, damn it . . .

Each trusted the family group around them. To an extent they trusted others who were "them." The few white-bread multicultural true-believers trusted all their little rainbow brothers, *of course*, until you got a few drinks in them and they started telling about their experiences. "And I never *did* get my lawn mower back!"

And nobody trusted the Police, the Fire Department or anything else smacking of the government. Most of the immigrants came from countries where that was just sense and police had a hard time dealing with those communities that closed around anyone, good or bad, when questions were asked. And *never* ask a fireman about responding to an "ethnic" neighborhood. You won't like the story if you like to sing kumbaya.

The kumbaya types didn't trust them because they were so *mean* to their little brown brothers. Fascists. General societal trust had been totally degraded.

You couldn't get people to agree on how to build a *playground*. Getting them to work together to fight a killer flu bug was so far beyond the pale it wasn't funny.

The specialists tried. Lord God they tried. The CDC worked around the globe. They knew what they were up against. They just didn't expect it to be this hard in the U.S. They had people that spoke just about every language on Earth but there were families that spoke Martian. They never did track down the snake-head that opened the container until he turned up at the hospital choking up his lungs. None of the Asians were willing to admit there even *were* such people. They found a few street-people who had been exposed. The other laborers, who had been working side by side with him? Nada. "Day laborers that were gathered on the corner? Which corner? We know nothing of this." They were never even able to track down the contractor until *he* was sick. And he didn't know any names or addresses.

It's hard to say whether "the rest of the first" could be called Patients Zero or not. The arguments are technical. I've monitored a few of the boards where specialists discuss it and tried to keep up. I'll just call them "the rest of the first."

It started mostly in the immigrant communities. The people traveling legally were stopped at the border and submitted to quarantine. Illegals, however, weren't interested in being stopped.

The Plague hit Mexico actually *after* it hit in the U.S. At least that was reported. The Mexican Territories were right on the edge of being a failed state back then. No way of knowing if it hit before or after. Didn't really matter. Immigration from Mexico, which had been high, exploded. It couldn't really even be called immigration anymore. Not with the Tijuana Riots and the border attacks in Texas and Arizona. It was an invasion of people desperate to get somewhere they might survive.

And lots of them were infected by the time they crossed the border. On the other side of the border were people willing to transport them to other areas of the U.S. Death crept through the land coughing quietly in the back of thousands of vans and pickup trucks headed for factories that no longer needed their services, farms that were looking at disaster . . .

Seattle, L.A., San Francisco, San Diego, Portland, *Cincinnatti?*, Atlanta, Houston, Savannah, *Indianapolis?*, NYC, Boston, Miami . . .

There was no pattern. There was no way to maintain containment.

It was like biological warfare except it wasn't. It was a Plague.

More came from *China* even until the West Coast ports just said "Enough!" and stopped accepting any shipments from Asia. Not that there were many by that point.

Big problem with saying "Enough!"

China was the United States' number one trading partner. And it wasn't just fold-out hampers you could get for a buck at the Dollar Store. (Remember those?) China supplied most of the raw steel, and a hell of a lot of formed, that U.S. industries used. (Not just because U.S. steel was more expensive but because Chinese was better. Big technical explanation but "trust" me, it was.) They produced parts to go in everything from cars to computers.

There's a really crappy book by Ayn Rand called *Atlas Shrugged*. It's a snoozer but I was really bored one time on an exercise and struggled all the way through that fucker. The basic premise, though, was simple. A guy who built a widget that was very important to, well, everything it turned out, decided to quit. The guys who took over building the widget didn't build it as well and society fell apart.

Societies are dynamic complex systems. It is not easy to break a society or an economy. You can't do it by missing any one widget. If the guys making the widget, now, don't make it well enough someone will come along who does. And probably better than the original widget maker. That's the whole point of a free-market. Command economy? Maybe. But then the KGB will come break down the widget maker's door and explain that he'd better get back to making widgets or he's never going to see his daughter again.

And *one* widget *never* does it. Ever.

One hundred thousand widgets? All those widgets that are in containers that might or might not contain infectants?

That will break an economy.

Look, our farm used only John Deere. Made in the USA, baby, best damned tractors in the world.

The wiring harness was assembled by slave labor in the good old People's Republic of China.

So were a bunch of other parts. The *steel* was Chinese. (Because it beat U.S. steel hands down.) They made the injectors for the engine in the U.S. It was Chinese material. They made the stanchions for the suspension in the U.S. The steel was Chinese. The computer chip that ran the engine? Taiwan, which fell about as fast.

If there had been time, if there had been warning, if the whole fucking *world* hadn't come apart, companies would have reacted, adapted and overcome. Many of them did in spite of everything. Things never really got to the point of complete Armageddon in the U.S. in most areas. (L.A. is an extreme example but Chicago was nearly as bad. Especially after the winter of 2019–2020. Actually might have been worse. Most of L.A. left rather than died. They're *still* finding bodies in Chicago.)

Forget a machine with sand in the gears. The economy of the U.S. had often been called the Turbine of the World. It sure came apart like one.

Ever seen a big turbine come apart? Think about the same quantity of plastic explosives.

Companies in those days ran on very thin margins and very small inventories. Various reasons. It was economically more efficient. After the changes in the '70s and '80s in the way that companies ran, the marketplace had become cutthroat competitive. There were a bunch of tax laws that pressured for it. Returns were higher. Everything depended on productivity, which was and is higher per man hour in the U.S. than anywhere in the world.

However.

That meant that when a company suddenly had a breakdown, the answer was to rush order whatever they needed. Don't want that parts inventory bogging them down. "Just in time ordering."

Only the parts were made in China. And while a middleman would normally have them, they were sitting in Port of Seattle under quarantine.

And what with the Plague spreading fast in Seattle there weren't any people to clear the container or guys to move it onto a train or even a train engineer to drive the train.

Not to mention that there weren't any more shipments. China was out of the widget business. Cheap hampers were suddenly a thing of the past.

So was the Dollar Store. Walmarts started closing. Whole companies went from "the fourth quarter will be a fully acceptable return period" to "here's your pink slip. I've already got mine" in mere *days*.

Various states became "reactionary." Technically, it was against the Constitution to close the borders of a state and people said that there was no way to do it.

First of all, by this time most people were trying to interact as little as possible. Even in areas where trust was high, Blue Earth for example, did you trust your neighbor enough to not give your kids the Plague? People, wherever possible, huddled in. Another reason for the economy coming apart so fast was people just stopped going to work. And the American Turbine ran on productivity. Companies kept as few people as possible and worked them hard. One calling in "long term sick-leave" might have worked. Half the work-force calling in was a different kettle of fish.

Businesses started slamming their doors. And it was happening so fast people couldn't begin to understand the effect. The President was dealing with reports that were a day old and during the height of the Plague that was like reading up on Darius the Great.

You know the greatest heroes in all of this? It wasn't the firemen and police and National Guard. It wasn't the guys from the CDC. They were all trying, hard, to stop the Plague and failing miserably. But they were innoculated and so were most of their families, officially or not.

No, it was the teller at the grocery stores. It was the nurses and doctors that opened their doors every morning, not sure how or if they were going to get paid all things considered, and dealt with patients for eighteen or twenty hours before going home to crash and come back and do it all over again. Most of the latter were vaccinated. Many of the truckers and stockers and tellers at the grocery stores weren't. They put on masks and hoped for the best.

Because people had to *eat*.

And then money started to run short at the same time as inflation hit big-time.

Explanation.

People were only buying what they considered essentials. Basically food and gas so they could drive to the store when they absolutely had to or to the hospital or doctor's office when they knew they had to.

But the distribution system for food and gas was getting shot. People were dying, yes, but even more weren't being heroes. It was a tough call.

Say you're guy working at a local fuel distribution plant. Your wife is, say, a teacher. She's on permanent leave and might or might not be getting paid. You've got two kids. They're both okay. You've got food in the cupboard, enough to carry you for a while. A few weeks at least. Surely by *then* there will be immunizations, right? There's some money in the bank. Not a lot; you live paycheck to paycheck.

Now, it's morning, there are reports of people dying all over the nation from this flu shit. Your kids are good. You don't want your kids to die. And, hell, *you* don't want to die.

So do you go to work that morning? And have to interact with a bunch of people?

The choice of most of the people who did get up and go out to try to keep things running was just that. They went out and didn't come back until the majority of the Plague cleared or they died. This was mostly males. Not all, by any stretch. But when it came down to who was going to survive and who die in a family, mommy stayed home and daddy went to work.

And about thirty percent of them died.

Mommy and the kids weren't doing so hot, either. H5N1 had a four day "latency" period. That is, it could sit around for four days waiting to infect someone under normal conditions. It also had a three day period before "first frank symptoms." You didn't sniffle for three days after you had actually picked it up. That combination of damned near a week meant that lots of people picked it up before they ever decided "enough's enough" and went home to hide. And even if family had been hiding before they went home, now everybody had it.

Let me talk a bit about the rest of the world before I get into just what that did to the U.S.

— CHAPTER SIX —

Daddy Is Under the Roses

H5N1 was spreading, fast, through the world. A few countries tried, hard, to close their borders. Some of them thought they'd done a good job. Cuba slammed the door fast but the sucker got in anyway. Then their "universal health care system" kicked in. Raoul wasn't as stupid as the Chinese; the soldiers he sent out were immunized. But the "universal health care system" in Cuba wasn't anywhere near what it was cracked up to be. If you weren't someone important, say a liberal celebrity licking a dictator's boot, you had to wait and wait for *any* kind of treatment. And trust levels were, to say the least, low. So when Cuba's patient zeros turned up it was the same problem as Chicago. People ran from the soldiers who weren't all that happy dealing with a plague. And when people went to the hospital because they were afraid they were dying they generally died. And infected everyone around them, some of whom could escape one way or another.

Then the soldiers started deserting and the doctors started deserting, taking as many medications as they could carry with them, and Cuba took right at 60% casualties, primarily among the mid-range of adults. Classic H5N1.

Britain's an island. It's hard to get to Britain if you don't have a plane or a boat. Britain cut off aerial communication with the U.S. when Ching Mao was reported. Didn't matter. A Thai doctor who was a British citizen landed at Heathrow the day prior to Ching's discovery. He had just returned from visiting family in Thailand via India. He landed in India prior to it cutting off contact with Thailand and India still wasn't on the quarantine list.

Two days later, Britain cut off all communication. But by that time it was too late. The doctor and nine other infecteds had spread out across the country. He was in frank symptoms for less than twenty-four hours when Dr. Van realized what he had and reported to his local health clinic. Where, despite being an MD, he had to wait. He'd worn a mask, not wanting to infect anyone else, and was gloved. He told the triage nurse he suspected he had H5N1. That was on the records of admission.

The records also listed his time of speaking to the first person about his condition. It was _nine hours later_ when he was _finally_ examined by the on-call MD who admitted him as a possible H5N1 patient. He was subjected to a battery of anti-viral drugs and put in quarantine while being questioned. He was fully conscious, in the first stage of bird flu. He gave a very comprehensive list of his contacts and had even taken the time in the waiting room to make notes.

During his stay in the waiting room, despite his best efforts, he was later determined to have infected eighteen persons. Total infectants was never quite determined but was believed to be on the order of two hundred.

Two things were important here. The first is that, as with any illness or injury, speed of the response _mattered_ with the Plague. Dr. Van died. Because he is one of the classic cases, there have been many articles written about Dr. Van. He had waited twenty-four hours after showing first symptoms, normal cold and flu symptoms, to go to the medical clinic. When asked why, he admitted he knew he would deal with much hassle and red-tape and hoped it was just a normal flu.

Even an _MD_ didn't want to deal with British Health.

He waited _nine hours_ for treatment. In the U.S., unless you were going to an emergency room with the flu, you weren't going to wait that long. Most people of any economic substance, and many who were on medicare or medicaid, had personal doctors. There were "emergency medical clinics" (Doc-In-The-Box) scattered at random.

From the first reports of H5N1 anyone with a sniffle flooded to their nearest MD. While in some cases there was little to be done, they were all instructed on basic necessities and in most cases pumped with anti-virals. The most effective in original tests, Zanamivir from Glaxo, had, again by the Chinese, been made useless. They'd used it in chicken populations in the years before the Plague and H5N1 had developed a resistance. A newer one, Maxavir, also from Glaxo, had just been distributed. Stocks ran out fast, but people who were treated in the first few hours of frank symptoms, instead of nearly 36 hours after the first sniffle, recovered at a rate of 80%. There was even an over-the-counter medication that increased survival rate if taken immediately on first symptom. Many people started using it as a prophylactic until it ran out and probably caused H5N1 to develop its resistance. But they survived.

Most of this wasn't available in a "socialized medicine" country unless you went to the local clinic and waited *all fucking day* to see a doctor.

Study done in 2004 by the CDC. The way that good science works is that the scientist looks at something and says "What if?" He then develops a statement from that (a hypothesis) then tries to disprove his hypothesis. "The sky is yellow." He first defines yellow. He then tests to see if the sky is yellow. If it turns out that the sky is actually blue, his hypothesis gets disproved. But he still publishes the paper and comes up with another hypothesis. Say that the world is really round. If he *cannot disprove* his hypothesis, it *then and only then* becomes a *theory*. This is Science 101. Man-induced global warming was an *hypothesis* that had been repeatedly *disproven*. Anthropogenic (man-caused) global warming proponents weren't scientists, they were religious zealots.

Anyway, the CDC *liked* "universal healthcare." It was a government health program and government health programs were *good*. *They* were a government health program so any government health program *had* to be good.

Hypothesis: "Universal health care will increase the lifespan and general health of a population over free-market health care."

Conclusion: "Fuck, we were not only *wrong* we were *really* wrong!"

How could that possibly be? Seriously. Universal healthcare is, well, *universal healthcare*! Everybody gets the same quality of treatment, young and old, rich and poor! Nobody is turned away! It's perfect communism! With doctors!

Yeah, everybody gets the same quality of treatment: Bad.

Look, if you're between the ages of 7 and 50, in reasonably good overall condition, don't have fucked up genetics and don't *really* lose the lottery, you *generally* don't really *need* a doctor. People between the ages of 7 and 50 rarely realize how bad socialist medicine is. Because they don't have to depend on doctors.

Try getting a hip replacement in a country with socialized medicine. Or a gall bladder operation. Hell, try getting drugs that improve a heart condition *without* surgery. And even though you can't, you also can't get surgery. Not in any sort of real time. Go rushing into a socialized medicine hospital with a clogged artery. You're going to get a stent if you're lucky. And get put on a waiting list for a bypass. For various political reasons, drugs that in free-market economies are the first line of defense just aren't available.

In the U.S. the standard time to wait for a gall bladder operation was two weeks. In the UK it was nine months. In the U.S., if you needed a bypass you'd be out of the surgery less than fourteen hours after emergency admission. In the UK it was emergency admission, minimal support therapy, months wait. Some 35% of persons waiting for a bypass operation *died* before they got one.

They found an interesting statistical anomaly as well. Death rates amongst the elderly climbed sharply as the end of the fiscal year approached.

Doctors in socialized medicine programs worked for the same pay whether they fixed people or not. But they had quotas for operations. As the end of the fiscal year approached, most of them had filled their quotas and went on actual or virtual vacation.

And people died.

Average population age in most of the socialized medicine countries were only starting to climb to the levels where death rates due to poor medical care were going to be noticeable. But the truncation of ages was clear. As were quality of life indicators.

Persons in free-market medical environments lived longer, healthier, less pain-filled lives. *Despite* the evil doctors and HMOs and pharmaceutical companies? No, *because* of the evil doctors and HMOs and pharmaceutical companies. All three groups had a vested interest in keeping patients alive as long as possible. The longer they lived, the more money the "evil" guys made.

The U.S. had been repeatedly castigated for the cost of healthcare and especially pharmaceuticals. Also for over-prescription of the newest and most costly.

But.

In Europe there was no pressure to use pharmaceuticals. With costs capped by the government, there was no incentive for the pharmaceutical companies. Modern pharmaceuticals are enormously expensive to field. The first problem is the cost of development. Many of them are derived from natural substances, but it takes relentless searching to find a new natural substance. Cancer drugs were derived from rare South African pansies, new antibiotics were derived from fungus found on a stone in a Japanese temple. Then they had to be tested to find out if any benefits could be derived.

Here's the numbers:

Animal (screening) in rats—about 1–2 years, cost about $500k/year, in monkeys—about 2–5 years, cost $2 million a year. Phase I in humans is strictly toxicology: 2 years, $10–20 million a year. If it doesn't kill anybody, then move to Phase II testing for effectiveness: up to 10 years, cost *$100+ million*/year. If statistics suggest a beneficial effect, then on to Phase III to determine effective dosage, side effects, other benefits and "off-label" uses: 5–10 years at another. *$100+* million a year. A (large) Pharma company will start with 10,000 compounds in screening, take about 200 into animal testing, then possibly get ten into Phase I to *maybe* get one into Phase II. In the last 10–20 years, about 95% of Alzheimer's disease drugs that got to Phase II on the basis of rodent testing were sent back because they had no effect in humans—hence the necessity for the added expense of monkey testing ...

It was a hideously expensive process. Again, Do. The. Math. Easily a *billion dollars* invested in *one drug*. The reason that a new pharmaceutical was so expensive was not just the cost of developing *that* pharmaceutical but the brutal necessity of so many *thousands and millions of failures* that that one new shining hope bore upon its back. Billions of dollars lost when "miracle" drugs failed at one step or another. And all that money only being recouped by those limited shining hopes that made it through the process.

But the results were worth every penny. New drugs that cut the need for bypasses; one of the most lucrative surgeries of the 1980s had been almost eliminated in the U.S. by the time of the Plague. Stroke reducing medicines, anti-cancer medicines, cancer prophylactics and, of course, Viagra, every old man's fantasy made real.

In Europe, in contrast, it was considered cheaper to just operate. Much more unpleasant for the patient but the doctors filled their quotas and the government wasn't forced to pay for the development of pharmaceuticals. Which was why most of the modern wonder drugs were coming out of America or from European businesses that were making most of their nut selling them in America.

Doctors in socialized medicine countries, and their bosses and the heads of departments, had *no vested interest* in keeping old people or the chronically sick alive. The doctors might have a personal desire to help people, otherwise they wouldn't have become doctors. But they had no actual *benefit* and if you've ever dealt with a bunch of crotchety old people you can see some of the actual detraction.

For doctors, hospitals and pharmaceutical companies in the U.S., those crotchety old people spelled money, money, *money!* So they researched and they worked and they studied ways to extend the time they could continue to suck the money out of them.

In the case of governments of socialized medicine countries, the primary users of the services, see: "crotchety old people," were their worst nightmares. The patients worked their whole lives, contributed to the economies of the countries and now expected to be paid back. Heavily. Socialized medicine wasn't the only benefit they expected. They retired early with pensions that nearly equalled their salaries when working. And they paid little or no taxes. And as any health insurance actuary will tell you, they consumed 90+% of the health budget. Mostly in their last six months of life. And what was the point of *that?*

It would be unfair to say that the politicians just wanted to see them all go away and that cutting off access to vital health services thus killed two birds with one stone. Save money and quietly kill off the primary users.

Or would it? Health care spending as adjusted for inflation had dropped steadily in socialized medicine countries in Europe even as the need had increased. All access to medicine was rationed. And in the Netherlands people who were "beyond help" were denied access to healthcare on a regular basis and even "medically terminated," put to death, against the wishes of their care-givers.

Not only old people but children with chronic health care problems. "Terminal" cancer? Which sometimes was treatable or even erasable in the U.S.? In the Netherlands, they just turned up the morphine drip until you quietly passed into the Long Dark.

A corollary effect was on the members of the health profession. A doctor in Britain who worked ninety hours a week got paid exactly the same as a doctor who worked forty hours per week. (Often they worked less.) And it was rare that there were any changes for quality. World-renowned surgeons in Germany and France made only a fraction more than less competent doctors.

In the U.S., on the other hand, they could write their ticket.

The brain drain was not severe at the time of the Plague but it was telling. More and more top-flight doctors had left to find greener pastures. For that matter, doctors in less developed countries had flooded into the U.S., where they might not make a fortune but they got paid in more than chickens and hummus. They filled the corner "Minor Emergency Centers" as well as being the front line general practicioners, a field most American born doctors disdained as the most plebian of medical fields.

This was what the good doctors at the CDC learned when they set out to prove that American healthcare, with its dependence on the free-market, doctor/patient choice, HMOs and pharmaceutical companies was far inferior to the enlightened healthcare of "socialized medicine" countries.

They discovered the irrefutable truth that when you put the same sort of people that run the Post Office in charge of your healthcare you get Postal Workers for health care providers. And more people die in less necessary ways.

So let's go back and look at the effect of H5N1 on populations.

In its initial discovery, mortality among affected populations, primarily Chinese poultry workers, was right at 60%. Two out of three who were infected died despite best efforts on the part of local (socialized medicine) doctors. This continued as a pattern during the long period that H5N1 was confined to avian to human transmission.

Across the board in unimmunized populations with access to "universal healthcare" the same pattern emerged. Two in three unimmunized patients who were admitted to healthcare environments (less than 10% of the affected at the height of the Plague) died.

In the U.S. the rate was *one* in three.

Thirty percent vs. sixty percent. Still a horrific number, total death-toll from direct effects of the Plague are estimated to be around a hundred million. But if the rate had been the same as Europe's, the death toll would have been *twice that*.

Why?

It had been a puzzler even before the Plague. One reason that there was a somewhat slower response among the public to H5N1 was that there had been an earlier scare involving something called SARS, Severe Acute Respiratory Syndrome. It had also started in China, there had been a cover-up that affected a large and never clearly documented number of cases with estimates ranging from five hundred to fifty thousand and mortality rates similar to H5N1. It had broken out into Thailand and Singapore and even spread into Canada. Everywhere the rate was the same, serious pulmonary distress that led to death in five of ten cases. Including in Canada, which was prepared for it and responded very fast to the discovered cases.

Cases that reached the U.S. were given a different name: MARS; Mild Acute Respiratory Syndrome.

Same exact bug. Fifty documented cases in the U.S. No. One. Died.

Why?

Think of Dr. Van. A *physician* who *cooled his heels* for *nine hours* in a *waiting room* after telling the triage nurse that he probably had a *deathly illness.*

By the same token, cases in the U.S. called their private general practitioner and told him that they were very sick. They were seen within no more than two hours and admitted within less than an hour afterwards to the hospital.

Cases in Canada which were detected through investigation got similar speedy care. More of them survived than those who were first cases. Speed of care was *preeminent*. Yes, too often it simply didn't work. And as cases burgeoned the healthcare system in every country became overloaded. But in the U.S., people didn't just have to go to the local health clinic. As hospitals became overloaded, doctors often shifted to the old fashioned home-visit. Where they could not, there were thousands of minor healthcare providers, mostly LPNs and Medical Assistants, from that increasingly lucrative industry who were pressed into service. The number of providers in the healthcare industry in the U.S. had been exploding as the population aged while it had been more or less stagnant in Europe. Because there was money in them there old people there were just *more healthcare workers per patient.*

Many of them worked through the height of the Plague for little or no money. The economy was tanking, fast. They worked in the hopes that they'd get paid and eventually most of them did.

This was one reason that the mortality rate from direct effect of the Plague was lower in the U.S. than in other modern countries. (Countries which *never* had their act together simply sank lower. I'll discuss my *personal* experiences of that later.)

A secondary reason is debatable. It had been debated as far back as the SARS scare and still remains questionable. But there is now some corroborating evidence based on analysis of mortality rates in various populations based on their lifestyle. It is, however, detested by most health care persons and every remaining "organic lifestyle" lover on the planet.

Hormones.

We're back to industrial farming. Yep, we injected our livestock with all sorts of shit. Growth hormones for the beef and goat stock. (Yes, we raised goats for meat. There was a pretty good market before the Plague.) Milk generating hormones in the milk cows. We used "genetically modified" seeds that were hyper-resistant to dozens of pathogens. We sprayed herbicides and pesticides and laid down fields with ammonium nitrate (the stuff terrorists use in big bombs) to increase yields. We used every trick in the book and most of the bigger farm corporations we competed against used the same tricks, just not as well as we did or we'd have gone out of business.

And you all ate it every day. For that matter, at the food factories, and there is no other term for the way that food was processed, it was then injected with more "stuff." In some cases it was vitamins. Preservatives. Colorations.

The U.S. was the most heavily chemicaled food on earth. Sure it had some effect. Was it a contributor to obesity? Don't know and there's no clinical evidence. Ditto "early maturation": those cute little girls that got their boobies *way* too soon. But it was in your bodies. If you weren't a health nut. And be glad you weren't.

One study that is roundly castigated still but pretty hard to argue showed that people who were "uncaring" in their food choices had a five percent *lower* mortality rate than people who were "careful" in their food choices. The language of "uncaring" vs. "caring" was explained in the codicil that "caring" meant they ate, to the greatest extent possible, organic and natural foods. Uncaring meant they stuffed whatever in their maw and didn't give a shit how it was raised or what was in it as long as it was tasty.

The problem with the study, with which I agree, is that there is *no mechanism explained for the effect*. Got that. But that was what the pope's Inquisition said about Galileo. Sure, *he thought* that the Earth revolved around the sun but he didn't have a mechanism. Gosh, he might even have evidence, but he couldn't show why that was the case whereas the "scientists" of his day had thousands of years of built-up stories about how the sun revolved around the Earth. And my answer is the same as his: "It still *moves!*"

In the U.S. SARS, a huge health threat everywhere else it touched, became MARS, a very bad cold.

Part of that was, unquestionably, free-market medicine vs. socialized. Absolutely. But another fraction, also as unquestionably, was that Americans had so much shit in their bodies it was amazing we decayed at all. All those chemicals had some negative effects, sure. But they also have some positive. That's the part that healthcare nuts and organic fruits don't want anyone to realize or talk about.

Fuck 'em. It still moves.

Here is another that relates purely to H5N1. It's just a hypothesis because nobody has been able to do a good clinical study on it. (Several people have tried.) And it's kind of weird.

Social distance.

First I've got to talk about, yeah, virology and binding. (Lord I was trying to avoid this.) Prepare for major MEGO.

The common "seasonal" flus are referred to as H3N2 and H1N1. Both have a binding protein that binds to specific proteins in the upper respiratory system. (Can you say sinus pain? And fever and all the rest once your good old immune system kicks in.) Then, maybe, it moves to the lungs and you get coughing and if it gets bad a secondary bacterial infection (pneumonia or bronchitis depending on how bad it is).

H5N1 in its classic "bird flu" form bound to receptors in avian intestines. (It's an intestinal flu for them.) Which was why at first only poultry workers got it. They got it from breathing in chicken poop. Because there are *similar* receptor proteins in *human lungs*. Not the same. Similar.

(By the way, on an interesting aside. Influenza, in general, may be the oldest pathogen around. The genetics indicate that it goes all the way back to intestinal flu in dinosaurs. So the next time you're sneezing and coughing, just remember: Species come and go but the flu is here to stay. Take it like a man. End aside.)

(Oh, serious technical note. The bird binding sites are referred to as alpha 2,3. Human lung receptors are alpha 2,6.)

What caused the pandemic was a switch in one little gene code. That permitted the flu to bind to the proteins in the lungs.

Which was a good thing. A "normal" flu that bound to the upper respiratory system with the same lethality as H5N1 would have been *truly* a world killer. What kept a lot of people alive was they just never caught the flu. Because it had to get all the way into the lungs. That required a much higher viral load.

Which gets to social distance.

Everyone knows what social distance is. "I need my space." In the U.S. it's about two and a half to three feet. Anyone who is "non-intimate" (which doesn't mean just family/lovers, get to that) coming inside that space causes a social reaction. People back up or a fight breaks out. I need my space.

Every society has a social distance. But "classic" Americans (white, black, you name it, but fully assimilated) have the *largest social space on the planet.* Arab social space is about sixteen inches. When they're just moving around. If it's crowded it can drop to ten or even in contact with no social issues. Asians (Orientals for the non-PC) are even closer. Standard is around ten. Africans even work closer than Americans. We're *very* stand-offish people. *Germans* get closer to each other than Americans and we probably got the social meme *from* the Germans.

Heavy viral load requires you to breathe somebody else's breath. In general, people don't do that much in the U.S. In Asian societies it's just everyday living.

The "in general" gets to "intimate contact." Intimate contact is getting down to less than arm's distance. People go "ain't happening" but it happens with several categories of jobs. Medical profession and early elementary teachers (K–4 more or less) being the top two. Kids, for that matter, get much closer to each other than adults do.

Guess which professions had the highest infection rates?

Probably one of the reasons that Americans just didn't infect as much as other societies is that we're grouchy, touchy SOBs. For that matter, it may be why some of the more "socially prominent" zones (San Francisco) got hit so hard. People were "accepting" of entrance to their personal space and it killed them.

The last factor is back to trust. Thought that was a big sideline, didn't you?

Let's go back to our standard family of four living in a house with a white picket fence. Mom's a teacher, dad works for a local gas distribution center and the kids are, well, kids. For this narrative we will make them twelve and nine, boy and girl respectively.

This is about to get . . . Well, those of you who were that family, you know where this is going. This isn't going to be your narrative, but most of you lived one like it.

The Plague is definitely spreading. Mommy and Daddy decide that they're going to sit it out with what they have in the house. They'd had a bad ice storm a while back and they have some preparedness. Daddy makes one more run to the store and the gas lines. He finally finds what they desperately need and comes home.

Doesn't matter. Daddy didn't bring the Plague into the house, Mommy did. She got it from one of her Hispanic kids who barely had the sniffles. She doesn't know it.

The nine year old shows the first frank symptoms. They all put on dust masks Daddy usually uses for painting and go to the doctor. The office is overrun. They do wait, probably two hours, to see a nurse. The nurse administers (at the doctor's orders as he shouts them down the corridor) an antiviral to all four. It's probably pissing in the wind but it's the best that you can do with a virus. The doctor doesn't have any immunizations; they went bad waiting for someone to figure out what to do with them. They are also given an antibiotic shot and a bottle of antibiotics for each of them. This is for the pneumonic stage so that there's a *chance* secondaries won't kill them. They're told the hospital is overloaded. Don't bother.

They go home. They hold hands. They watch TV. They get sick and then they get sicker. Mommy and Daddy take care of the children as well as they can until they are at the point of collapse then lie in bed to wait it out. There's a box of bottled water in every room and that's about all they can do.

They go through the pneumonic stage. Mommy and Daddy come out of it at about the same time. They check the children and make sure they're taking their antibiotics. The kids are both alive, thank God.

They relapse, almost at the same time. Mommy doesn't remember much of that period except shouting at her husband to stop screaming.

Mommy wakes up covered in sweat but clear-headed. Her husband is dead by her side. She finds her children in the kitchen eating cereal; the only thing they know how to make. There is no power and the water runs for a moment then stops. She hugs her children and tells them that Daddy has gone up to heaven. The children are shell-shocked. They know Daddy is dead. And he said bad things to them before he died. So did Mommy. They're terrified but she comforts them as well as she can and gets them something better to eat. That, at the moment, is the most she can do.

Mommy tells the children to go out in the front yard and not to come in the back yard or the house until she tells them. Weak, dehydrated and just recovered from a killer illness, she nonetheless drags her late husband's heavy body into the backyard. There she digs a shallow hole and puts him in it, wrapped in the sheet from the bed. It's spring. She looks around the yard and, despite her aching bones and fatigue, picks up the plastic tray filled with pansies that were supposed to eventually ornament a planter on the front porch and arrays them across the tilled earth that is all she has left of her lover, her friend, her mate.

Across the United States there are these small monuments to the horror and glory of the Plague and the response of just *everyday people*. Flower beds across our God-kissed nation rear up from the bones of the dead, their death bringing new life and beauty into the world they have left.

My father is buried under roses.

Yes, there were the charnel pits. There were the death trucks with their slowly tolling bell. Manned mostly by garbage men in cities they carried away thousands and do so still in places. But when people really grasped how messed up things had become and when they had the land many of their family members ended up in a flower bed.

Personally, I'd have preferred that, wouldn't you?

But then came the next step. What do you do when the world has so clearly come apart? Radio reports indicate that nothing is working, anywhere. The Federal government is telling people to do the best they can until help arrives.

I'll describe later what happened in low trust countries. But this narrative is about the happy suburban family, an environment where societal trust, believe me, is probably the highest it has been in recorded history. People growing up in suburbs just don't know how *unusual* they are. That "it looks the same all over" is boring as hell but it's a *function* of high trust.

The U.S. is a strange country. Growing up in it I never realized that, but spending those tours overseas really brought it home. We're just fucking *weird*.

Alex de Touqueville spoke of this weirdness in his book *Democracy in America* way back in the 1800s. "Americans, contrary to every other society I have studied, form voluntary random social alliances."

Look, let's drill that down a bit and look at that most American of activities: The Barn Raising.

I know that virtually none of you have ever participated in a barn raising. But everyone knows what I mean. A family in an established commuity that has gotten to the point they can build a barn or need a new one or maybe a new pioneer family that needs a barn puts out the word. There's going to be a barn raising on x day, usually Saturday or Sunday.

People from miles around walk over to the family's farm and work all day raising the barn. Mostly the guys do the heavy work while women work on food. That evening everybody gets together for a party. They sleep out or in the new barn, then walk home the next day to their usual routine.

ONLY HAPPENS IN AMERICA.

Only *ever* happened in America. It is a *purely American invention* and is from inconceivable to repugnant to other cultures.

A group of very near strangers in that they are not family or some extended tribe gather together in a "voluntary random social alliance" to aid another family for no direct benefit to themselves. The family that is getting the barn would normally supply some major food and if culturally acceptable and available some form of alcohol. But the people gathering to aid them have access to the same or better. There is a bit of a party afterwards but a social gathering does not pay for a hard day's work. (And raising a barn is a *hard* day's work.)

The benefit rests solely in the trust that when *another family needs aid*, the aided family will *do their best to provide such aid*.

Trust.

Americans form "voluntary random social alliances." Other societies do not. *Low trust* societies in the U.S. do not. The kumbayas trying to build swings for the neighborhood children assumed the willingness of their "rainbow" neighbors to form a "voluntary random social alliance" *for mutual benefit* and discovered how rare American are.

In other countries an extended family might gather together to raise the barn or some other major endeavor. But this is not a *voluntary random alliance*. They turn up because the matriarch or patriarch has ordered it. And family is anything but random societally. (However random it may seem from the inside.)

This leads to the next stage of the narrative of our family. The mother performs an inventory of what they have. She considers heading to the hills. Many did. But most, those that survived and lived in high trust areas, then did something unthinkable in most areas of the world: They set out to help their neighbors.

Note: In many areas of the world, most neighbors would be extended family. In those areas, similar things happened. But they *stopped* at the level of extended family. From there on out, it became the government's problem. The king is supposed to fix big disasters. Individuals help their family as much as they can and then it's up to the king. The king will tell us what to do.

The mother of this narrative, and it's documented in at least twenty studies that it happened in all "high trust" zones in the United States, then went next door. There she found one of her neighor's children dead, another alive and very nearly psychotic. The child clings to her and she comforts her. Then she suggests that the child go play with her children. Children will recover their feet quickly when given anything orderly and common. The child is marginally functional by the time she goes back to the house. Long-term effects may be high, but right now functional is all that matters.

She returns to the house. In this case the wife is dead and the husband in the last throes of the cerebral portion of the progression. She removes her friend's body from the bed and gives the husband as much support as she can.

Note: One function of the H5N1 is that children rarely suffered from the cerebral infection stage or did so moderately. This was across the board and the clinical rationale is still poorly understood. The *hypothesis* (unproven) is that kids' bodies, due to growth hormones and such, tended to hold the blood in despite systemic flu. Thus they didn't suffer as much from cerebral and other organic breakdown. No solid clinical data but that's the hypothesis.

Thus, unfortunately, children often broke out of their illness to find dead parents. Kids, keep that in mind when your parents are freaking out if you get a mild fever. The reason you only have one or two grandparents is that your parents found *their* parents dead of the Plague.

The support helps. One of the secondary mortality effects of H5N1 was often death from dehydration. She manages to get him to swallow some water, to take some analgesics to drop the fever. Perhaps she finds some remaining ice and, over his incoherent protests packs some of the precious substance around him.

She performs an inventory of her neighbor's material. While she is doing so a neighbor from down the street, well ahead of her on the curve, turns up to find out how people are doing.

The neighbor's final fever breaks. She informs him his wife and one child didn't make it and neither did her husband.

Yes, there is a new voluntary association starting to happen. Okay, it's becoming familial fast.

They bury the wife and child. They may rebury the husband deeper. Their children are playing with neighborhood children, recounting their tales of horror this time in whispers and even occasional giggles. Kids jump back fast.

People walk out on the road and look around. They start counting heads. Houses that still haven't suffered from the bug shout for them to stay away. Those who have stay back, not wanting to infect another family. But if one of those families gets sick, neighbors gather to help.

Neighbors gather to help. They bring over bottled water and administer medicines from their own dwindling stores. Larger groups gather and begin to inventory group material and food. A bit of shifting occurs. The female moves into the male's house and now has three children. There is a slight surplus of some food stock because of that. It is offered to others in the community.

Why? There is no benefit. Why minister to the neighbor? There is no fixed benefit. Loot the house? Fixed benefit. Provide your own precious bottled water to a man who may die anyway? Why?

Trust. Trust that when *you* need help, *they* will provide that help. That even if there's no policeman watching to make them return the lawn mower they will *anyway*.

This was not purely a function of the Plague. In every major disaster studied, response of random individuals in first moments was a key factor in initial recovery. "There's never a cop when you need one." By the same token, in a disaster during the first portion of recovery there is never a recovery worker when you need one.

All societies show an initial positive reaction amongst generalized individuals. Yes, there is also looting and scavenging (two different things discussed later.) But the "severe outbreak of violence" generally follows the disaster at long intervals.

However, in "high trust" societies, the "voluntary random response" continues and grows. In "low trust" societies it falters after a short period, usually less than 24 hours. See studies of the Northridge and Kobe quakes "individual persons response" vs. those in Turkey all from near the same time-period. For that matter, find if you can the study of "evacuation response" in New York post-9/11. A purely random and voluntary "Dunkirk" movement of boat and ferry owners evacuated *twice* the number of people out of New York as the "official" evacuation.

If you're going to be in a disaster, the best place to be is in a high-trust society. And if the disaster is Asian bird flu the best place is a high-trust, *standoffish* society.

Let's hear it for the red, white and blue and a chorus of badly sung "Star Spangled Banner." Just don't stand too close to me while you're mangling it.

CHAPTER SEVEN

Case Studies or the Grasshopper and the Ant

Was it invariably this clean? No, of course not. In any society there are those who consider trust to be aberrant and stupid. There were those who hoarded and looted even in high trust zones. But, by and large, yes, it was that clean. People gathered together in "voluntary random associations" for mutual support. And it saved our nation.

Case Study: Blackjack, Georgia.

Blackjack was, at the time of the height of the Plague, a town of two thousand in a very small rural county in south Georgia total population of thirty thousand. Counties in Georgia are tiny. I hunted around to find out why and learned it has to do with their charter, which was written right after the Revolutionary War. Basically, the county seat has to be "one half day's ride" from any point in the county. That was so voters (who at the time of the charter had to be middle class to wealthy white males) could ride into town, vote and ride home in one day.

Does any of that matter? Not really for this story. But it made doing studies county by county in Georgia a lot easier, which is why so many case studies of the Plague were done there. Also that the University of Georgia survived with so limited effect.

(Clarke County Health Department was one of those who got it right with the immunizations. It didn't hurt that the Tropical and Emerging Diseases Lab at UGA was immediately consulted and gave very professional advice, that was followed, to university, city and county administrators. No fewer than 90% of the students and faculty of UGA survived the H5N1 Plague and an astounding 70% of the residents of not only Clarke but the surrounding five counties. Athens has pretty much become the linchpin of Georgia at this point.)

Blackjack. The county health administrator was not the brightest light in the array nor were any of the other county politicians. Immunizations were not properly stored. They were administered purely by the two (count them, *two* for thirty thousand people) county health centers. All emergency services personnel, all county workers and administrators were vaccinated before the first local case of H5N1. (A Hispanic as was far too frequently the case.) Studies of the remaining doses indicated that they were probably less than 20% effective anyway. When the Plague hit in earnest, pretty much everyone went down.

When the wave was past, there were the initial voluntary associations. But once you've made sure your neighbors are okay, what do you do? Sit there and wait for the gub'mint to come help? Not hardly, brother.

There were many people in the county who needed assistance beyond just surviving the Plague. The elderly who had survived (a surprising number) needed assistance. Power was out and it was chilly that spring. There was food aplenty for the time being, but it was irregularly spaced. Bodies needed to be buried.

Did the county step up and get things going? After a while. But the next step was another "voluntary random association": Churches.

The preeminent church of Blackjack, as was the case of most areas in the deep south, was the First Baptist Church. The pastor was away on a missionary trip in, of all places, Thailand. Where he and his wife both died. The assistant pastor's narrative is unknown. He apparently took to the hills at the first suggestion of Plague and his whereabouts were unknown to the researchers.

This left the eldest daughter of the pastor in charge by a form of default. There were deacons of the church and such but they were doing other things to assist the community. The emergency services of *the entire county* ended up on the shoulders of a petite nineteen-year-old girl.

People who had special needs were brought to the church. A community kitchen was set up. Pews were moved and cots put in their place. People brought in food and supplies as they had them. Emergency crews trying to get power restored had first priority on food and beds. Then children. Then the elderly. Then "associated workers," that is everyday citizens who were helping out. Last were general refugees. If you were able-bodied and unwilling to help, you by God got the last of the food if there *was* any.

The priority was established by the preacher's daughter and *nobody argued with her*. And every time that things seemed to be on the brink of disaster, out of food, out of wood for fireplaces, out of blankets, in the words of the young lady in charge, "The Lord would provide."

Note: The limited effect of SARS and H5N1 leads people like this remarkable young lady to suggest the *real* reason isn't free-market medicine or hormones or "voluntary random associations" but that the Lord God looks over America. Given that "bigoted" and "stupid" and "backward" areas like Blackjack had lower mortality rates than more "enlightened" areas, even if similarly rural, it is occasionally hard to argue the logic.

They did not wait for the King to tell them what to do. They did not even wait for the local Lord, their elected county and city representatives, to tell them what to do. They just gathered in "voluntary random associations" and did whatever seemed to be the right thing at the time.

And it saved our nation.

Now we get to "who do you trust?" Well, you trust "us" whatever that "us" might be. Yes, if we're continuing this narrative, the white-bread residents of Smokey Hollow subdivision are not going to trust outsiders. They especially don't trust outsiders that don't look like them. Are they wrong?

Blackjack, again, was an interesting case. The local churches did not *just* take in those from their church. They ministered to anyone in need, which included Hispanic migrant farm workers as well as people who had become stranded on roads trying to escape the Plague. Did they trust those people? The answers given to the researchers were very Southern. Which means as opaque as a Japanese koan. "They were, by and large, nice people." "Did you trust them?" "They were, by and large, nice people."

The answer seemed to be "no." At least in the definition of "societal trust." But they also didn't turn them away. In places there were small towns and counties that closed their borders but Blackjack was, fortunately, far from major metropolitan areas and thus never reached the point of "overrun" with refugees.

The young lady in charge, however, only had problems from members of two minority groups: Hispanic males and African-American females. Neither group would accept her authority unless she brought in a male. Generally, that was one of the emergency workers who was catching a brief rest and a bite of whatever food was available. They were tired, they were frustrated already and they were very clear: You get what you're given, you give what help you can give or you get the hell out and go starve in the wilderness.

The news was still working and occasionally this sort of thing, or the "bigoted" counties that turned away refugees were pointed out on the news as signs of how "backward" such areas were.

Backwards and bigoted or just smart, wise even?

Let us take a look at our kumbaya brethren, what we *can* piece together of *their* narrative.

Comparing a city to a small, rural county would be ingenuous. I'll get to cities later. In the meantime, let's look at another case study.

Lamoille County, Vermont.

The county seat, Hyde Park, was a small town. The largest populated area in the county, Morrisville, had a population of 2000 just like Blackjack. The surrounding county had some farming but was primarily a "bedroom community" of mixed semi-retireds, "crafty" artisans and various others who for one reason or another could escape to the wilderness. Some of the homes were rentals but at the first touch of Plague the owners fled their suburban or urban residences and headed for the hills.

The county went 87% for Warrick. To call it bedrock rural "blue" is an understatement. The county government had issued nonbinding resolutions against the War in Iraq, the War in Iran, global-warming and every other cause celebre of the left. It had issued proclamations lamenting the fact that Lamoille was so intensively white-bread. Where are all our little brown brethren? Don't they know the Berkshires is the place to be?

Lamoille followed Frau Warrick's orders to the letter. Since they received a small shipment of vaccine, they were able to store about a third of their doses and kept the rest in styrofoam shipping containers. They violated the orders only to the extent of sending enough doses to the emergency services for them to spread their innoculations.

Instead of calling for people to come to the county health centers, though, they went out. They went first to nursing homes and innoculated all the old people. They got virtually every oldster that was in a nursing home or other care facility and that didn't object. Then they went to schools. That was harder. They had to get permission from the parents, first. Many of the parents were camped out at the, closed, county health centers so that was tough. They gave the schools a few days to get permission slips. God forbid they innoculate some poor dear when the parents objected.

The Plague hit Lamoille County in earnest about two weeks after they received the vaccine. Some of the vaccine had gone bad without refrigeration but not most. It was chilly in Vermont and it was stored in a back room. It, mostly, kept. But the only people vaccinated in the county, for all practical purposes, were the elderly, county workers, emergency service workers, some of the latter two's families and one school.

(Patient Zero at Copley Health Systems was a stockbroker from Massachusetts. His method of infection was never precisely determined. And many subsequent patients had never had interaction with him. But by then the Plague was really getting around.)

It took them two weeks to get to that point. At which point the schools shut down because parents were keeping their kids home, anyway.

It snowed that March in Vermont. It was a very cold and wet spring. People died. They were sometimes buried in backyards. People walked out and talked to their neighbors. There was some "voluntary random association" of local groups.

And at that point, it stopped. A few people, many of them long-term locals, gathered in larger groups centered around churches. The vast majority of the county, however, sat in their houses and waited for the King (Queen, actually) to tell them what to do.

Why?

Well, one reason was purely political. The vast majority of the "transport" population of Lamoille were liberals. Liberals Believe in the government the way that the young lady in Blackjack Believes in the Lord. It's almost a disservice to refer to such people as liberals. They were, in fact, aristocratists. They were very Old Country in that they felt that beyond their little fence it was the King's duty to fix things.

On average after one week they were out of Maslov's basic necessities, food, water. They then mostly drove to the nearest town to find help. They found dozens and hundreds of their mental brethren doing the same thing. The few "voluntary random associations" that had formed around churches or other societal groups tried to help at first. But there was no significant reciprocation. The transports felt that it was the duty of others to help them in need but not their duty to reciprocate. They wanted to be fed and watered and given shelter because it was a Right. From everyone according to their abilities, to everyone according to their needs. I have no abilities but I have lots of needs.

The voluntary associations, of necessity, started turning them away. Even if they had, societally, trusted the transports (and there had always been a degree of friction) they quickly learned that it was misguided.

En masse the transports complained to what was left of the county administration, accusing the voluntary associations of hoarding, bigotry, being badness. The county began rounding up supplies and distributing them, as was the *right* thing to do in any communist county. There was resistance from the ants that had prepared when the grasshopper, in a situation of survive or die and too many had already died, came to take his gathered seeds. In some cases, literally.

Farms were ordered to bring in all their food stuffs. Of course farms have *vast* stores of food. They're *farms*!

Uh . . . no. I mean, farmers tend to build up some personal stores in cans and such. Sure. But they don't store bulk grain, for example, on site. When they harvest it, it gets shipped to silos and distributed further. If they do have a couple of silos filled with what looks like grain, that's what's called *seed*. It's what you make *more* food from. Unless, of course, you eat it.

Farmers were preparing for planting season at that point. Some of them had seed in their silos. It was confiscated. Those that weren't already using "organic farming" methods or had genmod seeds were roundly castigated. A couple of the local farmers resisted, forcibly, having their seed taken from them. They lost in the end. More deaths.

And all the time the grasshoppers were wanting to know what the gub'mint was going to do to help them. They were protesting and shouting and generally making a nuisance of themselves.

Were all of them being idiots? No, no more than "random association" worked perfectly in high trust zones. But, statistically, "blue" counties had *lower levels of local volunteerism on every level*, from helping their neighbor to assisting in large-scale voluntary associations.

Why? These were, by and large, the people who spoke the most fulsomely of communal living, of everyone binding together in some sort of vast communistic surge to make the world a perfect utopia. And all organic, mind you. This general class of people, looked at in macrocosm, had the most experts in it on communal association of *any* class of people in the U.S. They should have been the biggest "voluntary associators" in the country.

Looked at in macrocosm. The hard-core believers in communal association, though, made up a small fraction of the overall "blue" group. Less than five percent. And most of them were already in "voluntary random associations." It's called a commune. And a commune where everyone voluntarily and randomly believes in communal living sometimes works. Sometimes. Generally, though, it don't.

Let's look at the most famous commune in history, even if most people don't know it *was* one: The Plymouth Colony.

That's right, the Pilgrims were communists. Oh, they didn't have the words and they sure didn't have Marx's great "From everyone according to their abilities to everyone according to their needs" line. But the original charter of the Plymouth Colony, the Mayflower Compact, was clear: Share and share alike.

This lasted through one year in The New World. A year with a death rate that made the Plague, at least in the U.S., look like a minor cold. They simply didn't grow enough food to make it to the next harvest. Various reasons. They were lousy farmers. They didn't understand the soil and weather conditions. But the most important thing they learned, forget putting fish heads under the corn if you got that in elementary school, was that if you treated the people who were doing the majority of the work exactly the same as those who would not or could not contribute as much to the community, the workers eventually decided to work less hard. And farming at that level is, trust me, very hard work.

Let's look back at Blackjack and that remarkable young lady. She looked at the situation very clearly and made a list of who really needed food and shelter. First, the guys who were officially trying to rectify things. They were out working hard every day to try to fix the disaster that was still ongoing. If things were ever going to get better it was going to depend, to a great degree, on them. Some of them were female. They got fed the same as males; take all you can eat, eat all you take. Then kids and the elderly. Okay, that fell into two categories but, face it, kids and old people don't eat much. And it was, after all, a church. Think "Christian charity."

Then the "random associators" got fed. These were the men and women that were doing things in the community to help out. They weren't going to save the world but they were saving lives and supporting the church's efforts. Farms get a mention here. At one point, according to the stories from that case study, they ate okra soup for three days. Why? Because there was a farm that just happened to have a bunch of okra. They offered it to the church for the refugees. One of the deacons from the church, a "voluntary random associator" went out and picked it up and brought it back. Those were the people who were next in line for food and beds.

Last, and certainly least, were the refugees who could help but did not. They were fed last, if there was food. Why? Because they simply didn't matter. If they all died, it wasn't going to offend God or Man because live or die they weren't fixing the situation. They were waiting for the King to make it Right. They were grasshoppers. They were the people that Da Vinci spoke of when he said "Most men are good for naught more than turning good food into shit."

Another true study. In any disaster situation, after the disaster is over and things are back to some degree of normal, ten percent of the refugees in temporary shelter have to be *forcibly removed*. No matter how bad it is, if they don't have to do anything they're content to sit on their ass. By the same token, there's another ten percent that, no matter how bad it is, *has to* help. Disaster professionals leave a certain number of blank spots in their response group because they know that there are going to be people who simply *cannot* sit on their ass and not help out. Giving them pre-specified jobs keeps them from being a nuisance. They're also very temporary slots because the same people will leave the refugee environment as fast as possible. Probably to head back to their communities and see *how they can help out*.

Grasshoppers. Ants.

Back to Lamoille County. The vast majority of the "transport" population, the crafty artisans and semi-retireds and such weren't true communalists. They were grasshoppers.

Look, I'll give you an example of the difference in another disaster: Hurricane Katrina.

Forget the suboptimal response of New Orleans, a city of grasshoppers led by a grasshopper, vs. Mississippi. Forget all the rest. This is a personal story from when I was a kid.

Like everybody else I watched the news when the disaster hit New Orleans. And I grew up on Fox or nothing. But even *that* left a bad taste in my mouth. Not because of what was happening, because of how it was being covered.

I recall this one incident clearly. It's never a thing they replay over the years when stuff comes up about Katrina but I recall it clearly as day.

Shepard Smith was interviewing people down by where the water stopped. When the TV crew first got there there was this guy standing up to his hips in that rotten fucking water. Skinny little black guy, looked like he might have had a drug habit or maybe he was a street person. I dunno, but he was skinny as fuck. He was, when they arrived, helping an old lady out of the water. Walking back to the land with her. When she got to land he turned around to go back out.

Shepard Smith stopped him and asked him what he was doing. The guy said he'd been there all morning, it was a bit after noon and looked hot as shit, helping people through the water. He hadn't had anything to eat or drink. (It's been noted that the news people never seemed to offer except to one lady with a baby that looked as if it was dying.) There was some back and forth then the guy went back out to help another lady.

This bitch, though, was about a hundred pounds overweight. She was bitching up a storm, too. She had on some sort of ID hanging on a lanyard, didn't see what it was. She was sure bitching, though. By God, where was the government! She'd been in her apartment for two days waiting for help and no help done come! Where the hell was the help! Nobody was helping us! We's got nothing and nobody doan care!

Did the cameras tune her out and go back to the good Samaritan up to his hips in water that was probably eating away his fucking legs?

No, they followed her. They caught every bitch and complaint. She just kept walking and they just kept following until the segment ended.

Let's be clear, here. This is a digression about the media. They had a fucking hero right in their fucking sights and they chose to follow a fucking complainer. Here is a guy killing himself to help others and they follow the overweight bitch that wants to know "why's nobody heppin us?"

But it's also about grasshoppers and ants. I don't care if the guy in the water was a heroin addict who lived by stealing purses. He was a fucking *ant*. When the shit hit the fan he helped others and didn't wait for the King to tell him what to do. He jumped into the fucking breach.

The fat bitch? Grasshopper. I don't give a shit if that ID was for some job somewhere and the guy in the water was a street person. She was a grasshopper, he was an ant. "I waited for somebody to help me. Why didn't somebody help me? You should help me. The government should help me."

Me. Me. Me. Me. Fucking Me.

(Ran into Shepard in Iran one time and was forced by higher to give him an interview. He tried like hell to be charming. I admit I was less so. I suppose some day I've got to explain why, but it's one of those things from your childhood you just remember, you know? You're trying to figure out how to be an adult and you look at that and go; "Well, I'm *not* going to be like that bastard Shepard Smith, giving the limelight to a bitching grasshopper while a hero toils away behind his back." Addendum: Turns out it was his producer's fault, not his. Okay, so I'm not perfect, I should have realized he was just the ventriloquist's dummy. In that case, his *producer* is an idiot. Sorry, Shepard.)

Me. It's all about me. Okay, they were *called* the Me generation. Yes, the vast majority of Lamoille County were baby boomers. "If it feels good do it" was the mantra. "It's all about me."

Well, you know in peace and plenty (brought to you in great degree by us ants) "It's all about me" works. It doesn't work for anyone with honor and dignity, but the "It's all about me" people don't care about that. They just care about themselves.

And even in a sufficiently awful disaster situation "It's all about me" works. If you can get out of the disaster area and stealing a car will get you out, you can go far using that technique.

But beyond a certain point, you need help. You can try to shoot your way to what you want, but eventually you're going to be outnumbered and outgunned. (That happened a few times in the U.S. Not many, but it happened. *Very* common in other countries, but I'll get to that.)

The wolf only ever gets to the door because it hasn't hit some blocking force before it gets there. Normally, that's people like me. "People rest safe in their beds at night because rough men stand ready to do violence in their name." I'm one of those "rough men" and proud of it. But when things come apart, hard, like an exploding turbine, well it helps to have a group gathered for mutual support. Lone wolves found themselves increasingly challenged in many areas (mostly red areas) by "voluntary random associations."

So what happened in Lamoille?

Foodstuffs down to seed were confiscated for "community benefit" kitchens. There were soup lines. (Well, they were all over for the next few years. Remember?) There was rationing. Remember the ten percent that *have to do something*? They were the first to leave, looking for somewhere less screwed up. Many of them were the natives of the area who were having their supplies stripped for the grasshoppers. They packed up and ran. Many of them to New Hampshire. Many of those counties weren't taking refugees, but a true Yankee accent could generally talk its way through. Especially if it was carrying supplies or had a sob story from somewhere like Lamoille.

Eventually things were getting bad and worse. There were starting to be some food shipments at that point. Things were starting to derandomize in the U.S. by May or so. Not anywhere near pre-Plague and there were still people getting sick, but it was starting to derandomize.

But it still wasn't great. And then there were the evil farmers who many were sure were still hoarding food. So many of the grasshoppers were moved out, or moved out voluntarily, to the farms.

This is called the Cambodia Syndrome. Also The Zimbabwe Method. In a situation where food is short, send people out to farms. There they can produce food for themselves and for the cities. More about *that* later as well. It's the explanation for 2020 and 2021.

In Cambodia it led to a 20% drop in the population. The farms were and are called The Killing Fields. In Zimbabwe it led to the "grain basket of Africa" entering a long-term famine.

Look, farming is *hard*. It's not only hard *physical* work, it's hard *mental* work. Farm boy, remember? Degree in Agronomy. I *know* whereof I speak. Sending a bunch of tofu-eaters out to rebuild the local farm economy, or even the semiretired stock market traders, or lawyers or power traders or whatever, was like asking a two-year-old to program your stock trading computer.

Especially the way they did it. And the weather didn't help much a-tall.

Most of the seed had been seized and eaten. But there was some left, at least for vegetables and beans. Little packets that had basic instructions on how and when to plant the crops. There was a county agent, a, you guessed it, expert on natural farming methods.

So people were sent out to farms and given the packets and told to read and follow the directions. How hard could it be. Put the seed in the ground and wait for the food to come rolling in.

Most of the packets had planting zone instructions. There were generally five, ranging north to south. Vermont (and Minnesota) were Zone One, meaning the last zone to be planted.

The seeds would give a time frame for planting in the zone you were in. Most of the seeds passed out that April and May were in the zone for planting. Corn, peas, even in Vermont they would *normally* be ready to go into the ground. Corn "knee high by the Fourth of July."

Big Chill, remember? Actual planting time, what you plant and when you plant it, depends on two things: soil temperature and projected growing season. (Wow, real farming information.) Seeds need the soil to be a certain temperature before they'll sprout. Plant them too soon and they're mostly going to go bad. By the same token, the plants need a certain amount of time to mature. Plant them too late and they'll get caught by an early frost or a cold front and be unharvestable. Or the harvest will be lousy.

My dad used to start pacing around March. He'd watch the weather reports like a hawk. He'd surf the Internet. He'd listen to the radio. He'd take soil temperatures. He was gathering all the information he could about how things were warming up, what they might be like that summer. He'd look, I don't joke, at things like the flight of birds. When they were migrating. How fast they were moving. It all went into that organic and extremely experienced computer in his head. And then he'd make a decision on just when we were going to plant and what.

The Big Chill was already setting in. Soil temperatures, which is what the little instructions were based on, were not following normal progression. The tofu-eaters and retirees and the rest of the grasshoppers who now thought themselves ants put the seeds in the ground and waited for the crops to roll in.

And, by and large, they didn't sprout. Some did, they happened to have gotten the soil temperature right. Those were, by and large, caught later by the fact that it was "a year without summer." Frosts continued into June and started again in August. Corn does *not* do well under those conditions. It can handle frost when it's near harvest. It does *not* handle it well when it has tassels.

Speaking of which: Then there was the insistence on "organic." I know, I know, how *many* hobby horses can one person *have*? But bear with me.

Up in Minnesota we've got our fair share of Amish. Nobody is bothered by them. They're not "us" but we're not "them" so it works out. Nobody wants to try to sing kumbaya with the Amish and the Amish won't even consider singing kumbaya with us. "Clannish" doesn't begin to cover it.

But they farmed organically. I mean, it was like their *religion*, right? They had been doing it for a long time and they were not stupid. They paid attention to what worked within the constraints of their culture. They used every trick in the book that wasn't a violation of their faith. They were, hands down, the best truly organic farmers in the United States.

Their harvests averaged half of my dad's evil farm corporation. The only reason they were able to stay in business *at all* was that they had so few needs and everyone worked for, essentially, no pay. They ate what they harvested and anything left over went to buy the very few things they couldn't make themselves.

They were excellent organic farmers. They were *not* excellent *farmers*. Excellence in farming is how much use you get out of a patch of soil. My *dad* was an excellent farmer.

The *best* organic farming in the world is *hugely* inefficient compared to industrial farming. All the kumbaya types that wanted everyone to go to organic farming *simply could not do math*. Say that everyone was suddenly forced, by some sort of edict, (like, say, The Emergency Powers Act and a fucking Presidential Order) to do organic farming. We won't even talk about horse-drawn plows, just no genmod seeds, no herbicides, no pesticides, no "nonorganic" (a contradiction in terms, by the way) fertilizers.

Look, the U.S. was and is beginning to be again the world's bread basket. We produced, and are getting back to producing, 15% of world agricultural production. With about a quarter the workers per ton. But if we had to go to "all organic farming" we'd have had to break *three* times the amount of land that was farmed. Why three? Because in areas that weren't rapidly urbanizing, *good* farmland was all in use. That means working the marginal stuff where production falls off, fast.

Three times as much plowing. Three times as much transportation. About five times (for some complicated reasons) the hands. There was already a notable shortage of skilled farm workers; I have no clue where we'd get the extra guys.

And you have to use *some* fertilizer. I can project places we could get it, they're called sewers. Do you transport it raw? I don't think even the tofu-eaters like the idea of honey-wagons all over the road and they would be *all over* the road. The transportation network for professionally produced fertilizer was very efficient. Trying to replace it with some massive network of shit carriers was going to be *ugly*. And then there's the energy involved in transportation.

Again, plenty of studies. Environmental damage from a total switch to organic farming would have been ten times that of the current conditions of mass industrial farming. Don't care *what* the tofu-eaters believed; that was the reality.

For every simple answer people don't use there are big complicated reasons they don't. But some people can't comprehend big complicated reasons so they cling to the simple answers.

Back to the tofu-eaters in Lamoille. The crops didn't sprout. Those that did did poorly. It was a sucky year to farm, that was part of it. The big part was that the tofu-eaters had no clue what they were doing. And they weren't willing to work *nearly* hard enough. If you're going to organically farm, you'd better be ready to work ten times as hard as an industrial farmer. And I mean "swinging a hoe" hard. And "picking the corn" hard. (The latter is not harvesting.) Why? Weeds. Pests.

Laying down a bed, industrially, works like this in the simplest possible way. (Understand, this is the farming version of C-A-T spells "Cat." Don't think this little paragraph can make you a farmer.) Start with winter fallow field. Spray with herbicide. Let sink in. Wait two weeks for Roundup to degrade. Spray with ammonium nitrate to "seal" the soil. Some stuff you have to combine these but that's getting into sentences and complex words like complex. Wait a short period of time for ammonia to do its magic. Check soil temperature (if you're good you've guessed the day perfectly) and start plowing and planting simultaneously with a John Deere combination planter. At specified intervals spray with insecticide and herbicide chemically targeted to miss your crops. Depending on what you're growing, you might have to do pollination. (Usually except for the low-grains like rye, wheat and barley.) Pollination is the one thing that is hugely manpower intense. (Oh and picking rocks. I can't believe I left out picking rocks!) Generally it happens in summer and you hire a whole bunch of the local kids to come out and hand pollinate. And they'd better be willing to work for peanuts or it's going to break you.

Harvest when it's ready and get ready to either do a second crop or let the field lie fallow for winter. Repeat.

(By the way, all farmers have some level of debt. Ever signed a mortgage and get the question "Do you want to pay monthly, quarterly, biannually or annually" and look at the banker like they're nuts? Monthly, of course! Are you nuts? Unless you're a farmer. In which case, it's generally yearly. You don't make diddly until harvest. That's when all debts get paid, payments on tractors, payments on improvements to the house, payments on your car. And you'd better have budgeted for next year, including the pollinators, or you're going to go bust. Farmers are planners.)

So, let's say you're growing corn and you don't do all that. You just put it in the ground (at the right time) and let it grow its own way. Okay, maybe you spread the field with "manure" (shit) before you plow. (The tofu-eaters mostly didn't.) But you're not going to use evil herbicides or pesticides.

Well, weeds grow much faster than crops. In fact, it seems weeds will grow like, well, weeds. They get up everywhere. Even in fields that have been sprayed over and over again, they spring up. They are transported by wind, by birds. Fucking thistles are the bane of any farmer's existence. They get carried on bird legs and birds *will* get into the fields. If you don't spray in a year or so you're covered in thistles.

But wait! I can hear the organic types screaming about burning and cutting and all that. Yeah. Tell it to the Amish. Go look at an Amish field right next to an "evil" field. Let's take wheat since it's easy to spot. Look at the "evil" field. You'll see, scattered through it, some brown looking stuff that isn't wheat. If you don't know what that is, it's called "Indian Tobacco." It's related, distantly, to tobacco but has no value as a crop. Period. It's a weed.

Look at the "evil" field. Maybe five percent of the total, usually less, is taken over by Indian Tobacco. Look at the Amish field. Closer to thirty percent.

And they burn. And they cut during fallow at intervals to catch weeds. Some of them, and there was a big debate about it, even used biological controls. (Pests that target specific weeds.)

And it's *still* there. Hell, it's hard enough to get rid of with herbicides. And its root structure strangles out everything around it. Let fucking Indian Tobacco get loose in a wheat field for long enough and you might as well move to Florida and retire.

And don't even get me *started* on mustard weed! I really fucking *hate* mustard weed!

But we were talking about corn. So let's talk about burcucumber. Sounds cute, right? It's a combination of two words, the first of which is "bur." Don't know if anyone reading this has ever dealt with burs. They're the things that stick onto your legs when you're walking through grass in summer. Burcucumber doesn't have really nasty burs, but it's a climber. It climbs like any viny plant. Let it get into a corn crop and it will climb right up and kill the plants.

And all weeds, no matter how minor, take away nutrients from your crops. They are a *pain in the ass*.

So, you can do industrial things to get rid of them. From a paper on weed management and burcucumber:

"Management: Soil applications of Balance Pro or postemergence applications of atrazine, Beacon, Buctril, Classic, Cobra, glyphosate, or Liberty."

You know, herbicides. Get out there in your spray truck. Call in a crop duster. Corn's a monocot. Burcucumber is a dichot. (grass vs. broad-leaf plant) Some herbicides (2-4-d: Brush-Be-Gone) only killed dichots. If you didn't get it with the first application of

Roundup you can get it with Brush-Be-Gone. In the case of soy, which had been "genetically modified" to be resistant to glypho (Roundup) you can go ahead and spray 'em anyway. I do so love modern bio-tech.

Or, you can manage it by tilling fallow fields (not a great use of anyone's time), burning at appropriate times and, most especially, weeding. (All but the last, by the way, causing *more* damage to the environment.)

Weeding. You know, get out there with a hoe and hack away at the weeds. Better make sure you get *all* the roots and especially get them before they seed. Or next year is going to be worse. And worse. And worse. Gonna spend a lot of time on your knees. Backbreaking work. Stoop-work, the worst kind. It will kill you fast. Ask any Mexican farm laborer.

But those guys were mostly doing it at harvest. You'd better be doing it all summer. Hell, spring, summer and fall; there are weeds that spring up all three seasons and you need to get them young.

If you've got an area that's large enough to support four people and some to sell, you're going to be weeding *all the time*. Or you're not going to get enough to support the foursome.

And you *still* will have more weeds than those evil bastards using chemicals. Ask the Amish.

Then there's pests. We're sticking with corn again. Corn borer. Ever picked up fresh corn at a roadside stand and when you're shucking it there's this big fucking caterpillar which has eaten, like, half the kernels? You go "Yuck!" and toss it out. But a bunch of the rest has the same shit?

Corn borer. And your friendly roadside farmer is an organic nut. Welcome to the reality of organic farming on the sharp end. If it doesn't have a worm somewhere, it's industrial. If it has a worm, it's organic. If you're eating something organic, there has been a worm involved. Guaran-fucking-teed.

And if the worms are eating it, people can't.

Prior to the advent of modern pesticides and other pest prevention methods, pests and infections (corn gets sick, too) caused a loss of 25% of all crops before they could be consumed. That's *a lot* of fucking food.

Digression again. Ever heard of a guy called Thomas Robert Malthus? As in "Malthusian Equations"? There was a book called

The Population Bomb that was based on Malthusian Equations. Basically, according to Malthus, people reproduce a lot faster than food production can be increased. (Geometric vs. arithmetic.) Thus every so often you're going to get a massive famine since the amount of mouths outstrip the production.

Malthus did his study and wrote his treastise just as the industrial revolution was getting into gear. And *for his knowledge of the day*, organic farming by human and animal labor, *he was absolutely right*. There was a regular cycle of population growth stopped by famine throughout the world prior to the industrial revolution. See the upcoming thing about Marie Antoinette. Not to mention Les Miserables.

What changed it was *industrial farming methods*. Period. Dot. Everybody on earth would occasionally be going through a widespread killer famine if we all went back to organic farming worldwide. Simple as that. I hate "all organic" nearly as much as I hate mustard weed. More, probably. Mustard weed just evolved. Organic farming nuts have brains. They just can't use them.

But the good organic farmers (oxymoron, I know) are going to use tricks to keep it to a minimum. They'd pick the corn. Very labor intensive, again, but get a bunch of people out there looking for the corn borer eggs on the surface. Getting the eggs off. Looking for caterpillars or grasshoppers (they're fucking locusts, okay?) and picking them off by hand. Have a big fry at the end of the day since you might as well get *some* protein from your fields.

The tofu-eaters were *not* good organic farmers. They were not good farmers. They were not good horticulturalists. They thought they could be grasshoppers (fucking locusts) and just prop their feet up and wait for the food to fall into their mouths.

"Summer time, and the living is easy . . . "

No. It's not. Traditionally, spring and summer were when people *starved*. Back in medieval times the lords would store the grain and if you had been a good worker, when your personal stores ran out you could go to the lord and get grain to feed yourself and your family. If not, starve. Sometimes stores didn't make it all the way through the next harvest. They had *huge* problems with pests. (See above.) But that was the general idea.

There wasn't any food. Crops weren't coming up. There was nothing to eat.

There was *nothing* to eat.

This is referred to as *famine*. It hadn't happened to the U.S. in a century or more. And even then it was, to an extent, localized. 2020 was the first widespread famine the U.S. ever had. In 2019 it was still localized until the example of Lamoille became fucking *national policy*!

But I digress . . . Again.

There was still a certain amount of fuel. Most people had run their fuel out but there was still some. And there was always the leather-personnel-carrier. (Shoes.)

People started wandering. The tofu-eaters started looking for food, any food. The grasshoppers were turning into locusts and starting to fly.

There *was* food. Grain stores from the previous year were at near record highs. Even the winter wheat harvest hadn't been awful, despite the weather. And there were, alas, fewer mouths to feed. By June there was some movement on emergency distribution.

And then there was the Big Grab.

But we'll get back to that.

Okay, last bit on "organic" farming.

It's bad for the environment. It's sucky efficiency. Trying to go to it as the only way that farming was done *caused* the famines of 2019 and 2020. And then there's the whole pest thing.

Sure, there are more worms but, hell, it's *healthier* for you! Right? Well, there's the part about hormones and their effect on H5N1 but that's sort of specious. Let's talk about *real* health and safety issues.

What do they use for fertilizer? Shit. Okay, dress it up in any pretty language you want, "manure," "fully natural plant food," whatever. It's shit. It's what came out of your anus and you flushed down the toilet. It might come from cows or horses or whatever. It's all shit.

Don't get me wrong. It's a pretty good fertilizer. Especially horse shit. Very balanced. Also less smelly than the cow shit. (Which means, by the way, less nitrogen.)

But it's shit. It's made up of e coli bacteria. And the good organic farmers not only use it to prep their fields, they spray it (using a tractor and a manure sprayer) at times during the growing season. Because while it's *pretty good* fertilizer, it's not as good as the industrial type.

Yes, that's right folks. That organically grown food you just ate at some point was sprayed with shit. In many cases, it's "debiologicaled" shit. That is, it's been heated to the point that the germs should be dead. Doesn't always work out that way. And that kind is more expensive. Anything that's not cooked—lettuce, celery, green onions—generally got "debiologicaled." And sometimes it wasn't quite debioed as people would prefer.

Look, bottomline: Of the ten major e coli outbreaks of base food materials in the five years before the Plague, *one* was associated with industrial farming. One. The other nine were products that were "all natural."

Way more people died of "all natural" food that was contaminated with some "all natural" toxin than people who stuck to that icky "evil" food.

Back to trying to avoid famine.

CHAPTER EIGHT

Let Them Eat Cake

Food distribution centers had been set up in some areas. But they, by and large, had not gotten to small towns like Morrisville, VT, or Blackjack, GA. Never really did. Those areas were supposed to be *producing* the food, not *drawing* on it.

Initial movement during the Plague had been out of the cities. As the summer (what there was of it) kicked in, the movement was back. There wasn't any food in the countryside. Oh, there was, just not what most people recognized as such (yet). And the locusts wanted the government to feed them. Which it did. I wasn't on that detail but I've heard the stories.

Food distribution was very much on the classic methods used in Africa during famines. People got in long lines and were given some basic food materials. Semolina (cream of wheat for those of you who don't know the name, couscous for the hoity toity) was a base distribution as was cornmeal and beans. Why those? You could put it in a pot and boil it up and eat it. That simple.

"How can I boil it? I don't have a pot!" "I've got a pot, where's a stove?"

The answer is "find a pot, cut down a tree, boil the fucking water."

Believe it or not, there were still "environmental activists" being interviewed on the news who were complaining about the ENVIRONMENTAL DAMAGE that was being done from this sort of distribution. Trees were being cut down. (There used to be these things called "greenbelts" around subdivisions. I kid you not.) Fires were adding carbon dioxide to the atmosphere. There were even *lawsuits* seeking *injunctions* against *fires* used for *cooking food*.

Due to the way that the population had ebbed and flowed, most of the food distribution centers that were getting heavy traffic tended to be in the outer edges of cities. Central areas had some commerce as well, but people were clustering *out* of cities and, well, there were "issues" in the cities. Which wasn't good for the economy. Cities were and are the mitochondria of the economic animal.

But that's where most of the people who were coming to the food distribution centers were. And they included the "random associations" from suburbs. Side note again.

According to orders, the only people who got food were those that came to distribution centers. The Bitch again. I'll get into her hate affair with her crisis management specialists, including the head of FEMA, later. But that was the Rule.

Very few local officers paid attention to it. The majority of the distribution was going through the Army and what remained of the National Guard and reserves. The NG had had widespread desertions when they were called up. Go take care of others or stay with your family? About 20% chose the latter. There were also screw-ups with their vaccination program. They ended up at about half strength.

Oh, why weren't there more widespread desertions in the Army? There is no better place to be in an emergency (generally, we still haven't gotten to me, right?) than the Army. The Army *always* gets fed. Rations may be short, but it gets fed. And it generally takes care of dependents.

Dependents near bases went to the units when things got bad. They got some medical care, unit family support groups gathered in "less than random" associations and, well, supported each other. The troops were away. Rear area detachment personnel weren't going to turn away their wives when said wives turned up with kids in tow, hacking and coughing. (And in some conditions girlfriends or even "close personal friends" of the same sex. You can turn a blind eye to all sorts of shit in an emergency.) But even the dependents, those that lived on or near base, mostly got innoculated. And while power might be out in the local town, it stayed up on bases. There was food, water, shelter, medical care and clothing. As things started to get humming again there were even jobs.

There's a reason for this. See the difference between the National Guard and the Regulars. The Regulars stayed on the job in droves, less than five percent desertions, no matter how nasty those jobs were. (Body clearance in Miami was high on the list according to a buddy in the 82nd. He's challenged by a couple of officers in my unit who were involved in breaking up the food riots in DC. Clearing already dead people in hundred degree heat or killing American citizens? Tough call. *I* didn't get to find out, fortunately. Sort of. But, truth to tell, I actually enjoyed Detroit. Sometimes you can do good works in very bad ways.)

The point being that most of the work at the grunt level was *not* being done by FEMA, which never had many bodies, or even by the National Guard, which should have had many more bodies, but by Regular Army units. They'd been flown back starting in April when it was clear things were going to hell in a handbasket. At first the generals stuck with the pre-disaster plan until they got ordered to follow the Bitch Plan under Emergency Powers.

Okay, okay, damn. Sooo much to cover.

There was a Plan. Like all emergency plans the Post Catastrophic Disaster Emergency Rebuilding Plan left out, well, the Emergency. But it was a plan. It was a plan nobody wanted to implement but it was a Plan. It amounted to nationwide triage.

Triage is a word that comes from the old French word "trier" meaning "to pick or sort." Triage on a battlefield (where the word originated in the Napoleonic Wars) came down to three choices: Those that don't need help right now, those that can survive if they get help right now and those that are probably going to die whether they get help or not. Three choices. You send the bulk of your resources, doctors in this case, to the cases who had to have help right now, but that were probably going to live if they got that help. The lightly wounded could wait until later. And for those for whom there was no help, you sent *no help*. You put them together hopefully somewhere far enough away from the rest that their groans and screams wouldn't bother anyone and you Let Them *Die*.

It was an ugly, ugly, ugly plan. Basically, the Powers That Be, notably the military and FEMA, would determine zones that were recoverable fast. Energy would be concentrated on those zones first. As they got back on their feet, they would be used to springboard movement into zones that were just so totally fucked up they hadn't been recoverable. Lightly wounded (not many of them, NYC comes to mind) would be more or less on their own.

So now we turn once again to the Bitch. Tum-tum-ta-dum-tum, Hail to the Chief and all that.

She's been going quietly insane in my opinion. The news media did not agree. The Democrat Congress did not agree.

Everyone else in the *world* fucking agreed.

In March, in the midst of the worst of the Plague, the Congress had passed the Biological Crisis Emergency Act, effectively surrendering power to the President "for the duration of the biological and economic emergency."

Biological *and* economic.

What is the definition of an economic emergency? Okay, the world's economic turbine coming apart like an explosion is one definition. But what constitutes the *end* of the emergency? According to the news media, blips in the stock market pre-Plague were "emergencies." A quarter point rise in the unemployment index was "an emergency."

Okay, okay, fifty percent unemployment, as far as anyone could determine, (and, remember, *thirty percent* population drop) was an emergency. But at what point did it *stop* becoming an emergency?

Fortunately, they put a sunset date of one year from its signing for it to end but there was a proviso for an automatic renewal with a simple majority. And there was no stated limits. It suspended just about every right a person could have. Notably, habeas corpus *and* property rights.

Okay, there were "issues." There were a lot of dead people and stuff that was lying around that could be used. Factories that had been owned by families, the local members of which were dead and the distant ones unreachable. Or, hell, the corporation had just shut its doors and was in receivership. Farms that were lying fallow due to the Plague. Fine, whatever. There's a term called "eminent domain" for those. Basically, if there wasn't an immediately recognized heir or owner the government could and should take it over. Then sell it to someone who can run it.

The Emergency Powers Act cut through that. It also meant that there were no legal roadblocks to forced immunization. (Not that the Bitch *ever* got around to that.) And there were areas where social order had broken down completely. They were supposed to be placed in the category of "let them die" but . . . There's the Bitch deciding what is Right and What Should Be Done. Despite experts who were advising her that SHE HAD CHOSEN for their EXPERTISE.

Bush had been lambasted for his response to Katrina and New Orleans. Incorrectly IMO; the people who really cocked up were the local authorities. Look at Mississippi if you can find the information. There were entire counties that were wiped out. The storm surge that hit the Mississippi coast was *higher* than the tsunami that had hit Indonesia. There were bodies on top of a *Walmart*. They just picked up and did what they could. They called for Federal assistance right away, they followed their pre-disaster plans.

But the bottomline was Bush got hammered. And one of the things he got hammered on, justifiably, was his choice of head of FEMA.

I won't get into the hundreds of thousands of words I've read on that particular issue. Bottomline was that Michael Brown was not the guy to lead the agency. For so many different reasons it's scary.

But FEMA's actual *response* was as near *textbook* as you could get. Mostly because Brown realized he was totally out of his depth and let his people handle it.

The problem being, nobody really understood disaster response in the media. And they fucking *hated* Bush. Even Fox didn't really like him.

Look, in a local major disaster like that, FEMA wasn't even supposed to be up and running for *seventy-two hours*. Three days. That was after they were requested by local authorities.

But on day two, hell with the skies barely clearing, people were asking "Where is FEMA?"

FEMA doesn't actually have all that many full-time employees. Disasters, by their very definition, don't occur all the fucking time. So most of its response specialists are contractors who do other things, or are retired and hang out, waiting for the next response.

They had to be called in. People had to go in and find areas to set up. It takes *time*.

Even then, they don't do most of the work. They *coordinate* the work. More contractors, and military, and local government do the actual work. Federal Emergency *Management* Agency.

Asking "where is FEMA" in a disaster is like asking "Why aren't the managers here?" The managers are important, don't get me wrong. But they don't get the bodies cleared.

So Bush was roundly criticized for responding in damned near textbook manner. Despite Michael Brown.

Warrick, though, knew it was a major political point. So even during her campaign, she found a person that she said was to be her head of FEMA in the event of her inevitable election.

Brody Barnes was a former Army colonel. He'd started as a tanker but then got into specialized areas of what's called "civil affairs," that is dealing with problems of a local populace.

He'd been an unnoticed but major reason that the rebuilding in Iraq, which went *way* better than the media ever could realize, went as well as it did. His main degree was industrial management so he wasn't an engineer but a guy who understood how to get very disparate parts of a complicated system to start working together.

He retired at twenty years and got a job almost immediately as assistant director of the California Emergency Management Agency. The director was a politically appointed position. A year after Brody joined, the director "voluntarily" resigned and Brody was appointed by the Republican governor. Like similar positions in the federal government, it required the consent of the very liberal California Senate. He passed the vote with acclaim. He was definitely a rising star.

By the time the election of 2016 rolled around he'd dealt with multiple major brushfire outbreaks, three minor earthquakes, mudslide seasons aplenty and one fairly major earthquake. He also looked good on TV. Square-jawed, soft-spoken, dry sense of humor, good soundbites.

He accepted the nod as a potential FEMA head and spoke widely in favor of Warrick. He liked her domestic policies. When asked about her military policies he politely declined to comment. Not his area. Ask someone else.

He was appointed head of FEMA one month after Warrick went into office. He was head of FEMA when the Plague hit.

He was one of the people with testicles trying to get Warrick to stick to *some* sort of plan. Wasn't happening.

You see, he had been a convenient tool to aid a close election. But he wasn't one of Warrick's inner advisors. Not that Warrick listened to them much. She knew what was Right and so on and so forth.

Warrick had Her Plan. And everybody else was going to follow the Warrick Plan.

The first part of the Warrick Plan was the distribution Plan. Pancake.

The second part of the Warrick Plan had to do with the economy. Okay, Wall Street fucking tanked. It made Black Friday look like a minor blip. The Dow was riding high at nearly 16,000 points before the first word of H5N1. By the time trading was "semipermanently suspended" it was below *5,000.*

Well, if corporations couldn't handle a minor matter like a plague that had wiped out their workforce and their customers and their distribution systems and the economic underpinnings that they depended on for sustenance, they would just be *nationalized.*

How, exactly, she expected that to help was never quite clear. They were to be nationalized. The Government, in its infinite wisdom, would take over their facilities and get them back in running order.

Banks closed. The one smart thing she did was stop all foreclosures from banks. The stupid thing she did was continue to permit *tax* seizures. The idea of tax seizures is that the government grabs the goods of a person or company who refuses to pay taxes. Then they sell them.

There were effectively no buyers. Oh, there were some. That money in the stock market had gone somewhere. Mostly it had gone into the first people to bail out. They were sitting on money in various places. Some of it evaporated. When banks closed, if you had more than the federally protected maximum in it, it disappeared. Not exactly but it was tied up in loans that, for the time being, couldn't be recovered and might never be. But the truly rich were covered on many fronts and held onto portions of their assets. And they then used them to buy up properties at firehouse prices. Some of them were in eminent domain because there were no heirs. But the government was seizing a lot of stuff that was because people suddenly found themselves unable to pay taxes on it.

Farms, factories, equipment, there wasn't a huge market but

there was a market. The problem being that just as basic necessities, food and clothing, were getting astronomically expensive, things like a dump truck were going for pennies on the dollar.

The next thing she did was declare a fixed price on commodities. Oh. My. God.

Look, in a free market economy stuff sells for what people are willing to pay. If the commodity, pork bellies for example, is in big supply and low demand, it sells for less. If the commodity is in big demand and low supply, it sells for more. Supply and demand.

Go back to the seizures. A loaf of sliced, wrapped, packaged bread in the few remaining open grocery stores, if you could find one, was going for ten dollars. Knew somebody who had paid $500 for a pound of coffee. You could buy an F-350 pickup truck in nearly mint condition for not much more. The supply of useless vehicles was high. The supply of food was low.

Supply and demand.

The Bitch decided that she was going to put a stop to that and ordered all basic commodities to be repriced at pre-Plague levels.

Which just meant that people who had any money left stripped the shelves and because it was costing more to produce a loaf of bread than ten dollars, the few remaining businesses that were making bread went out of business. So there was no more bread.

Ever hear the whole thing about Marie Antoinette and "If there is no bread then let them eat cake." She wasn't a cold-hearted bitch as is normally thought. She was a liberal airhead.

Think I'm wrong?

There was a famine going on at the time, a Malthus special combined with, hey! look! a global cooling event. The French agricultural economy had reached its carrying capacity just as there was a turn-down in the thermostat. One bad harvest and people were starving. The king ordered that the price of bread in Paris and other cities be fixed at a certain level so that people could afford to eat. The only problem being the *farmers*, who had limited supplies from the bad harvest, weren't willing to sell it to the *bakers* at the cost necessary for bread to be that cost. So the supply of wheat ran out for bread.

The king had also decreed that if there was no bread flour, then cake, which was from much *more* expensive (less supply) flour, was to be substituted.

So she was making, within the "command economy" mindset, a perfectly plausible statement. If the bakers aren't making bread, then the poor get to eat cake.

The only problem being, there wasn't enough flour for cake, either. And either way the bakers were going to go out of business.

There were stores of grains still in silos. It could be argued that locking in their price to what they were worth pre-Plague was reasonable. Except that the people who owned them now had much higher expenses across the board. And if they went out of business, somebody was going to have to run the silos. Okay, the government. Are we going to get to full communism? If Warrick had her way we would have.

But even if you fixed the cost of those, that didn't get it to mouths. You had to transport it. The fuel delivery system was shot. (Take our dead husband in the suburb and multiply by fifteen million.) What fuel was available was expensive. Law of supply and demand.

Okay, then fix the price of fuel!

Truckers had gotten hit hard by the Plague. By definition, they traveled and were exposed all over the place. So there were fewer truckers. And most of them were independents. There were fewer loads, but there were *way* fewer truckers. They could pick and choose their cargoes and if they had one that was willing to pay more, say a load of critical components that a company was willing to pay through the nose for, rather than, say, a government priced shipment of food, they went for the filthy lucre.

Seize the trucks!

Thus was the Big Grab started. And it went on and fucking on. Sure, she had the Right under the Emergency Powers Act. It was, however, very fucking stupid. It did more lasting damage to the economy than the Plague. We're *still* trying to unfuck it.

There's a personal side to that but I'll get to that. I promise.

But while the Big Grab was still getting rolling, and understand it was never quite a full governmental program, just an ad hoc response as things came to the Bitch's attention, the Bitch implemented the next stage of her Plan.

There was to be *no* triage. Not as such. Areas that were recoverable weren't to be designated. Areas that were write-offs weren't to be designated. She and her advisors would determine which areas were to be concentrated on, first.

Well, go figure. Looks like the blue states won out big-time. And especially blue counties.

Only one problem. If Brody Barnes had been asked, his contention was "they're mostly gone for the time being."

Go back to the trust thing. Think about multiculturalism. Look at Morristown vs. Blackjack. And blue counties tended to be heavily urbanized.

The cities were just a fucking wreck. At least for a time in almost all urban areas "essential services" broke down. Essential services are Maslov's hierarchy. Food and water are the big two. Security isn't really mentioned but *before* food started to run out looting became a major issue.

Ah. Looting vs. scavenging. In a disaster situation, there is a difference between looting and scavenging. Scavenging is a person coming out of a Winn-Dixie or Meijers with a shopping cart filled with canned goods and bottled water. Looting is a person coming out of Walmart with five TVs.

You help scavengers, you shoot looters. (Okay, okay, shoot me. It was too good to pass up! But I'm getting ahead of myself again.)

Inner city neighborhoods that had been the target of "specialized policing" were the absolute worst. These were the grasshoppers gathered in force. Trust barely existed within family groups. There was little or no social cohesion.

After the first wave of the Plague they were free-fire zones. I'd have rather walked down a street in Qom butt-assed naked than drive through South Detroit in a Stryker.

But not only were those areas where the bulk of her voters came from, they were where the news media was. If it bleeds it leads and it was bleeding hard in South Chicago, Detroit, Watts, East L.A., Washington, DC . . .

The *worst* spots were to be the target of the most concentrated effort.

There's a military term for this. It's called "slamming the wall." The basic concept is that if you take your enemy's strongest position, it will break him. It's also called "suicide." Porkchop Hill, the Somme, Coldwater Harbor. Historical examples of "slamming the wall." Also historical examples of highest casualty assaults. And none of them did a damned bit of good in the end.

Neither did pouring vital supplies into the free-fire zones.

And then there were the Rules of Engagement. They went way beyond "do not fire unless fired upon." Warrick was, after all, a lawyer. Written out, they went to five pages of flow diagrams. They were worse than the ones issued towards the latter part of the Iraq Campaign. Essentially they came down to "do not fire." Period. If you shot anyone, for any reason, you were probably going to jail.

Soldiers were prosecuted, during that period, for firing upon people who were actively firing *at them*. Guys went to Leavenworth who had *bullets in their body-armor*. Dozens of food shipments were lost to gangs that forced the soldiers to turn them over. It was that or have a fire-fight. And they were not permitted to fire. When it was more or less one on one, and it often was, not firing first meant heavy casualties. The leaders, and I don't blame them, were willing to give up the shipments rather than take the casualties.

Units were required to "maintain a minimum presence of force." That is, they weren't supposed to ride into the neighborhoods like an invading army. No matter how violent they were. Habeas corpus had been suspended but you couldn't tell it if you were a soldier. Unless, of course, *you* were up for punishment. Then you hadeus no corpus.

And some very heavy weapons had gotten into the hands of these gangs. One Stryker was hit and destroyed by a Javelin while escorting a food convoy. *Most of the units doing the escorting* didn't have Javelins issued. (A Javelin is an anti-tank missile. More about those, later, too.)

So while the red counties, the rural counties and smaller cities that made up "fly-over country" were organizing and recovering and hoping for some help, however little, the "blue" counties, many of which had gone completely bat-shit, were having food and medical supplies and emergency supplies shoveled into them like coal into a furnace and for about as much result.

Okay, they were not all losses. Notice I didn't mention Harlem, Queens or the Bronx. That's because they didn't ever get that bad. Not even close. Part of that was because the mayor refused to let it get that bad. Mortality had been incredibly low. Less than 20% and that, frankly, tended to be among grasshoppers. Police presence was high and the local National Guard unit had been turned into something closer to the New York militia. When they were ordered to displace to handle problems in New Jersey—Newark *was* one of the war zones—the orders were ignored.

Food shipments got to where they were supposed to go. Bodies were collected. Order never really broke down in New York. It's possible for at least a local government to maintain near normal conditions even in densely populated areas, even in a disaster as bad as the Plague. But it took strong and effective leadership. People have got to *trust*. Let's all work together said "I'm trusting you to trust me to not screw you." Enough people got the idea that it worked. The few "random associators" among New Yorkers supported the mayor. And the "King" types were willing to follow a strong man in a time of trouble. Call it a cult of personality.

Like I said, if Cranslow runs for President, I'll work with him. He's even a fiscal conservative. What the hell.

CHAPTER NINE

Random Associations

The majority of the functional distribution, therefore, happened *outside* cities. Much of it was illicit. That is, food convoys were ordered to Philadelphia and "broke down" before they got there. And set up distribution stations. And fed people that needed it and weren't going to try to steal it. And, often, turned bulk materials over to "local random associations" for distribution.

Okay, the gangs were, often, local random associations, more or less. Some of them, especially Hispanic and Asian, were at core familial based. (And by Asian I don't mean just Chinese. Note the Caliphate.)

But they were not going to be, in turn, acting as useful distributors. The food was used for internal power. There was a touch of that in places with the churches and other associations (VFW did enormous if unheralded good during the Time). They had the food and they made the choices who ate and who did not. Generally, this was not race based as was often reported. It was, to an extent, based on trust issues. But mostly it was based on the same reasoning that young lady in Blackjack used. Feed local emergency services personnel first. Feed kids and elderly next. Feed random associators next. Feed the grasshoppers last.

There was a degree of blending and bonding during the Time which was unprecedented in American history. Generally, for actual biological reasons, people *do* differentiate on the basis of color. (Yes, babies do not. Children, by and large, do not. The trait kicks in at puberty. It can be culturally adjusted, but it's a defined human trait. A white child raised among Chinese is going to trust Chinese over whites. True study. Another urban myth trashed.) And there were then and are now bigots on that score.

But due to societal factors, random associators had a fair slice of military personnel in their midst. And military personnel deal with *all kinds of colors* when they're in. It's hard to be in the military for any time and not become to an extent color blind. They may look at *cultural* factors, but they tend to look past *color* per se. The two are *not* equal.

(Had a bit of an issue on that part just before the last Iran deployment. We were having a hard time getting a widget out of one particular supply unit. I paid them a visit to try to sweet-talk. Ended up talking with the unit commander. Didn't get far. And then the fuck-head had the audacity to say "I guess you're just not part of the African-American mafia." So I laughed and admitted I wasn't. And then I turned the whole thing over to the IG. Along with my report of the meeting. About three weeks later the unit commander was on his way out of the Army.

By the same token, Colonel Richards, just about the best fucking battalion commander I ever had, was black. Culture *is not the same* as race.)

So when a white kid walked up to one of the white distributors and asked for extra food to take back to his family, he was judged on his social appearance. Did he have his pants hanging down to his knees and his ball-cap on sideways? Was he wearing an earring? Did he look "ghetto"?

He'd better be known to the people doing the distribution or they'd tell him if someone had a chance they'd take some over but right now it was line up or nothing.

A black guy walking up to a line of distributors from a very white church might get the same perusal. If, however, he was neatly dressed and well spoken, and especially if he offered to help, he was likely to be trusted. He might be given food for more than just himself if there was extra.

Yes, there were those that used that to their advantage. But by and large judging on the basis of culture for trust works.

It was not only white churches that got largess from military units who were, increasingly and against orders, turning away from downtown areas. Any random association that seemed functional and valid might get a drop of food and medicines. A fucking *mosque* in St. Louis was eventually considered the best place to drop shipments. They handled them evenhandedly and very efficiently. Charity is one of the few things that Islamics get right.

Larger associations formed, very very much "back channel."

Example:

A white church in suburban Boston was running low on food. Suddenly, a convoy destined for the center of Boston "broke down" nearby and had to unload most of its supplies. Convenient?

A black church in Arkansas had received a similar largesse, in part because the first sergeant of the National Guard company doing the delivery had family in the church and they were *not* interested in going into the portion of Little Rock they were destined for.

The two churches, widely separated, were "sister missions" to each other. That is, there was some reciprocation of ministers and support. That mostly came down to the more wealthy church having, over the years, given financial support to the less wealthy. And, yes, that is white and black. And even after the Plague they had kept in contact through several means.

In this case bread upon the waters, as Jesus said, worked out. The XO of the National Guard company had been a member of 10th ID. He called one of his old bosses and mentioned that he'd heard there was a church group doing good works but struggling near Boston. 10th ID was working the Boston area. Voila "breakdown."

Bread upon the waters. Random associations.

Where there was not direct interference, it was random associations that started to rebuild the country. The economy was just screwed. But that didn't mean people didn't work and businesses didn't function to some extent. It was strange. There was a labor shortage and *at the same time* high unemployment. It was like the cost of goods. There were many hands that wanted to work and companies that were opening or managed to hang on and stay open that needed to fill the slots left open by deaths. It took *time*, though, to get those two together.

Communications never went down completely. There were times when it was impossible to get a phone call through to certain areas. And the Internet was a spotty thing. Not so much because of the trunks but because of local providers, functionality thereof.

But commo was spotty and screwed up. And there would be various scares of a new plague breaking out. It did in places. Miami had a cholera outbreak, more deaths. L.A. . . . Well, despite the best efforts of Warrick, or possibly because of them, L.A. was fucked. Cholera, resistant tuberculosis, typhus, they all broke out. And then there's the water situation. But that's a sideline I'll see about covering later.

And whenever there was a scare, the phone lines went down. All the connections weren't in place and as soon as anyone who still had access to a working phone heard a rumor, or a news report, which was often the same rumor, that a new plague had broken out they called friends or relatives in the area. And commo went down.

So let's look at an example.

Let's go back to the suburban family. The father was a guy working at a local fueling center. Now, this is a pump farm where the trucks that fuel gas stations go to fill up. Sometimes they're owned by one oil company but fill up all the trucks in the area, regardless of whose gas it's supposed to be. Not usually, but it happens.

Anyway, working one those places is a semi-skilled job. At the very least, a knowledge of the basic safety and emergency response is useful.

By and large, such places stayed up. Fuel was central and critical. They might not be going to a dozen gas stations anymore, but they were providing fuel to *somebody*. The military bought from such stations, fueling *their* fuel trucks at them.

But they'd taken hits in personnel. One in three, more or less at random. And as things started to reform, they were getting more and more trucks wanting fuel. Sometimes they ran out; it had to come from somewhere and the distribution system was in chaos. But the bottomline was, they needed bodies.

Say that the first family was in suburban Cincinnatti and the fueling station was, too. The husband was dead and buried under pansies. They get to the point they need a new fuel guy. Everyone's working overtime, for sometimes no pay but the company is making sure they get food, and they're getting worn out. They need another body. A warm one. Not the guy under pansies.

So they put out the word. They need a trained fuel technician.

All sorts of people walk over to the place. It's a job, man. Jobs are scarce. And the fuel company is making sure its people and

their families get fed. But these are just bodies. They need someone with experience handling big quantities of fuel. They're too
overworked to train someone, much as they need the body.

In the suburbs of Beltsville, itself a suburb, there's a former
webdesigner who, during a single stint in the Army, worked a fuel
distribution point in Iraq. She is a trained fuel transfer technician
and has experience. But the place that needs her experience is
in Cincinnatti. She's more than willing to go there to get a job
and assured food. Maybe a bit of money left over for more than
bare survival. It's a *job*, man.

Say that she still gets some Internet access, somehow. (Librar-
ies still had some functionality.) Say that she finds the want ad on
MonsterJobs.com. (Which came back up in June of 2019 and stayed
up to this day.) How does she *get* to Cincinnatti? Note the "she."
Hitchhiking is a choice of last resort. Major league trust issues.

In this case, not quite a random association. She puts her
experience on the website along with a phone number at her
local association (the VFW in her case, yes, it's taken from a real
person's experience) where she can be reached.

The manager of the fuel point sees the hit and nearly jumps
for joy. If it's legit. They'd had lots of people who could talk a
good line about being experienced. One who was *very* good at
talking had nearly blown the place up.

They get in contact. He quizzes her. She sounds good. But so
did the nightmare. But how to get her to him?

Hey, fuel moves.

Mostly it moves by rail to distribution points like that. But
they also handle more minor materials such as volume grease
and oil. The military term is "POL": Petrol, (gasoline for Americans) Oil, Lubricants. Oil and lubricants, to a great degree, still
moved by trucks.

There was a fuel point, from another company, near Beltsville.
It had all the people it needed, but it also had trucks going north.
The truckers, in this case, were known quantities.

Calls were made. E-mails were exchanged. (The oil companies
had ensured their own connections to backbones long before the
Plague. They were going to be hooked tight into the Internet if
anything happened. They also had satellite connectivity if even
that went down. Oil companies tend to be planners, too.)

She met a trucker at the "other company" fuel point who carried her to the outskirts of Philly where there was a distro point still open. From there, with the knowledge of the distro point manager, she caught another ride to another point. And so on. She had someone who knew who she was, where she was going and when she was supposed to arrive at each point.

She wasn't, really, a hitchhiker. She was a commodity being moved for the good of the companies. And while the companies were cutthroat, normally the exact opposite of "random voluntary associations" they also understood scratching back. When a favor was needed, it would be called. They trusted the other company, especially in these conditions, to be good for it.

She reached Cincinnatti and went to work.

By the way, there was a certain ignoring of paperwork in those days. Green cards were not necessary. Social security numbers were not necessary. Pay, by the same token, was spotty. Really long-thinking companies like oil companies tried to keep their people fed and mostly succeeded.

But it was still maximally fucked up.

The point to all this is that you can have massive unemployment and still have a labor shortage. Even if things are sort of bumping along, sort of, maybe, the "disruption" means that bodies, parts and everything else that is needed to keep any business going is scattered in the wrong places.

What saved the U.S. was a lot of people at fairly low levels working very hard to keep things going using any means necessary to do so. Like moving a skilled worker around via trucks that had strict regulations against picking up hitchhikers.

What nearly killed us were people in positions of power who wanted things to work the same way as pre-Plague.

There were articles and news reports on various "irregularities." Okay, that was a minor one and mostly overlooked even though she didn't file taxes for the whole of 2019. (Thank God for the Amnesty Bill is all I'll say.) Hell, she didn't officially work for Exxon for most of 2019 . . . Oops, did I say that out loud? ☺

(Wife edit. Thanks a lot. If you think *you're* getting any for the rest of the year, think again!)

(Hell, most of 2020 you worked for the feds! Back off.)

(And it was a *nightmare*.)

But the worst "irregularities" were "price fixing."

Sigh. The *government* could do price fixing but not *companies*. *Especially* not oil companies.

Sigh.

Look, things were total suckage. People were still dying. There were very few truly functional banks. Nobody could figure out if we were dealing with run-away inflation or runaway deflation.

So a bunch of managers getting together and saying "We need to call a truce" just made *sense*. Don't compete. Associate for the common good. Wait until things cool down to go back to stabbing each other in the back as hard as we can.

They had a far better idea of what valid prices were than Warrick. They knew their costs, they knew their inventories (and when the on-hand inventory was out, it was going to be a while getting more oil on a national level. There was no chance of getting out of the Middle East, I can tell you that. Not sure of deploying troops to cover the pumping and transfer. Which we got around to eventually.) They consulted, they planned, they projected, they shook hands and they set their prices.

And they got hammered.

Oh. My. God. The news media led the charge. The evil oil companies were screwing the American People. Profits were soaring as prices were fixed by an unnamed cabal.

So Warrick nationalized the oil companies and arrested the "conspirators."

And *that* worked real well.

At that point she was nationalizing so many industries, many of which were effectively defunct, that she didn't have government employees to run them. Sure, she could just say "all of you are government employees" but who bells the cat?

Okay, take the oil companies.

Running an oil company is, at almost every single level, a very complex business. Receptionists are about the only people who don't require hours and weeks of training before you can let them do anything on their own. One wrong turn of the wrench in a refinery can mean a big boom. Figuring out how to get just the right inventory to Peoria, Kansas, means having figured out which ten thousand gallons of fuel from which tanker at what point in its voyage is going to go there *months* in advance. Not exactly, but functionally.

What does "you are nationalized" mean?

Well, in the case of Exxon (oops, sorry) it meant choosing a crony to become the CEO with all the perks, pay and privileges. Said crony being, effectively, a tofu-eater. Notably, the person put in charge of Exxon had, upon a time, been a senior member of Greenpeace. And an "environmental lawyer."

Metaphors on that one are tough. I guess putting Osama Bin Laden in charge of the Defense Department works.

The crony brought in more cronies who brought in more cronies. Their job was to make the oil company less evil *not* make sure it ran efficiently. Profits were no longer their objective; "serving the world" was their objective.

Some of the "service" that was required of the company during the brief reign of what were and are called "the fucktards" were odd to say the least. Okay, so they had to be even more environmentally conscious than they already were. I'm not an oil guy, that would be someone I know and she's not a guy, (Thanks) but there's this thing called "the law of diminishing returns."

Look, refineries were already about as clean as they were going to get. Spills were a major response issue. Emissions were pretty low, all things considered.

Getting the emissions lower required engineering that was horrendously expensive and, at the time, unavailable. The refineries were having a hard enough time just continuing to function. Installing more and better emission systems simply *was not an option*. Who was going to *make them*? They don't grow on trees! They grow in *China* on trees!

But they had to get lower. And gas has to get cheaper. Oh, and you need to start contributing to various funds. Greenpeace, Sierra Club, Environmental Defense Fund. And pay these huge numbers of grasshoppers exorbitant salaries so that they can get back to their grasshopper lifestyle even though they're not actually contributing anything but bitching to the company.

And contribute to the presidential election campaign, by the way. I mean, I'm the CEO. I can cut a check if I want to.

First of all, there *weren't* profits for the first two years of the Time. There was also no infrastructure renewal, damned little maintenance and there was barely money to pay the workers. The oil companies had been providing fuel to major farm corporations in return for food that was then distributed down to, well, the level of a lady working in a refueling plant.

That was illicit collusion and had to stop.

Because most of the tofu-eaters didn't understand the oil business, or any of the many other businesses they were put in charge of, they were often flat ignored. They did so love meetings, especially meetings with obsequious and chastened oil company executives bowing and scraping and giving long PowerPoint presentations. They were taken to refineries and shown all the new "environmental improvement systems," many of which were cobbled together from spare pipe and flashy lights, and generally led around by the nose in the hope that grown-ups might get back in charge.

And in cases where they weren't ignored, or things fell apart anyway, the government then had to pick up the slack and actually try to run things. That worked about as well as any communist-run organization. And there were cases where workers rioted or quit despite the employment conditions or went on strike and had to be told "get back to work, slaves!"

Another lovely job of the Army. In that case, the rules of engagement were somewhat reduced.

The Army had long experience of mob control, though, if not in the U.S. And commanders tended to negotiate rather than open fire. The workers, many of which had a certain respect for the military, tended to talk things out as well.

(This, by the way, was slightly different than the case of the Long Beach Oil Terminal. In that case, the strikers were led by a very hard-core union group that stated that it had "seized the means of production for the people" and was less than willing to negotiate. Actually, they didn't want to negotiate, they simply had demands that had to be met or "the oil terminal would be destroyed." When President Warrick dithered the commander of SOCOM ordered Delta to deal with the situation. Delta dealt. The remaining strikers, with ten dead ringleaders being carried out by their heels, went back to work. The SOCOM commander was court-martialed as was the group commander who carried out the mission. Delta got gutted. But oil flowed. Ex-General Pennington is being bruited for the next secretary of Defense. Got my vote.)

Look, civilian control of the military is a very important thing. If the military doesn't obey their civilian commanders, sooner or later you get Generalissimo Jones trying to run things and making things worse. We knew that. That bedrock belief went all the way back to George Washington who, when some of his officers wanted to mutiny, ordered them to swear an oath to always obey the orders of the government, no matter how bad they seemed. It was the foundation of The Society of Cincinnatus. I'm not a member since I'm not descended from any of them. The S-4 in Iran was, but that doesn't reduce the importance of the concept.

But we were being told to do things that were *clearly* unconstitutional, and the *Constitution* is what we swear an oath to not the *President*, while simultaneously being told to do things that were suicidal.

Did we ever slip control, totally? No. But at first at lower levels then at higher and higher we started to ignore The Bitch. When told to do something clearly illogical, we tended to tune it out and do something more logical. Or at least survivable. We got people fed when we had the food. We distributed to groups we trusted. We were color blind on that but not culture blind and sure as hell not tactically blind.

On an actual *functional* level, we implemented the original Plan, even if we didn't realize it at the time.

We reacted, adapted and overcame.

Which, *finally*, leads to "let's talk about me."

BOOK TWO

The Last Centurions

— CHAPTER ONE —

Stick, Shit End, One Each

So there I was, no shit . . .

January we got our warning on H5N1. February, late, we got our innoculations. By then there were more reports around and Patient Zero in Chicago. March was when the Plague hit in earnest in the States.

We were sitting in Fars Province as things went from bad to worse in Iran. It didn't take the Plague hitting (it hadn't, really, yet) to screw things up in Iran. All it took was Iranians.

Look, Iranians are, by and large, good people. I'm not talking about the jihadi assholes, obviously. I'm talking about your regular low to middle class Iranian. They like to talk, they like to share green tea. They're even reasonably hard workers (unlike the fucking Arabs).

But they're also massively screwed up. There's a bunch of reasons, but I can easily detail two.

One: They're arrogant as fuck. Look, ever seen a movie from pre-Plague called *The 300*? Bunch of stupid Greeks hold a pass against the whole Persian army. (That would be Iranian, by the way.) Three hundred (actually, more like a thousand with battle squires and allies) against two *hundred* thousand. Go with the thousand number; they're *still* outnumbered two hundred to one.

Worse, back then Persia (Iran) was The big superpower. Persian emperors spotted a place they liked, invaded and took it over. They were too large and powerful not to be able to take anything they wanted.

Back then, Persia was *The Thing*.

(Of course, not too long later historically they were subjects of the Greeks, but I'm not writing a book about the ascent of democracy and why shock infantry always wins over alternatives.)

Iran, even in pre-Plague days, was a third class power.

First Class powers were ones that if they got really busy were going to trash the shit out of any non-First Class opponents. Basically, just pre-Plague, that came down to the U.S. and China. The U.S. because we had, hands down, the best military in the world and we were "the world's economic turbine." China because it was just so fucking big and so was its army. They might not have been able to trash *us*, (see Greeks vs. Persians; size does *not* always matter) but if they got it into their heads to invade, say, Cambodia, Cambodia might as well roll. And they were pretty powerful economically as well.

Second class were places like Japan and Western Europe. They had large economies, they were world players and they had small but functional militaries. (Some very good. Australia comes to mind. Then there's the French. It varied.) Throw "academia" and "artists" into this if you wish. Military and economic were usually followed by more or less equal values of the other.

Third class were countries that had some economic power (mostly oil), some semblance of a real economy and were regional powerhouses. They were often big frogs in very little ponds. Brazil, South Africa and Iran all come to mind. Russia might have been second class, might have been third. Not worth debate.

The problem is, Iranians just could not get over the fact that they *used* to be the big frog in *any* pond. *They still thought they were.* And because of that, they thought they knew *everything*. How could some upstart from a country only *two hundred years* old know how to do something better than *they* did?

Well, maybe because the world's changed and we're not still doing it the way that Xerxes wanted it done.

The second problem with Iranians might be an effect of Islam (it's certainly consistent in most Islamic countries) or it might have been something that was a long-term meme. Don't know. Read well researched arguments for both. Anyway, the second problem was they were fatalists.

Look, anybody who has ever been in heavy fire and survived mentally is somewhat fatalistic. "I'm alive so far but if there's a bullet with my name on it, oh, well . . ."

But Persians raise this to high art. The term is "In'sh'allah." "It is as Allah wills."

Bus about to fall off a road in the mountains? "It is as Allah Wills." Circuit board not precisely put in place. "It will work if Allah wills." Foundation for a building made out of quicksand? "It will stay up if Allah wills." In'sh'Allah.

Need a group of workers at a certain place at a certain time? "They will be here if Allah Wills."

For a Midwestern farm boy and military officer, dealing with In'sh'Allah was less than pleasant.

Kipling wrote about it once, talking about people who are *not* like that:

> *They do not preach that their God will rouse them a*
> *little before the nuts work loose.*
> *They do not preach that His Pity allows them to drop*
> *their job when they damn-well choose.*

Ayrabs and Iranians are *not* the sons of Martha.

But the point is, when the first news of the Plague hit, the entire country went into a spasm. Trust? Familial trust society. If you're not family, you're nobody. You'd better have a hard power control to get anything done.

Familial groups started shifting and contacts started dropping off the screen. Getting anything done quickly became flat impossible. Except getting shot at and bombed which continued right up to the point of Plague hitting Iran in earnest and then just got more random.

Meantime, things were going to hell in a handbasket back home and we were stuck in the ass end of nowhere attempting "reconstruction duties" while the world was deconstructing around us.

March 5th I got the e-mail I'd been dreading. It was from Bob Bates, Dad's senior manager and vice president of the corporation. Dad had contracted H5N1.

Mom died of ovarian cancer when I was ten. I didn't have any brothers or sisters. (Turns out Mom's uterus was pretty screwed up to start with.) Dad was all I had left.

Growing up with Dad had never been real easy. Don't get me wrong, if he backhanded me or gave me a spanking I deserved it.

But while "negative conditioning" was high on his list, "positive conditioning" was less so. The flip side is, when he gave praise it was because you *deserved* it. That made the slightest hint that you'd sort of maybe not screwed up *entirely* worth gold. I learned a lot about leadership from my dad.

But Midwestern farmers, despite this little missive which is much bigger than I'd intended, don't talk a lot. They spend so much time in their own company, they just learn to absorb the silence. Slowly over the years they tend to become more and more like a Minnesota winter, cold, silent and powerful.

That left me wondering what to say to a man with whom I'd exchanged barely ten words in the same number of years and yet whom I loved beyond measure.

"Get well soon. I love you."?

Oh, GOD no.

"I need you in my life so you'd better pull through."?

If he *did* live he'd *kick my ass*! (And despite being in his fifties he could probably do it.)

"Dear Bob:

"Tell Dad that if he doesn't pull through he's a wuss."

Yep, those were the last words from me my dad ever got.

I'm morally certain he understood the love buried deep within them.

The rest of the e-mail from Bob, and it was long, was about the farming situation. Distribution was getting bad. They had laid in rye for the planting season but he wasn't sure when they could get it in the ground. Even rye needs a certain amount of soil temp to sprout and soil temperatures weren't even beginning to flicker upwards. By early March you usually saw some thawing and it just wasn't happening. He also wasn't sure about getting a herbicide and fertilizer delivery. They might have to do some "organic" stuff but that required hands. Which were *not* available.

They'd also gotten word that the big combines might not be available for harvest. They could till with the cultivators on the farms if they could get the bodies but those were scarce. They'd had to close one of the milk farms because they didn't have the four guys to run the milking machine.

Hell in a handbasket.

March 21st was the day I got word my father was gone. The Iranian New Year. Normally a time of high holiday in Iran with lots of celebrations going back *before* Persia tried to knock off Greece. Not much celebrating going on in 2019, though. The Plague was starting to spread and people were dying like flies.

Also the spring solstice. There wasn't much spring in the air in Fars province. It was a high plateau more or less surrounded by mountains, and the major farming area of Iran. It generally had the weather of Virginia in terms of temperatures.

This year it was more like Minnesota in the spring. A *normal* spring.

The funny thing was, I knew there was a "cooling trend" going on. The *Army* knew there was a cooling trend going on.

Couldn't tell it by the news. We were still getting CNN and between the reporting on the Plague they had occasional weather reports. I stopped counting the number of references to "global warming" I got after fifteen in two days. I just quit listening after the damned meteorologist said:

"We're having a cold and wet spring on top of everything else that's going on due to global warming affecting world-wide ocean currents."

Ocean currents.

Ocean currents have a lag that runs from five *hundred* to ten *thousand* years. Anything that ocean currents were doing, *now*, was because of something that happened a *long* time ago.

And there was no "global warming" anymore. Yeah, there had been a slow warming trend going back to a mini-iceage back in the Middle Ages. But we'd stopped warming. Given that it was Old Sol driving it, we might go back to warming soon. From the solar physicist's predictions, though, it wasn't going to be any time soon. Not the rest of 2019 for sure and probably not 2020.

We were cooling off. *Fast*. And people were still beating the drum of "global warming."

Here's how it really works. And it's more complicated than "CO2 makes the temperature rise! Reuse, reduce, recycle! SUV owners are global terrorists!"

But not a lot.

Cosmic rays are produced from big stars exploding a long way away. They're all over the place in any galaxy and Earth is constantly bombarded by them.

Cosmic rays hitting water droplets in the upper atmosphere form clouds. Those clouds cool the Earth.

Cosmic ray impact is controlled by solar winds. What are solar winds?

The sun is a big ball of fusing hydrogen that pumps out an *enormous* amount of power every second. It not only emits heat and light but particles that fly out headed for deep space. Solar wind. When there's a lot of solar wind, it "blows back" the cosmic rays so less get to Earth.

Less cosmic rays, less clouds. Things warm up. More cosmic rays, more clouds, things cool down.

Decreased solar activity equals decreased solar wind. Decreased solar wind equals more cosmic rays impacting the Earth. More cosmic rays impacting the Earth equals more clouds. More clouds equal cooler temperatures.

QE fucking D.

That can be reduced to: Less solar output equals cooler temperatures.

But not by direct effect.

This had been studied repeatedly, proven rigorously and *was* the reason for Earth's long-term heating and cooling trends. Or, hell, *short* term.

"But CO2 tracks with temperature!"

Sort of. CO2 increases *lag behind* temperature increases. CO2 increases in the atmosphere are a *result* of temperature increases not the *cause* of temperature increases. They track *eight hundred years later*. Something that changes *eight hundred years later* cannot be a *cause*. It's an *effect*.

Why? Boyle's Law. Go see "oceans as CO2 repositories." It's okay. I'll wait.

Back? Okay.

Less solar output equals colder temperatures. (Also, in eight hundred years, less CO2. In the meantime, it's going to keep increasing.)

Sunspots had been tracked for centuries. And sunspot activity had been found to be a, pardon the pun, stellar indicator of solar activity.

The sunspots on the sun were going away, one by one. They had their own lag. But the layer of the sun that *caused* them had gone into "recessive condition." That is, it wasn't working.

Bottomline, the sun was cooling off. Big time. And so was the Earth. Because less solar wind equalled . . .

And all the fucking weathermen could talk about was "global warming."

AND PEOPLE WERE *STILL* BUYING IT.

Christ. I lose hope for humanity sometimes.

The same lack of sunspots had last been observed in that mini-iceage back in Medieval days I mentioned. Reporting on its effects when it first kicked in was spotty. But archaeological evidence showed that it kicked in *fast*. Bogs have been found that had frozen practically overnight and then been covered by glaciers. Things got cold, they got cold fast and they stayed cold for a long time.

It looked as if that was what was happening. And the people responsible for reporting the weather were *still* talking about *global warming*.

(Yeah, kids, I know. What the Fuck? I mean, *you* all know that they were fucking idiots as you wrap up in your coats and blankets. But back then, Global Warming was going to end civilization as we knew it. And it was all Man's fault. If we only cut back on CO2 emissions we could all sing kumbaya. I know, it's hard to believe. But go look up things like "The Dutch Tulip Frenzy" and "The Internet Bubble." Humans are pack animals and when the pack stampedes they tend to follow.)

Don't get me wrong. There were people out there saying the opposite. Climatologists were *screaming* about it. But the ones who were doing the screaming were "global warming deniers" and had been put in the same category as Holocaust deniers (not going to explain that one, go look it up later) and thus were tuned out by the "balanced" news media. They were getting *no* airtime. "Too busy reporting on the H5N1 catastrophe and how our Glorious Leader . . .sorry, our First Female President is gloriously responding! All is well except for that continued pesky global warming and, you know, this Plague thing."

Lose. Hope.

Anyway, it was getting cooler, H5N1 was running rampant and the world, warming, cooling, whatever, *was indeed* approaching the end of civilization as we knew it.

The support contractors were already pulling out. International air travel had been suspended but they could still get charter flights under local government (where they were landing that is) rules. There was fucking nothing we could do positive in Iran and we sat there all through March, watching the reports from the U.S., getting hit by the occasional attack, people starting to line up outside the FOBs looking for safety, food, shelter, anything to survive.

April 1 we got our warning orders for movement. The U.S. military was pulling out. Everywhere. We had too many problems at home to try to deal with the rest of the world's problems.

But.

This was only a *temporary* emergency. Warrick had stated that we were going to maintain our *international obligations*. And since we were coming back, any day now, well . . .

Okay, we *couldn't* move all the fucking equipment we had in the Middle East. Just wasn't feasible. Moving it over there had taken *years*. Minimum redeployment time, under optimal conditions, was considered to be six months. A. We needed to get home, now. B. These were *not* optimal conditions. Most of the ships we would have used to get us home were either sailing in circles trying to avoid the Plague or tied up alongside piers with mostly dead crews or crews long disappeared.

This didn't even *cover* the stuff we had in Europe, Korea, Japan . . .

But the troops were going home. We mostly had unit "sets" (all the equipment a unit needs) Stateside as well. So the troops were pulling out.

What to do with the equipment? We're talking about billions and billions and billions of dollars worth of inventory. One report I saw said that the pre-Plague value of the total mobile overseas inventory of the U.S. was at least one *Trillion* in old Dollars.

Well, in countries that were allies instead of totally fucked like Iran, we could just leave it. The units pulled their equipment and supplies, all of it, into holding areas and from there it was up to the local government to secure.

In countries which weren't allies and in which we had "security concerns"?

We were leaving it. With guards to "maintain and secure" it "until relieved."

Each area was different. I can only speak for Iran. (MY can I.) We had six brigades and all their supports in Iran. We had four separate major logistics bases and I don't know how many FOBs and COBs.

The Big LOG base, though, was in Abadan. Abadan is a city that sits on the Shat Al Arab, the confluence of the Tigris and Euphrates, and is right on the border with Iraq. For a lot of reasons, (security) we used Abadan rather than Bandar Shapur or Bandar Abbas for our prime logistics base. And it was a *monster*. Keeping six brigades fed and watered, not to mention the units that fed and watered them fed and watered, was a major undertaking.

People just don't understand the enormous mass of materials that modern units require to keep doing their jobs. I'll put it this way. Think of a really big football stadium. Now, imagine filling it to the rim with . . . stuff. You don't want to break stuff so you put tanks at the bottom. Put armored personnel carriers on top. Keep stacking. Fill it from side to side and all the way to the top. Ammunition, parts, rations, tents, snivel gear, weapons, batteries. (My God do we use a lot of batteries. Remember, I was responsible for making sure the guys in my battalion had all this shit. I know whereof I speak.)

That's the logistics we had in Iran for ONE brigade. A full *stadium* of . . . stuff.

One.

We had six in country. And all the supplies for the camp followers. (Support and supply.)

Over the course of April and into May we moved it all back to Abadan.

Well, okay, some of it we left. We left a lot of rations in place. Units that were in the last detachments to pull out said that there were riots as people flooded in to strip the camps. We left most of the tents and shit that couldn't be used directly as weapons.

We pulled out everything else (and most of the rations) and moved it to Abadan. And piled and piled and stacked and parked and stacked on top of parked and parked on top of stacked.

An ammo dump is a very scary place under any circumstances. Good ammo dumps have massive internal berms (big dirt walls) or big *really* tough bunkers to prevent one set of ammo going boom and making all the others go boom. And only ammo that is pretty much assured not to go boom should go in an ammo dump. And only so much in each sector.

We had to build another ammo dump for all the ammo that was brought in. And we were still stacking it to the top of hundred-foot berms. It was very spectacular when it finally got blown up.

Rations?

The Army does not run just on MREs. Most "long storage" rations are in large cans (called Number 10 for really obscure historical reasons.) Unless you've got really huge hands, you can't get two around them.

We had forty-two ACRES of "long storage" rations. Boxes of Number 10 cans stacked two *stories* high. We had another *fourteen acres* of MREs.

When you're discussing MREs in terms of acres you know something has gotten truly screwed up.

The total coverage area of all the mass of material that was to be "left in place" and "secured" was right at *two thousand* acres.

Unless you live in someplace like Kansas or Nebraska, you've probably never *seen* two thousand acres. That's *three square miles*. Think a box a mile and three quarters across and wide covered in . . . stuff. Tanks, trucks, water blivets, stacked tents, weapons, internal bermed areas for ammunition dumps. Concertina wire, thank God.

It was amazing to look at. And very very scary. Especially when there was just one.

As units finished their "phased redeployment" (euphemism for "run away, run away!") they were flown out. Yeah, international air travel was suspended. Which just meant there were a lot of planes sitting around. And pilots could be scrounged up. We had 747 after 747 roaring out of Abadan airport (which we secured) morning, noon and night.

And then there was one.

Somebody was supposed to stay behind "until relieved" and "ensure inventory, maintenance and security" of the enormous mass of material.

Units were needed in the States. Things were going to hell and the Army had a job seeing that things didn't come apart entirely. Every body that could be spared was going home.

I don't know what fucking lottery led to *our battalion* being tasked with leaving ONE COMPANY to do the job of a fucking BRIGADE but we got handed the shit end of the stick.

Remember me mentioning the Bravo Company commander? One of my former JO's and not the battalion commander's fair-haired boy?

You guessed it. The battalion was tasked with leaving "one company of infantry and minimal necessary supports" as security for an area you couldn't *walk* around in an hour.

And "a logistics officer" to maintain inventory of the "stored equipment."

Gulp.

— CHAPTER TWO —

There's this Duck Video . . .

The Emperor Trajan once ordered a legion of Roman soldiers to "march east until you come to the end of the world." Everything but that is spotty history but they're believed to have been destroyed in battle by, well, the Iranians somewhere not too far from Abadan. They're remembered in military legend as "The Lost Legion."

(It's possible, though, that some of them made it as far as Western China. There's a *very* odd tribe over there. But that's ancient history at this point.)

As we watched the last trucks headed for the airport, watched the eyes of our fellow soldiers who were headed home, leaving us behind to "maintain security" over an area that was impossible to secure . . .

Well, we wondered what history would call us. If anyone remembered us at all.

We weren't the last people in Titan Base. (Don't know who named it originally but it had gotten fairly titanic that's for sure.) All the contractors hadn't pulled out. There were a few Brits left. They'd been in charge of the mess section for the original Titan Base. They, however, had to leave on a plane at the same time as our guys or they figured they'd never see balmy old England again.

They were *in charge of* the mess section. They didn't do the scut work. The scut work had been done by a lot of different laborers. Most of those had gotten out. But they still were in charge of sixty Nepalese.

135

And while there was transport for the Brits, there *wasn't* any for the Nepalese.

The guy in charge had been a British Army cook then worked in one of the universities. He was a specialist in producing large amounts of good to excellent food. He also was a stand-up guy. Which was why he stopped by my office as the battalion was loading up to "redeploy."

"Old chum, got a bit of a bother."

(Okay, he *was* a stand-up guy. But he also had a very affected Oxford accent. It's a Brit thing. Think *Keeping Up Appearances* but a guy.)

"Go," I said, not really paying much attention. Look, Captain Butterfill was, technically, in charge of security. But, one I had time in grade on him and two he wasn't in charge of inventory for all this shit. I was up to my eyeballs in the paperwork regarding inventory for two fucking *divisions*.

Look, nothing *had* been inventoried. What I had were the inventories for the units. And inventories, notoriously, are inaccurate. Oh, not stealing. The Army had an incredibly minor problem with that. Usually just bad paperwork.

But in this case, shit had been picked up and then dumped off. There'd been a *general* with a *huge* staff in charge of the base. *Before* all the shit was "redeployed."

I knew, deep in my bones, that at some point someone was going to be asking me pointed questions about where a case of DL123 batteries went. Okay, *four truckloads* of batteries.

It took me a couple of days to grasp the futility of my job and revel in the fact that I really didn't give a shit. But at the time I was trying to be a good little Assistant S-4.

"I don't have transport for the Nepos."

"Nepos?" I asked, wondering what in the hell Britishism that was. Soap? Guns? Hell, with Brits it could be anything. They were worse than pharmaceutical companies. Why not just call Viagra "Dickerector"? I think it's a plot with the Brits.

"The Nepalese," he said, pretty patiently given that his driver was honking the horn. "The cooks and whatnot. Been screaming to home office about it but Nepal's gone quite isolationist what with the whole birdie thing and Foreign Office won't take them in. The rest have gotten transport out or bunked off. But there's the Nepos, you see."

I did see. What he was telling me was that there were a bunch of foreign civilians left on the base with no way home.

What to do? It wasn't like I could just kick them out. The Nepalese are not Iranians. They couldn't get integrated into the society. And things were coming apart, fast. Hell, there was still, technically, a government in Tehran but if it controlled anything past the city borders I'd be very surprised. Kicking them out into the wilderness Iran was quickly becoming would-be murder.

"Vaccinations?"

"Up to date," he said, handing me *more* fucking paperwork. "Good chaps. Willing. Couple of them speak English. Sort of. Don't suppose you've got a Gorkali speaker?"

"No," I said, coldly. We had one translator, an American born Iranian who'd been raised learning Farsi. He'd grown up in L.A. and really wanted to go home. He also spoke a smattering of Arabic. I'd been told by one of the Iranian officers I met that he was very nearly incomprehensible in Farsi. Basically, what he spoke was the Farsi equivalent of Ebonics.

"And?"

"I can't be sure *we'll* survive, much less your 'Nepos,'" I said. "But I'll do everything I can to keep them alive."

"Thank you," he said, clearly moved. It was apparent he liked his "Nepos" and felt like shit leaving them behind. Well, there was a lot of that going around. "Good luck, old chap."

"Same to you."

Well, I learned why he liked his "Nepos" over time. Pretty quick I *started* to learn but it took more time to *truly* learn. If there was ever a race destined for greatness who just ended up at the wrong place and the wrong time, it's the fucking Nepalese.

I've dealt with lots of cultures and races in my time. Most of them I don't care much for. Arabs are lazy as hell, Iranians are arrogant. But Iranians don't have a touch on the French and probably work harder even if they fuck much of it up. (Call it the Active/Stupid culture.) Kurds and Americans get along pretty well, all things considered, but Kurds treat their women like shit.

If there is a finer group of non-Americans than the Nepalese I have yet to meet them. They're some of the hardest workers I've ever met, tend to be fairly intelligent, have got a very broad sense of humor and are just tough as fucking nails. Disciplined, too.

Ghurkas, who are some of the finest infantry in the world,

are drawn from some of the Nepalese tribes. Our guys weren't (mostly) Ghurkas. But working with them I learned why Ghurkas are so highly regarded. If the Ghurks are *better* than my Nepos, that's pretty fucking scary.

But at the time it was another pain in the ass I didn't care for.

So about that time Butterfill stopped by.

"Yo, Bandit. What did the Limey want?"

He was a captain now. He could call me Bandit.

"He couldn't get out his Nepalese. They're ours now."

"Well, that's the mess section settled."

"So, what are you going to do?"

It was a big question. As in, square miles and umpteen billions of dollars of gear big.

"I have a very complete action plan provided by the battalion commander. Actually, the S-3 working from the BC's concept plan."

"Uh, huh."

The S-3 was a pretty good guy. But if he had to create a plan from the BC's concept, it was unlikely to be good.

"We're to maintain continuous three-man roving patrols around the perimeter," Butterfill said. "Six of them, which means a platoon on patrol all the time. And one platoon on standby for reaction."

I winced. What he'd just said . . . Well, there were *so* many things wrong with it.

First of all, three-man patrols in uparmored humvees *or* Strykers were just waiting to get picked off. Attackers weren't going to hit us near the main base. They'd wait until a patrol was on the far side, separated from other patrols, and set off an IED or burn in with RPGs and light them up.

In a high-threat environment, and we were a very big and juicy target which was going to make this a high-threat environment, you did *not* send out three-man patrols.

The other thing was, there was no downtime built in. Eighteen guys on patrol meant a full platoon on duty at all times. They could do that for twenty-four to forty-eight hours, max. Another on "standby" and covering internal guarding meant *they* weren't exactly getting downtime. It would be better than being on patrol duty but not much.

And there was stuff that would have to be done. Technically, we were supposed to keep up with training. I figured that was out the window but still. And there was maintenance. Stuff did not run itself. We'd been left with one "support" platoon, most mechanics, to keep stuff running. But they didn't have enough hands to do it all. And, hell, if something broke it's not like we couldn't go out and find a replacement. But there was work other than patrolling that was going to have to be done.

Nobody would have so much as a day of downtime. Of any noticeable degree. And if we got hit by a big attack, we'd have a third of our unit scattered to fuck and gone. If the attackers were *smart* and put in an attack on a patrol, pulled out the duty platoon . . .

"And your opinion of that, Captain?"

"Six patrols aren't going to be able to prevent pilfering . . ."

"Pilfering, hell," I said. "I'm worried about getting fucking overrun."

"And then there's that."

Even the core base was too large for one company to secure in the event of a heavy attack.

"Technically," he added, causing more heartburn, "You're in charge."

"*You're* in charge of security," I pointed out. "*I'm* in charge of the support section and 'responsible,' fuck me, for inventory of all this crap."

"You're the senior officer."

"Oh, thank you very much."

"So if you have any . . . alterations you might suggest, I'd be under orders to implement them."

"Putting *me* in the position of violation of a direct order."

"There is that. On the other hand . . ."

"I don't want to end up as a trophy for some fucking RIF."

Well, hell, all that material was just *sitting* there.

The whole camp was protected by berms. But you can climb a berm. Teams of guys can climb a berm and "pilfer" quite a lot of stuff. Like weapons. And ammunition to go with the weapons.

Berms weren't going to keep the majority of them out. The roving patrols might slow them down. But only slow them.

So I started looking in the inventory.

Concertina is a razor wire that's wrapped in big rolls that open up into about three-foot circles. You might have seen it up on fences around prisons.

It's very nasty stuff. One strand was not so much. A *bunch* of strands made for a very tangled situation. You could *get* through it, but not easily.

You don't want to know how much concertina was in the inventory. More, by volume, than the MREs. Acres.

Wire, by itself, though, wasn't going to stop the RIFs.

Want to take a square area guess how many *mines* we had in the ammo bunkers? Cubic, actually, their boxes stack quite well.

Army engineers are normally the guys who put in major defenses. There had been a lot of engineers in Iran. (Sorry for calling you guys and gals "camp followers.") And over the years they've gotten tired of doing things by hand so they have some interesting equipment to do it for them.

They had, I shit you not, a big ass semiarmored . . . *thing* that could put in fence posts (big ones, twelve feet high) and hook fencing to it, all automatically. It looked like a big dump truck crossed with a factory. Another big ass . . . thing from the same family could lay down concertina at the rate of one mile an hour for as long as you fed it concertina.

Last but not least, they had an armored vehicle that could emplace mines for you as long as you fed it mines. In series, which means not just one at a time but three in a pattern.

And, hell, the Nepos were just sitting there.

But we didn't start with securing the whole base. First things first; make sure we survived.

Titan Base had had a permanent population of nearly five thousand, with military personnel and contractors, as well as a floating population (since it was used for replacements) of another thousand or so at any time. Since everybody was in tents and trailers, that was . . . Think acres again.

The core of the base, though, was smaller than a FOB. That is, the central offices and some senior officers' quarters that were still trailers but with slightly better amenities.

The latter, however, wasn't disconnected from the majority of the base in any way.

Well, the bulldozers were just sitting there, too.

I don't think the last plane was off the ground before we got started. One of the mechanics knew how to drive a bulldozer.

Look, technically we should have taken down the tents and possibly moved the trailers or something. We didn't have time and we didn't care.

Over the next three days we bermed the central area, renaming it Fort Lonesome, and started laying in wire. There were three kinds: Military link (sort of like chain-link but welded and much thicker), barbed wire and concertina.

Eventually, over the course of the next several months (yes, people, months) we got Fort Lonesome to look like this:

Tanglefoot barbed wire (barbed wire strung tight at about shin-height) covering a thirty-meter cleared zone all the way around the fort except for two entrances. Get to them later.

Six strands of concertina piled against a twelve-foot military link outer perimeter fence. Three strands on top.

A cleared zone that was mined like a motherfucker. You had to work *hard* to get to the mines. Anybody that got to the mines got what they fucking deserved.

Another set of tanglefoot, this one laced with command deto-nated mines (claymores).

More concertina, staked down.

Berm with ground-level sandbagged bunkers heavy enough to shrug off a 105 round. (Aluminum aircraft pallets are *great* for making those. Don't know why we had . . . well a bit less than an acre of pallets but . . . They were just *sitting* there.)

All of the bunkers mounted M240 medium machine guns except for "heavy defense points" which had .50 caliber. I thought about putting .50 caliber all around and we might have gotten to it, but . . . Ah, hell, getting ahead of myself.

We weren't done.

The area was flat as a fucking pancake so a raised central defense area was out of the question. But we put the final defensive zone in the middle. There we had another berm with three exits, more con-certina, mines, fences, etc. Covered *trenches* to the central redoubt. And enough armored vehicles that if it got down to brass tacks we *still* had a chance to fight our way out. I brought in two Abrams, along with six Strykers and two Bradleys. We also had fuel trucks, maintenance equipment and what-have-you in there.

That was Fort Lonesome. Inside its nigh impregnable defenses we could lay our heads with peace.

About the Nepos.

So while Butterfill was getting his act together, I wandered over to the mess area to see what I'd been left.

The barracks for the Nepos were halfway across the compound

but most of them were gathered in the (vast) combined mess hall. And they looked dejected. About the only time I ever saw Nepalese looking depressed.

"Who speaks English?" I asked walking across the mess hall.

Lemme tell you about that. Imagine a high-school gym. No, imagine an *aircraft hangar*. Fill it with tables and those benches you ate on in school. Position lots of garbage cans. Have a serving area at one end. Cordon off a small area where there are more "civilized" tables and chairs and, you know, tablecloths and silverware.

Behind the serving area is the kitchen. You don't want to try to imagine the kitchen.

These guys were sitting or standing down by the serving area. The mess hall was, otherwise, completely empty and I'd never realized how much it echoed until I had to walk the whole length in near isolation.

"I am speaking English, sir," one of them said. "I am Samad."

Samad was not a Nepalese name. I, to this day, don't know why my friend is named Samad. I've never asked and hope to be able to refrain.

Samad was the straw-boss for the rest of the Nepos. Mainly because he spoke some English (it got better) and because he was a former Ghurka. He says he was a subadar major, a sergeant major or master sergeant. I figure he was a sergeant, maybe even a private. But I've never challenged him on it.

Ghurkas (okay, technically "Ghorkas") are all Nepalese but not all Nepalese can become Ghurkas. Ghurkas are recruited from four tribes in Nepal and the position has become to a great extent hereditary. And there's not much you can say that distinguishes Ghurkas except they're short, tend to be kind of barrel-like, have very tough skulls, smile a lot, are very disciplined and fight like ever-loving bastards.

Samad was the only Ghurka among the Nepos but all of the Nepos turned out to follow the same pattern. I told Samad that we'd been left behind and that they were working for me now. He translated and the whole group started to give those grins that are the trademark of their race. They had somebody to tell them what to do again. What it would be didn't matter. Just tell them what to do.

There was a lot of initial movement. The company wasn't

barracked near the area we were planning on building up. Stuff had to be toted.

There were vehicles but it wasn't that far to walk. The guys picked up their personal gear and walked.

I told Samad the Nepos were going to have to barrack in with us and we headed over to where the procession was forming. The Nepos didn't even ask for orders, they just started grabbing gear, including packs from the troops. That took a bit of sorting out and we finally convinced them that infantry could carry their own packs a few hundred meters.

Samad was everywhere. At the time he had no real clue about how to expand on an order and acted a bit "active/stupid." Some of the things he had the Nepos doing were useless or counter-productive. It's one of the reasons I think he was a private not a sergeant major. But eventually we got over it. Took a while. I'll cover "training" later.

We moved. And we moved again. Then we started clearing.

We did send out patrols. One. Two fully loaded Strykers moving together. It was a deterrence patrol, not a guard.

You see, Titan Base was well out on the plains east of Abadan but people were making the trek anyway. Abadan was headed for the sort of hell only the *worst* areas in the U.S. experienced (see L.A. and Detroit) and people were trying to get away from the Plague and the chaos. People may rant and march and burn effigies about the U.S. when things are good, but as soon as the shit hits the fan they turn to American troops. Trust. They may not trust their government but all the propaganda about "abuses" in the world doesn't break the trust of people in the American soldier.

Problem was, one company could not do shit for them. Later on we figured ways to help, a little. H. R. Puffinstuff; we could do a little but we couldn't do enough. But that was later.

We moved. Then we started tearing down and rebuilding.

My office had actually been in the central command zone. I'd had one over in the Battalion S-4 shop but as part of the "reconsolidation" I got a new one, with more paperwork, in the central area. Actually, all the paperwork wasn't in the office. There was a trailer next door that had all the paperwork. All I had in the office were the summaries of the summaries of the summaries of what was in the trailer. And on my computer the "physical location for inventory" of all the fucking stuff that had been dropped off.

It had been a scramble pulling all the stuff in. And some of the stuff wasn't where people said it was. But given the scramble, the place was amazingly well organized. That general and his staff knew their stuff.

My main worry was the ammo. Without the ammo all the Tinkertoys we had stored weren't worth dick. But even the ammo bunkers, which were mostly on the other side of the base from our area, covered one hell of a lot of ground.

It was actually while we were moving, the first day, planes barely off the ground, that the "deterrence patrol" had to do some deterring. Two "military grade" trucks with Iranian Army markings came up the road from Abadan and turned towards the entrances nearest the ammunition depot. The patrol had been on the far side of the area when they started out and only got up to them when they were nearly to the gates.

They stopped when the Strykers came in view and a man in "military garb" got out of one and waved for the Strykers to approach.

Only problem being that the drivers of the trucks weren't in military garb. Oh, maybe they were laborers and maybe the guy thought he had some right to U.S. Army ammo. Didn't matter. The lead Stryker fired a burst of .50 caliber off at an angle while the trailer moved over to the gates.

The trucks turned around and went back towards Abadan.

It was duly reported and the deterrence patrol continued.

They also ran into clearly civilian groups. People were walking or driving out. The gates to the place were shut and the patrol fired warning shots to scatter them. We just couldn't do a damned thing for them. Not then.

Normally, American soldiers ride fairly openly and are notorious for handing out candy and food. Kids love them and vice versa. We *couldn't* be kind. We had *way* too much to do.

People started camping out. We were in the middle of a flat fucking plain ten miles from the nearest town, Abadan, and people just trickled out there. I don't know what they thought *we* were going to do for them, but they came in droves. And they stayed in ramshackle huts cobbled together from shit people dragged from the city.

Living on a desert plain with no water or food in sight is not a good option. Unless the alternative is worse. Gives an idea what it must have been like in Abadan.

And they died. We weren't interacting with them *at all* at that point. The patrols had orders to keep people at least five hundred meters from the berms and any time people tried to approach they'd open fire. Usually a warning burst from a .50 cal would turn people away. Not always.

Fucking drivers in the Middle East are the *worst* drivers on earth. And more totally oblivious than a blonde on a cell phone. They started to get the point after the fifth or sixth shot-up wreck on the road to the base. Yes, they were civilians. Probably. None of the cars blew up. And, yes, there were women and kids in the cars.

Did we like it? No. Was it necessary? Yes. Why?

Follow the logic. By the end of the first day there were three or four hundred people gathered not far from the main gates. The gates had six guys on them, all we could spare. They were in bunkers, but only six guys. Everybody else was busy creating someplace we could huddle "until relieved." Two Strykers trying to cover the entire perimeter and six guys on the gates.

So we let a car come up to the gates. People go in the direction of the pack. All those people wanted inside our walls for protection from . . . Well, it was probably pretty bad in Abadan.

If they weren't firing to kill, think six guys could keep three or four hundred desperate people from overrunning them? And then there would be three or four hundred desperate people running around the base. Think we could have maintained any semblance of order with a bare hundred soldiers? While trying to keep the rest of the base under control?

Later we helped out. Things got complicated. But for then, there wasn't anything we were going to do.

Oh, except keep it from becoming Abadan.

The evening of day one people had settled in. And two "military style" trucks approached the main gates, then turned off into the area where people were huddling. At that point, they barely had any shelter. It was just . . . people. Sitting in a fucking desert. (Yes, it was fucking with us, okay? We're American soldiers. Believe it or not, most of us are paladins somewhere in our heart of hearts. We *did not like it*.)

The trucks stopped and "males in civilian garb" began unloading and "attacking" the refugees. They were stealing what little food and water they had and apparently engaging in some rapes. Or started to.

The gate guards put in a call for the on-call platoon, which was mostly still engaged in moving shit, and the roving patrol. But the roving patrol was up by the ammo bunkers, about a mile away.

The main camp of people was about five hundred meters west of the gates. Five hundred meters is a long shot for any sniper especially into the sun, which was setting.

Captain Butterfill, however, and it was his idea not mine, had put two of his company snipers on the gates. Not a normal choice but it turned out to be prophetic. They "engaged the attackers at long range with careful aim." Apparently got three of them before the rest got the idea. Some people might have been kidnapped from the refugees. See also "raped." But the two "military grade" trucks drove off. Last we saw of that group of problem-makers but we were to have many *many* more.

By evening the movement was complete. Nothing else but we were centrally located and close to the gates. (We hadn't been before.) Units were rotated. A third Stryker was parked outside the gates. There were Klieg lights over the gates (and all along the berm although most eventually had to get shut off). They could still see the edge of the refugee camp.

A mortar carrier was sent out with an infantry Stryker in support. The Stryker stayed back while the mortar carrier approached the refugee camp.

Look, we're human, okay? People were dying in the desert and God wasn't raining mana. Well, maybe He was but the "mana" said "U.S. Army" on the side and it came in brown plastic packages.

Somewhere in the mass of shit were large numbers of "emergency civilian disaster support packages." They were sort of like MREs but they were made to fit just about any religious taboo and came in yellow packages instead of brown. We didn't have the time or interest to find them. We had MREs. We took MREs.

And bottled water. We had that, too. Not quite acres but a shitload. We also had a water processing plant and all sorts of shit we didn't know how to run. We were to figure it out.

In the meantime, we had bottled water. We took that and MREs out to the refugees.

Mistake? I dunno. Maybe. Maybe if we'd been hard-hearted enough to just ignore the people dying in the desert they would have gone away. Or maybe not. Maybe we'd have had a few hundred or thousand corpses from dehydration and malnutrition.

Saw this clip one time on a funny video show. First part was two ducks swimming in a pond. Mallards. The people were ooing and aaahing. Cool! Ducks in the pool.

They apparently fed them and the ducks eventually continued their migration well fed and able to prosper.

The next bit was the following season. The ducks had apparently reproduced or found friends. Ten ducks. Cool! Ducks in the pool.

The next bit was some following season. Must have been over a thousand ducks trying to get in the pool. Water was splashing twenty feet as they nose-dived into the throng.

Yeah. It was like that.

But we knew not what we did.

There were no attacks and people weren't trying to overrun them. They handed out one MRE packet and two bottles of water to each person who approached. They had extras and they left them behind. I'm sure that the toughest and the strongest grabbed the extras. Law of nature.

The guys also dropped off shovels and pointed to the corpses which, thus far, had been left to rot.

There were no major incidents.

Day two was spent digging out stuff we needed to toughen up our defenses. We found the engineering equipment we needed right where it was supposed to be. You couldn't miss the wire storage area; piles of concertina *that* high are noticeable. We drove construction equipment over and got to work.

More refugees. Hovels were going up.

This time *before* dark we sent out the food wagon. The corpses were just sitting there. The guys on the mortar track pointed to the corpses and went away.

Some people tried to run them down. The Stryker fired warning shots.

About an hour later, the gate guards reported that some people were burying the corpses of the guys who'd been shot the day before. When the mortar carrier went back out, the guys on the gate went with them. (There were replacements on the gate.)

They pointed out the guys who had been on the burial detail. They got extra rations and the translator told them to dig some slit trenches or find somebody to dig them for latrines. Or the food wouldn't come out the next day. And if there were dead bodies, bury them.

Day Two: No major incidents.

Oh, one but not about refugees or attackers. The BC called. He told us we were doing a great job and that our contribution was extremely important. I asked how long we were going to be stuck in this armpit. He said that hadn't been determined yet but finding out a fixed timetable for redeployment was at the top of his list.

Yeah. Right.

Day Three.

Everybody didn't walk out to the refugee camp. There was a fair car-park building up. People were using them for shelters and such.

A line of "civilian style trucks, vans and cars" came out from Abadan.

Same shit as Day One. Guys started unassing and robbing everyone in sight.

The ROE had been adjusted. And this time we had a response platoon. (The Nepos were taking up a lot of the work.) But we didn't really need it.

The gate Stryker rolled out. It got close enough to "engage the vehicles with careful, aimed fire" and started shooting them the hell up. It continued rolling forward to the edge of where the refugees' shit was scattered and fired more shots over the group.

Now, by this time the attackers and the refugees were sort of mixed up. The refugees were mostly trying to run away, but some of them were fighting. The stuff they had was all they had. They weren't just going to give it up.

Many of the "attackers," though, were armed. And quite a few refugees got shot by them.

But when the Stryker rolled up and started lighting up their rides, they fired at the Stryker, which was buttoned up and thus a lousy target, and started trying to run.

We did not give them the opportunity. Every single "armed person" was engaged and all the "convoy" was fired up and destroyed.

Quite a few bodies to bury, though. So we rolled an engineering vehicle out and dug a slit trench. We were going to roll it out the next day but somebody had already filled it in. And the bodies were gone.

Were there wounded among the refugees? Probably. Were we going to send one of our two medics out to find out? Or if anybody had eye problems or goiters or a host of other shit we'd fixed around the world?

Nope. Not then.

There were some shots from the refugee camp that night. Didn't know at the time if it was happiness that they had weapons or people settling personal disputes. But there weren't any bodies in the morning.

There were the day after. And pretty much *every* day as time went on. But they got buried and that was all we cared about.

Was there "pilfering" going on? Yeah, probably. Some. But, remember, we were in the middle of a big ass flat fucking plain. I mean flat like the flat parts of Kansas. And we were slightly elevated. (Slope of the plain coming up from the river. There weren't any hills, trust me.) We could see all the way to the Shat Al Arab, Abadan and the refineries. The closest point of concealed approach was about four miles and that was from a line of trees by the refinery. That was to the west and southwest. To the north there wasn't much but the trace of the highway (big one) running to Awhaz. To the south, flat plain that eventually became one of the world's biggest and flattest salt marshes. On a clear day, and there weren't many that clear, you could see the edge of the Gulf.

To the east, *way* the fuck away, were the Zagros Mountains. You could tell the progression of the seasons by the way the snow on the top slid up and down. Point is, you could see them.

Anybody approaching with any sort of vehicle we were going to detect miles away. Well, once we got eyes in every direction. That took about four weeks.

CHAPTER THREE

Pax Americana

What was happening in that four weeks?

Inside the berm, a lot of changes. We cleared an open area around our zone and rebuilt a FOB inside the LOG. (Fort Lonesome.) It was pretty big for even a company to hold but every time Fillup and me figured we had *everything we could possibly need* we thought of something else.

I'm from Minnesota. I don't know any Minnesotan, not a *real* Minnesotan, who's not a pack rat. It's in our genes. I could *never* have enough parts, rations, water, fuel, to satisfy me. Okay, maybe I *was* in the right place being an S-4. I hated being left to guard this fucker, but *having* it all? Mine all mine? The only person to tell me I didn't own it a face on a videophone who was *way* too far away to force me to do anything? Heaven.

Mine, mine, mine.

Speaking of mines.

We got Fort Lonesome minimally prepared to withstand a significant assault. Then we got started on securing the *whole* base.

We shouldn't have had to do it. But the ROE that came down on high (which we were still, technically, under) did not permit laying in mines. Don't know why we had so many of the fuckers, but we did. And we didn't lay the mines down first.

First came the outer perimeter fence. That was just to keep kids and dogs out. It took two weeks to lay in and used up just about all of our remaining military link. It was right at six and a half miles around the perimeter. That's one big fucking fence.

We put in gates by the main gate. (Later we played with that extensively.) The main gate had a series of berms, concrete barriers and such to keep suicide trucks from getting to it. The fence linked into the edge of those and we put in outer gates.

Then we got started on the inner defenses. More concertina. (The stacks were, to my amazement, dropping. Who could have known?)

Most of this was getting done by the Nepos. We had multiple patrols working, the gate guards, security for the workers on the fence and a reserve force. The troops didn't have *time* to do the manual labor.

I'd been pissed at getting the Nepos dumped on us but they were a godsend. Okay, first of all, the troops were, by and large, lousy cooks. The Nepos were decent. They tended to start to cook some odd shit without their British supervisors. If you let them get away with it we would have all been eating vegetarian curry and vindaloo. I'll admit I got a bit of taste for vindaloo but it was not shared by all the troops.

The nice thing, in my opinion, about vindaloo was that it was pork based.

There were problems. Oh. My. GOD were there problems. I'm not talking about security issues, either.

Electricity.

The power plant for the base was a big gas-turbine fucker. Nobody but *nobody* had any clue how to operate it. But there were back-up generators that were, essentially, diesel-electric railroad engines. Those the mechanics could figure out. And we had one *fuck* of a lot of diesel in the tank-farm.

We only needed power for the area we were inhabiting. The mechanics and a couple of the Nepos that had some clue about electric got those buildings hooked up to a couple of the generators. But we had a problem with power surging.

So we got on the phone to back home. No, we have no fixed date for your redeployment. You're doing a great job. Keep the faith.

(*My fucking* dad *is dead you bastard and I'm stuck on the ass end of nowhere. All of the troops have gotten word that somebody in their family has died and to say the least morale should be shot. We're keeping it up by giving them shit to do but that's only going to last so long . . .*)

Fine, fine, but we need to find somebody who has a clue about generators . . .

Hello. Commo. We had one radio tech. He was *not* a satellite radio tech. We had this big fucking communications van and no clue how to run most of the shit.

Fortunately, one of the privates in the company had spent time before enlisting working in a satellite shop in a cable company. He wasn't a satellite engineer, by any stretch, but when we lost commo with home for three days he finally figured out how to get us back up. (Without SkyGeek, in fact, this book would never have come about.)

The water for the base was a pipeline from the Shat that ran to a water processing plant. The plant was called a ROWPU. I had to look that one up. Reverse Osmosis Water Purification Unit.

About week three some bastard cut our water line. We had water for about three weeks at current use (*big* fucking tanks) but after that *we* were going to be dying in the desert.

Turned out the original base had been supplied by a deep bore well. There was water down there. We weren't all that far from the Gulf and the Shat. Water percolates. There were even limestone layers that carried subsurface water from the Zagros. That was actually what the well was tied into. Crisp, clean water. Don't know why they ever put in that fucking line. It was a tactical weak point.

Only one problem. The well had been rather radically disconnected from the water system. It wasn't even left as backup. Don't know why.

So we had to figure out how to reconnect it. We were not plumbers and so proved figuring that out. And then figure out how to get the very deep water up to the surface.

"Head pressure" does not always have to do with something obscene. I'm a farmer. I understand head pressure. Farmers use wells a lot. However, this one was a holy mother of a bitch of a big, deep well. We got it done.

React, adapt, overcome. We did one hell of a lot of that.

We got the mines laid in. We even found a stack of signs that warned of mines in multiple languages. We shot some guys in a pickup truck who were trying to sneak in the back way. We filled in all but the main gate entrances to the base.

It took two months of work, mostly by the Nepos. But we

got the base surrounded by multiple lines of fencing, mines and such whot. We even found a complete "video surveillance" system that had never been installed. We installed it. The reserve platoon monitored.

We fed and watered refugees. There had gotten to be a fuckload of them. And they'd apparently established some sort of governance body. At least there were guys with guns (scavenged from attackers) who strutted around with angry expressions on their face.

Feeding and watering of the refugees had gotten to be a massive chore. Again, handled mostly by the Nepos. We now had to send out *two* mortar carriers to carry all the rations. Each of them towed a water buffalo. (A large water tank that had spigots on it.) The refugees would get handed a meal. (We'd found the yellow stuff by then. Some people waved the old MRE wrappers after the first couple of "refugee" meals. Apparently they hadn't realized that was a pork patty and wanted more.) They had to figure out how to get their own water. Doing it that way increased the time but just handing out *that many meals* increased the time.

Sometimes the guys with guns took a meal away from somebody right in front of our eyes. That really stuck in people's craws. But we weren't going to get off the tracks to give the meal back.

A couple of weeks after that sort of thing started to happen, one of the guys with guns took away a meal from a woman and then started beating on her.

Each of the tracks was manned by a track commander at the .50, two Nepos to hand out meals and three guys with rifles for security.

One of the guys with a rifle shot him.

There was a lot of shouting. More guys with guns came out. The woman ran to the track. The TC jacked a round into the .50 and fired a burst over the camp. The Stryker that was sitting back on overwatch gunned its engine and rolled forward a couple of feet.

Things settled down. The lady was allowed to scramble on the track. Others came over. They were shooed away. Meals were passed out until they were gone. The tracks came back to base with an extra body.

That was the first refugee we let in. It wouldn't be the last and, yeah, that had issues, too.

Specialist Stephan Noton's ass was in a very deep crack and he knew it. The track commander wasn't real happy, either. He had just brought a refugee into the camp.

What was worse was, well . . .

Salah wasn't gorgeous. But after this long in the desert and no fucking women around at all . . . She was seventeen according to the translator and as far as she knew all her family was dead. She had lived in Abadan all her life and was a very good Moslem as far as that sort of thing went. She was a nice girl. We didn't question her about specific events. I didn't want to know if she'd been raped or how many times. Yes and many was probably the answer. I also didn't want to know how she'd been surviving in the camp. But apparently whatever she'd been doing wasn't good enough for at least one of the guys with guns.

I could *see* the thought percolating through the heads of the troops. Most of them had, at this point, been out feeding the refugees one time or another. And despite the conditions there were quite a few females out there better looking than Salah. And we'd been away from women a *long* time.

And when you've been starving to death in a desert, you'll do a lot for a cracker and a bottle of cold water.

Hell, *I* was thinking it.

But I had *some* capacity to think with my topside head. And various thoughts were percolating. Some of them had to do with maintenance and support.

The Nepos were doing most of that. But as the major construction ran down, I'd been thinking about other uses for them. A company was not enough guys to hold this place against any sort of serious attack. Yes, we could draw back into Fort Lonesome but that wasn't the mission.

We believed as an article of faith that sooner or later we'd be "relieved." Maybe some other unit would be sent out to replace us. Maybe we'd be ordered to just leave all the shit behind. My personal choice was to destroy most of it in place. But something was going to happen. Uncle Sam was *not* going to leave us out here to grow old and die.

But if we got a serious attack, and one was bound to happen sooner or later, we couldn't do much about it. Unless we had more troops.

And the Nepos were just sitting there.

Well, no, they weren't. They were cleaning our clothes and fixing our food and maintaining some of the support equipment while we were defending the base. Sidenote: It takes ten people to keep one infantry soldier functioning in battle. Yeah, many of those are really "rear echelon motherfuckers" (REMFs) but that also includes cooks, techs and whatnot that are absolutely vital to an infantry unit. We'd been left with a few techs but damned little "other support." "Other support" was what the Nepos were doing.

But as the main job of getting the defenses in place was winding down, I started to give some thought to other uses for them.

Yes, they weren't Ghurkas. But at this point I trusted them to hold a gun while behind me. At least if they could hold a gun and not have an AD. Thing being, I wasn't going to tell the troops they now had to cook. Laundry, sure. Cooking? Not these guys. And the troops were already busy.

Women could probably figure out how to cook and clean. And, hell, it would relieve some *other* pressures. Might create new ones, but there were some pressures building up right before my eyes I did not care for.

By the way, the Nepos were not entirely straight. Oh, I'm not saying they were all queer as a three-dollar bill. I think it was more like prison, maybe a function of their culture. Samad had a slighter built Nepo who always seemed to be hanging around and that he bunked with. Sure. They were just friends.

For that matter there was, I was pretty sure, at least one "couple" among the troops. I didn't give a shit as long as it didn't affect the unit and it didn't seem to. Don't ask, don't tell.

(For clarification: Once Samad got a wife, I never saw hide nor hair of male "close personal friends." And he thinks the question is funny. Most things the Nepos and Americans see pretty eye to eye on. Some things not. Different cultures.)

So. There was an argument for bringing some of the refugee females, if they were amenable, into the camp. When we got relieved, pardon the pun, we could write them off as "locally hired support staff." Whoever was incoming could deal with that.

The question was, what would the nature of our "relief" be? A new unit to sit on the junk? Or leave it all behind? Or destroy it in place?

In the first case, well, camp followers rarely worry about which camp they're following. There might be some broken hearts and pining. Get over it.

In the last two, though, which at one level I considered likely enough to be formulating plans in the back of my mind, there were . . . issues.

Say that we were told "destroy everything, we're coming to get you." (By the way, that would mean coming in by helo. There was no way we were going to work through the airport at this point. Iran *had* no government. The place was slowly being reorganized under local strong-men. It wasn't until later that such got functional in the Abadan area and when it did . . . Well, ahead of myself again. Point is, we weren't going out by 747.)

If we got extracted we might be able to argue for extracting the Nepos. But a bunch of local civilian women? Uh, uh. Which would probably leave them worse off than before.

I knew my logic was getting messed up. Normally, I could see a situation and make a decision without any real difficulty. Things were black and white. This looked like shades of gray and I wasn't good with gray.

So I took a walk.

Somebody, probably an overzealous engineer lieutenant, had put a "sentry walk" up on the berm near the main area of the base. It was a lousy item, defensively. We didn't have sentries walk the parapets because normally they'd be dead meat for a sniper. But the area faced southeast, where there was fuck-all for miles and we had thermal imagery cameras set up so anyone approaching, especially at night, would be detected at artillery ranges not sniper ranges.

It was, therefore, a decent place to walk and pace.

I think it was the character Horatio Hornblower who used to pace all the time. I didn't. Pacing, to me, was a sign that the commander didn't know what to do. But the truth was, I didn't. And pacing did help me think.

So I put on my battle rattle, headed up to the parapet and paced.

The night was clear and damned cold for Abadan in the summer. The wind was from the east, down off the mountains as it often was. And it was a cool breeze, lemme tell you. But it also helped me think.

I knew that two aspects of the question were fucking with my logic. The first was "female" and the second was "refugee." I'll take the second first.

About fifteen years back was the only time I think it made the news. But UN aid workers in two or three areas were trading refugee supplies to underage refugees, male and female, for sexual favors.

That was, to say the least, a violation of honor. The people were, hands down, scum. They were given a trust and they violated it.

I was contemplating doing something that was, on the surface, identical. Violation of honor? Would I be "scum" even in my own eyes?

The answer depended simply on whether it was the logical decision given all the factors. That led to the "female" part.

Males have a notable fall-off in long-term critical decision making in conditions of sexual cues. And this situation was one huge sexual cue. So I first had to eliminate, for the time being, the term "female."

One way would be to ignore the females, maybe do something to improve the situation but not bring them into the base, and bring in males.

I could not, in good conscience, take in the local males. After disastrous experiences in the first part of the Iraqi occupation, the military never hired locals or even Islamics for anything where they could be a threat. One remaining hardcore that we let in undetected could gain access to the ammunition and explosives on the base, there was no way to control internally with the forces I had, and do untold damage. Bringing in male refugees for support was out of the question.

Females, by the way, did not have the same security risk. Females in most of the local societies were trained, very early, to be nonviolent followers. They were extremely compliant. That would create its own issues, but it virtually eliminated them as a security threat.

I also was going to have to dig out another decision making tool I often used when unsure. "What would Sergeant Rutherford do?"

Sergeant First Class Rutherford had been my platoon sergeant when I led the Scouts. A harder, colder, more stoic NCO I never met. Talking one time he told me that his secret to getting things done was "Do one thing every day that you don't have to do immediately and you *don't want to do*." A better definition of stoicism I've never seen. And a better way to get stuff done I've never found.

But the question was, what would he do in this instance? How would he make the decision?

Frankly, he would be able to ignore the fact that he was considering females. Not because he was gay, but because he was an ultimate stoic. I was not, and knew it.

So I did a little change in my mind. I quit thinking of females.

I imagined that there was a group of males, say Salvadorans, who had somehow gotten caught in the refugee camp. Because they were not locals, they were being abused by the guards.

Item One: I needed more hands. There were too many tasks I felt necessary to complete the mission for the personnel I had on hand.

Item Two: I could not trust the local males.

So I imagined the females as these hypothetical Salvadorans. If I had a group of non-Islamic males in the camp from a friendly country, would I bring them in to help out?

Oh, hell, yeah. The logic, that way, was clear. Thinking of the potential support in terms of a bunch of Salvadoran former workers that got left outside the walls made it clear it was a rational decision. What would Sergeant Rutherford do? Bring in the Salvadorans.

Okay, but they're not Salvadorans. They're females. They are compliant local females who will do just about anything for a cracker and some water. If they weren't that compliant before, they were now from the reports I was getting from the camp.

That left the question of how to deal with them inside the walls.

Rule One included the rule "No Fraternization." Fraternization is a nice way of saying "Don't fuck the local females." (It was assumed soldiers wouldn't fuck the local males which in numerous instances turned out to be erroneous. But I digress.)

The way that the Army maintained Rule One with a bunch of horny young soldiers was to virtually eliminate contact with local females. Units went out from the FOB on missions and then returned. Mostly for very good security reasons. But the point was, there were no local females inside the base and when males ran into them outside they were a) on a mission, b) in the company of a large number of other males and c) not going to be around long to chat.

In this case, they were going to be in long-term contact with local females.

A military maxim says: Never give an order you know won't be carried out.

Giving an order you know won't be carried out just makes the commander look like an idiot. "Rule One is still in effect" and mixing horny soldiers with compliant local females wouldn't work. Period. Why?

Some of the soldiers were just going to flat ignore it. They, too, would be affected by the reduction in critical decision making in the presence of sexual cues. I'd have guys slipping away from security posts to screw because that was when they could get away with it.

And the girls weren't going to stop them. Why? Compliance and "anything for a cracker." They would also see the males as their protectors.

Giving an order that's unenforcable reduces trust in the commander's decision-making capability. How can you trust somebody who's stupid enough to give an unenforceable order? That means that unit combat efficiency goes down as the troops second-guess their commander.

Trying to enforce Rule One would, therefore, be worse than saying "Here's the girls. They're yours."

If, however, I put in place logical and rational restrictions under the circustances, it could be handled. Rotas, etc. If the guys knew they didn't have to slip away for a quicky, they wouldn't. They'd do their jobs.

Some of the guys would probably be such paladins that, at least at first, they'd take their "rota" as a chance to snuggle with something comfortable. Others were going to use the girls like the Kleenex and towels they were jacking off on already. There would be issues between those two types. That's what sergeants are for.

And they'd get their tubes cleaned. With a bunch of testosterone laden males stuck in the middle of nowhere, no real way to get home, etc. I was looking at the sort of potential mutiny that led to the *Bounty*, anyway. Right now, if the guys mutinied, they could set themselves up as local lords and *fuck* Rule One. There was no indication, at all, we were going to ever get relieved. I'd had the question practically every day. I *knew* there was talk. Heading that off was a good thing. Getting their tubes cleaned was a way to head that off.

In the end I made, I think, the logical decision. The haunted eyes of Salah, multiplied by hundreds in my head, had nothing to do with it. I'd eliminated that, I'm pretty sure successfully with the "Salvadoran" argument. I think Sergeant Rutherford would have approved. (Found out later he died in Savannah. So I never got to ask. Voodoo fuckers.)

The question remained: How to bell the cat?

Up to this point we were having as little to do with the refugees as possible. We tossed them food from the safety of our tracked vehicles. We treated them like a pack of wild dogs.

But we had Salah for information. Apparently after the attack when we'd killed the whole convoy, some of the men of the camp had grabbed the guns. The leader, at this point, was called Abu Bakr. That probably wasn't his real name, since it was the name of one of the successors of Mohammed. But he had the largest family group in the camp and his family had managed to grab the most guns. The shots we'd heard had *not* been happy noise. His family or people he trusted had the guns. She'd been on the outs with one of his cousins which had led to the incident that had her in the camp.

She didn't know a whole bunch of the people in the camp. But when it was tacitly suggested that we might, maybe, be interested in bringing some women in for support, she nearly broke down. Apparently things were not going well for women at the moment.

Side note: Any feminist who is against modern technology is an idiot. Okay, I'm being redundant but it's true. Women seem to make up a large majority of the "if we all just returned to nature" kumbaya movement.

Modern technology and Western culture are the only things keeping women from a life of utter hell. Every society where social order breaks down it's not necessarily "the poor" who get hit hardest, it's the *women*.

Kumbaya only works when you've got guys like, well, me keeping guys like Abu Bakr from making your life hell.

End of side note. I could go on, but I won't.

Maybe later.

Was I going to be a total paladin? Oh, hell no. I told her what I needed, about thirty females, young, decent looking, who would cook, clean and provide other "support functions."

Note, I was working through Hollywood, the translator.

"Other support functions, sir?" Hollywood asked.

"What's that Shia thing about "temporary brides"?"

Shia and Sunni. Think Catholic vs. Protestant but more so. I'm not going to get into a five thousand word treatise about the difference. I did note, though, that Abu Bakr was normally a name that would be associated with the Sunni and this was a Shia region which made things in the camp . . . interesting. But one of the things with Shia is that they have this . . . tradition called "temporary marriage." A mullah can "temporarily marry" a Shia female to a guy and for the time that the temporary marriage lasts, say one hour and that will be two hundred bucks, she is legally married and thus does not suffer "dishonor." The "mullah" gets four and you get one, go find another sucker with two hundred bucks, bitch.

Use "pimp" as a translation for "mullah" and you're getting a very accurate picture.

"Uh, we'd need a mullah for that, sir."

"Yeah, and it's a violation of so many regulations I don't want to begin to list them. Rule One, for example. But we need the hands and we need to be relieved. You an Islamic?"

"Uh, technically, sir."

"Good. Then tell her you're a mullah. I'll get you a pimped out Caddy when we get back to the States. Spinners and what-not. Maybe a big hat with a feather."

"I'm not a *mullah*!"

"I don't care *how* you explain it to her, as long as she gets the *picture*."

I don't know how he explained it. She got the picture.

She didn't even *mind*. Let me put you in her perspective.

You're a seventeen-year-old girl. Your father—who has been your boss your whole life and will be until you are married and your *husband* becomes your boss—is dead. Your whole life has been ripped apart. You are barely holding onto life in a desert. You have no control over your life or over your body. Once a day a big metal tracked vehicle comes out of a place and there is food and water. Maybe you are allowed to keep some of it. From the look of Salah, not much. You only get a bit of water, less than most Americans drink in an hour. And it is hot (not as hot as normal, but up in the 90s) and men take you whenever they please and any way that they please and usually more than one at a time.

Beyond the berm is paradise. So far, despite being surrounded by men, you have not been raped. You have been given more food than you've seen in months. You can have all the water to drink that you like. You can even dream of having a shower or a bath, something you haven't had in months. You're in *air conditioning*.

And all they are asking, *asking* mind you, is if you're willing to work at cooking and cleaning and, oh, yeah, spending some time on your back. Probably in a *bed* not the hard desert floor. You're not being *told*, mind you. You may not quite realize that, you may be thinking that they're being nice now but will change their mind soon. But you're being *asked*. And asked if others would be willing.

Oh, HELL yeah.

When you've been slowing dying in the desert, you'll do a lot for a cracker and some cool water.

I knew that was the reason she was answering in the affirmative. Did I feel like a heel?

Oh, HELL no.

Because I knew that my guys, and the Nepos, would treat them gently or I'd damned well beat the shit out of them. We'd *seen* what was going on in the camp. We'd seen the *lines* from time to time. That was probably when some girl, maybe Salah, was being put in her place. Rape is a technique of power. You teach a bitch, be that a guy in prison or a female under your control, who is boss by raping them. It is very nearly the ultimate loss of control over one's body.

I couldn't take in all the female refugees. But I could do *some* good in the fucking world. Gray good, but still good.

But how to bell the cat?

I decided that the best way to bell a cat is kill it. Hell, talk about *good* in the world ... Hmm ...

The next day, bright and early, Strykers started rolling out of the front gate of the camp. Nobody was moving in the direction of Abadan except the continued trickle of refugees. There were, in other words, no secondary threats. Good thing because most of the company was buttoned up and coming to call on the refugee camp.

At first people got up and started heading towards the road thinking that it was the daily food and water ration. We'd shifted to morning for various reasons so that was reasonable.

But as more and more Strykers rolled out, the people set up a wail. They thought we were leaving.

The Strykers formed up around the gate, then rolled down to the camp. Then they spread out to surround it.

Each of the Strykers had the commander "out and up" in his cupola. The Strykers had been slightly redesigned over the years so the commander's cupola was now a circle of armor which just his head peeked over. They were *not* good targets.

What *were* good targets were the two guys on the top deck. Of course, each of them was holding a military grade sniper rifle. So you weren't going to get many shots.

Behind the Strykers were the mortar tracks with their water buffalos and a ten-ton truck.

The lead Stryker waited until the rest were arrayed and some communications were effected. There wasn't much cover in the refugee camp. Hell, it was surprising that everyone hadn't died of exposure. I was getting ready to start fixing that.

But the first and most important thing was to establish who was boss.

When everything was in place, we rolled up to the edge of the refugees.

Let me try to do justice to this picture.

Take seventy-four cars and array them randomly in the desert. Not all were cars. There were four SUVs, nine minivans and fifteen pickup trucks.

Off to one side put more cars and such but they're all blackened piles of rubble.

Scattered in and around these cars and such, place whatever you can imagine for shelter. Tarps held up by twine. Plastic sheets. Blankets serving as tents.

Into this throw garbage. No food, mind you. Call it trash. Inorganic. I was getting ready to deal with the organic trash.

Add in some small personal posessions. Pile those somewhat less randomly around a cluster of six of the minivans and two of the SUVs. Anything of any real value, put in that cluster. Hell, there were even some unopened MRE and "halal" bags.

Throw in about a thousand people. All of them unwashed. Most of them not in amongst the cars. Just scatter them around the desert, just sitting there. No fires because the nearest wood that wasn't under our control was ten miles away.

There is an almost unnoticed open area between the majority of these survivors and the cluster.

Add in some dug holes that were supposed to be where people shat and pissed. They weren't used much. Add in a lot of piles of human dung, huge clouds of flies around same.

Picture Strykers opening up around this area that covered maybe four acres of hell. Troops unass and start moving through the outer periphery of the refugees. They stop well away from the cluster. They are moving in three-man teams. One guy turns to the rear, the other two face inward. All of them, as if by magic, take a knee with their weapons pointed at the ground. They're in the midst of the crowd.

The crowd gets the picture and starts moving. Away from the cluster.

All of this takes place before the troop door of the lead Stryker lowers. Around from the back comes an officer in a dapper uniform. He is carrying not a single weapon. He holds a swagger stick and uses it to wave away the flies. He is, however, wearing a radio and headset.

He is wearing sunglasses.

He is followed by six troops in heavy armor. Their weapons are *not* down. They are up and training on anyone near him who might be considered a threat. Two face forward, two to the side and two backwards, walking carefully to avoid the filth.

In the midst of this cluster of troops is a seventh, equally well armed. He is followed by a young woman in a blue jumpsuit that looks as if it has recently been removed from a package. Her hair is clean and brushed. *She* is clean and brushed.

The Stryker has parked as close to the cluster as it can without running over refugees or their meager posessions. It is a short walk to the edge of the cluster where a number of armed men are now up clutching AKs and looking very angry.

The unarmed and unarmored officer does not appear to care if they are angry. He doesn't appear to notice them. He is whacking at flies and smiling and nodding at the few refugees who are too tired or despairing to move out of the way.

Out of one of the minivans comes a large man. He is at least six feet two inches tall and broad with a hard, dark face and black hair. He is carrying an light assault machine gun and bandoliers crossed across his chest. Also two pistols and at least four knives. He is clean shaven but otherwise closely resembles the sort of pirate Sinbad may have had to deal with.

The officer, by the way, is looking *down* at him. The officer is . . . not small. However he *is* unarmed.

There are more armed men emerging. They appear to have been resting in the clustered vehicles. A few young women follow them out. Some of them *very* young.

Do you have this picture clearly? Fourteen armed and angry men. An unarmed captain who is clearly happy to see them. Refugees scrambling to get out of the line of fire. Heavily armed troops in an array that can cover *most* of the angles of fire.

It's a clear morning, just after dawn, still reasonably cool but looking to be another hot one.

"Hollywood," the officer says, languidly, raising the swagger stick. "Front and center."

The large, armed, man starts saying something angrily. The interpreter cuts him off and gestures to the officer.

"My name is Bandit Six. I am the commander, pro tempore, of Titan Base. Translate."

This is translated. The large, angry man says something and the others laugh.

"Yes. Having completed all of our initial preparation missions within the base, it seems time to do something about the situation outside the walls. We also require some assistance."

A glare.

"Indeed. We will be taking thirty of your ladies to handle camp chores. And they *will* be the younger and prettier ones."

A female head is peeking out of the minivan the large man had vacated. The girl is probably twelve. She has a large bruise on her cheek and a cut lip. Her clothes are tatters.

The large man is now more angry and speaking quite angrily. He reaches for one of his pistols and draws it, possibly to wave in the air.

"Open fire."

The officer does not flinch. The six troops and the interpreter hit the ground and light the area up. The young woman hits the ground.

The officer stands there. The large, angry, man explodes apart from a .50 caliber round, blood and less identifiable bits splashing on the officer. The officer does not flinch. He simply waves away some more flies. Rounds crack past his ear, he feels a tug from one on his lower left arm.

When the firing stops, he smiles.

Troops move in and ensure all the vehicles are clear.

"Hollywood, find someone in this rat-fuck who can be put in charge. Have Salah start rounding up the girls. All of these for starters. Don't add any of these below the age of . . . sixteen to the thirty count. Any chosen who have children can bring them as well. And if they might not be *their* children, that's okay, too."

The camp was moved. Some of the refugees had to be carried, but they all survived. It was moved to the other side of the road. A man who said he was a mullah was put in charge. He never carried a gun. (He was later recognized as one of the "diggers" from the first few days. The guys who got off their ass to bury the bodies. Good enough.) Others were found to carry the guns. The example of Abu Bakr was pointed out to them. Food and water distribution was rationalized. Tents and cots were brought out. A roadblock was put on the road to control who came out to the camp. Latrines, eventually a kitchen, etc.

Of course, that brought more refugees. But . . .

Some good in the world. For a time. A moment.

Pax Americana. It's like a gnat in a blast furnace in the Middle East.

- CHAPTER FOUR -

We Get Ammunition?

Did I get my tubes cleaned?

Dude, I was the base commander.

Her name was Shadi. She was eighteen. The reason I know is that I had a conversation with Hollywood.

"How old is this young lady, Hollywood? She's eighteen, right?"

"Uh, sir, she said she thinks she's . . ."

"Eighteen, right?"

"Yes, sir! She's eighteen, *sir!*"

She was eighteen and she looked, even after all that time in that fucking place, like a god damned model. Long legs, gorgeous face, high cheekbones, aquiline nose, gigantic dark eyes and very nice hooters. She was, by a smidgeon admittedly, the best looking of the young ladies who had chosen to enter the employ of the United States Army.

She was my "personal maid." She kept my quarters straight, shined my shoes, cleaned my clothes, made sure I ate . . . Stuff like that. She also, yes, participated in the general housekeeping chores for the unit. That was the point of it, not to get a personal concubine.

Butterfill got one too. Rank hath its privileges. The lieutenants, four, had two. The senior sergeants I'm not sure how it broke out. And *really* don't ask me about the troops. I know there was a rota of some sort but I did *not* get into it. That's what first sergeants are for.

Were there "issues?" Oh, hell, yeah. Guys in their twenties fall in love with anything that's got pussy. But the issues *paled* before the benefits. I'm not talking *personally* although the benefits were nice. I'm talking about troops who were more alert and with *soaring* morale. My morale was better than it had been in a year. And, hell, the girls weren't exactly unhappy.

By the way, did the boys have problems with "rank hath its privileges"?

I'd just stood there cool as a cucumber in the middle of a firefight. The boys do love someone with big brass ones. Those who hadn't previously served with Bandit Six had heard the rep and might have believed it and might not. They *knew* it now. *Big* brass ones, calm as hell when the shit hits the fan. Bandit Six rocks.

(I did *not* tell them I was nearly peeing myself. There'd been a lot of reasons, including the above, that I did it that way. Didn't mean I liked it. Rank has way more to it than privileges.)

Did the boys have problems with "rank hath its privileges"? No. They would have for the fucking battalion commander who hardly ever left the fucking FOB and created no end of trouble when he did. But not for Bandit Six. Or Fillup who was a stand-up guy.

We eventually dipped further into the well for some more for the Nepos. The girls that "assisted" them were getting a bit ragged.

Some of them had kids. *Their* kids? I dunno. Didn't care. Some of them, despite my best efforts (there was a supply of birth control pills on the base, naturally, and I kept *telling* guys to use fucking *condoms*) got pregnant. Or were pregnant when we brought them in. Deal with that bridge when we came to it. Hell, we were *bound* to get "relieved" . . . more relieved sometime.

Or were we?

Look, the U.S. was a shambles. The military, Army, Air Force, Marines, even the damned Navy, was stretched to the nth degree trying to keep things from coming totally apart. People thought they *were* apart. They weren't. Hell, television stations were still broadcasting. CNN was up. Fox was up. Networks were mostly showing repeats but if you had satellite and power you could pretend things were normal if you didn't watch the news.

Civilization in the U.S. was hanging on by a thread. Civilization *everywhere* was hanging by a thread.

Europe looked as if it might survive or it might not. Besides all the shit the U.S. was going through, its average mortality, despite an I'll admit better distribution of the vaccine, was higher than that of the U.S. See that long bit about why and pick what you're willing to believe. Bottomline, they'd gotten hit *massively*.

Oh, yeah. Might be time to talk about how effective the vaccine really was. They *had* distributed vaccine. And gotten a goodly part of their population. Type one vaccine. Turns out that the strain of H5N1 that actually broke out almost *all* had mutated binding proteins.

(What the hell? Mutated what? You mean it stalked around growling "Braaaains . . ."?)

Here's what a flu virus does. A flu virus is a little packet, it can't really be called a cell, that looks sort of like a robot and acts a lot like one. Depending what kind of cell it's "targeted" on, it finds that type of cell and hooks on with proteins that look remarkably like hooks under an electron microscope. Then it shoots a package of DNA into the cell. The package of DNA first tells the cell to make a shitload more viruses then kills itself (lyse) so they're released.

This is the way that *immunization* works.

Immunization doesn't attack the flu. It tells your body's defenses what the flu is going to look like when you get it. It's sort of like giving the body's policemen a picture of that flu bastard and telling them "Shoot to kill." So when the flu attacks, your body produces a bunch more policemen (antibodies) which attack the flu.

The problem with most flu vaccines is that the "picture" that the antibodies get only describes those hooklike proteins. And it, chemically, describes them precisely. If the antibodies see *different* proteins, they ignore them. Otherwise you can get what's called an "autoimmune" disorder where your antibodies are attacking *you*.

A virus can only mutate in a host, therefore *who* it infects is as important as *how*—certain human genes control how and when the virus mutates—a blended genetic culture such as U.S. is much less likely to produce a uniform mutation that could spread (see Patient Zero discussion)—so the monocultures in the rest of the world were much more likely to be infected by a resistant mutant that was practically *tailored* to wipe them out.

Okay, so sometimes there's a point to multiculturalism.

H5N1 had been mutating fast. It had to to become as lethal as it was. Part of that mutation (just minor changes in genetics; not weird zombies) was in its binding proteins.

Slippery little sucker.

Type Two, on the other hand, described the *coat* proteins of *all* flus. The outer case of the robot if you will. They all "look" the same. (Bit like R2D2. With claws.) It worked on just about any flu. I haven't had the flu since that one injection that I was bitching about.

That's why I was such a fucktard. I was bitching about the only immunization that really *worked*.

All the H5N1 that spread didn't have the mutated binding sites. There were, it was later determined, six different "strains" of H5N1. Did they all come from Jungbao? Probably not. They probably mutated later by cross cellular chain mutation . . .

(What's . . . ?)

Look, I'm not going to give another fucking class in virology, okay?

The point being, even when people *got* the vaccine, it didn't always work.

Europe got hit hard.

But that was only the beginning of their problems. Europe had been "aging" for quite a few years. That is, they had less and less native population peoples to keep up that elaborate retirement pension plan and socialized medicine. More and more of them were retiring.

The bright plan to take care of this was to bring in immigrants. Might have worked, if they'd worked a little harder on being a melting pot. Instead, the immigrants had often created their own internal communities that were reflections of the "Home Country." The U.S. had that a few times, too, but never to the degree that Europe was experiencing before the Plague.

This had created . . . issues. On the surface the Europeans were very kumbaya. That was the official line and nobody was allowed to stray from it. "Multiculturalism is good because we *say* it's good. Alles in ordnung!" Underneath, however, was the very European mindset that there were US and THEM. No matter how many generations you family had been in Germany, you were not granted full German citizenship if you weren't ancestrally German. France had a slightly different way of segregating the minorities. The basic lesson was clear; you're here to take care of us in our old age but that doesn't make you important.

I don't like radical Islamics but doing something like that would make *me* radical. It did so in Europe. That was causing problems, bigger and bigger problems, well before the Plague.

Europe, Western Europe, had had a very European response to the Plague. Not "new Europe" which was all sweetness and light. No, it was an "old Europe" response. You know, the one that gave us words like "pogrom" and "Holocaust."

Germany and France, what was called often the Franken-Reich, were the centers of power in what was called back then the European Union. Each had their own way of dealing with the Plague and their "restive" immigrant population.

France dealt with it by how it distributed the vaccine. It didn't go to every clinic, everywhere, all at once. It went to selected clinics on a "trial" basis. This dissuaded some people from seeking it out. But the point was, they weren't doing the "trial" on the Wogs. They were doing the "trial" in clinics that were in primarily native French regions, down to neighborhoods. And there was a shortage of the vaccine. Gosh, before the Plague hit they never *did* get around to those Moslem neighborhoods!

Germany's was a doozy. It was a very German approach. On certain days, everyone with last names starting in, say, F to H were to go to their local clinics for vaccination. Alles in ordnung! But. The first round of the vaccine was to go to persons with "full German citizenship."

Hey, why didn't you just put a yellow star on them for Christ's sake?

Germany was having riots before the Plague. Which they put down with Teutonic efficiency.

But when it swept through, they hadn't gotten most of their "native" population vaccinated, anyway, what with one thing and another and almost none of their "immigrant." Between that and the fact that the vaccine wasn't all that functional, Germany and France were both hit hard. And the remaining immigrants had gotten *really* untrusting. There also wasn't much of a military in either country to help out. Germany had a "social service" obligation that was supposedly the same as the draft. But most of the people serving in it did "social services" rather than military service. And most of them were less than available in a disaster.

They were sort of hanging in there. Sort of having a civil war along with eveything else but sort of hanging in there. All the Western European powers were *sort of* hanging in there. Worse than the U.S. or better? At *that* point, nobody could tell. It was all a toss-up.

Eastern Europe... Poland was doing pretty good. Lower level of immigration and higher trust levels. Pretty good vaccine distribution. Death rates about like the U.S. In the late summer of 2019, Poland looked a good bet to make it.

I could go on. I won't. The "European Union" was hanging by a thread. But it was hanging. They might or might not go into a thousand year night.

In many places civilization was *gone*. Iran was one. Most of the Middle East. China, southeast Asia except Thailand and Singapore which were just very bad. Vietnam, it depended on which station you listened to. It sounded sort of like they were going back to North and South. Russia... depended on if you believed the government or the few news reports still coming in from refugee interviews. I believed the refugees.

China, a Tier One nation, was gone. It had gotten hit brutally by the Plague and it never was really high function anyway. All it had had going for it was a lot of people and some of them very bright. The Plague hammered them.

Japan was hanging. It had been distributing vaccine while the Plague actually spread. (It got hit *early*.) High death rates. But the Japanese are sort of used to that. They were consolidating in the way the Japanese always do. Economy wrecked but, hey, look at where they were in 1946. At least this time they didn't have atomic ruins to deal with.

The point to all of this being, the U.S. military may care for their troops but the last thing on anyone's mind, right then, was a company of infantry left in fucking Iran.

Problem was, things in Abadan were starting to shape up. And not in a good way. Actually, things in the region were shaping up in an *un*good way.

We first got wind of this from refugee reports. We were in contact, now, and stayed that way. Refugees were still trickling out of Abadan and we knew, more or less, what was going on in there.

There were three factions holding various parts of Abadan. The Mahdi Army, The Warriors of Victory and Shia Liberation Front. All three had been at their core local "militias" we'd been fighting and trucing with since we'd been in Iran. Well, most of the Warriors of Victory were the remnants of the local "security forces" (Army, police and such) we'd been training. But we also knew they were connected with the Warriors at the time. Such is the nature of the Middle East.

When the Plague hit, the Warriors had a problem. They were not a family grouping. We'd worked hard on breaking up the clan structure in the "security services." But when the shit hit the fan, they didn't have their old, tried ways to fall back on. So they broke up into small bands.

The Mahdi Army *was* a family based structure. Oh, it had peripheral families allied to it, but it was mostly clan based. So it had coalesced faster than the Warriors and eaten up some of their little bands.

The Warriors reunited, sort of, in defense against the Mahdi.

The Shia Liberation Front was a minor faction. Very hard-core Islamicists, more hardcore than the Mahdi, who were more interested in secular power. The SLF thought this was the Apocalypse and the 12th Imam was coming any day and they were preparing to fight the great fight, blah, blah.

I *think* the first guys in the trucks were probably a Warrior faction. But who knows or cares?

Basically, what it was were three gangs controlling the city. There was some fishing going on in the Shat and out in the Gulf. That was where most of the food in the city was coming from along with a little bit of agriculture that was getting going again.

Every now and then there'd be some open fighting in Abadan between the gangs. We'd hear about it in time, but we always knew it was going on when refugees picked up on the road from Abadan.

The SLF were the smallest faction, but they were going to be our biggest problem.

Started off with a probe. A group of three "military style" vehicles came out of north Abadan across the plain. Nothing to stop them; it was *really* flat. There were a couple of small wadis but nothing you couldn't negotiate.

Now, we could see Abadan. By the same token, they could see us. They had watched us put in the perimeter fencing and decided they had a way to breach it.

As the three vehicles approached the fence, the drivers jumped out of the lead truck and ran. The other two stopped. The truck hit the fence, knocked down a big chunk and then blew up.

The reaction platoon Strykers were rolling out of the gate by then. I mean, they'd had to cross nearly six miles of desert. We had time to get the reaction platoon up and going.

The truck bomb probably took out most of the mines. It also tore up the fence and some of the internal concertina. Guys jumped out of the other trucks and tried to make it up the berm.

We had guard posts on the top of the berm for a reason. They were taken under fire.

By that time we had the mortars up, too. Oh, you think we forgot indirect fire? Hell, no. We'd even set up some Paladins, 155mm tracked artillery, oriented on Abadan just in case we needed it.

Point was, the guys trying to climb the berm came under fire from the machine guns on the berm guard posts just about the time the first mortar round was starting to fall. The mortars never got properly adjusted but they were falling.

The guys on the berm got slaughtered despite the bunker being damned near a klick away. The reaction Strykers were faster across the desert, and much more heavily armed, than the trucks.

Game, set, match.

The next stage was negotiations.

A Humvee (we'd provided quite a few to the Iranians) came rolling up the road from Abadan with a white flag on its aerial. It stopped for the refugee guardpost then came rolling up to the outer gate.

We rolled out the Gate Stryker. I got called.

There was an officer in Iranian Army dress uniform. Think Hussar in an opera but gaudier. Had the epaulets and such for a colonel and covered in awards. I could read the rank but not the awards and didn't care about the latter. The uniform was a bit big for the guy but one thing or another he might have lost weight.

Colonel Reza Kamaran. He was commander of Iranian security forces in Abadan. And he demanded weapons and supplies to be used in restoring order in Abadan.

I said I'd have to get back to him on that. Not my orders. I'll have to call my boss.

It is as Allah Wills.

He said he'd wait. I suggested he come back tomorrow. He insisted he'd wait.

This conversation took about an hour. That's the way Iranians talk.

I went back to the commo shack. I tried to get ahold of the BC. He was "unavailable." I talked to the duty lieutenant for a while. The battalion was trying to feed Savannah and get the port back up. They had had no luck on either score. Shit was bad. Fucking BC's back at Stewart in the rack. Or just hiding. He's not saying much these days. Casualties from gang fire. Voodoo priests. Shit's bad.

Hmmm . . .

My senior officer is unavailable. Come back tomorrow. In'sh'allah. Okay, whatever.

Note. Time difference meant I had to be up in the middle of the night to talk to the BC and vice versa. Actually, if I called in the evening I'd get him in the morning. I called in the evening. He was in a meeting. I left word that we had been contacted by a local group about giving out free weapons and ammo as party favors and I was thinking about it. (The last part being a lie.)

Fucker called me back at 2AM local time.

Don't give out anything. Secure and maintain.

Says he's a colonel in the Army, yawn. Don't know. Name. Local allies.

Don't give out anything until I check with higher.

Okay. When you getting us home.

Top of my priority list. No transport at this time.

Want a security update?

Send me a memo.

Colonel came back the next day.

Where's my stuff?

It is in consultation among my bosses. Come back tomorrow. In'sh'allah.

I quit going out to meet him. I sent the BC a memo. After a week or two he quit coming out. I don't know if he'd gotten tired of the drive or died. Didn't care.

Here's the thing. The refugees, who I trusted more than this guy, said there wasn't any "Iranian Army" in Abadan. There was the Warriors, who were made up of gangs that had fractioned off the Army and police, but they weren't the Army. They were a fucking gang that didn't even give the pretense of being a formed unit.

I figured the guy was one of the Warriors, probably a lieutenant maybe captain by his age, who'd gotten the uniform and decided to come out and stroke me out of gear.

Absent a direct order, wasn't going to happen.

But it got me thinking. More.

Sooner or later somebody was going to come and try to take this shit away. And although we were supposed to "secure and maintain" it, I wasn't going to have a pocket mech division's worth of gear fall into the hands of these yahoos.

The Nepos were, at that point, just sitting there.

Well, sort of. I'd put Samad in charge of training them for guard duty and such. Not Ghurkas, but somebody that we could use as spare rifles if the crunch came.

That was kind of funny. I told him that they needed to be trained. I had them set up a short range inside the perimeter. I told him to take over. Get them to be reasonable soldiers.

Look, the rest of us were busy. I was busier than a one-armed paper-hanger keeping everything working. Shit was always breaking down, working with Fillup on security, I was finally getting the sort of busyness I prefer. Basically, I'm pretty lazy but I get bored if I'm not given something to be lazy *about*.

I didn't notice for a couple of weeks that I hadn't heard any shots. Well, the boys were starting to use the range a bit, but I didn't hear the sort of crackle you'd expect to find if sixty guys were being trained in marksmanship.

So I went poking around.

Found Samad and the Nepos in one of the areas that had been emptied out to make the defenses. I think it used to hold concertina.

It had been marked off with chalk in a very precise square. The Nepos were out there in what looked like British combat uniforms (turned out they were, don't know how I missed *that* line item) doing close order drill.

And they were good at it. Damned good.

Of course, when they hadn't been doing their other duties they'd apparently been out there *every day, all day*, doing close order drill. For two fucking weeks.

I waited until the end of the day to pull Samad aside. I'd taken some time up to write up a training schedule. I suggested to him that maybe just maybe it was time for his guys to start training on something other than close order drill. Like, you know, weapons training, field sanitation, first aid. Here, I have a list.

He looked at it in puzzlement.

"You mean we will be given *live rounds* to practice?"

There was the fucking ammunition for a *division and thirty days of combat* sitting in the ammo dump. There was no way that it was ever going to be "redeployed." It was either going to sit there until it rotted or we blew it the fuck up.

"I think we can spare some, yeah."

"Very *good*, sahib!"

That grin. Okay, so sometimes you had to give him kind of detailed orders until he got the hang. But he had a great grin.

You can't turn raw recruits into a good reinforced platoon overnight. Not even Nepos. But we got them started on the path.

I gave him two weeks of "additional training" before I started my next little scheme. I mean, the demo was just *sitting* there.

— CHAPTER FIVE —

Unofficial? You're Fucked.

I know I'm sort of jumping around but we were getting into late August at this point. There'd been a couple more probes. No more negotiations. One what looked like an attack on the refugee camp. Convoy of vehicles, some of them with weapons on the back (called "technicals" for some reason.) Gate Stryker drove it off by taking them under long-range fire. Might have been an attack on us. Don't know. Wasn't getting close.

But sooner or later a big force would get in motion. Refugees were still coming in and they all said that everyone knew how much booty was in our walls. And people wanted it. Most of them to just fill their couscous bowl but the gangs wanted the weapons, ammo and equipment.

I'd set things up so that we could roll out at any time. There were enough Strykers, trucks, fuel trucks and all the rest, including one hell of a lot of parts, lube, ammo, food, water and most especially batteries, that we could roll to Israel if it came down to it.

That was my plan. If everything exploded we were going to roll out and head to Israel. Israel had held on, more or less. The Plague had hit their enemies worse than them. Maybe they put lamb's blood over their doors, I dunno. But they'd taken about 20% casualties and were still hanging in there.

Oh, that's something I mentioned a while back. All the models said at the point that a society took 20% casualties from a disaster, especially a plague, it broke down.

The H5N1 Plague disproved that. What it proved was that *certain types of societies* broke down at that point. The models and historical records had never accounted for modern, technological, democratic, high-trust societies. All the previous societies hit with that sort of plague had been preindustrial, nondemocratic or functionally nondemocratic, low-trust societies.

Every society like *that* on Earth that got hit with H5N1 *had* broken. Iran and Iraq might have been notionally democratic societies, ditto Turkey, but they were not resilient enough to withstand their casualty rates (which, anyway, ran into the 50–60% range).

The "good" societies held together. Hell, *Thailand* held together. And they had 60% mortality.

Nobody knows, to this day, what it takes to destroy a society like the U.S. or any of the other Anglosphere countries. Or Japan. Or Thailand or Singapore or (South) Korea. What we know is, it takes more than the Time of Suckage.

But getting back to the point, at some point I figured we were going to pull out. That we'd either be extracted or, it was looking increasingly like, have to self extract. Getting to the U.S. was going to be . . . interesting. Among other things there was an ocean in the way. Flying back was optimal, but we needed to have an airport to do that.

And when we pulled out, whether I tried to pass it off as an "accident" or just bit the fucking bullet, I wasn't going to leave this shit for the enemy.

Got any idea what it takes to *really* destroy an Abrams tank? I mean, so it's not even *vaguely* useable as a tank *ever again*?

Yeah, neither did I.

Or a Paladin. Or a Bradley (we had a lot of those). Or a Stryker.

Trucks and such were pretty easy. Oh, it was time intensive and manpower intensive but the Nepos were just sitting there.

Take one 155mm round. Place it on the engine block. Place another in the cargo compartment. Daisy chain them together with det cord and a small "initiator" package of a half a block of C-4 per round.

All that could be left to the Nepos. At this point you have two explosive rounds that aren't going to go off short of blasting caps (which weren't installed) and maybe not even then tied together with some funny looking cord.

In the meantime, the boys of Company B were getting an *intensive* course in demolitions safety. This was not "do I put the blasting cap under the sandbag before installing the claymore?" demolitions safety. This was "if you don't do it in these precise steps, *everybody* is going to blow the fuck up including you."

You see, none of that stuff was going to blow up short of blasting caps. Military explosives are very resilient. They have to be; they're handled by soldiers. Soldiers can break just about *anything*.

Stuff like 155 rounds were designed to survive handling by soldiers. They were tough as *hell*.

But put blasting caps in the mix and you are dealing with a different situation.

Frankly, I would have preferred that all the blasting caps be put in place and wired by myself or Fillup. But that simply wasn't possible. He had good sergeants, though, and we were very careful.

Wiring the whole damned camp, though, took a long time.

Oh, we didn't wire everything. I mean, I figured leaving all the food and shit was fine. But just wiring the vehicles and ammo was interesting.

How *do* you bust an Abrams tank so nobody was ever going to be able to use any part of it again?

It's not fucking easy. There are *five separate sealed compartments* on an Abrams. Each of them is, more or less, capable of withstanding any reasonable explosion in the other. Driver, control area (turret and crew compartment), engine and chassis. That's four, right? The *gun* is such a tough motherfucker it's going to resist most explosions. And it's the part that, in the end, counts so I wasn't going to leave any functional if I had my way.

The tanks were *not* loaded with their rounds. All of the vehicles had been stripped of ammunition before parking. (Ammo specialists had destroyed most of the onboard munitions; they weren't considered safe enough to store.)

Well, the ammo was just sitting there.

Five 155 rounds in the central compartment. Another in the driver's compartment. Another in the engine. Anti-tank mines under the chassis. A tank round up the breach preceded by a charge of C-4. Partially close the breach. When the round detonated *something* was going to happen to the fucking gun. Didn't know if I could destroy the fucker, but *I* wouldn't want to ever use it again.

Daisy chain. That is, hook them all together so they'll go off at once.

The problem being, I'm doing all this *without orders.* I'm getting prepared to destroy a whole bunch of billions of dollars worth of Uncle Sam's equipment (nineteen billion and change) and nobody in my chain of command has *suggested* that is a good idea.

It was early September when we started. Compared to some deployments we hadn't actually been left in place all that long. Three and a half months since we'd been left.

But this wasn't a normal deployment. Look, we had one guy get sick. Doc didn't know what was wrong with him. Thought it was appendicitis. (Turned out it was food poisoning. His honey had fixed him some "special" food and hadn't been quite as sanitary as she should have been.)

I got on the horn to the States. Got a soldier with possible case of appendicitis. Request evac.

Nada.

Fucking NADA.

The U.S. mililtary *does not leave you to die.* They've killed crews trying to save *civilians.* What they do for their own sick and wounded is astonishing.

There was no way to get us. No. Fucking. Way.

The only possible choice was to move a whole fucking Marine Amphib unit into the Gulf and fly helos up to us. Maybe just a frigate.

Only problem was, *all* the ships were back in the U.S. zone.

The nearest "stable" zone, barely, was Israel. And there wasn't a helo on earth that could make the run. Oh, there was a way to do it with tankers and special helos. But the Israelis didn't have the capacity, even if they were willing, and our tankers and helos were in the States saving lives.

We didn't have a doctor. We didn't have a hospital. (Well, we had one but no clue how to use it.) We were on our fucking own.

The point being, this was not a normal deployment. Hell, women cooking and washing and providing "aid and comfort" weren't a normal deployment. I cannot for the life of me recall where I heard the line. Something about "and the last centurion took a barbarian wife . . ."

That was *us* as far as we could tell.

I didn't want to start up a local dynasty. But if I *did* start one, I wasn't going to let all this ammo and gear fall into the hands of my enemies. And it was *way* more than *I* could *ever* use.

And if we did what I figured was most likely, the bug-out boogie to Israel, I wasn't going to leave it to the RIFs. Surely there was an adult in my chain of command who could get *that* logic.

The problem being, the next guy in my chain of command was the battalion commander.

Chain of command is holy writ in the Army. You *do not violate* the chain of command.

But I was getting dick all from the BC. I violated the chain of command.

We had commo information for higher command levels. Hell, this thing had a commo link to the National Military Command Center but I wasn't going to call NMCC. I called the Brigade S-3.

Yo, Bandit, wassup? (He'd been a company commander in a sister battalion when I was a lieutenant. He could call me Bandit, too.)

What the fuck? No medevac. No deadline for "replacement"? What the fuck?

No medevac?

Appendicitis, we thought. Got over it. No evac.

Fuck. Bad shit here.

Bad shit everywhere. Refugees. Attacks. Replacement?

No fucking idea.

Plan if we get hit bad? Bombers? Nukes?

No fucking idea. Battalion?

()

Okay, point. Plan?

Blow and run.

()

Go-To-Hell-Plan. Replacement. Reinforcement. Redeployment. What The Fuck Ever. None? Blow and run.

Battalion? Told?

(Video link. Stand up and wave hands around ass.)

Okay, point. Send memo. Chain of command.

(Stand up . . .)

Situation? Seriously.

Official or unofficial.

Official then unofficial.

Official: Nominal. Security Threats. Action plan. Insufficient force. Unofficial: If we knew when we were going home and weren't worrying about getting overrun, not bad. Nepos and local civilian personnel left behind. Gets weird.

Try Savannah. Voodoo doctors. Send memo. Stay frosty.

Fuck you.

Sent the memo. I attached my full "action plan" in the event of "action by superior enemy force." Which amounted to "kill as many as we can, blow the place the fuck up and run like hell."

Rigging the place had *required* a detailed destruction plan. I attached it.

Got a call two weeks later from the *brigade* commander.

"Bandit, Colonel Collins."

"Yes, sir."

Shit bad here. Unofficial: You're fucked.

How fucked?

"There are no forces capable of evacuating your unit closer than Japan. And they're not going to be redeployed to pick up a straggler company of infantry. The shit everywhere is just too screwed up. There's a MEU (Marine Expeditionary Unit: Brigade of marines and ships) in the Med but they're tasked out. The official line continues to be that all stored material is to be "maintained and secured." Think *you're* bad off? We left a damned unit of SF in Colombia. They've dropped completely off the net; no clue what happened to them. Unofficially, and I'm told from a very high level, in the event you are hit by forces you cannot resist, blow it the fuck up and run. But you'd better be able to justify it pretty well. And even then, I can't guarantee that you won't end up in Leavenworth even if you *do* make it back to the States."

"Yes, sir. Can I get an official order to implement my action plan in the event this unit is faced by an overwhelming force?"

Long silence. Much forehead rubbing.

"Send your action plan to your battalion commander." Hand goes up to forestall protest. I wasn't planning on making one except in my head but he must have seen my face. Of course, he also had to deal with my BC on a daily basis. "Send it to your battalion commander. It will be approved."

"Thank you, sir."

"What, you think I *like* one of my fucking companies being

left out to rot? But shit's bad everywhere. If you lose commo for any reason, all I can say is good luck and good hunting."

So I sent the action plan to the battalion commander.

What the fuck? No fucking way! Are you crazy? If you were here you'd be relieved and I'd make sure you spent the rest of the emergency as a private, you complete dickhead moron, who the hell could think you had the authority to blow up nineteen billion dollars worth of . . .

A week later I got the action plan back. Redlined. That is, he was telling me all the things wrong with it and wanted me to do "corrections" of all the items.

Which was weird because that meant it was conditionally approved.

Of course, it was also fucked up because he'd left out blowing up half the shit and most of the changes meant nothing would get blowed up. Most of it had to do with "demilitarization" of material. Yeah. Like we had a few thousand people available to do that.

(Demilitarization: Drill holes in the guns. Drilling holes in an Abrams gun requires very serious drills which we didn't have. Thermite barely scratches the motherfuckers. I know. I experimented.)

And we'd already done most of it my way. Sure as shit wasn't going to do it *his* way.

I sent the redlined plan off to the Brigade S-3. Then I wrote it up his way. Hell, he wasn't going to know if I did it that way or not. I was seven thousand miles away and it wasn't like the fucking IG was going to drop by.

Two days later I got an action plan from the BC. Less redlining. Still stupid.

Off to Brigade S-3.

Got back the original plan. Approved. By the *Brigade* commander.

Good thing, too, because we were about done.

Talked to the S-3 later. Apparently it had gone like this.

Battalion commander gets the plan. Throws a shit fit. Chews me out. Starts charges.

Brigade commander, a few days later, calls him up and asks what's happening with Bravo Company.

Battalion commander sucks ass. All good. No issues.

No issues? Evac?

Minor issue.

Security situation?

No problems.

Any Go-To-Hell-Plan?

No need. "Secure and maintain."

Get Go-To-Hell-Plan. SF battalion. Bad shit. My boys. Send me copy. Out.

I get GTH redlined. Send back corrected plan. Copy to Brigade. BC sends to Brigade.

Brigade commander. Don't like. (He'd seen my original *and* the redlined one.) Like it *this* (my) way.

Battalion commander sends up next plan.

What is it about "do it *this* way" you cannot understand? Original plan approved.

I now had legal authority to blow the place the fuck up if I had to.

Which was good. Because we had to implement our "Go-To-Hell-Plan" sooner than I'd thought.

— CHAPTER SIX —

Actioning by Transformational Defenestration of Obstructors

What is it about Mondays?

Okay, so you had a good weekend and maybe you had a bit too much to drink. You don't want to go back to work. Mondays suck.

But that wasn't the case with Iran. We were working every day, more or less. Oh, there was a rotating "down-time" schedule but with increasing probes the guys weren't getting much rest.

So what *is* it with Mondays?

Guess you figured it was a Monday when the shit started to hit the fan.

Actually, we got some wind of it early. Scatter of more refugees. Then the food detail got told there was a new problem.

Remember the Shia Liberation Front? Seems they'd maintained communication with fellow travellers. Said fellow travellers, the "Husayn Ali Martyrdom Brigade" (HAMB) had managed to avoid enough martyrdom to consolidate their hold in Awhaz and were now looking to establish "true shariah" in a wider region. Which really threw a monkey wrench into the whole Abadan area.

Okay, background:

Who or what the fuck is "Husayn Ali"?

Husayn ibn Ali ibn Abi Talib was a grandson of Mohammed by one of his numerous wives. (Mohammed's wives that is.) Husayn is one of the guys who's a founder of Shia. Remember the whole thing about Shia and Sunni? Most Moslems are Sunni. Iranians and a cluster in southern Iraq and down into Saudi Arabia are Shia. I won't get into details about the Umaayids and shit. He revolted in favor of "true Islam" and got his head cut off. Just know he's one of the Shia's big "martyrs." Got killed near Al-Najaf where there's a big temple in his honor and, I shit you not, every year guys gather there and whip themselves with flails. I've seen weirder shit, but not much.

But the Husayn Ali Martyrdom Brigade wasn't just religious wackoes. It had been formed around the family of an Iranian colonel up around Ahwaz. Was *he* a religious wacko? Sort of.

Okay, one of the "lessons" we learned in Iraq was "don't completely dismantle the standing government and military." We shut down the Iraqi Army in Iraq and then tried to rebuild it "right." The problem being, that when soldiers are out of work they'll work for anybody. And a lot of the guys we were fighting, at first, were former soldiers all the way up to senior officers.

So when we went into Iran, we kept the Army together as much as possible. Oh, some of the units like the Revolutionary Guard and stuff were stood down and mostly rounded up for questioning, etc. But we didn't stand down the whole Army.

Well, the mullahs had wanted to keep the Army under their thumb as much as possible. So a bunch of senior commands were held by "fellow travellers," guys who thought the way the Mad Mullahs in charge thought or were family. (Which amounted to the same thing.)

Farid Jahari was one of the guys who wasn't rounded up for questioning. Oh, later, I found out he had been tagged as hardcore Islamic, but he was making all the right noises and following the New Way so nobody fucked with him. Despite "credible" reports that he had maintained contact with the RIFs and might be supporting them.

Whether he'd been playing both sides against the middle or what, when the shit went down, he managed to hold together a "coalition" in Ahwaz. It had taken him several months to consolidate his power and get things functioning. Now it was time for the next step.

Shooters he now had aplenty. What he *didn't* have was equipment.

And guess where the biggest store of equipment around was?

The "probe" with the truck was probably his idea. And they'd apparently been watching how we were guarding things.

The first inkling we had that things were going to be going astray was increased traffic on the Ahwaz Road. (Highway 9 for people who care.) Vehicles were headed into Abadan. And then the flow of refugees picked up as street fighting broke out.

The good colonel had the cachet of being military. The Warriors and the SLF, now a branch of HAMB, called a truce. Together with some "special warriors" from HAMB they took down the Mahdi Army in about two days' fighting.

Didn't hurt that they took out the command structure, first. They called for peace talks to "begin the reunification of our peoples." Not all the senior people from the Mahdi Army turned up, but enough that it mattered. They weren't trusting, mind you, but they also weren't expecting a big truck bomb.

We heard that on Monday. Big ass explosion down in Abadan kind of near the docks as far as we could tell.

Took the Warriors, SLF and HAMB about three days to clear out the Mahdis. Some of the refugees we got were "dependents" of the Mahdis. That's where we got the story. (Also a couple more workers. The Mahdis had clearly been picking and choosing carefully. Woof!)

(Wife Edit: It's amazing what you've left out over the years. I thought I knew *all* your stories.)

Fuck.

Anyway, we *really* knew shit was bad mid-week when two T-62s and some trucks came rolling down from the direction of Ahwaz.

Found out, later, that was the sign Herr Colonel had come down to show the flag. Until Abadan was "secured" he'd stayed up in Ahwaz. Now it was time to spread the joy.

So we got another delegation.

This time it was a civilian truck but the guy who got out of it was in uniform. Pretty correct. Unlike the first joker he seemed to fit it and it wasn't exactly loaded with medals.

I got called out.

"General Farid Jahari, Commander of the Faithful, Sword of The Prophet, Warrior of Islam . . ." etcetera, etcetera, etcetera, "sends you his greetings. In his beneficience and munificence, his overriding goodness that extends beyond the ability of mortal men . . ."

We had three days to pull out. We could take anything we could carry. We had to leave all the rest and open the gates.

Took, like, fifteen minutes for the guy to get to the point. I said: "Ain't happenin'."

"Captain, you cannot understand. The armies of the Prophet cover the ground like the sands of the desert . . . !"

We know your strength to the last Nepo. You're badly outnumbered and we're going to kick your ass.

All I could do was fall back on something I'd heard back in ROTC and many times since over the years.

"Convey my message to your commander exactly. This is the message. Nuts."

Okay, so it *was* an airborne unit. Big fucking deal. It was a good line.

What *wasn't* good was what we didn't know. The Commander of the Faithful was not an idiot. We had a fairly good feel for the numbers in Abadan at that point. The Warriors, if they hadn't taken a bunch of casualties, could field maybe six, seven hundred troops. The SLF had been about a hundred. From the count of vehicles going to Abadan, we were looking at, at most, another hundred or so.

Okay, say a thousand against our one company. Two tanks. I knew how we were going to deal with *them*. Adverse correlation of forces, but we had pretty good positions and good vehicles. And we had them in view the whole approach. They were going to get slaughtered.

Well, I *thought* they were going to get slaughtered. But I hadn't figured on the Commander of the Faithful being smart.

Ahwaz wasn't on the Shat, but it wasn't all that far, either. You had to cross into Iraq to get to the river (the Tigris, actually) but nobody gave a shit about borders. Turns out he'd sent a *bunch* more fighters down on barges. And we didn't know about them. The refugees had cut off to nothing. No satellite intel . . .

Okay, I had a couple of UAVs in the place. I'd even gotten a couple up and ready to go. But they weren't Predators, they were short range and duration. Even if I *had* gotten them out and done some surveys, I wasn't going to get any more intel.

Now, a thousand vs. a little short of two hundred with the Nepos might have been enough to change a guy's mind. Maybe should have been. But American forces had faced odds like that before and won.

Problem being we were going to take casualties. And there wasn't a doctor nor any evac.

That was going to purely suck.

So I called home. I didn't bother with calling the BC.

"Brigade S-3. Assistant S-3 speaking. How can I help you sir or ma'am?"

"Tell me to cut and run."

"What's up?"

"Security is no longer nominal."

Thousand of them. Two hundred, sort of, of us. Three days.

"What did you tell them?"

"Nuts."

"That's what the 101st said!"

"I couldn't think of better line. Go fuck a camel just wasn't as succinct." (Heh. I used a big word.)

Chain of command.

Duck's bottom.

Call you back.

Ring, Ring!

"Fort Lonesome. We've got the ammo if you've got the money. If not: Go fuck yourself."

Call your boss. Brigade Commander said "Nuts" though and he couldn't think of a better line, either.

Yo, BC, security situation no longer nominal.

You're a bad boy! You should have negotiated! Bad boy! Bad boy! No biscuit! Take off your skin so I can use it as a shawl!

Gotcha. Give 'em the stuff.

Calling higher.

"Fort Lonesome! Security situation is in degradation mode and headed for sucky!"

Brigade Commander said "Nuts."

The 101st said that. Couldn't he think of a better line? Medevac?

Nope.

Reinforcements? Fighting soldiers from the sky?

Nope. Get fucked. Bad things here. And where's that human skin I ordered?

Blow it and run?

Maintain and secure.

So then things went from weird to weirder.

Friday, I think, evening, anyway, I was "pondering the security situation" when I got a call at the office.

"Bandit, sir, there's a reporter on the video link. She wants to talk to you."

Now, this is a *secure military video link system*. How the fuck a reporter could have gotten onto it was beyond me.

I never considered the incredible boneheadedness of my boss.

So some reporter from CNN is chatting him up as he is delivering "aid and comfort" to the voodoo doctors in Savannah. (There's another essay there, but it's not mine. Things got very weird in Savannah at one point.) Good people doing good work for good people who are all good and it's all good and we all love each other.

(The battalion took more casualties in Savannah than *we* did during most of this mission. Khuwaitla, Instanbul and all.)

And somehow the point that he's only got two companies helping comes up. And, wow, there's a company in Iran? Really? Could I talk to the commander?

I don't know *how* she sweet-talked the BC into *that*. Bandit Six was the *last* guy he'd ever want to give air-time. That would take it away from *him*. And I don't know what strings he pulled to get her on our vid-link. Maybe CNN did it.

Fuck.

I got out of bed with Shadi, checked to see I was shaved, put on my battlerattle and went over.

"Captain Bandit Six. What's it like in Iran?"

"Our mission plan is to maintain and secure."

"Have you had any problems?"

"We have rectified all our action issues with transformational deconfliction."

(*That* one I remember. What a classic. I saw it one time on a poster and nearly shit myself.)

Refugees?

Adjusted with transformational synergy. (I think. Something like that.)

The last fucking thing I wanted to do was tell a reporter:

"Well, we're outnumbered something like five to one, and some of our 'one' are Nepalese tribesmen that just learned to turn on a light-switch and you got me out of bed when I was 'aiding and comforting' a refugee. And if we get hit we're going to blow this pizza joint sky high."

I doubt she understood word one of any of my replies. I don't think *I* understood most of them and I'm pretty good at buzz-word bingo. I *do* know that the troops were laughing next door so hard I could faintly hear it through the extremely soundproofed walls of the commo van.

We were deconflicting and transforming faster than a battle-bot. We were synergizing and action iteming like a couple of water beetles in mating season. We were defenestrating obstructors at one point, I think.

Went on for about fifteen minutes of me just a shuckin' and jivin' as fast as I could.

There's a point to the media in a democracy. It's there to make sure that people have the information they need to make rational decisions about their actions. Especially their actions in regards to who is going to be elected King or Queen or Duke or whatever.

I won't go into media bias. There's reams and reams of papers on it at this point. And it's *still* biased. It's going to stay biased for another fifteen years or so until the people who have lived through the Time end up as bosses in the media and start choosing different producers and editors. Hopefully, they'll choose wisely.

But at that point, the media was the military's worst enemy. They were the *enemy*, no more and no less. They *never* reported anything straight and *always* took the side of whoever was shooting at us.

They weren't fucking murdering terrorists who killed their own people faster than they killed us. They were "freedom fighters" or "irregulars." *We* weren't the freedom fighters, oh no! How could we be? It was rare that they called us what they really thought of us, but every now and then one would slip. *Mercenaries. Murderers.* Continue in M and go back and forth for every evil word for people you can dredge up.

When one of our number, usually a grade A asshole to start with, would fuck up, it was "all soldiers are like that! They're *all* evil murdering lying scum!" When one of *their* number fucked up, if you learned about it, they were "confused" or "overwrought" or there was nothing fucking wrong with them at all. Circle the wagons. We'd sit there and *prove* that some story about atrocities was bogus and the fucking media would sail on as if nothing had happened. Anything *bad* about soldiers or the very hard job we did was major news. Anything *good* we did wasn't covered.

Don't think that the Plague had changed anything. Every fucking screamer with some sob story, no matter how wrong, was instant headline news. The 4th ID got reamed when some woman got a reporter on ABC to put her on telling about how a whole bunch of those poor fucking grasshoppers had been "gang raped" by a bunch of soldiers.

Was there ever any proof? Not a fucking shred. As far as anyone can tell she made it up.

Back in the Iraq Campaign there was some fucking Air Force sergeant who got some reporter to repeat her sob story about "thousands of women raped" and how she had been.

Were female military members raped in Iraq? Yep. And any time we could track down the bastards that did it we'd put them on trial and sentence them to max punishment. But when you have males and females together, you get rape. It's like sunshine and flowers and April showers. Fucking happens. Pardon the pun.

Were "thousands" raped? No. Despite there being nearly a *million* females rotating through the AOR over time. The rape rate was *way* lower than on a college campus despite pussy being rare as hell.

And the Air Force sergeant in question?

Not only was she not one of the "thousands," at least she'd never reported it at the time or since, *she was never in fucking Iraq*! She'd made it all up. And the news media fucking ran with the story *anyway*!

Any lie by anyone who hated the military was repeated endlessly. Any truth was ignored.

I did not and *do* not like reporters. Is that clear? Even after the whole *Centurions* thing I maintain my opinion.

Sherman said it well:

"If I had my choice I would kill every reporter in the world but I am sure we would be getting reports from hell before breakfast."

Oh, and about democracy.

The purpose of a free press, in which I believe believe it or not, is so that people can make rational decisions in a democracy. They'd already perverted the process so bad that was hard, but the point is valid.

So why give her the runaround? Why not answer the questions straight?

There was still Plague running around. Most of the cities were (or should have been) free-fire zones. People were starving to death. And there was an impending climate catastrophe *they were completely ignoring.*

What the *fuck* did a company stuck in Iran have anything to do with making rational decisions about how to survive in the current conditions?

Nada. Dick. Nothing. The closest you can get is deciding whether Warrick was a fucking idiot and the reality was all around you. It didn't take a rocket scientist. Not that the *media* was going to admit their annointed was a fucking fruitcake.

She was going for a "human interest" story, that most idiotic of media exercises.

Well. Fuck. Her. Try making a robot interesting.

The company dayroom was right by the commo van. When I stumbled out, unbuckling my helmet and swearing under my breath, the troops had lined up to give me an ovation.

"God *damn*, sir, you sounded like a Pentagon spokesman!"

"They're going to put you up for Chief of Staff!"

"Defense Secretary!"

"Fuck you all. I'm clearly not working you hard enough."

In truth, I wasn't. I wasn't working *them* hard, I wasn't working *me* hard, I wasn't working *Fillup* hard. Why? Because I knew we were *all* going to be working our asses off soon.

Bill Slim was an interesting guy. British General in WWII. Probably the best Brit general of his generation and certainly the best one that got anything done. (*Way* better than Monty.) Wrote a hell of an autobiography. One of the things he said stuck with me. (Well, a lot did, but I'll just get into this one.)

"A General should take as much rest as he can in peace because when battle rages he will get none."

Paraphrase but that's the general idea. I knew the shit was about to hit the fan. So I and everyone else was getting as much rest, food and water as possible.

Good thing I did.

— CHAPTER SEVEN —

All Good Things Come to an End

Yeah, that was Friday.

Friday is a holy day for Islamics. Not quite like Sunday or Shabbat, but it's the day they sort of celebrate the same way. They sure as hell weren't going to kick off an assault on Friday.

Saturday? Don't mean dick to them.

The best time to assault somebody is right before dawn. It's called "Before Morning Nautical Twilight." (BMNT) Its that time when the world is still and the light makes things look sort of blue. You can't tell a white thread from a black. It's not dawn; it's not night. Night vision systems get screwed up by the light levels.

It is, generally, when people are at their lowest ebb. Sentries are sleepy, those who are sleeping are generally sleeping hard and don't wake up well.

You'd have thought they'd attack at dawn. Think again. Iranians, remember. In'sh'allah.

I don't know if they *meant* to attack at dawn. I do know that our sentries, who were very bright eyed and bushy-tailed, let me tell you, said that there were some vehicles moving around down by Abadan and the refinery. It was easy enough to see them with thermal imagery cameras of which we had a fucking *slew*.

So I set up in the command post. Things had adjusted. The Nepos had positional security on Fort Lonesome. The U.S. infantry were taking the gate, surrounding bunkers and such. But mostly they fell out and into their Strykers.

We sent out a team to tell the refugees that things were about to get busy and they were not going to like the neighborhood soon. They were in a truly fucked up situation. The armed guys wanted to help us, or said they did. We weren't having any of it. We just told them to move off to the side with what they could carry and dropped one more set of rations. It was more than they probably could carry, we used a couple of forklifts to carry it out. But that was the point.

Temperature-wise, it didn't get hot. Not a bit. Abadan in mid-September is normally hot as shit. Not that year. We hadn't had a snow, yet, but you could see it creeping down the mountains. That day it never got above about 70.

Got pretty fucking hot otherwise.

So some vehicles came out. And went back. And came out again. The troops opened up their battle rattle and snoozed. We'd been up since before dawn. I called the Nepos and had them get the girls working on a hot meal. There was time.

The guys ate chow. It was about nine AM before there was much movement. More vehicles came out. Some started to head up the Ahwaz highway and then turned and headed for the end of the base, the end with most of the ammo bunkers on it.

I let 'em come for a while. They were probably going to replicate the suicide bomb truck trick. Okay, got something for that, now.

When they got to about two klicks, two kilometers, I told the Mk-19s to open up. Mark-19s were originally developed for the Navy but the Army fucking loves them. 40mm grenade launchers, they pack a hell of a punch and just keep on firing.

Bud-a-bud-a-bud-a-bud-a-bud.

Three Mk-19s opened up from bunkers. Two klicks is a long range for the Mk-19. Max effective range is 1600 meters. Max range is only 2200.

The point wasn't to kill them. The point was to throw off their aim.

Fuckers kept coming. Don't know if it was a suicide run or what.

So they got down to the range that they could be engaged effectively and started getting hit.

Three "military grade trucks," Mercedes ten-tons, probably loaded with ammonium nitrate and all the rest that makes AMFO, and four pickup trucks loaded with guys with light weapons. The pickups were keeping wide of the big trucks, which gave me a clue they were bomb trucks.

The Mk-19 is a pretty effective "anti-material" weapon. It's even better when it hits a big assed bomb.

The term is "secondary explosion." One of the Mercedes just fucking disintegrated. I mean the fireball was probably a hundred yards across and made a mushroom cloud. Very big explosion. Another one rolled over. The third continued on. For a while. Until a couple of rounds hit the engine. Then it rolled to a stop smoking. The driver got out and ran for it.

Not far. By then the group was in range of all the bunkers on the berm. And both the Mk-19s *and* the .50s were lighting them up. They wiped them out.

Here's military law. Don't ever imagine I wasn't skirting some issues. Use of "local" personnel for "aid and comfort" was against so many regulations I don't want to start. But we're talking about military *law*.

In a combat situation a military unit *must* give the other side a chance to surrender. Under *certain* conditions.

1. The enemy clearly signals a desire to surrender or is hors de combat.
2. Taking the enemy prisoner will not endanger the receiving group.

That's right. During most of the War on Terror we'd been accepting surrenders that, under the laws of war, we *did not have to*. A side that uses "irregulars" has three days to give them all some identifying mark saying "this is our side." If they don't, they are known as "illegal combatants" and have exactly *no* rights under the Geneva Convention or any other law of war. They are legally the equivalent of spies with guns and the Convention is clear that you can shoot spies. They're given a swift and not particularly just trial, guilty unless proven innocent, and after six months you can justly and legally shoot them.

That'd clear out Guantanamo.

Okay, so we're the good guys. We cut the bad guys some slack. I get that.

You think I'm going to take prisoners when I've got one company of troops cut off so far behind enemy lines you can't see the good guys with a fucking *satellite*?

Not hardly.

My orders had been simple. "No quarter. We can't afford it."

The boys had no qualms with that. They knew what a cleft stick we were in.

So there was a blown-up truck, another rolled over and a bunch more shot to shit.

Round One: Bandit.

At the same time there'd been some movement from town. More vehicles. Including the two tanks. They were followed by a whole *bunch* of people. More people than I thought were living in Abadan at that time.

We didn't have a way for me to automatically use any of the sights we'd set up. I had somebody hand zoom on one.

The vehicles had stopped. The people were herded out. And I do mean herded.

The front rank was women and kids. Mostly. There were some old farts.

I don't know how they'd been chosen. Never did bother to find out.

Bottomline: The fucker was using us being the "good guys" against us. Behind the women and kids were more soldiers than I'd thought could be in Abadan. That was when I knew I wasn't holding the base. It's also when I figured there was no way I was going to lose.

They were headed for the same part of the base as the trucks; the part with all the goodies. That was fine by me.

Fillup started getting queries when they got close enough most of the bunkers could see what the group was made up of. They'd put the vehicles, "technicals" and the tanks and one APC that was a surprise, in behind the women and kids. But most of the "soldiers" were interspersed. There was no way we were going to be able to take them out without killing the noncombatants.

Again, there's a military law that covers this. I could have lit them up. My boys would have done it if ordered. I'd have been covered, technically. My name would have been mud, I wouldn't have liked myself much and I don't want to think what it would have done to my All American boys. The Nepos would have just been professionally chagrined.

Thing was, I figured I didn't have to. Oh, to hold the base and all the gear I would. But I'd kissed *that* goodbye the moment I saw how many soldiers we were up against.

"Make sure we get fucking video" was all I said.

The whole group shuffled forward. They weren't moving fast. A few fell out, heat stroke, exhaustion, whatever. Some more were shot "pour encourage l'autre." We just let them shuffle.

Six miles from their main point of departure to the fences. Gave me time to get a good look at what I was up against. Couple of 20mm anti-aircraft guns mounted on trucks. More with machine guns. Couple without any weapons. The two tanks. One APC with a 30mm gun. About *six thousand* infantry. That had required some logistics, that.

The plan was, apparently, to just shuffle up to the fences. I was good with that. Was interested to see what they'd do about the mines.

Six miles. Took three hours. It had taken them about an hour to get set up. Was two PM before they got close to the base. They stopped about a half a klick out.

The three trucks that weren't carrying weapons pulled through the group. They weren't moving fast; getting the civilians out of the way wasn't easy.

"Get some Jav teams up on the berm. Let them get a look at what they're facing. Don't show the Javs."

The trucks eventually got through, spread out and headed for the fence.

We'd repaired the previous damage. They derepaired it. All three took out sections of fence and the concertina.

"Tell the gate guards to get ready to open up and then hunker."

"Roger."

"Samad?"

"Yes, sahib?"

"May be some leakers. Do not let them take my whiskey."

"They will not pass us, sahib."

God, I love the Nepos.

They hadn't opened fire at us. We weren't opening fire at them.

I started to wonder just *how* much this colonel knew about our internal defenses. I'd made sure that once the girls came into the compound, they didn't leave or pass messages out. I wasn't going to have the sort of intel we were getting from the refugees get out to my enemies. But he clearly knew we were on this end, primarily. He was staying well away from our living area. Like he was saying "We're just here to take the silverware. Don't mind us."

The problem being, he was going to have a hell of a time getting everything out over the berm.

Which meant he probably intended to assault through the holding encampment. More cover there so it made sense. Use the people to get up to the berm, blow the defenses, charge over the berm then fight forward through the gear in the base.

The big question was when he was going to drop the civilians. He'd do it at some point. Keeping them would make a battle impossible. At least coming through the gear park.

The answer was, as I'd guessed, at the berm. Some of the infantry, along with some civilians for cover, cleared out the last of the concertina. Then they formed up a wall of civilians on the berm as cover and started marching over into the gear park.

Worked for me.

Remember, it was rigged like a motherfucker.

We could hear them hooping and hollering all the way to the base. Most of the civilians, with the "infantry" over the berm, were beating feet back to Abadan much faster than they'd come. They left a trail of stragglers behind including some kids. See what we'd do about them later.

The colonel apparently had good enough people they stopped the sack before it got started. The thing was, to get it all out, short of major engineering, he had to take Fort Lonesome. We were blocking the gate.

We had internal cameras. I could see them moving through the stacks of gear, the tanks, the Bradleys, Strykers and Humvees. I was wondering when they'd notice all the wires and shit.

"Get ready to roll," I said as soon as most of the guys were over the berm.

I saw at least one of the guys who caught a clue. Young guy, looked about twelve which probably meant seventeen or so. He saw one of the wires and followed it back to the hood of the Humvee. Looked under the Humvee. Got up and started shouting.

There was more shouting by that time. But the guys were spread through the park and didn't have much in the way of commo. Some of them were heading back. There were arguments.

Iranians and Arabs are okay fighters until you throw them a

loop. So far, everything had gone according to plan. The plan had just changed.

Bunch of them had gone into the secondary ammo dump, the one where we'd dropped most of the ammo from the FOBs we'd had scattered around Iran. I figured I'd light them up first.

Wow, that was exciting.

I'd *tried* to make sure shit actually blew up. You'd think ammo would just blow up and stay blowed up.

Now I knew why those ammo guys had so carefully fired every single Carl Gustav.

The explosives went off then the ammo started going off. Or not going off. Some of it was just flying through the air. In every direction.

Big, big, big explosion. Lots of secondaries. Lit up the sky despite it being broad daylight, sort of an orange-purple. And it kept going. Shit going off overhead. Shit hitting the ground and exploding.

It was hitting *us* and exploding.

Oh, not a lot. And we were mostly in bunkers. But it was popping all over the place. We didn't take any casualties but it was mighty damned exciting.

"Right, Fillup, get rid of their vehicles for me."

Javelin is one hell of a weapon. Absolutely sucks to be up against, mind you. But that's the point if you're holding one.

They make, like, no signature. The missile pops up under very low power and then ignites about twenty feet up. And the signature even then is really small. Something about very efficient combustion.

The really nice part, though . . . Well, there are *so many* nice parts about Javelin.

Nice part one. They're fire and forget. You lock them on the target, fire them and they just track right the fuck on. Forget the old days of having to keep the sight on the target like TOW and Dragon. Fire and *fugedaboudit*. Fucker is going to hit the target five times out of six.

Second nice part. The target *is* going to be smoked. Take a tank. Armored like a motherfucker, right? Sort of. They can't armor them like a motherfucker everywhere. So the majority of the armor is up front, where you'd *expect* a round to hit anyone but the French.

Javelin? Comes down from *way* the fuck up. They went damned near vertical at that range. Came right the fuck down. On the softest part of the tanks.

Third nice part about Javelin? Really easy to fire another one. Drop the launcher, slap on the sight, get another target.

Fourth nice thing about Javelin? Range. Dragons were about a klick. The vehicles that were the target would have been out of range. (*And* Dragon had a *minimum range* of six hundred meters. So you had a *four hundred meter* engagement basket. Sucked. Oh, and they used to blow the fuck up when you fired them. Better than nothing if you were up against tanks but not by much.)

Now, the *manual* said that the maximum range on Javelin employment was 2000 meters. At the range, it had been found to be at least 2500. And one SF team in Iraq had gotten a kill at over *3000*.

These guys were at about 1500 meters from the Javelin teams. Clap shot.

They could have fired back if they were looking the right way. And if they'd seen the teams pop up and fire. They didn't get much of a chance.

The company had four Jav teams. They'd talked it out and engaged the two tanks, a 20mm gun and the APC first. The thing about the Javelin was . . . Okay, another nice thing. They went *way* the fuck up. Time of flight for a short range shot or a long range shot was about twenty seconds. If you were in a hurry to take somebody out, not so good.

If you were in a hurry to take out a bunch of things, pretty good. Because our guys could reload, target and fire in less than ten seconds.

Second flight was off before the first had hit. Targeted at . . . the two tanks, a 20mm gun and the APC.

Never do unto others unless you do unto them *hard*.

Then they slid down the berm and displaced. Just in case.

Meantime, the guys in the gear park were freaking out. Some of them were running forward. Some were running back. The ones near the ammo dump were just rolling around on the ground.

I do so love my job.

So I figured, what the fuck? Everybody survived the *first* ammo dump . . .

I had no need for any of the ammo. I had all I could carry in Fort Lonesome and then some. And, what the hell, ammo is cheap.

This one, fortunately, was further away than the first. It was also bigger. Less rained down on us. More rained down on them. Most of it didn't explode, mind you. Clearing the area was going to be an interesting job. And, okay, there was going to be some ammo for the locals to pick up and use. It was going to be on each other. They'd been doing that since Sargon; some scattered and very fucked up ammo wasn't going to change things. But the "Husayn Ali Martyr Brigade" was *not* going to be using it if I had my way.

So three "technicals" had survived, all mounting 14.7mm machine guns. They were now looking for whatever had killed them. I doubt any of them had ever faced Javelins. They were pointing the guns into the sky.

The Jav teams displaced. They popped back up. They only fired once this time.

Smoke three more technicals. Round two to Bandit.

Now, the gear park was about a *mile* long. And it could be confusing as hell if you didn't have a map, which I trusted they didn't.

Well, I more than trusted. I couldn't figure out, anymore, who was trying to attack us and who was running away. Except the running away ones were probably the ones running up the berm and sliding down the other side.

Into concertina. Hadn't *intended* it for that use, but it worked.

"Barriers that are not covered by direct fire are of no use except annoying an enemy." Don't know where I heard that, AOC maybe, but it's true. If you put out barriers, wire, mines, tank-traps, and don't have fire on them all they do is slow the enemy down, slightly, and annoy him. You might kill a few but most get through unscathed.

Unless they're panicked and stuck in concertina. In which case, as soon as they get unstuck, they start running again. Into mines.

And then they had to get past the fence. Which most couldn't. And thus tried to run to the openings. And if they hadn't seen their buddies getting blown up, they ran into mines. Those that *had* mostly hunkered by the fence and wept.

Let's go for round three. I hit my last charger and started to watch umpteen billion dollars of Uncle Sam's gear go up in flames.

Most of it was pretty unspectacular. A tank getting hit, when it's fully loaded, is an awesome sight. A pillar of flame from its exploding ammunition, turret flying off, etc.

The ones hit by the Javelins had just burst into flame and cooked the crews. Not too spectacular. I was disappointed.

The mortar carriers were okay. They tore apart. Trucks went up like bombs, as should be.

Strykers, even, were quite spectacular. One round on the engine, two in the crew compartment. They really tore into ribbons.

Fucking Bradleys?

Same load out. Turret came off of a couple. Burning like shit, don't get me wrong. All sorts of plastic and stuff. But not the earthshaking kaboom I'd hoped for.

The damned *Abrams* with *five* God-damned artillery rounds and C-4 and tank rounds in them?

Puffs of smoke. I couldn't even tell for sure if they were damaged. Pissed me off.

Oh, the guys caught in this?

Man, we'd put all *sorts* of explosives in there. And when shit blows up, it throws stuff around. Think various sized pieces of metal, wood and plastic going through the air at a very fast rate. Not pleasant to be around. Then there were the fuel trucks.

Now, they were empty, mind you. But I'd sort of forgotten there were going to be fumes. And fumes, generally, blow up better than liquids.

Okay, *they* were spectacular.

I was running out of eyes at this point, there had been various effects on my video surveillance system, so I got on the radios.

"Samad?"

"Are things going to stop blowing up, sahib?"

"Yeah, pretty much done. Hey, *you* guys did most of the work. Good job, by the way."

"Then may Buddha forgive us, sahib."

"Still some guys crawling around in the ruins last time I'd looked. Keep an eye out."

"Your whiskey is safe, sahib."

(Oh, where'd the booze come from? This was a big ass LOG base *before* we packed it with all the shit from Iran. Yes, Rule One, no drinking, pornography or such was in effect. But when big civilian brass visit they don't want to hear about no fucking Rule One. One of the things I'd found in the inventory was the storage for booze for the Distinguished Persons. And, trust me, brother, it was the *good* shit.

(Okay, logistics sidenote. I didn't know that there was booze out there in a CONEX. But after Samad turned up those Brit uniforms, I decided to see what weird crap was stored here. Figuring that "weird" meant small amounts, I sorted the full computer inventory of the original LOG base for smallest number of items. Also where I found the swagger stick, which I still have. As well as a bunch of really odd things. I don't know what *dip-shit* left behind several pounds of *gold* in thin sheets but it was packed on the evac vehicles along with a stash of random currency *also* left behind. Really, you wouldn't believe some of the shit I turned up. The "less than twenty items" went to fucking pages and pages. Most of it "case, one each." I kept expecting to find the Ark of the Convenant.

(I said I didn't *like* being a logistics puke, never said I wasn't good at it. End sidenote.)

(Wife's Edit: Is *that* where that silver tea service came from?)

(Shhhh! And the answer is sort of complicated . . .)

Where was I? Radios. Oh, yeah.

Wasn't really radio. I just swiveled around in my chair.

"Fillup, I think the rest of the party is yours. I'm going to go hang out with Samad."

"Roger," Captain Butterfill replied, heroically or some shit. "Thanks for leaving *something* for us to do."

So the Strykers rolled out the gates and turned north, up the outside of the base. There were now some of the bad guys up on the berm. Some of them shot at the Strykers. They didn't get more than one shot.

Two platoons unassed by the breaks in the berm. Where the footprints crossed the gaps it was clear the mines were gone. They got up on the berm and started working the remains of the gear park.

The third platoon, which was short because it had supplied the guards on the gates and in bunkers, continued a sweep around the base. Any enemy they spotted they engaged with "direct fire."

A few of the guys had made it through the gear park, what was left of it, and into the open area in front of Fort Lonesome. I got to the main control bunker as firing started up from the lines.

"Samad. What are you doing letting people get this close to my whiskey?"

"They will not get your whiskey, sahib."

"Or my women."

"Or your women."

And they didn't. There was some long-range fire that might have been an issue if a. the Nepos hadn't been in bunkers and b. the RIFs could shoot worth a shit. Since a. equalled value "yes" and b. equalled value "no" it was a nuisance not a threat. And the Nepos had gotten to be some really good shots. I wouldn't trust them on a patrol, not yet, but firing from their bunkers they were racking up some kills.

But there were still guys in the gear park and they were going to have to be combed out. With a bunch of unexploded ordnance in their midst.

It wasn't, by the way, getting dark. I looked at my watch when I got to Samad's bunker and it was 1430, two thirty PM.

The whole "battle" had taken thirty minutes. Round Four was done.

So what to do next?

Wait for dark.

Fillup arrayed snipers up on the berms, including what was left of the ammo berms. Sometimes they took fire from rats hiding in the remaining gear. We couldn't actually level the place and there was plenty of cover.

Then we waited. And had a drink of water and some cold MREs. I ordered Fillup and Samad to rotate guys for downtime; it was going to be a long night.

When it got dark we went to Round Five.

It was tedious and it was dangerous but that describes a lot of shit that soldiers do.

As soon as it got dark, it started without any help. The RIFs, thinking they could escape under cover of darkness, started trying to slip up the berm and away.

Sniper rifles come with thermal imagery scopes.

Our enemy did *not* have thermal imagery equipment. It was a moonless night and just about as black as pitch with all our lights shut down.

To them, we were invisible.

They *glowed* in the fucking dark under thermal imagery.

I moved over to the berm to watch. The whole group was arrayed on the west and north sides of the berm. Samad had the south exit from the base covered.

The guys had been firing at the RIFs hiding in the garbage

during the afternoon. The RIFs knew they were on the west and north side. They'd figured out, from the firing in that direction, that the south was blocked. They went east.

To get out on the east side, they had to climb the berm.

That was not a fast exercise. It was fifteen feet high and steeply sloped. And there was, mostly, an open area before it.

And they glowed.

Under thermal imagery, good thermal imagery and the scopes were sixth generation, a person glows white-hot. Their *footprints* glow white for as much as twenty minutes depending on conditions. When they move through concealed areas, the heat of their body rises, as it did this night, and you can see a faint trace like a ghost moving overhead.

And if you're a sniper with an assigned area you wait for that trace to come into view and you shoot the guy in the chest. If he's still moving, then, you shoot him again in the head.

The base wasn't a box. It was a long oval, more or less, curved a bit like a kidney. It was seven hundred meters across most of the base, berm to berm. Long shot for a sniper. But they'd gotten settled in, stacked sandbags, used laser rangefinders. There wasn't any wind. It was still as death. Except for the occasional crack of a shot, echoing off of the berms. Sometimes there'd be another. Not usually.

I didn't interfere. I just walked behind them, listening.

"Sector two-five."

"Fucker is smoking a cigarette. How fucking dumb can you be?"

Pause.

Crack.

"Hope he liked his last smoke."

A sniper works with a spotter. The spotter, well, spots the targets and gives the sniper information on distance, weather, what he should have eaten for dinner.

All the sniper has to do is dial in the information on his scope, take a good steady stance, breathe deep the gathering gloom and terminate.

Bravo company had some *very* good snipers. Lord Love my boys. Okay, Fillup's boys.

I also had some good guys at "Close Quarters Battle." Not that, I hoped, there would be any of that tonight.

But when the movers settled down, the guys still in the area apparently being of the correct opinion that trying to leave was suicide, the rest of the company had to get into action.

Teams spread out and moved through the park. They'd done it before and knew their way around. But it was somewhat different after a. murthering great explosions and b. said explosions having scattered unexploded ordnance around.

The teams, though, weren't there to fight. They were there to flush. They, too, were using thermal imagery and were in contact with the snipers. Very direct contact. As that part of the battle started, the snipers shifted around. Each was assigned a sector and a team. And the two talked. A lot.

"Okay, you've *got* me, right?"

"You're right by that fucking blown-up Humvee."

"That describes a lot of this sector. There's, like, two hundred Humvees here, all blowed the fuck up. I'm waving a chemlight over my head. You've *got* me, right?"

(To add clarity to this exchange: A chemlight is a plastic tube that has some chemicals that mix when you bend it and make light. Think those necklace thingies. Well, the military has chemlights that give off *invisible* light. I shit you not. There are both infrared and ultraviolet. If you break one, you can't see the light unless you've got thermal imagery in the first case or UV imagery in the second. This is the type of chemlight the guy was waving. The world is a very strange place when it has chemical lights that *don't give off light*.)

"So is . . . Second Platoon's One Alpha, I think. Yeah, man, I *got* you. The dumbass by the blown-up Humvee waving the UV chemlight. The other guy is by an Abrams."

"Okay, we're moving south at this time."

"Trust me, I've *got* you. I could smoke you and fuck your girlfriend. And there's a heat source in that next Humvee to your . . . left. So watch your *ass*."

Unexploded ordnance *could* get one of the guys. If he wasn't very damned careful. It was all *over* the fucking place. One thing I hadn't counted on. Also fires which fucked with the thermal imagery.

But what I was really worried about was one of the snipers taking out one of the flushers.

Seemed to be working out all right.

It took all fucking night. Snipers got rotated. You could only look through a scope so long before your eyes started getting fuzzy and we did *not* want fuzzy snipers. The guys doing the flushing went in then out and got some downtime, if nothing else a few minutes to not be in wracking terror between stepping over unexploded cluster munitions and not knowing if some RIF was right around the corner. The Nepos got some Zs. I forced Samad to rotate them; he thought they were just being lazy. I forced *him* to rack out.

Me? I kept moving around the base. There were problems, there always were. That was what I was there for. Me and Fillup who also didn't get any sleep.

By dawn's early light the broad stripes and bright stars were still gallantly waving. And, yes, there *was* a flagpole. Before the rest of the fucking Army pulled out, along with all the Non-Governmental Organizations and the Press, there had been, like, nine flags up. Ours, Iran's new/old one, various countries (Britain) that had something to do with the LOG base, a fucking *UN* one.

When everybody left we took them all down. (We burned the UN one. *And* the French.) Except the Stars and Stripes. And we had fucking reveille every morning with a raising and retreat in the afternoon complete with badly rendered bugle over loud-speakers.

I'd left it up that night. And there she was in the morning, Old Glory still gallantly waving.

Okay, she was sitting flat down the pole because there was, like, *no* fucking wind. But work with me here. Point was, the flag was still up and the enemy was toast.

Of course, our mission was *also* toast.

— CHAPTER EIGHT —

It Seemed Like a Good Idea at the Time

So it was time to report in.

I'd prepared for that pretty well. Okay, I'd been out with the some of the sweep teams. There were burning vehicles. (Not the fucking Abrams, of course!) You had to get in close to those to make sure nobody was still hiding out. Very smoky, very sooty. Fun as hell.

I'd checked myself in a mirror before calling in. Stubble check: Manly. Soot-covered face? Stopped in a line where my helmet band crossed my forehead. Quick wipe with a cloth and the soot was mostly standing out in the scars on my left cheek.

Perfect.

"I need to talk to the battalion commander. We had an incident overnight."

BLEW IT ALL UP? Bad boy! Bad boy! No biscuit! Flayed Skin! Still beating heart!

Yes, sir. Request new orders since "maintain and secure" is now inoperative.

Bad boy! No biscuit! I'll get back to you. Bad boy! Flayed skin!

So then I took a shower while Fillup and his XO and Sky-Geek did some good works. They'd actually starting working on it the night before. The brigade commander was not going to be impressed by stubble and soot. He'd had plenty of stubble and soot in his time.

"Did you *really* have to blow it up?"

Freshly pressed uniform (thank you, Shadi, and for the quicky), cloth cap neatly placed, destubbled.

"I'd like to squirt you some video, sir. It's about ten minutes long. I'll include everything in my full report. In my professional opinion, we're lucky to be alive. Sir."

Sent him the video. Said he'd get back to me.

Now, it's night in the States. Getting on to, anyway. Sunday. Colonel is still at work, though. Good man.

Called me back *two hours* later. Middle of the fucking night.

What was on the video?

Shots of the approaching army with close ups of the civilians in their midst. *Good* view of the Abadan refinery for perspective.

Close ups of the tanks.

Troops rolling out of the barracks in battle rattle. (Did not note that they'd done that *hours* beforehand.)

More of the approach. Let that one loom. It looked like "all the sands of the desert" if you didn't notice that more than half were unarmed women and children.

Them blowing the fence with the suicide trucks.

Thousands of heavily armed shooters pouring over the berm and celebrating.

Explosions. More explosions. One shot caught bodies, literally, flying up in the air. Well, parts.

Javelins firing.

Tanks blowing up from Javelins. Technicals blowing up from Javelins.

The Nepos holding the compound. We had to work with that one to make them look really seriously endangered, but the geek managed.

The Strykers rolling out of the base in an unstoppable wave. (Again, *careful* editing.)

Snipers on the berm. Day shot.

Thermal imagery of the sweep teams and a *really* lucky shot of one of them engaging a small group of hide-outs. Guys dropping from snipers.

One totally trashed compound. Bodies scattered everywhere.

A last shot of the stars and stripes waving in the wind.

All to music from the Halo movie. Well, and "O Fortuna." "O Fortuna" and Mjolnir Mix for the approach then "Blow Me Away" for the rest. Okay, it's more like 11 minutes. I didn't hear any bitching.

(And, okay again, the flag was cheating. There was this video that was like some sort of marketing video for Titan Base. Didn't know the U.S. Army did marketing videos. Oh, well. Anyway, we took it from that. But work with me, here. A flag hanging limp wasn't going to do it. SkyGeek was a real find. Same guy that fixed our satellite shit. I was protecting him *very* carefully.)

Did we carefully edit for "we're going to get fucked" and then "we survived and kicked ass!"? Oh, hell yeah. Was it propaganda? Yeah, probably.

But I'd just trashed something like nineteen billion dollars worth of stuff. (Actually, less, but none of it was coming home.)

I *needed* some propaganda on my side.

So the brigade commander called me back.

"That wasn't, exactly, a report. Where'd all that video come from?"

"We had prepared the base with an extensive surveillance system, sir. We were only one company and it was a very long perimeter."

"And some fencing, I noticed."

"Yes, sir."

"Busy little beavers. Actually, that was the corps commander's comment."

"The Nepalese did most of it, sir."

"The ones you armed. That was your battalion commander's comment."

"I have been doing the best job I can, sir, to maintain and secure this environment. I may have taken some unorthodox steps, but I considered them necessary to ensure the security of myself and the troops and noncombatants I am responsible for. Sir."

"The corps commander's question was actually 'Where'd he get the fucking *Ghurkas*?' I explained. He felt it was 'a pretty optimal use of available personnel.' He also mused about whether we can keep them."

"Yes, sir."

"What was your count on the threat? I was looking at better than two grand. I thought you said there wasn't that much threat in the area."

"Faulty intel and things accelerated, sir. Sir, we're one company. I don't *have* an intel guy. Or overhead. Sir. And our rough count was six thousand. We've got enough video to do a hard count when it comes to it. But that was our estimate."

"*Before* I showed it to the division commander and his staff I asked for their count of what they considered 'overwhelming force' in the circumstances. His answer was around a thousand. Same for the corps commander when he was asked. He's sending it on to FORSCOM with his comments. But you're going to need to do an actual report."

"Yes, sir. Breaking the chain, sir. Extraction?"

"Still nothing. Brought *that* up, too. You're probably going to have to roll to somewhere. Ensure your own security and make plans for that. The last is probably redundant but you didn't destroy *all* your ammo and equipment, right?"

"I'm an S-4, sir. You *really* think I'd destroy all my equipment, sir?"

"Yeah. We need to unfuck that when you get back."

Yes!

"Out here."

So we were out of the woods for now. The Chief of Staff might be less forgiving, not to mention the Secretary of Defense, and I figured it would get that high what with a billion here and a billion there.

But for now, we were out of the woods.

Well, actually we were stuck deep in them. But we could see some paths and shit. Maybe.

Then we had to deal with the State Department.

Most of the "governments" in the world were, essentially, thugs. We'd had embassies overrun in a dozen countries. And then gotten in contact with them and said "no harm, no foul." (Look, a dead ambassador, not to mention the Marines, was *foul*.) The "governments" were whichever group happened to have commo with the States at any moment.

I'll give you an example that actually mattered. Turkey.

The capital of Turkey is Ankara, which had been a fairly big city in the middle of fuck all. Our embassy, there, was evacced by that MEU in the Med when "the security situation deteriorated."

Subsequent to that, the U.S. had been contacted by three separate groups, all claiming to the be "the official government of Turkey."

The "official" official government was the one that the Turkish ambassador to the U.S., who lived, said was the official government. Sort of.

See, the Turkish Ambassador to France was buddies with a different faction. So the *French* were recognizing *them*.

The Turkish ambassador to the *UN* had also survived. And *he* was saying the *third* faction was the "official" government.

And the State Department was in a dither. Which was the official government of Turkey?

I can tell you that from my experiences. None of them. They were three groups of thugs who had satellite phones and the ears of three more thugs who happened to have the ear of idiots.

There was no "official" government of Turkey if you count "official" as having control over most of the territory. Or even a big segment of it. Say, half. Not at that time.

There *was* an official government of Israel. New prime minister; the vaccine hadn't worked for the last one. Somewhat reduced Knesset was in session. Elections were in the planning stages.

It was willing to take us in. But not the Nepos.

What the fuck?

They were still afraid of the flu. Okay, there was some constant to that. But I had documentation that the Nepos had been vaccinated with Type Two. (I wasn't mentioning the girls *at* all. Just a vague mention of "local contract staff." Besides, we'd vaccinated *them* too.)

For some reason, well some pretty obvious ones, they were willing to take a company of American infantry, but not the Nepos.

And then there was the problem of how to get there.

Remember my discussion of Turkey?

To get to Israel, we'd have to pass through Iraq and Jordan.

Get this, there were *four* semi-official governments in Iraq and three more in Jordan. The really "official" government in Jordan was the one led by the son of King Hussein. Kid was a former tanker and he'd actually managed to gather a pretty decent body of troops and stake out some serious territory. But there were two more who were recognized by various ambassadors who'd survived.

The King Hussein faction was okay with us rolling through. Actually, they were asking for our *help*. The other two were against it and raising holy diplomatic hell.

Then there's Iraq.

Okay, one of the factions I could dig with. The Kurds had managed to hold things pretty much together. Really high death rate, but they were tribal based already and the tribes had things worked out between them pretty well. And the Kurds just react, adapt and overcome. I'd say it's a mountain people thing but that doesn't explain the U.S.

Anyway, the Kurds were one faction. They didn't say they were the government of *Iraq*, they were the government of *Kurdistan*. Which by *their* maps included some parts of Iran and Turkey.

They didn't have an ambassador in the U.S. The State Department didn't recognize them at *all*. Of course, they just had the most effective control over the largest area in the Middle East. But they were, officially, nonexistent.

Then there's the other three (major) factions.

Note, these guys weren't, any of them, as big as HAMB. At the rate General Dead Meat had been going he was well on his way to taking Iraq and turning it and Iran back into the Persian Empire.

But all three of these guys were recognized by one or another government and none of them were willing to let us through "Iraq."

Truth was, territorially, we weren't going to be dealing with but one of them, depending on our route to Israel.

If we even went to Israel.

"State Department thinks they can talk the Iraqis around. But Israel is *not* going to let your Nepalese in."

I'd stopped dealing with the BC. I mostly was talking to the Brigade 3 these days.

"I'm not going to leave my Nepos behind."

"With the Jordanians?"

"I'm taking them to the States. If I have to canoe over."

"Nobody is willing to let you through."

"And that's going to stop me exactly *how*?"

I didn't know how much hell I was causing at home until one of the guys called me in to watch TV.

Yeah, I know. Here we are in a compound filled with rotting bodies and still burning equipment and the guys are watching TV.

What else were they going to do? There weren't enough hands to bury all the bodies.

Actually, we'd done something on that score. Basically, we sprayed as much of the compound as we could reach with diesel and lit it up. Burned for a day or so (we used a *lot* of diesel and it soaked into the soil) and most of the bodies were crispy.

But we couldn't get all of it and they were a health hazard. People were staying inside away from the flies as much as possible. Flies that have been on rotting bodies are not good for the body. We were immunized against every fucking thing in the world but they still weren't good.

"What's up?"

The day room is the province of the troops. Good officers go in only on duty or if called in. The lieutenants and I had our own official "O Club" which we had tarted up with some stuff from the "low-inventory" stores. Would you believe there was a fucking *Ming vase* in there?

(Wife Edit: So *that's* where that came from.)

(Shut up.)

So, anyway, I was walking out of the commo van after another fruitless conversation with Brigade when one of the troops waved me into the day room.

There, large as fucking life, on fucking *Fox*, was our video.

Oh. Holy. *Shit.*

The troops loved it. They'd replayed it a couple of times themselves for shits and giggles and then played around with the video some more. That one concentrated more on dying ragheads.

But this was the one I'd sent to Brigade and then had, apparently, been marched up the chain. Fucker was *supposed* to be secret.

Holeee shit. I was fucked.

Don't get me wrong. It was a good video. For a certain audience.

But viewed in the wrong context? Scrambled around a little bit by the media? With CAIR doing a voice over?

Holeeee shit.

"Hell, yeah!" I said, grinning. "You're all fucking heroes, now."

Hollllleeeee SHIT.

I went back to the commo van. The on-duty RTO was already running to get me.

Fecal storm *incoming.*

— CHAPTER NINE —

Cross that Strait
When We Come to It

Nobody knew how it had leaked out. I guess we did too good a job. Some Fobbit SOB just *had* to send it to some friend on the Internet and then it had all gone bad. It had one of the highest hit counts on record on YouTube (which was back up). I tried to figure out if there was some way we could get residuals, given that we'd sweated blood for it. And were about to sweat more.

But that wasn't the problem.

Was all that force *necessary*?

They destroyed *how* much equipment?

Why was the equipment still *there*? Hadn't all the troops come *home*?

Why did we still have troops in *Iran*?

Are we still going to have to fight terrorists *as well as* the flu? Isn't it time for *peace* to have a chance?

Where had the *Ghurkas* come from?

Britain had sent an official query asking how an American unit had come to be in command of their troops. So had Nepal but that one took longer to be noticed. Except, as far as either knew, they weren't *missing* any Ghurkas. But they had on the right uniforms. They were even wearing kukris. (I *told* you there was some strange shit in that place. Hell, there were cavalry sabers and saddles and . . . You wouldn't *believe* the list. I wish I could have kept it but there was no fucking way.)

Congressional investigation. Congressional fucking investigation.

Except for one problem.

Witness A would be me. And *I* was in fucking *Iran*.

They wanted to video-conference me in.

It ended up with the Army Chief of Staff explaining. On national TV. Bet he loved *that*.

"By order of the President, we *had* over *fourteen* 'support and maintain' detachments scattered in as many countries around the world. Six were evacuated when the security situation reached critical. And in all six cases the equipment on site had to be destroyed or fall into the hands of the enemies of the United States. As of this date, there are *two* units responding, *including* the unit under the authority of Bandit Six. The other *six* units have all been *lost*. Two we do not know what happened to them. They simply stopped responding to requests for update. The other four are confirmed by reports at the time and satellite imagery to have been overrun. Total lost military personnel over *one thousand*, making it the highest KIA/MIA single action operational loss since *the Vietnam War*! *One* of them destroyed some or all of the material under their control. That was Bandit Six and he was under orders to do so rather than have it fall into the hands of enemies of the United States.

"I've been watching my men being overrun one by one sitting on material that has exactly *no* value to the United States under the current world conditions and you want me to explain why a captain and one company, *a hundred and sixty troops*, had to destroy the material in the face of SIX THOUSAND? Is *that* what you want me to explain, Senator? Senator, I'm glad my boys are ALIVE!"

Most of the damned session, as is normal with congressional hearings, consisted of fucking idiots talking about nothing and then asking a koan. Four minutes of the importance of the Health of Children Opportunity Bill followed by "Why did he use rock and roll music?" I swear, they must slip some sort of fucking psychodelic into the water in DC. But a few of the questions, from Republicans naturally, were on point. Okay, actually the best Q&A came from a Democrat.

"You were ordered to leave the equipment in place by the President?"

"Yes, Congressman. There was no logistical option. That is, we couldn't pick it up and bring it home. Things were and are in a situation such that disaster relief takes priority."

"Understood. And to bring back all but, and I quote, 'absolute minimum forces. No more than a company to be left behind.' Is that correct?"

"Yes, Congressman. That was the order from the President in consultation with the Secretary of Defense."

"What did you think of that order?"

"I was given an order by the Commander in Chief and carried it out to the best of my ability. In situations where a company was unavailable I tried to leave equal or better forces. Such as the SF battalion in Colombia which had the approximate firepower of a company. And which was the first we lost contact with."

"But what did you *think* of the order?"

"I thought I was being given an order, Congressman."

"You're a member of the Joint Chiefs, correct?"

"Yes, Congressman."

"And your job, as a member of the Joint Chiefs, is to advise the President on military matters. Were you asked for your advice in this case?"

"Yes, Congressman."

"And what did you advise?"

"Destruction in place and recall of all personnel. Barring that, choosing force levels sufficient to ensure security and maintain an ability for extraction."

"And your advice?"

"I was given a different order, Congressman. I carried out the order I was given."

"General, I was a captain in the Army, you know that, right?"

"Yes, Congressman."

"General, you left units scattered all over the world with *no way to get home*. No *plan* to get them home. Thousands of troops that could have been brought home if we just destroyed the equipment in the first place. I'm not asking about how you felt about the order. I'm asking how you felt about that *situation*. It's a subtle difference; I want to hear your answer."

"Congressman, I was ordered to leave guys out in the wilderness to *die*. The fact that we got back six of the packets is a miracle. If we get back Bandit Six and his boys or the unit in Kazakhstan it's going to be *more* of a miracle. How do you *think* I feel about that, sir?"

But the classic was:

"I don't understand why there are Chinese troops there, General. Can you explain that? Aren't they a risk for the H5N1 virus?"

They're Nepalese not Chinese. Look, let me show you a map. I thought this might be asked. See? Different countries. Good light infantry. Also some other contract personnel . . . Hoping to get them all back to the States for either residency or eventual repatriation when that becomes possible.

So the Chief of Staff was on record asking for me to bring back the Nepos.

But the Israelis were still balking.

Then The Bitch apparently got involved.

People had a different opinion of the world, and of soldiers, after the Plague. The good people of America were getting fed by soldiers every day. They were getting medical attention from the Army. They were, now, interacting with soldiers day in and day out. If there had been a military coup in late 2019 nobody, I think, would have batted an eye.

Sure, there were lots of bitchers about the government. And every bitch about soldiers was being picked up by the news media. Fewer were getting broadcast about people bitching about The Bitch. That didn't mean they *weren't*.

Warrick wanted me off the news. Big time. The "Lost Company" was now big news. Human interest. Actually, maybe it *did* make sense.

The majority of the print and broadcast media, Fox being an exception, was pitching us as murdering and destroying bastards. The "nineteen billion" number was repeated again and again. Along with suggestions that we'd fired on the civilians.

Fox was showing the RIFs pouring over the berm in an unstoppable tide.

Thing was, people still didn't have power and TV, period. But that didn't mean that stuff wasn't getting around. A lot of radio stations were back up. They were the main medium of news. I hadn't realized it at the time, but that really helped.

You see, most of the news stations were still "talk radio." And *that* had been dominated by conservatives for a *long* time. Liberals had tried again and again to break into it and bounced. You had to have some logic to be able to work in talk radio. Not to mention a sense of humor which tofu-eaters were notably lacking.

Oh, there was some backlash. Warrick had used her FCC and

"Emergency Powers" to shut some down for "hate speech." Which got broadcast by others. Which had caused a bunch of questions in Congress. Which was getting restive under some of the shit she'd been pulling.

Elections were coming up. Everybody wanted to blame somebody else for the fucking disaster in the U.S. Deflect *some* of the fucking damage, politically.

The one group that was coming out smelling like a fucking *rose* was the U.S. military. The congressional investigations about my little destruction spree were supposed to kill that, to tarnish our image. Make it look like Abu Ghraib or some shit.

It was doing *exactly* the opposite and they quickly saw that. The Army, which was the only group that seemed to actually be *doing* anything for people, had been ordered to abandon its troops, *America's* troops, in wastes far from our blessed shores by the *same woman* who had screwed up *every step* of the disaster.

Warrick wanted us off the news. To get us off the news she had to get me back to the U.S. and into a quiet *grave* if she could arrange it.

But the Israelis were *still* balking. Warrick had pulled some shit about Israel in her time. She was *not* a fair-haired girl in their estimation. They shucked and jived very good. They'd gotten better spokespeople lately. Flu threat. Security problems. Flu.

Send a MEU?

The one in the Med was on its way back to the States. They'd done all they could do. And send a MEU for one fucking company? That would look great on the news. Helos, ground threats . . .

Fly us out?

From where? Abadan airport was too big for us to hold. Any airport capable of supporting planes big enough to fly us out was too big for us to guarantee security.

I got told by the 3 that somebody, I think it was the BC, had suggested dropping a *Ranger Battalion* in to hold the airstrip while we evacced.

Look, Rangers are tough. I went to the school. Yada, yada. But my fucking *company* had more firepower than a Ranger *battalion*. Rangers are always portrayed on the news like they're the heaviest infantry in the world. Not hardly, brother. Heaviest infantry in the world was a full up Mech unit with Bradleys. Next down the way is *us*. The Stryker boys. When you care enough to send the very best. Sending a *Ranger* unit to "support" a *Stryker* unit is like sending a PeeWee league to pitch for the Yankees.

The order, for once, was not micromanagement on her part.

"Tell them to get *out* of Iran and *off* of the news."

We were headed home.

But how?

Israel was saying not only no but hell no.

There was a port in Jordan down on the Red Sea. There was a bare possibility of getting a ship in there.

Only problem was, it was held by the wrong faction. And they were tough. We, possibly, with the help of Hussein, Junior, could have shifted them out.

But we'd take casualties.

And there weren't many ships.

Fly out from Jordan?

Again, no good airstrip and birds were blocked out, big-time. I think that the brass were, at that point, using us to stick it to the Bitch. Just being passive aggressive. "Can't do that, can't do that . . ." Wasn't sure how I felt about that at the time. Despite the hell we went through, I'm good with it, now.

Why? Because the Bitch needed to be taken down. Not by a military coup. By showing the American people what a fucking fruitcake they'd elected.

I don't get or like human interest. Back before the Plague, it had ruined all sorts of stuff. The Olympics for one. Back when I was a kid, you'd watch the Olympics and it'd be about sports. By the time I was a teenager it was all about "poor Bobby was born with a heart defect but he managed to overcome it and become an expert male syncronized swimmer!"

The fucking Olympics are about who wins and who loses. Period fucking dot. I don't *give a shit* if Bobby has a heart murmur. Did he get a gold? No. Fucking loser.

But, I don't get most people. The world's a very black and white place to me. That's good in a soldier. Not so good in a politician. And to be a senior general you *have* to be a politician. It just goes with the fucking job. You *cannot do your job* if you're *not* one.

Well, we were *good* human interest. Poor homeless waifs that, nonetheless, were carrying the flag. Good boys. Have a biscuit.

It pissed the hell out of me, but there you are.

Questions about the Battle of Abadan were opening up other questions. Why had the immunization distribution been fucked up? Why weren't we cracking down on the violence in the cities?

The latter had started to spill over. With most of the food shipments cut off, the gangs had been moving out looking for food, loot, women, whatever. There had been "encounters" between them and not only military and police units but some of the "random associators."

(Fox called them "local volunteer organizations" which was pretty accurate. Every other broadcast and print news organ seemed to call them "right-wing militias." This, of course, being a code for "Bad Dog! No Biscuit!")

Warrick realized her orders were being circumvented. But even the Mainstream Media couldn't always cover up that the people *she* wanted supported were mostly murderous thugs. So she didn't push the issue.

But she also didn't push for a crackdown. "Negotiate." "Collaborate." "Minimal force." Kumbaya. Whether, at that point, it would have worked or not, I'm not sure. But the point was, she was sitting on the fence as much as possible.

And things were getting ugly. Er.

So more and more questions were getting asked. Not congressional investigations. Oh, no. Democrat Congress. They could squash those.

Right wing radio? Oh, yeah. Fox? Some.

Internet?

Oh. My. Fucking. God.

It seemed like the whole Internet had shifted. Most places it still wasn't up. But the places it was up all seemed to be in the "red" zones. That is, fly-over country.

Things were coming up in fly-over country *much* faster than in the kumbaya lands. This was pitched by the media as some sort of plot. Possibly by the military.

Nope. It was just that the people in fly-over country weren't taking the shit that the "blues" were accepting. Governors were using state police, National Guard where they could get away with it and even "right-wing militias" to take back their cities. With very liberal Rules of Engagement.

Things were starting to resemble civilization in parts of fly-over country again.

The lower population density and survivablity, in general, also worked.

And in "blue" country, times they were achangin'.

Okay, maybe it's time to talk about California.

California is a desert. Not quite, but close enough. Southern California, at least. Northern much less so especially in the Valley. But southern California is a desert made green by much effort.

California was also densely populated. After the Plague it was still pretty densely populated. Temporarily.

Most of southern California's water came from a *very* complicated system of canals, tunnels and pumps. They had some local reservoirs, but mostly it came from *way* back east. They'd been in "drought" conditions (actually, quite normal conditions) for fucking ever. They were *always* short on water. And power. And everything else that makes for a modern industrialized society except people.

When the Plague hit, they lost a good half their population. It had a lot of people. It even had areas of high trust. But they were, pretty much, fucked.

California had a lot of agriculture, too. But much of it was dependent on irrigation. The whole Imperial Valley for starters. And there had to be people to run the irrigation canals and weirs and locks.

So they ended up short on food and short on water. Things got very ugly very quickly. Lots of low trust areas. Borderline civil control in a lot of areas already. No food. No water.

L.A. pretty much started to empty out by May. The only problem being, there weren't any better areas around. Water was scarce *everywhere*. And going east was just going into areas with *less* water.

San Diego was a bit better off. They had Pendleton Marine base and a Navy base there. The Navy ships, those that weren't tasked elsewhere, had big desalinators for water. Between the Marines and the Navy they managed to keep civil order. Wasn't easy. There was pretty much an invasion going on from Mexico. The Marines had machine guns.

A lot of people from L.A. headed south. Not all of them bad people, mind you, but there were enough that it mattered. There was a lot of killing in the areas south of L.A..

But it's a *long* way to San Diego on foot. And much of it is

Pendleton, which isn't exactly overrun with food and water. There are a few streams. The term here is "dysentery." Which means you dehydrate faster than you consume.

Cars? California was the car capital of the U.S. The roads were choked. As in, not moving.

It was a fucking death-trap.

Marines and the few National Guard that had assembled did what they could. And a couple of NG units were wiped out for it. But something like two million people are believed to have died in the area south of L.A. That's on top of the estimated four million from the direct effects of the Plague.

Some made it over the mountains into the Valley. The Valley was better. Services were starting to come back, there was more water and such.

Then Fresno got hit by about a million refugees from Los Angeles. Most of them the toughest and meanest. Things were ugly for a while.

Estimates again. Deaths in the L.A. metropolitan area, total population about 12 million pre-Plague.

Four million direct effects. *One* in three again.

Maybe another four million in the first breakdown of order.

One million or so from secondary effects and secondary epidemics in the next four months.

Evacuees?

Well, Orange County, as of last census, has about a half a mil as noted. Rattling around like peas. Total L.A. metro area is a mil and change. Say a mil and a half.

And most of those went there after the Plague. Still not a bad place to live. If you're not addicted to water.

Like I said, it emptied.

Point is, a lot of the "blue" areas were like that. L.A. is worst case, but it's not completely off.

San Francisco got hit *hard* by direct effects of the Plague. Okay, one of the reasons, frankly, was AIDS. The drugs that HIV "sufferers" took kept them alive. It didn't rebuild their immune systems. But that was, at most, a couple hundred thousand. Nobody quite knows because the records were "secret" and nobody's bothered to dig out the no longer secret records.

But they had something like 40% mortality rate from direct effect. Worst noted mortality in the U.S. Reason? Nobody quite knows. See all the previous factors and reverse them is my guess. Low societal trust, healthy eating . . . Water, again, became an issue. They got it from across the Bay. Pumps weren't working. No water eventually equals death. Movement started, north and south.

South was The Valley again. The Valley had gotten hit, too. But there were big pockets of "high trust" zones. Suburbs, yeah, but farming communities, too. Those that hadn't gotten eaten by the suburbs.

The Valley mostly was able to absorb the refugees from the Bay area and even L.A. Not easily and the fringes in both directions got hit, hard. But they managed to absorb the blow.

Thing about it is, the Valley was one of the most conservative areas of California. The "blue" people from the cities were dependent on the charity of those evil "red" people. Who were clearly busting their ass to help.

Bottomline: Various and sundry effects of the Plague hit liberals hardest. Oh, the "poor" too. But if you look at the demographics of the Democrats they tended to be *upper*most echelon of income and *lower*most echelon of income.

The Plague, except for the tiny fraction at the very top, tended to hit both groups harder than middle class.

And if you looked at the demographics of the Republicans, they tended to be middle class.

There's one last point. Prior to the Great Depression, the Democrats were a minority party. The Grand Old Party (GOP: Republicans) had dominated every Federal office since the Civil War.

Hoover killed that. His response to the Great Depression was to tell people to pull up their socks and quit complaining. *Not* a functional response. People couldn't afford socks. It went over as well as "let them eat cake."

FDR simply did things that made sense to people. Oh, they were considered "communist" at the time, but they made *sense*. He put people to work. He made sure people got fed. He led. "A chicken in every pot" was his mantra. (Back then, chickens were *high*-cost food. They were hard to raise and focused primarily on egg production. The modern chicken farming industry was started at least in part by it being a "Hero Project" if you will.)

Warrick's response to the Plague had been:

Screw up the vaccination distribution. (The vaccine worked *sometimes*.)

Bitch about conspiracies.

Ignore all the experts on recovery.

Pour all her efforts into places that were free-fire zones.

Play the victim card.

Start seizing every business in sight and proceed to run it further into the ground.

Talk about the wonders of socialized medicine.

Talk about the environment.

Play the race card . . .

It was getting old. People were as tired of her "Plan for the Future" and "Conversation with America." They were tired of her waffling and she was starting to look a bit *weird* every time she was on TV. Like a robot or a brain-eating zombie. (Heavier and heavier doses of tranquilizers as it turns out. *Good* ones, too.)

Even liberals will see sense when survival was on the line. Just as a lot of Republicans saw sense in 1932. It's hard to call someone a "mindless myrmidon" or a "babykiller" when he's handing you food. And looks at your kid and gives you some more under the table.

Point is that a lot of good, devout, tofu-eaters were starting to go the other way. And the problem with unthinking zealots is, they tend to *stay* unthinking zealots.

When a long-term vegan has to eat meat or die, they have to rethink their morals. When a PETA "animals are people" lover has to kill and eat a house cat to survive, they then have to *justify* their choice. To themselves if to no one else. Ditto some long-term gun-hater who gets a gun for self-defense fighting her way out of L.A. and has to *use* it. Multiple times.

And if they are truly unwilling to adapt, they just die.

A conservative is a liberal who's been raped. There'd been a lot of that in places like L.A.

The Plague and the depression that resulted were causing a lot of grasshoppers to choose being ants or die.

Warrick was looking at taking her place in history next to Herbert Hoover crossed with Saddam Hussein.

The last fucking thing she needed was her former radical liberal tofu-eaters, now quickly becoming radical conservative fire-eaters, swooning over a company of Hellenic Mold Heroes cut off in Iran.

I was told, later, that my "winning looks" had a part to play in all this. Given the sexual orientation in some of the "switchers" I'm not sure that was a good thing.

And the Brass was being *notably* passive aggressive.

Then I got The Call.

So there I was, trying to stay away from the flies . . . Really, it was the only reason I was lolling around in bed. Oh, that and that it was, like, 2AM again.

And the phone rings.

"What *now*?"

"Sir, you've got a call."

The on-duty RTO wasn't real happy. It was either brass or reporters again.

"I'll be right over."

"It's . . ."

"I'll be right over."

So I sit down, wearing my best uniform and at least half awake. Guy comes on. Colonel in dress uniform.

"Captain Bandit? Stand by for the President."

"Roger."

Oh, holy FUCK. No, no, no, NO!

Yes.

So there's the robot bitch. And to add to the misery, there's the fucking Chief of Staff and the Secretary of Defense and the Secretary of State on other screens.

I'm a captain. They're the Gods. This was *not* going to be good no matter *how* it turned out.

Look, yes, I hated the Bitch. Still do. But she was, after all, the President. Anybody who sits in that chair carries a certain mystic chill. The weight of history, etc. She was sitting in the same position as George Washington and Lincoln and Reagan. Yes, she looked as if she wanted to eat my brains. But she still was the President. Making fun of her in abstract was one thing. Looking her in the eyes was another.

I resolved to put the words "robot" and "zombie" out of my lexicon.

"Captain, I'm told that all standard conceivable methods of extracting your force are impossible to effect at this time."

"Yes, ma'am?"

"And you have . . . issues with moving your troops over to Israel."

"Yes, ma'am. The security situation in southern Iraq is notably unstable and the Israelis refuse to accept my Nepalese attachments or the local contractors. It would be . . . dishonorable to simply leave them behind. I hope to get them to the U.S. Barring that, to some area of relative safety."

The "security situation" I'd thrown in just to throw her. But the Nepalese were a major telling point.

The "Ghurka Meme" had infected the reports. Overnight, it seemed, we turned from being evil murdering destroying bastards to "heroic fighters." You see, the news media had noticed that we had little brown brothers we were helping. That made it all right and good.

Getting the Nepos out was probably right up there with getting *us* out in her mind.

"So how are we going to get you home, Captain?"

"The Ten Thousand, ma'am."

"Excuse, me?"

Yeah. Shows how much *she* knew about military history.

Group of Greek mercenaries from various city states at one point hired out to a pretender to the Persian throne. This was between when they'd kicked Persian ass at Thermopylae and Marathon and before Alexander ended up teaching the Persians who was the *real* boss.

Their side lost. Not far from here, again. Hey, there's a lot of history in this area.

Anyway, they ended up fighting their way home. Look up "Anabasis."

What I was proposing was the same thing.

We were going to march to the sea. The Black Sea in this case. Well, part of it. Sort of.

"Anabasis?" the Chief of Staff asked.

"Yes, sir. Bosporus, actually. I think the Greeks might be more willing to take us in."

"Turkey is not willing to permit your movement," the secretary of State said, cutting off that suggestion.

"There *is* no Turkey," the Chief of Staff said, giving him the exact value he deserved. "How are you going to cross the Bosporus, Captain? There's a very unfriendly Caliphate in the way."

Fuck.

"Dardanelles?"

"No bridges."

"Cross that strait when I come to it," I said.

The Prez might have been a fuck-up but she wasn't a complete moron.

"So you're suggesting that you march through Turkey to Greece, Captain? Can you do that?"

"Yes, ma'am," I said. Fuck it. I was fucked anyway. If the Chief of Staff didn't like it he should have sent me a fucking MEU. Or something. "I have sufficient supplies to take the full unit, including attachments, to the Bosporus. And beyond."

"The security situation in Turkey is not the greatest, Bandit," the Chief of Staff said.

"Yes, sir. Duly noted. I'm better prepared than the Ten Thousand and I've got better troops."

The last was debatable. Those Greeks were kick fucking ass motherfuckers. But I *had* to say something.

"Approved. Break this down."

That was it. No "good luck." Nothing. Just "Approved."

You know, Johnson used to get on the radio and order around companies. We lost that war.

Then there was the question of the Greeks. Would they let us in? All of us?

"Oh, sure. No problem, buddy. By the way, could you bring some supplies?"

There was one Greek government. Not four. One. All the surviving ambassadors agreed and there was even a U.S. Embassy still open. They'd had some major issues, still did. But they were, well, the *Greeks*. Sure, they hadn't won a war since Palatia. But they'd been fought for and over and through for centuries and they just kept being Hellenes. As long as there was enough mutton, retzina and ouzo they were good. A company of infantry replicating the Ten Thousand's march. Oh, hell, yeah! Come on over! We'll bring the ouzo! You're cute, you know that? How's your butt look?

Great. Problems settled. All we had to do was fight our way through Iraq and Turkey, over some stone bitch mountains which were already starting to fill up with snow, dragging along some Nepalese irregulars, who might be some good in the mountains come to think of it, and a trail of camp followers.

This was starting to feel *too* much like the Ten Thousand.

And I hadn't even found *out* the bad parts, yet.

CHAPTER TEN

Uno Problemo

There were a few details to work out. I paid my second in-person visit to the refugees.

The "mullah" who had taken over was a guy in his forties. He had, somewhere, scrounged up traditional Islamic dress and never actively carried a gun.

Let me explain the quotes. A mullah is, technically, nothing more than a teacher. That's actually the translation of the word: Scholar. He's not a priest specially annointed by God through a chain from some distant past. The Islamics simply don't have that. They have some people, like Hussein Jr. in Jordan, who are descendants of the Prophet and therefore specially important. But they are not necessarily or even commonly mullahs. A mullah is more like a rabbi, but even rabbis tend to go through an elaborate preparation for their posts. The only fixed requirements for a mullah is that he has completed the Haj, the annual pilgrimage to Mecca, and that he reads Arabic so he can translate and "explain" the Koran, which is a fairly baroque and in place opaque document.

(These "explanations," by the way, are called "fatwahs." A fatwah is not always a license to kill although it often seemed that way to Westerners since those were the only fatwahs we ever heard about. A fatwah can be something as simple as whether you can talk on your cell phone while doing your morning ritual washing. No, by the way. And, yes, there's a morning ritual wash. Why do Islamics often smell like the backside of a camel? Because it's based on people washing in the DESERT. Water is not required.

Trust me, as OCD as Mohammed was (and he was *very* OCD) if he'd been around for modern conveniences he'd have added "And use *water* you morons! And *soap*! And maybe some fucking *deodorant*! You all smell like camels' butts!")

Down south and to a certain extent anywhere in the Bible belt you'll find small churches all over that are set up by a "preacher" who then brings his personal version of the Word of God to people every Sunday. Such preachers range from guys with multiple degrees in divinity (one of the schools Al Bore failed, by the way) or theology to some guy who can barely read the Bible.

Now you know what mullahs are. They're guys who a) went on the Haj, b) can or fake that they can read the Koran and c) convince people to give them money to preach.

And among the Shia they occasionally act as pimps. It's a funny old world.

This mullah seemed a decent enough guy. Whether for propaganda reasons or faith he seemed, also, to be trying to live the life that Shia mullahs had tended to live prior to the Mad Mullahs taking over Iran. That is, he advised and suggested how things should run, but didn't actually run them. Not under "shariah law." It's kind of like, a guy may be one of those small town preachers. He can still run for office. But if he's smart he doesn't bring God into every discussion of a bill. By the same token, his advice and suggestions were taken. Look, I wasn't going to tell them how to run their little society as long as it *ran*.

They'd gotten the gist that we were pulling out. And, of course, they'd been around for the earth shattering kabooms. The fight, fortunately, hadn't spilled their way but with no defenses and no chance of decent survival if we lost they couldn't have been real happy. And they weren't real happy we were leaving.

People were trying to kiss my hand. I hate that. But they apparently hadn't cared much for HAMB, either.

"We're pulling out. We have a way we can get home."

Hollywood duly translated.

Mullah: That sucks. (This, of course, took about ten minutes.)

Yeah. Well, things suck all over. We're not leaving you in the lurch. You've done good by these people and I hope things go okay for you when we leave. To help with that, we've left all the noncombatant stuff in the base intact. Food, water, a water plant and of course the defenses. Even some AK ammo for your boys.

You rock. (Another ten minutes.) Guy was crying. Yeah, I probably would have cried too.

They were figuring we were pulling out and destroying all the food and shit. I'm a farmer. Food is *my* religion. Well, and killing all enemies of the Constitution "foreign and domestic."

Bandit: Got a problem, Mullah. The girls. Our "temporary wives."

We'd explained to the girls what the plan was. Then we had to explain again, in more detail.

Look, most of the girls were from pretty reclusive families and they might have been taught their ABCs but that pretty much covered it. Girls only had to know three things in Islamic society: How to cook, how to clean and how to obey men. They mostly figured out having babies on their own.

The world had already gotten to be a very big and unpleasant place with the Plague. Trying to explain to them what was about to happen was hard. Think cheerleaders but with even *less* knowledge of the world. Not bright, ignorant and with a very short attention span.

When it was finally explained to them so that they understood, and I could see it sinking into their tiny little brains, I explained that it would probably be better for them to stay. We weren't sure we were getting through and if they got captured when we lost, it would be bad for them.

Problem being, it was going to be bad for them *anywhere*.

Islam was really strict about the whole "premarital sex" thing. The penalty for being raped, not for the *rapist* but for the *girl who was raped*, was *stoning*. Generally the family of the rapist paid a nominal fee and it was all good. Rape was, in fact, a way of exacting punishment on someone in (really backward) Islamic societies. Say a guy was caught stealing. Technically, the punishment was losing his hand. But say that he was the sort of lout who comes from a good family that's politically connected. Just one of those fuck-ups you get when power is in the wrong hands.

Say he has a sister. The penalty for *him* and for his *family* was often for the *sister* to be raped. Not because they cared about the sister as a human being, not because he loved his sister (they never did), but because it was dishonor to the *family*.

Then to purge the "dishonor" the *sister* would be stoned to death and everyone was happy.

I am totally not shitting you. There is some shit you just can't make up. We *saw* it, later. Another story I'll get to. The basis of "Stones."

Technically, if we left the girls behind they'd all be stoned to death. More likely, they'd end up as concubines doing scut work for the rest of their lives.

(Yes, they'd been concubines doing scut work for *us*. But *we* treated them with respect. The same would *not* be the case in most Islamic households. Mohammed the OCD also included precise instructions for how wives and daughters, any women, were to be "instructed" using a cane "no more than the width of a man's thumb." At the time and society, this was actually enlightened like a lot of Islamic law. Problem being, times had changed.)

I told them I'd do what I could to make sure they were better off than that. And this was me trying.

Mullah: This is a problem. I'll do what I can. (Ten minutes.)

Bandit: Yeah. I'm sure that will work. You're a good Islamic preacher, right?

Mullah: Yes. (Maybe three minutes.)

Bandit: Women can inherit under Islamic law, right?

Mullah: True. But a man must manage it.

Bandit, pulling out a bunch of paper: This is the printed out inventory of what's left in the camp as far as I can figure it. I, a male, am gifting to *them*, for their extraordinary service to the United States Army in times of peril above and beyond the call of duty, all the materials in the camp. Actually, I'm gifting it to their "temporary husbands" who in turn are willing to turn it over to *new* husbands. Each of them has some of the materials, basically broken up by areas and what I figured you guys would value. Guys who marry these girls, under all official Islamic law and the blessing of Allah the Beneficent and the Merciful, get the goods. As long as they remain their husbands. By the way, the prettiest one was my temporary wife under Shia law. And she got quite a bit of shit. More than the rest is all I'll say including all the ammo and the water supply. *How* many wives do you have?

Look, I said I didn't *like* Islamic law, never said I wasn't *good* at it.

We stuck around long enough for the weddings. All the girls decided they were staying. I had a talk with a couple of the grooms on the subject of how we really liked our former "wives" and that some day I *was* going to be back and they'd better be *just* as happy and smiling.

(By the way, they were never in any way officially or unofficially, Shia or American or Chinese law, our wives. I lied. He knew I was lying. He also saw it as an excellent out. Good guy, like I said.)

Did I miss Shadi?

Pussy like Shadi's is *very* nice. Do not get me wrong. But I like someone I can talk to. And even after Shadi got a few words of English, we really didn't communicate very well. I'd gotten her started on reading before we left but it was at C-A-T equals Cat and then explain what a Cat is.

(She also got me learning Farsi and Arabic. It's called a sleeping dictionary. Most military guys learn the local language that way. For that matter, it's how English came about. No shit. There are benefits to "fraternization" I don't think the brass ever consider.)

I'd done the best thing I could for her. I'd married her to the local strong man who also seemed to be a pretty decent and wise guy. Right age difference according to Islam, etc. We were going where angels feared to tread. Leaving her in the care of a good man was the best I could do for her. But I *was* going to miss her.

Pax Americana: Like a gnat in a blast furnace in the Mideast.

(Sort of. The mullah? *Thaaat* would be *Mullah Rousham Faravashi*. Yeah. *That* Mullah Rousham Faravashi, former Ambassador to the U.S. and current president of the Persian Union.

(You know his *really* hot oldest wife? The serious "Islamic women's libber" who goes around unveiled and is on all the talk shows? "Gorgeous eyes?" Also a former ambassador? But more importantly the current head of the PU Secret Service and touted as the *next* president?

(Shadi is going to fucking kill me. She's got *lots* of assassins on her payroll. I'm going to fucking die.)

(Wife Edit: So *that's* why we get that big box of almonds every year. I'm not eating any when *this* comes out. You can have them *all*.)

So we rolled.

I'm not going to do an Anabasis and give a blow by blow account of the whole trip. Basically, it sucked. Not quite as much as it sucked for the Ten Thousand, but it sucked.

Oh, hell. Okay. I'll do the whole fucking Anabasis . . . Even if most people have seen it in reruns.

We were starting off, by then, in late September of 2019. We left on September 25th.

Now, in late September in Minnesota, back then you could get some frosts.

Abadan is on the same latitude as Jacksonville, Florida. And for some pretty straightforward meteorological reasons, it has a hotter climate. *Way* hotter in the summer, rarely as cool in the winter.

The day we had the wedding it snowed. Let's just say that it didn't used to snow much in Jacksonville anytime and it hadn't snowed in Abadan in recent memory even in the dead of winter.

Snow in September.

Yep, classic Big Chill weather. We all know that. *Intellectually,* I knew that. Problem being, we were headed *north*.

So that's the climatological issue covered for the nonce.

Second "issue."

We didn't want to go over by Ahwaz. There were still probably remnants of the HAMB over that way. My plan was, as much as possible, to get through all areas with as little incident as I could manage. I knew that there *were* going to be incidents.

("Incidents." Hah-hah-hah-hah! This is me madly chuckling. "Incidents." Bwah.)

I took a look at a lot of maps and had traced out a route I figured was going to keep us away from the majority of problems. We weren't going near any big cities and were going to skirt towns as much as possible. Unfortunately, for some really simple terrain reasons, we were going to have to get closer to Baghdad than I liked. And because we were moving to the east of the Tigris, which was the wetter side, there were going to be a lot of water crossings. That was going to totally suck.

Might as well talk about equipment, which has to cover personnel as well.

We'd dumped the girls. So there were three groups under my command and control: The infantry company under Fillup, the Nepos, and the technicians under their NCOIC.

One thing I'd done, coldheartedly, was to figure out which were the most important to the mission of getting home and the order was: The technicians, the U.S. infantry, and the Nepos.

Why?

I only had a few technicians. (The satellite/internet/electronics geek from Fillup's company was now in that crowd.) We were rolling with a lot of wheeled and some tracked vehicles. Wheeled and tracked vehicles break. They need maintenance that goes beyond "filler up and check the oil." Commo breaks. Weapons break.

We were going to need to have most of this stuff most of the way through the mission. I *needed* those techs to keep it running. Lose one grunt or Nepo and I was out a shooter. I had lots of shooters. Lose one *tech* and I was probably fucked.

So the technicians were going to need careful handling and feeding. They were all, basically, Fobbits anyway. Oh, they could handle themselves in an ambush if they were firing from a vehicle but I wasn't going to be using them for any assaults even if they weren't as valuable as gold.

So the techs had to be protected.

Fortunately, there was a way to kill two birds with one stone.

Military equipment is very heavy. It's got lots of metal parts and then, of course, all that armor. With a few exceptions (and we weren't taking any Humvees at *all*) you can't tow it with your neighbor's car. You need big fucking metal to tow a Stryker very far.

Thus you have the armored vehicle recovery vehicle. (Heavy Equipment Recovery Combat Utilty Lift and Evacuation System: HERCULES.) Hercules looks sort of like a big fucking tank without a gun. And it's got more power than God. It can tow, I shit you now, *two* Abrams tanks at the same time. (The suckers weigh in at 73 TONS *apiece* to give you an idea what I mean by "more power than God.") It's not real fast, unfortunately, but it could keep up with us. We weren't going to be going fast.

There were over a dozen of them in the base. I'd pulled out four before rigging. We ended up taking two. Why two? Redundancy. More on that later.

Now, this was a big motherfucker. And it was designed to carry a "recovery team" of three guys. In other words, I could fit six techs in those.

Then there was another necessity. We were going to be crossing a lot of watercourses. Some of them we could ford. Some of them there were bridges strong enough to take even the recovery vehicles. Others we *were* going to have to bridge.

Big bridges were out of the question. They take, like, a fucking engineering battalion to put up. But the Army also has a cute little "fast bridging" armored system based on an Abrams chassis.

It was the only Abrams chassis we were taking. I do love those big motherfuckers, even if they are hard to destroy. But they just sucked so much gas and were so hard to move through certain areas I had to leave my last two. (And I didn't destroy them. I left them for the mullah. Seemed like the Christian thing to do. And they had ammo.)

Point was, it could span a thirty-foot watercourse. Crew of three. More techs. They could learn as they drove. Driving an Abrams is *not* hard.

So I had lots of heavy metal wrapped around my techs. It gave me warm fuzzies.

We took two of the big rolling command post/commo vans. They were Strykers with a big ass box on the back and could keep up satellite commo and local radio even on the move. Lots of electronics I rarely fiddled with. They were supposed to be for battalions and above. What the fuck, I was a reinforced company. Close enough. Later I got closer. I'll get to it.

Then there were the Strykers. We had enough for all the guys and most of the Nepos. We could have had them for all the rest of the Nepos but I had another use for them.

Now, Napoleon said "An army travels on its stomach." Since I wasn't planning on walking to the Bosporus, much less low-crawling, this army traveled on more than its stomach. All those vehicles took fuel. Lots of it. Military vehicles are graded in gallons per mile not the reverse. (Strykers are a bit better, but not much.) We were going to need a lot of fuel.

Since I wasn't planning on looting local villages for olives and shit (see Anabasis) we were going to need food. That was mostly going to be MREs and BritRats. The latter were for the Nepos. And they'd brought some of their own food that they might get a chance to cook.

We were going to need water, both for the vehicles from time to time and for our own consumption. Most of the vehicles were towing a trailer. Some of them were water buffalos. We also had a portable ROWPU we could figure out how to use. Had an onboard generator. Quit working? Why do you think I brought the techs?

We needed ammo. We might need lots of ammo. There's never such a thing as *too* much ammo. There's only too much ammo to carry.

Sideline: A lot of people over the years have dissed the M-16 series of weapons that we were still using in the form of the M-8. It wasn't all that different from the M-4, just a slightly longer barrel and it could be "modulated" for different weaponry and stuff you could hang on it. It fired a dinky little 5.56mm diameter round. That translates as .221 caliber, same as a .22, basically. Big diff.

The difference matters, though. Because it went very fast. And, honestly, with good shot placement was very lethal.

The Army had used .30-06 rounds in WWII. Those were big honking man-killers. Then they'd gone to the .308 which was still pretty hefty. It was what we used in our medium machine guns.

Why go to the 5.56?

Took up less room. More rounds for less weight.

Lots of arguments both ways, but when I was figuring cubic space to carry all this shit, I was glad I could pack 30% more 5.56 into the space the .308 took up. And it took up less than .30-06. And waaay less than .50 caliber. All of them took up less than mortar rounds.

Yes, we brought two mortar Strykers with us. Indirect fire is a good thing. I'd have taken more but I was getting pack-rattish and I knew it. It wasn't the vehicles, it was the *ammo*. And the fuel to *haul* the ammo.

Most of this shit was going to have to go on trucks. Several trucks. The trucks were going to be our most vulnerable targets. Therefore the Nepos drove the trucks. They were the least vital group.

Why were the Nepos our least vital group?

It wasn't because they weren't Americans. I'd grown to love the little bastards like they were my own boys back when *I* had B company. But they simply were not as important as the U.S. infantry. Why?

The Nepos were shaping up to be good irregulars. Given enough time and opportunity and some more trainers I probably could have gotten them up to the point they were just as good as the U.S. infantry guys.

But they weren't. They were good cooks, some were sort of mechanics and they were decent irregulars. They wouldn't run from a fight and they could sort of shoot. Quality on that was coming up and would come up more.

But they were semiskilled. The U.S. infantry were *highly skilled technicians* on the subject of war. Let me try to explain.

The Nepos could fire their individual weapons pretty well, clean and strip them and put them together. The ones that had been trained on machine guns could fire those machine guns, clean and strip and clear basic jams. They could slap a compress on somebody who had been shot.

The riflemen in the Stryker unit could: Fire their individual weapons, clean, strip, detail clean and in many cases do minor repairs. They could do the same on a pistol, squad automatic weapon (SAW), a medium machine gun or a heavy. Didn't matter if that was their primary job. The Javelin gunners could do the same and most of the guys could work a Javelin about as well as the gunners. They could do close quarters battle, movement to contact on foot or in vehicle, set up an ambush, react to an ambush, perform battlefield first responder actions up to and including inserting an IV and in many cases stitching a minor wound. They could lay in claymores and in many cases more advanced demolitions. They could call for fire from the mortars. They could land navigate using GPS and/or map. They could perform fire and maneuver. They were trained in night movement either in march or combat.

They could all work a radio.

The Nepos, mostly because we simply had not had the time to train them with everything else going on, couldn't do most of that. And most of them, still, didn't speak English. So whether they could work a radio or not was sort of moot.

I didn't want to lose the Nepos. But if it came down to losing them or the guys who were highly trained specialists at survival, I'd take the highly trained specialists over the semiskilled any day.

So the Nepos drove the vulnerable but incredibly important trucks.

The problem being, most of them didn't know how to drive a *car*.

Foreseeing this as an issue as time had passed, I'd taken some of their training time to ensure they could all drive military trucks.

Driving military trucks is *not* like driving a car. The ones we were using were HEMTTs (Heavy Extended Mobility Tactical Trucks.) Think a four-wheel drive tractor trailer. Bit smaller than a tractor trailer but not much. They are big, boxy trucks designed to go anywhere tanks or Strykers can go.

Teaching the Nepos to use them was . . . interesting. Among other things, the Nepos turned out to have a repressed size inferiority streak. Putting them in big-assed trucks with cabs six feet off the ground suddenly put *them* in charge of their destiny.

It's very hard to roll a Hemitt on flat ground. They managed it. Fortunately, they had very hard heads and we had *lots* of Hemitts. (It's how it's pronounced.)

They eventually got the picture and got over their tendency to race each other.

Strykers:

We had a lot of Strykers. We had more Strykers than we needed. Why? Since they all used fuel?

Look, I'm a big fan of the Stryker. But the things just *break* a lot. All military equipment breaks. It's a function of how it's used in part. (I won't get into deep conspiracies about companies that then get to provide parts.) And who uses it. Soldiers are specialists in breaking things, not keeping them going. And they're complicated compared to the average car.

But Strykers break a lot. They were, in fact, overengineered. They had way too many moving parts. Frankly, much as I liked Strykers I wished they'd have gone with something like the LAV. Not as complicated and broke less. "Keep it simple, stupid" is a military acronym that weapons designers and generals often forget.

I had lots of Strykers because I figured by the time we got to the Dardanelles at least half of them were going to be scattered on the road behind us. I was planning on fixing any that we could. Barring that, they were going to be left behind.

We had three types. The mortar carriers. These were the latest and greatest things and actually *were* pretty cool. They were 120mm automortars with automated tracking and guidance. That is, instead of manually moving them around, when you got a call for fire a computer figured all the corrections and they automatically fired. Assuming everything worked. If everything didn't work, there were manual overrides including a way to work them around by hand.

But if we got in the real busy, they might come in handy. Two of them, again. For one thing, the more mortars the better. For another, redundancy. I was hoping that those wouldn't be the Strykers that broke.

Then we had Assault Gun Systems. These had, originally, been the "Mobile Gun System" with this weird-assed 105mm "semi-recoiless" cannon. That had lasted, from what I heard, five years after deployment. Then they all got converted to "Assault Gun Systems." Difference? The well-tested 25mm Bushmaster from the Bradley replaced the 105. The 105 was supposed to be an "anti-tank" gun system. It couldn't stop most modern tanks straight on. Neither could a 25mm but it could from the *side*. Just like the 105. And it didn't break as much and you got more shots.

Besides, we had Javelins for tanks.

Most of them were "Infantry Carrier Vehicles." Just big rolling boxes filled with shooters and a commander's cupola with a .50 cal. Some of the commander's cupolas had Mk-19 40mm grenade launchers.

Oh, and six recon vehicles. Those were, basically, AGS with more ammo and less room for shooters. Also better commo including a satellite and meteoric bounce system if they got too far away for radio.

All the vehicles had "Block Five" Blue Force Trackers. That is, they would continuously tell me and Fillup where they were and more or less what their status was. There was an automated ammo counter we'd long before learned to distrust.

With all the vehicles, most of the team was driving Strykers at first. Or commanding them or gunning. I figured that would "consolidate" over time. And the Nepos were cross-training on Stryker driving.

I wasn't planning on stopping for much if I could avoid it. I figured that RIFs along the way, if they heard we were coming through, were likely to pile on just to take out an American unit. Not to mention the loot. Oh, speaking of which.

We had ten trucks, two supply, two food, three ammo and three fuel. One Nepo driver and an AD in each. AD manned the .50 caliber. In the case of the supply and food trucks we'd also mounted them up on the back with two more .50s in ring turrets and welded armor.

We did *not* have enough fuel to make it to the Bosporus. I was hoping for some Islamic charity along the way.

The basic plan was to stay off road as much as possible. The Strykers would stay in a ring around the trucks. Scouts out.

The Scouts were most of Third Platoon. Why Third? I drew

it out of a hat. They loved the fuck out of it. Third Herd usually has a touch more esprit than the other two platoons in any company. Why? Well, they're the only one with a cool name, I guess.

They each carried a crew of three and two "dismounts." The dismounts carried rifles and there were some Javs in the vehicle in case it got real busy. Javs were good against not only tanks but anything else that was big as previously proven.

Spare weapons for when one got totally fucked up, spare batteries, spare clothing, parts, tools . . . I created one list that had us with eighteen trucks. Wasn't going to happen. I winnowed it down. Forgot stuff we'd really need. Went back up.

It was the best list I could create is all I can say.

So we rolled. And then we stopped. Did I say something about watercourses?

Iraq, which we entered almost at once, is part of the Fertile Crescent. If you didn't get the Fertile Crescent in school I'm not going to be explaining. See there are these two rivers that run through it, the Euphrates on the west and the Tigris on the east.

We were running along the east bank of the Tigris. The Tigris is the big river in Iraq. It's not huge by American standards, not a patch on the Mississippi, but it's pretty big.

And my God is it farmed. It's been farmed since time immemorial. This is ancient Babylon, Sumeria, Ur, cradle of civilization, blah, blah . . .

So there are, like, four hundred and twenty-nine *billion* damned irrigation canals running off of it. *Especially* to the east.

We spent the first *week* working our way through that fucking maze. Setting up the temporary bridge was fairly quick. Taking it back up not so quick. And when you're looking across one irrigation ditch, which is *just* too deep and steep for your vehicles to negotiate, at another five hundred meters to the north, well, you tend to see if there's a bridge you can use. Only problem being, most of the damned bridges were designed for farm trucks. So the answer, especially in the case of the HERCULES was: No.

Bridge. Roll. Stop. Bridge. Roll. Stop. Bridge.

It was during this period that we developed the habit, that we kept even during minor skirmishes, of "afternoon coffee."

Yeah, we had coffee. I know there are people who lived through the times that are gritting their teeth. We drew on a big fucking LOG base and I made sure we carried plenty of coffee. An Army runs on coffee. We had coffee.

Specifically we had it every afternoon at 1630. (That's 4:30PM for all you non-mil types.) And we did it right.

All the officers had somehow ended up with Nepo "orderlies." I swear to God it was never ordered. I think Samad did it. But we all had "orderlies" whether we wanted it or not.

Things had gotten pretty weird, obviously. Back in the LOG base we'd had our "temporary wives" and, well, we were stuck in the fucking Middle East with no clear route home. Things had gotten weird.

I remember the day I decided it was a good time to do "coffee." We were rolling out on the second day and I wanted to sort of "brainstorm" what some of our potential threats and weaknesses might be. How to do it? With Samad? He hadn't a real clue. He was coming along in the "anticipate and intelligently expand orders" area, but he wasn't really any sort of military expert. Surprising inputs from time to time ...

So I decided to do an "officers' call" and "council of war." Those were the technical American Army terms for it. We did "coffee." I called for all officers to come to the commo van at 1630 to "talk shop." Told Samad he was included and suggested we might have some coffee and maybe some MRE crackers or something.

Should have known better than to get Samad involved. Remember, he was trained by the fucking Brits. And he'd participated in packing the supply truck.

So at 1600 my orderly comes into the commo van carrying a fresh uniform. We hadn't stopped. He just opens up the back and pops through, fresh ACU over his arm.

(Despite my repeated discussions of "safety" the Nepos considered the exterior of moving Strykers, at almost any speed, to be quite convenient ways to get around. I swear they were half monkey. But I digress.)

Sahib will be pleased to change before his conference?

Huh? How the fuck did you get here? Why would I change? Sure, I've had the uniform on for a couple of days but, hell, it's good for ...

Sahib *will* be pleased to change before his conference.

So I changed.

1615 the orderly opens up the door to the commo van. A thing drops down.

Ever moved yourself with a U-Haul? They've got this sort of ramp thing that you extend and stuff.

Call it a gangplank in this case.

The vehicles have all slowed as if for a LOG, which wasn't scheduled.

There is now this gangplank sort of thing hanging off the back of the commo van. Fillup, in a fresh uniform, looking a little confused, walks down. It's got a railing. It's riding on the front slope of his Stryker. All he had to do was crawl out the TC hatch, grab on and walk down. Simple. Scary, bad safety, but in a way *very* fucking cool.

One of the Nepos who had sort of taken the position of senior sergeant is standing by the door, on the outside, holding on.

"Bravo Company . . . arriving!"

One by one, all the officers show up. In fresh uniforms. *In order of seniority.*

"Number Two (XO) . . . arriving." "Weapons (mortar platoon leader) . . . arriving." "Scouts . . . arriving." "Second Platoon . . . arriving." "First Platoon . . . arriving." "Auxiliary Force . . . arriving." (That would be Samad.)

From somewhere, a silver tea service has been obtained. (See, honey, *I* didn't grab it!) Coffee is served by the orderlies. There are little baked things. There are finger crackers. There are linen napkins and a tablecloth. (Laid over the map table. It is, by the way, a very *crowded* commo vehicle at this point.)

Sure, all that stuff had been in the LOG inventory. *I* hadn't brought it.

I think Samad had just been pining for some good old Brit pomp and circumstance.

And here it was.

But we also had a good conversation. The . . . formality of the thing caught us by surprise at first. But after we got over that, it worked out well. There was a point to the way that the Brits did some things. When "it's just you" surrounded by howling savages, remembering you're a civilized being is sometimes a good thing. Yeah, they could take it overboard but . . . Remembering you're civilized is a *good* thing. Take it from this borderline barbarian.

So that's the story of "afternoon coffee." Just in case you were wondering. And, yeah, we once had it while a murthering great battle was raging but there wasn't much we could do about it at that point so we had "coffee."

Back to the run.

The good news was, there were no major threats. I sweated blood at first figuring we were going to get hit by RIFs from every side. Shouldn't have bothered. The area was more agricultural than the Midwest. And while it was more densely populated, it was spread out.

See, they didn't do the whole "industrial farming" thing with giant combines. That area, you were lucky to have a tractor. Bunch of it was done by ox plow. Good in one way; they had less to fall from the Plague and shit. But not particularly efficient. See "Organic."

So you'd have a farmhouse surrounded by a few trees and some fields. Farming less than a hundred acres cause that's about what you can do with oxen and shit. Then another down the road not too far.

And the area had been hit hard by the Plague. No medical facilities to speak of, not many cities and few towns. Just fucking farms and irrigation ditches.

Most of the farms were fallow and I could tell the irrigation system was breaking down. Places where the water had spread out over fields and was still there. Places where ditches were dry.

We didn't see many people. There must have been a shitload before the Plague but I figure they took at least 80% casualties between the Plague and secondaries.

Up side was that there was probably enough food stored.

But harvests had gotten fucked up by the Plague and the weather. That area normally had at least two harvests a year, three if you did it right. Most of the wheat, millet, peas and what-not was still standing. Most of it was all fucked up for that matter.

There were some fields active. I taught the Scouts to recognize those and we avoided them as much as possible. These people were going to need the food. We could go through the fallow fields.

Not that they were probably going to be allowed to keep it. Places like this never did. Somebody more powerful came along and took it away to feed an army.

We ran into that around Al Amarah. Actually, near a village called Al Halfayah. Group of thugs in a truck rounding up food from one of the functioning farms.

I wasn't going to get into it. Pax Americana. See also: Gnat/ blast furnace.

Problem was, one of the thugs spotted our Scout vehicle and took it under fire with an RPG.

Which was really *really* stupid. The max range on an RPG is about 300 meters against a moving target, which the Scout was. And they were almost a klick back.

The 25mm, especially with stabilization systems, has a max effective range of *2000* meters.

So they lit up the thugs' truck.

We carefully maneuvered around the farm but I sent the gun Stryker with Hollywood on it over to parley and gain intel.

The "tax collectors" had been from a group called the Al Sulemani Warriors' Brigade. They were the big local group based in and around Al Amarah. The farmer didn't know much about them except that they were taking his food and telling him he was now under their rule.

There was a lot of that as we headed north. Every little city had its rulers and was, in effect, a city-state. Al this and Ibn that and... They sort of blended.

Mostly we tried to avoid them. When it did come down to getting busy, it was usually against a small detachment like the "tax collectors" that got stupid. Sometimes we saw guys who were less stupid who just let us pass through.

More or less stayed the same until we got up around Baghdad. At which point three things happened in pretty rapid succession, Bad, Good, Really bad. (Or at least I thought so at the time.)

I'll take the "good" first since it leads to the "bad" and the "really bad" is pretty unconnected.

The good was that we finally got ahold of the Kurds.

I've spoken about the Kurds a little but I figure I'll add some detail.

The Kurds are a mountain people found in the mountainous triangle of what used to be Iraq, Turkey and Iran and is now Kurdistan good and proper.

They're pretty much descended from the Hurrians (look it up) and have been in those mountains for fucking ever. Like the Nepos there's some basic similarities between all Kurds:

They're generally fairly tall for the region, not giants just a bit above average.

They're very straightforward compared to anybody else in the whole fucking area, even to an extent the Greeks. You don't spend ten minutes exchanging polite inquiries about their family with the Kurds; you get to the point.

They love Americans despite the fact that we've regularly fucked them over. (Ditto British.)

They treat their women just about as badly as any other group in the Middle East. Perhaps a touch worse. By the same token, they're pretty okay with women in positions of soft power like doctors.

They are hard-core, in-your-face, one-of-us-is-going-to-get-fucked-up-and-it's-*you* fighters.

Since back in the Bronze age they've gone through periods of conquering the lowlands around them, getting pushed back by a big "settled" empire, raiding said empire until it takes them over, fighting against the conquerors until nearly wiped out, becoming the best fucking fighters the empire has after it tacitly lets them run things in their own area, waiting until the empire falls and repeat.

Suleiman, one of the most famous warriors of Islam and the guy who kicked the fuck out of one Richard the Lion Hearted? Kurd.

That's the Kurds in a nutshell.

So we finally got ahold of the Kurds when we were southeast of Baghdad and trying to screen past.

To our east were the Zagros Mountains. As a foretaste of what was to come they were covered in fucking snow about two thirds of the way down. They also had a bunch of bad-boy Iranians in them and we'd picked up indicators of some organization, a couple more city-state groups, around Ilam and Khorambad. They were reputed to be remnant Revolutionary Guard back in command and had some fair forces. We did not want to tangle with them in mountains. Especially mountains covered in snow.

So we were keeping to the lowlands, hoping to slip through between Baghdad and the mountains and avoid major conflict.

My initial goal was the Kurdish region. Why besides the above?

During the latter reign of Saddam Hussein the U.S. had established a "no-fly" zone over the northern part of Iraq. (And the south but it was different there.) They also sent in SF teams to work with the Kurds.

With no more than "keep the helos and planes off of us" and some spare equipment the Kurds kicked the shit out of everything Saddam sent at them on the ground and established their own local democracy. Saddam purely *hated* the Kurds; he'd used poison gas on them in his time. He wanted to be one of the guys that conquered them. Good luck, the Kurdish Perg Mersha were not going to be beaten by a bunch of lowland driven wheat-farmers.

But they really appreciated the help, little as it was. And when we went in and hung Saddam, the "Kurdish Provinces" were the only areas we didn't get fucked in.

There were, basically, four cities in the "Kurdish Provinces." Two of them were pure Kurdish; the other two had been "disputed."

The pure Kurdish were As Sulymaniyah—and, yeah, that's "Suleiman"—and Kirkuk. The two "disputed" were Mosul and Irbil.

See, Mosul and Irbil, pre-Saddam and during the first part of his reign, had been pretty mixed cities. They were about 70% Kurdish with the rest being Assyrian Christians, Turkics and a smattering of Islamic Arabs. More or less in that order.

There was just one problem. Oil was discovered in the Mosul Province. And a refinery got built. And what with ongoing resistance from the Kurds, Saddam couldn't trust them around oil.

So he purged a lot of the Kurds (and Assyrian Christians and such) out of Mosul and Irbil and settled "safe" Sunni Arabs in the area.

(See above about the history of the Kurds.)

When the U.S. came in, the Kurds got a partial benny on resettlement. A lot of the Sunnis hadn't wanted to be up there, anyway. As they left the Kurds moved back in.

But a lot of the Sunnis, who made up the most hardcore faction of the Resistance, fought back. So Mosul and Irbil remained war zones until the Sunni were more or less wiped or driven out. (The reason the Iraq campaign really started winding down.)

Even before then, the Kurds had established a "no travel" zone in their core areas including Kirkuk and Sulamaniyah. That is, they'd take in anybody but an Islamic Arab. Turkic? Come on in. Assyrian Christian? Love you guys. Fucking Sunni or Shia Arab from down on the south plains? Fuck off.

Which is why when U.S. units crossed the borders into what *everybody* called Kurdistan, you could take off your body armor and relax. You could walk around in a market with no more bother than kids pestering you for treats. People fucking *handed* you stuff like fruit. They *loved* American troops.

But the battles around Mosul and Irbil never really stopped. The Sunnis always got weapons, money and people funneled into Iraq right up to the time of the Plague. See, Saddam had been a Sunni. Most of the surrounding countries, especially Syria, Jordan and Saudi, were either controlled by or predominately Sunni countries. They did *not* want the Shia in control in Iraq. That would create the possibility of a Shia Union with Iran.

(Which is more or less what the Persian Union is, except it's secular. Well, as much as the U.S. is.)

And the Sunni didn't just try to take back their "core" areas around Baghdad (what used to be called the Sunni Triangle and through which we were about to pass) they wanted the fucking oil around Mosul and Irbil.

So we get to the good and the bad.

We'd kept in contact with the Kurds. They'd gotten hit, hard, by the Plague. Not as hard as some areas, though. One; we'd made sure they had vaccine through the military. Two: they distributed it pretty effectively. (More in their core areas than around Mosul and such, obviously.) Three: They had, as a culture, high-trust and a huge degree of cohesion.

So they'd lost a lot of people. And they had then reacted, adapted and overcome. Bury the dead, sow and reap.

Oh, things weren't great. But they were hanging in there.

Which, when I found the right guy at the Pentagon to tell me that and give me some phone numbers, was great news. I was going to need a fill-up and *some* friendly faces would be nice to see. They had fuel and friendly faces, just like Sunoco or whatever.

Which brings us to the bad.

Unlike Iran, which was not yet up to the level of "pacified" whatever policy maker thought was good enough, Iraq was not considered a "threat country." They were an "associated country" with "good relations" with the U.S. Not quite an ally, but on the way.

(I would have begged to differ, but we're talking about policy makers. State was involved.)

So they could be left with all the gear we were leaving behind under the assumption it would be put to good works.

Now, having just described what great fucking people the Kurds are, where do you think we parked all that fucking equipment?

The Shia were marginal allies of the U.S. They hated the Sunni and Saddam and we'd kicked Saddam out and given them a chance to get out from under five hundred fucking *years* of domination by a Sunni minority. They were, of course, like any fucking Arab or Persian in that you couldn't trust them as far as you could throw the Great Pyramid. And they had lots of guys who wanted to team up with the Mad Mullahs and kick our ass. But, overall, they were nominally on our side.

The Kurds were just our fucking right damned arm. They thought we rocked, most of the guys who worked with them thought *they* rocked. They could be trusted like the armor on an Abrams.

The main problem, beginning, middle and right up to the end in Iraq, were the fucking Sunnis. Whether the RIFs that trickled in from other Sunni countries around the world with the intent of blowing up an American for Allah or the Ba'athist party thugs who wanted back into power so they could go back to dominating the Shia like a good Sunni should. They were the motherfuckers we were constantly fighting.

And they were concentrated, to the very end, around Baghdad, up to Tikrit and over to the Syrian border.

So where did we park our equipment?

That's right, right in the middle of the fucking Sunni Triangle.

What. The. Fuck?

We get back to the tofu-eaters. Sort of. Actually we get back to State.

State had a long-term suck affair with the Sunni.

Part of that was just numbers. There were way more Sunni countries than Shia. The only major Shia country, Iran, we didn't have diplomatic relations with until we invaded. (If you can call that diplomatic. Most did not.) So there were just more slots for State pussies to suck Sunni dictator dick than Shia dictator dick. So they learned to suck Sunni dick. They "spoke the language" in diplo-speak. "Would you like it slow or hard?" in Arabic appropriate to the local grammar and norms.

The other part was, frankly, money. Filthy lucre. Graft.

The Sunni countries, many of them, had shitloads of oil money. And they tended to throw it around. The UAE, a tropical desert country, built a giant fucking tube of steel to use as a snow skiing slope. I shit you not. Huge motherfucker.

They gifted "chairs" at prestigious universities. They funded think tanks.

Eventually, every government service worker, including soldiers, wants to get out and do something else. For some of us it's buying or returning to the farm. For others it's getting a good academic position or a think-tank position or a spokesperson's position or a lobbyist's or ... You get the picture.

Pre-Plague the average salary for an ambassador to a "top-flight" nation was $175,000, most of it untaxable, and quite a few perks. Nothing to sneeze at.

A retiring ambassador to Saudi Arabia left government service and was hired into a "think-tank" that "considered Middle Eastern relations with the Western World" for *two million* and change.

Guess where the money came from? Bunch of small scale middle-class American contributors?

Don't think so. Whole think-tank, all American citizens and mostly former State employees, was funded by the Saudi Arabian government. The former ambassador had been handed his watch by the U.S. government and a Rolex factory by the Saudis.

So where do you think his *real* interests lay? Including while he was ambassador.

Oh, of *course* it was *never* money! Heaven forbid. The Sunni were our closest allies in the region. Sure, just ask the *Sunni* guys flying the planes into the World Trade Center. Most of them Saudi citizens because a *Saudi* citizen could get a visa, from *State*, *without any review whatsoever.*

State considered Shia to be unwashed monkeys. What they thought of the Kurds, those violent inbred rednecks of the Zagros and Tauric mountains, you don't want to know.

(The Shia, by the way, were mostly Persian or Persian oriented, even the Arab ones. They'd had a burgeoning civilization when the ancestors of the Sunni were still trying to learn how to herd goats and our ancestors in Europe weren't even doing *that*. Which was why the Shia, and especially the Iranians, called them goat-herds. Or, more often, goat fuckers. And the Iranians didn't think much of us, either. Discussed that.)

So, and yes it was under "advisement" of the State Department, the DOD was told to park all its shit under guard of the guys we'd been fighting for damned near twenty years and fly home.

Did the Sunni bastards grab all our gear? No, but they grabbed enough before the Plague hit to start a decent little, and entirely unreported, civil war to retake the Sunni Triangle. Then the

Plague hit. They got hit at about 60% rate. Things fell apart but they fell apart for everybody.

The Sunni, though, had managed to spring back. Now, there was another park of gear down in the south, very dominated by Shia, area. The Sunni had more and better tanks. But the Shia were still more numerous and even if they were a bunch of groups, the Sunni weren't entirely cohesive.

There was an uneasy truce between the Sunni and Shia. Problem being, while central Iraq had all the government buildings and monuments and museums and even some factories, it had *dick all* for oil. And eventually the tanks had to be filled on those tanks.

But the *Kurds* had oil.

And the Kurds didn't have tanks. Or even much in the way of APCs. We hadn't left them much at all, in fact. Just some ammo dumps with light to medium weapons.

Think that the Sunnis, once they got reconsolidated over the summer, immediately kicked the Kurds out of Mosul and Irbil and took over the oil fields?

Think again, brother. They were up against *Kurds*. Who at least had *some* shit to fight with this time.

Did I find this all out at once? Nope. But I found out a bunch of it pretty fast.

I finally got the phone number, sat phone, for one of the big Perg Mersha commanders.

Oh, the Perg Mersha. It means "fighters to the death" or some such and was sort of a National Guard. More like the original U.S. and Swiss militia. The guys were farmers or factory workers or whatever. Every now and again, on a rota, they'd get called up and either train in peace or raid in war. Every male Kurd had a weapon of some sort ranging from a rifle to heavy machine guns. They'd come in with their weapons and some ammo, get more ammo then gather under a tribal boss soldier and go fight like fucking demons.

Don't get me wrong. They were *not* shock infantry. Shock infantry goes back to the Greeks again and their hoplites. Every other fighter in the world, back then, were essentially "raid" infantry or cavalry or whatever. They'd charge and poke then run away. Charge, poke, run away. Do that until one side backs up from too many (low) casualties.

It's very conservative of losses. Also a good way to lose a battle if you're up against the alternative.

The alternative is "we're going to keep rolling forward until you're either dust or we are."

Think the difference between soccer and American football. One of them is all about swift moves and GOOOOOOAAALLL! The other is about slamming bodies together until you've forced the ball up the field. Oh, maybe a bit of throwing and such. But without the slamming bodies, the quarterback's toast.

Think of Three Hundred Spartans facing two hundred thousand Persians and allies. And kicking their ass. Marathon: Ten thousand Greeks (Athenians mostly) vs. about two hundred grand, again, this time on a flat fucking plain. And they smashed the Persians.

Put the Kurds on the plains against us or even the Iraqis, who sort of had the concept of shock infantry, and they were going to have a hard time. But the shock infantry people were never going to have a bit of rest. And in any sort of terrain, including urban areas, raid can counteract shock if shock's not done right. (Which *nobody* did except us in those days.)

So I called this Perg Mersha commander.

Bandit: O Great One, commander of the faithful, a descendent of Suleiman . . . (Three minutes.)

Kurd: American! Dude! Amigo! Great to see you! (Pretty much that.)

Bandit: Sorry, man. I've been dealing with fucking Iranians for *so* fucking long . . .

Kurd: American! Dude! Amigo! No problemo!

Bandit: Uno problemo. Need a fill up. Willing to trade some gear and shit.

Kurd: Dude. Bummer. Got a problem.

They didn't hold the oil refinery. Or the tank farms. Or any significant stock. And to get to them I'd have to hit the Iranian Sunni force anyway. Maybe they could sneak us up through the mountains. But then we'd be bingo on fuel.

Mother*fucker.*

This was getting to be *too* much like the Ten Thousand.

(By the way. If you ever read the Anabasis or one of the really good historical fiction accounts, the guys who *really* fucked up the Greeks in the mountains? Kurds.)

Okay, well if that was how it *had* to be.

They don't call us Strykers for nothing.

CHAPTER ELEVEN

He Turned White. Well, Whiter.

So here I switch right into a battle chapter, right? Good patterning. Build up and then fighting.

Dude, life is *never* that simple.

I don't know how they found me. They never told me and the investigation has never concluded who gave them the data.

Look, I was up on commo with the States. We were using BFTs. Everybody in the Pentagon and various other places with the right clearance could tell where we were and our more or less status as well as I could when I was in the van.

One of these days I'm going to find the guy with the "right clearance" and feed him his ass. And other parts. Slowly. Without mustard.

We're in consultation with the Kurds. We're going to heightened alert with what they've told us. They don't have much intel on the threat in our area but we're getting some.

We're sweating bullets. Somewhere up ahead is an armored force that's guessed by the Kurds to be about a division in strength. I didn't buy it. The one thing about the Kurds is that they *always* overestimate. But say a battalion. Even a brigade.

It's way more complicated than this, but this is military structure 101. Three platoons in a company. (You'll already notice ours has four including mortar platoon. And then there's the techs and Nepos . . . Like I said, this is *101*.) Three platoons in a company. Three companies in a battalion. Three battalions in a brigade. Three brigades in a division.

More complicated but you get the idea.

Basically, if we're looking at anything like a normal battalion, we're outnumbered and outgunned three to one. And they've got *our* Abrams tanks, which are a bitch and a half to kill. Not to mention Strykers and Bradleys. Those were all confirmed as well as we could confirm it.

If they've got a brigade, we're outnumbered nine to one. And way outgunned. Then there's artillery which is going to way out-range our mortars. Their mortars.

There were also aircraft. Fighters dropping dumb bombs and some helicopters including a couple of Apache gunships. Those, right there, could rip Strykers a new one without breaking a sweat. The trucks? Toast.

We are on a heightened state of alert.

We've moved to constant movement for the time being. I want to get past Baghdad as fast as possible. The main force seemed to be to the north but the fucking Baghdad area is never good.

So we're moving by day. And I get word that there's a visual contact on a plane. Whoa.

Context for the young people: Back before the Plague there were always planes in the sky. Fucking always. One of the weirdest things about the few days post-9/11 was the lack of planes. And when they started coming back we all cringed. Compared to the Plague, 9/11 was a kiss on the cheek. But it was all we had as comparison back then.

They're coming back, but still not up to the level they were in 2018.

Since the Plague, if we saw something in the sky it had been a bird. I'd never even launched our UAVs. (Hadn't had to. The Scouts had them at the moment and we still hadn't used them.)

Zero planes. Nada.

So when we got reports of a plane, we went on *really* high alert.

Okay. The LOG had had a lot of shit in it. Among other things, it had had Stinger missiles. Not sure why. The only air threat around was the U.S. Air Force. And while having been under blue-on-blue fire once I could see some benefit to blowing up an Air Force plane, they frown on that sort of thing.

But the fucker had had swaggersticks. What can I say? Maybe the guy running it was from Minnesota.

Point being, we had Stingers. We didn't have any qualified

Stinger guys, but we had Stingers. And it wasn't as if my guys couldn't read the manual. And a Stinger is very easy to use.

So we might be able to take out a fighter if it got low enough for a good bomb drop. Probably wouldn't, but then we'd just take our chances.

Problem being, the guys said this was a big one. A transport.

This I had to see.

That was tough.

The commo van didn't have a good way to see out except the commander's cupola. So I pulled the commander out, over his protests, and climbed up in his seat.

Binos. Old fashioned optics.

It was a plane. A big transport. And it was just sort of lazing around up there.

Suddenly it turned and passed south down our west side near Baghdad. Banked around and headed back.

The edges of the Baghdad suburbs were in view to the west. Barely. We were staying as low as we could given the terrain. But while there was some terrain it was mostly pretty flat. There was a bit of haze and I hoped that would let us get past unnoticed.

But this transport had apparently noticed us. I thought, maybe, possibly, could it be a supply drop? Nobody had called ahead. Didn't seem likely.

I had to climb up on top of the vehicle, not a good exercise normally, to see over the box on the back. There were grab handles, thank God. It was lining up behind us. It was a transport but transports can drop bombs. Didn't seem likely, but I was starting to get a puckering feeling. It *definitely* seemed to be looking for somebody like us.

Passed overhead at about two thousand feet over ground level. Flaps down, going *slow*. Russian Antonov. What the *fuck*?

We're still on that flat fucking plain. Still farms and occasional irrigation canals. More widespread on the latter, bigger on the former. More "industrial." Sunni Triangle. Saddam made sure the *good* farmers got the good *equipment*.

So we're bounding over this field at about thirty miles an hour and I'm trying to get back in the commander's hatch when the bird starts dropping shit. Not bombs. First there's a set of personnel parachutes. Standard static-line drop, the easiest kind in the world. Then a bunch of parachute bundles.

Are we getting reinforced?

I get back into the commo van and everybody is "what the fuck"ing. So I spread the word we don't know what it is and the scouts are to check out the drop. And I go "what the fuck?" and get on the horn to Brigade.

Brigade knows fucking diddly. No, no transport drops. No transport planes that they know of outside U.S. states and posessions. Most grounded. Cannibalization. Bad here.

Scouts come back while I'm on the phone with Brigade.

"Sir . . . No threat. Need you up here."

It's *reporters.*

Flying assholes from the sky.

They're scattered across a field but the scouts have helpfully gathered them up and gotten all their bundles for them. It's a team of *six.* One of them I vaguely recognize.

"Graham Trent, Skynews. Bandit Six, I presume."

(Look, it was *his* reference, not mine.)

Most people have probably heard the story. It's still in reruns. If you haven't, here goes.

Skynews (I tend to call it SkyNet. Kids, get your parents or grandparents to explain the reference) along with Fox and a bunch of other "media" holdings were owned by this guy named Rupert Murdoch.

Fairly conservative, for a Brit, and a bit of a character. He'd used the character, and a fucking ruthless business sense, to build up a pretty fair business empire.

Skynews was a British satellite news service. The Brits, then and now, had the BBC, the Beeb, which was paid for by the government. (From taxes on TVs. If you had a TV, you paid a yearly tax to watch it, I shit you not. And it went to the Beeb.)

Going up against a government monopoly was hard. But Murdoch knew there was money in giving people something other than the relentless propaganda of the Beeb. Oh, the Beeb occasionally had "alternative view" programming, but not in its news. It's news was pure liberal tofu-eater, rainbow this and global warming that.

So he founded Skynews. And it had made a fair amount of brass. (Brit for change. Got brass in pocket. Money.) That was, up to the Plague when shit was falling everywhere.

The Brits, despite being overall much more socialist than the U.S., had not been seizing businesses left and right. But they also weren't propping them up. And they especially weren't propping up Murdoch. He was barely holding on. He knew that he needed a gimmick to get some viewers. Preferably something he could sell to other networks that still had money.

(Oh, the U.S. "networks," NBC, CBS and ABC, were all being supported by "government emergency support spending." Fox, which was owned by Murdoch, was not. CNN somehow, though, had gotten in on the money. Politics? Nah.)

He needed a show that people were going to watch.

What was the biggest news story in terms of viewership in the U.S. and Britain?

You guessed it.

(The U.S. for reasons previously described. The British because they had a thing for the Nepos as well and, having a bit better history program in school, the whole "Ten Thousand" thing had caught on.)

So he, and it was Murdoch, got a brilliant idea. Send out a news crew to embed with us. It was going to take cash he didn't have, but if it worked it was going to be big news. His stocks, where stock markets were still trading, would go up. He would get more viewers. Might sell subsidiary rights.

He was putting most of his remaining wad on a roulette square marked Bandit Six. Yeah, some days I still dream about walking up to him and whispering "Residuals."

I got this, more or less, from Graham Trent when I pulled him over to the side to get a brief conversation away from the troops. By then the rest of the unit had caught up. Scouts were out forward, the unit had spread automatically. The Nepos were grinning in their turrets. No immediate threats.

There was some sort of building. A pumping station, something, by one of the irrigation canals we were going to have to cross. I could get out of sight for the conversation by pulling him around to the side. Unfortunately, that left us nearly at the waterline.

He laid this all out for me grinning ear to ear. What a lark! Wasn't this grand! Russian bird. Flew in from Greece. Good luck we found you, eh? Make you famous.

I'd asked what was going on and since then just nodded. Calmly. He was pumped up. Turned out they hadn't practiced the jump at all. First time out of a bird. Flying on that adrenaline high. I'll give him credit for brass ones.

I grabbed him by the front of his fucking safari jacket, down to the water, into the canal and then pressed his face under the water. Looking up. I wanted to *watch*.

I kept him there, despite his struggles, until I could tell he was about to pass out. Then, against my better judgement, I let the fucking idiot have air.

What? What? What's all this, then?

"Listen, you little pissant," I said, slamming him up against the wall of the concrete building. I don't even recall carrying him up the pretty steep and slippery slope. And he was not a small guy. Didn't matter. "Let me tell you what you and your fucking boss have done. You have just probably killed us. All of us. Including you. I figured we had about a *one in seventy* shot of making it to the fucking Dardanelles. We're looking at having to take on *three to ten times* our numbers in firepower to have *any* shot. You've just added six fucking useless mouths to my force. Six seats I have to find room for. Six slots to load gear into. *And* you're going to want to give fucking 'regular reports' since you're in the news business and every last fucking RIF with a damned satellite dish and power is going to know we're coming and more or less where and when. Last but *most assuredly not least*, you just did a fucking drop *in full view of Baghdad* which I was *sincerely* hoping to slip by *unnoticed*. My first thought is to just kill all of you. Nobody would ever *know*. Overrun by RIFs before we got to them. Poor brave reporter bastards. Never stood a chance. Are you *listening*? Do you *clearly understand my dilemma*? That dilemma being whether to push in with my forearm and crack your hyoid to leave you to choke in your own blood, walk around the corner and say 'Kill them. Kill them all.'? Because my boys won't bat an eye and they will never, ever talk."

He'd gone white. Whiter. He'd gone white when he realized I was drowning him and not just kidding around.

"We hadn't realized it was that bad . . . I'm sorry. Sorry."

He wasn't pleading to live. He clearly understood what I'd said and realized how badly he had screwed us.

I doubt I could have killed him if that *hadn't* been his reaction. But I was sorely *sorely* tempted.

"You're working for me, now. Not Murdoch. You will send *what* I say and *when* I say. You will explain to your crew, who I hope all include smart people, just what a fucked up situation they have dropped into."

"You've got it."

"It's going to be censorship."

"If it keeps us, *all* of us, your Yanks, the Nepos, my crew, alive, I can work with that."

"You fell in the stream. We laughed about it."

"Got it."

The fucked up thing was that I knew what I was going to do before I'd ever pushed him underwater. I knew in a *moment* while he was talking. Oh, not the details but the outline and it never was much more than an outline.

I hadn't pushed him under because I was negotiating. I really had had as my first plan killing them. Nobody would ever know.

But I went with Plan B.

Rupert Murdoch wanted news to prop up his flagging networks?

We'd give him the same kind of news the MSM had been sending for years: We'd be sending entertainment.

The only thing was, I was hoping to send much *much* more.

Get news back to what it was *supposed* to be.

If we survived.

We rolled out. Fast.

Didn't matter. We got hit, anyway.

I had the Scouts echelon to the west towards Baghdad. I figured if there was going to be a threat, it would be from that direction.

Sure enough, they spotted a line of trucks, couple of military grade and more pickups, some of them "technicals" rolling down the highway to cut us off.

When the trucks, in turn, spotted the Strykers some of them pulled off the road. Guys started bailing out. The technicals opened up and started weaving across the field.

Our guys started backing up. There were two Strykers moving by fire and maneuver. One would fire up the convoy moving slow while the other backed up fast, also firing but not as accurately. There was a line of trees they were headed for to get behind.

A bunch of the RIFs had dived into an irrigation ditch. Some of the technicals were smoked.

One of the Scout Strykers blew up. Just blew the fuck up. No clue why.

The other one backed up faster and started maneuvering. They didn't see anybody bail out of the other, which was billowing smoke.

I could see the smoke from the commo van. It had external viewers even if they were lousy for spotting planes. I told Fillup to maneuver his unit and find out what had killed them. There was a marker for the enemy unit where the scouts said it was. Pretty much a klick from where they first engaged, klick and a half to where the Stryker was hit.

Second Stryker maneuvered into the trees. One of *them* blew up but the Stryker lived.

They had Javelins.

Only two, thank God, but that's what we found when we rolled over their position. One sight and two expended launchers. For one of our vehicles.

DOD, on orders from the Secretary of Defense under consultation with State, gave the whole damned LOG base in Iraq to the fucking Sunnis. Including the Javelins.

We checked out the Stryker. It was toast. They don't have much in the way of internal blast control. The Javelin had hit just behind the commander's cupola and just blew the Stryker up like a child's toy. You could see the little-ass hole where it hit. Little hole, big boom.

We pulled every last body out and into body bags. They went on the supply truck.

I thought about Javelins as we rolled. That and the reporters. At one of the "rest" stops I tossed everybody but Graham out of the commo van and we "talked."

I said "rest" stops because we never really rested through those few days. It went like this. The Strykers had to fuel. Drivers got tired and logy and that led to accidents. Etc.

The guys could sort of rest riding in the Strykers. Not well, but it was "military rest." Like "military law" and "military music." You could close your eyes. If you were very experienced you could sleep the sleep of the just. Generally you sort of floated in a white daze that sort of helped.

Most of the infantry could come out of it fighting as fast as if they'd been awake.

But the drivers had to work, constantly. You had to rotate them. The AFV and the truck and the rest.

We'd gotten it down to an art. I'd order a rest stop at a certain point followed by "Logging." That's what it's called. As in "Logistics resupply."

We'd stop. Drivers would switch. New driver would hop in the seat, old driver would grab a spot and we'd roll on. Took about ten seconds. Think "Chinese Fire Drill."

Then we'd roll *slowly*. We had four trucks lined up. Food truck, ammo truck, fuel truck, supply (trash) truck.

Stryker would come up on either side of the food Hemmitt. Track commander would hold up fingers if he wanted cases of MREs. Number would be tossed. Speed up a bit to the ammo truck. Shout what they needed. Cases of ammo would be tossed. Speed up to the fuel truck. Grinning Nepo would toss a fuel line. Guys would drag it to the fuel point and fuel as the truck and the Stryker drove alongside. Fueled up, fuel line goes back, roll up to the (supply/trash) truck. Any critical supply needs? No. Toss me your trash. Bag of trash (mostly MRE bags, empty) would go over. Stryker would speed up and get into security position.

We only *had* to stop moving to change drivers.

The Navy calls it "UNREP," underway replenishment. We called it "logging."

When we had eight trucks and plenty of room, we could do two simultaneous loggings. Later we only did one. Eventually, we'd do a halt. Things were just too fucked up, guys were too tired, to trust logging.

But for then, we could unrep fast.

And later, well, there weren't as many Strykers to fuel.

So while I thought about the fucking bind I was in, I talked with Graham. And, yes, I could multitask it.

I asked him what the normal method of sending out this sort of stuff was. Turned out the answer was "it's complicated." Generally is.

There are two sources of any news, print, video, whatever. The first is "primary source" news reports. That's when you've got a known person standing in front of a news camera or a known "byline" reporting in paper or a known voice doing radio. Twenty-four-hour news cycle, they get a few minutes a day. Unless they get really popular, then they get their own show and eventually become an anchor and senior producer and such. Won't go into career progression in the news field.

But most video people saw on TV, and most news stories and

most written stories that got converted to voice, was done by "secondary" sources. Stringers. Stringers were usually locals who had developed some connection within their news area. I'm going to stop talking about print because here's where it got interesting.

Stringers didn't sell to the networks. A bit more about print. AP got most of the news from stringers and then sent it on, sometimes with editing that was a bit, ahem, slanted and getting to pick and choose what was going to be news (people defending themselves with guns was *never* news, gays beating up straights or blacks attacking whites for hate reasons was *never* news). That was print. Also much of the Internet news and news reports read on radio. About eighty to ninety percent.

AP controlled all of that news. If *they* didn't think it was news, it *wasn't* news. Talk about a monopoly.

Video had avoided that for a long time. In the '60s and '70s, TV news was the networks and they filled a bare hour or two of mostly repetitive news. News from distant lands came in by film and then video tape. It was edited at the national studio, script was written and then broadcast. Local news followed the same pattern but without the flying it in. They got that from their parent network.

And all the networks had fair sized "bureaus" in major capitals. So did print.

But with the advent of the 24-hour news cycle they needed more and more video. So there started to be stringers. They'd go through the local bureaus.

But they needed more and more and more. And at the same time they were cutting back bureaus and foreign reporters.

So the media got together and formed a third party that would collect all the stringer videos. Most of it wasn't used. That got cut. Unimportant? Who knows. Nobody ever saw it. What *definitely* got cut was anything related to context and the networks never saw *any* of it. All there were were clips of dramatic shots.

The networks paid for the clips and then did voice-over based on the description the *company* gave of what the clips meant. That was for, call it "Western" news channels. For other countries, for more money, the company also did voice-over in local language.

Follow the money. Here's the thing.

Most of their clients for voice-over, more money, were in the

Middle East and dictatorships with an axe to grind against the U.S. and Israel. So, you've got a clip of Palestinians shooting at Israeli soldiers, Israeli soldiers returning fire and a kid dead in his father's arms.

You're cutting that down to thirty seconds. You've got excellent shots of each of these if each is held as a chunk: twenty seconds of Palestinian fire, twenty of Israeli and ten of the dead kid. (Which is just a shot of a dead kid and a grieving father. No clue what kind of bullet.)

You can make one for the Western market with the Palestinians shooting and one for the Arab market of the Israelis but that takes time. And time is money.

You're a company out to make a buck. Your best paying clients are Arabs.

You make a clip of Israeli soldiers shooting and a dead kid in his dad's arms. The voice-over can be very plain. Just "an outbreak of fighting between Palestinian and Israeli forces left three dead including a twelve-year-old boy."

People *never see the Palestinians shooting.*

Nobody sees it. Not the networks, not the Arabs, not the Israelis who are watching "Western" TV news. As far as they are aware, the Palestinians were just peacefully singing kumbaya when the Israelis opened fire and the kid can *only* be dead from the *Israelis* because *only the Israelis are shooting. Right?*

In the 1990s the company, based in London, was bought by a holding company from the network "cartel." The holding company was owned by the Saudi Royal family.

By 2001, the vast majority of the employees of the company were Islamic. Sunni to be precise.

And it controlled the broadcast news for the *entire world.*

Plot?

You betcha.

During a seminar in Arab-Western relations in the 1980s, the future king of Saudi Arabia said that "nothing is more paramount than gaining favorable media attention to the plight of the Arab peoples."

This from a guy who owned more Rolls Royces than you could stick in a very big LOG base.

Well, the broadcast news world was in tatters. It was barely functioning even *with* government largesse. And the Saudis, for the moment, weren't producing oil or money or anything else. The whole region was a vastly overpopulated desert. It had been L.A. times ten and wasn't coming back soon. I had no clue what was happening with that company in London. (And, no Graham didn't tell me all that. He told me bits, how he and Skynet did things, and I had other bits and I worked the rest out in research later. But I'd heard the basics long before.)

We wouldn't be going through that company, though. The way that Graham did stuff was he shot a bunch of clips, whatever struck his and his producer's fancy, then sent them back to London and Skynet. It all got edited there. They might get a request to concentrate on something after a bit. A particular human interest angle, for example.

They'd gotten video of our blown-up Stryker. Also of the dead Iraqis. Also of the Javelins.

We'd gotten video of them dropping out of the sky. Not as good as theirs but very close.

And while they had good uplink/downlink, *we* had better.

I also had a couple of aces in the hole.

So I told him what we were going to do. And he got white again. Whiter.

CHAPTER TWELVE

Go Do that Voodoo

But, hell, I sort of needed permission.

See, there's this thing. Generally, it's best to do it and ask for-giveness. Especially in the military. Except when it comes to clear and unquestionable violation of regulations. Sure, I could ask for a lawyer but I might as well ask for a last cigarette if I let Graham start broadcasting as an "embed." There was a process.

(Okay, the girls had been a violation of regulation. If it had come up, I was debating the lawyer or the last cigarette. They're both bad for you but cigarettes kill you slower, less painfully and are cheaper.)

I wasn't going to ask full permission, mind you. I was going to present it as a fait accompli. But sending anything out needed some sort of stamp of approval.

Turned out it wasn't as hard as I'd thought.

Brigade S-3: No, we don't have any help to send you. Would you like to call back again when we have some?

Bandit: Bandit.

Wassup?

Know that drop I asked about? Reporters. Skynet. Murdoch. Embed. Kill them? Nobody know.

Shit me?

Shit not.

Be back.

In the meantime, I got my satellite/commo . . . I got the geek. Here's what we're gonna do . . .

Boggle. No fucking way!

Authority. Boss. Bad dog!

Oh, then "No fucking way, *sir!*"

Did before.

Geek babble saying "No *fucking* way, sir! Other simple. No way. No how. No can do. Nada. Zip. Nichts. Nein. Nyet. Impossible."

Don't talk geek. Do.

Try.

There is no try.

That *is* geek-speak, sir.

No. Because there is no do or do not. There is only do. That is Army-speak.

In the meantime Graham had a chat with his chaps.

You might wonder, as I often have while driving a combine or worrying that some Afghan who knows this terrain *much* better than me is going to hear or see me sneaking up on his lines not that I've *ever* done that, how a scene in the news is actually shot.

Here's how it works. There is normally a four-man crew. They have a mobile system that can move the video, live or "canned" (prerecorded) back to the studio, home-office or that place in London. (Which, I found out later, was still in business but now owned by the BBC. Sigh. I suppose it's better than the Saudis.)

The crew consists of the reporter ("the dummy" in news-speak), a sound-man who is almost invariably between the ages of nineteen and twenty-six, has acne that he covers with a scraggly beard and in his off-time is a world-reigning champion at God of War, the cameraman, often on his second career, who is between twenty-three and fifty and whatever his age is developing a beer gut, and the producer, who is either a former dummy or a female "communications major" from a school to the left of Lenin. The producer is, in either case, generally to the left of Lenin or his or her bosses wouldn't let him or her be a producer.

Six is a bit odd.

In the case of Graham's chaps, the producer was a former dummy from the BBC. Never a star dummy (as in a ventriloquist's dummy) he got into producing and jumped to Skynews for the better pay just before the Plague. Nice chap. Bright. Amenable. Ambitious. Which was the card I played.

The sound-man was 22, developing a gut, had a straggly beard and was a world reigning champion at HaloV. I know because I tried to play the bastard in deathmatch and despite the fact that he had the good grace not to respawn camp he waxed my ass so hard I gave up the game in disgust and have never played it since.

Camerman. 28. Second career. First career was British Royal Marines. Six years. Did a stint in Basra. Thought he'd see how Iraq was shaping up, don't you know? Wasn't Para. Silly of me. Better out a fucking plane than bobbing around on a small boat!

He had a beer gut. He looked as if he could chew railroad spikes. I eventually realized that he was wasted on England. He needed to move to Texas.

The other two?

Half-trained camerman and a guy who was sort of thinking about getting into the sound business and could sort of run the equipment. Sort of porters. Sort of supernumeries. Sort of spares "in case."

Sort of dead weight?

Former SAS. (Special Air Service. Brit version of Delta.) Former SBS. (Special Boat Squadron. Brit version of SEALs.)

Told you Murdoch was a character.

Of course they didn't have weapons. Didn't do with reporters old chap. Until I bundled some out along with spare gear and told them to *rig the fuck up.*

Graham had a powwow with them. I had a powwow with them. The only slight balk was the sound-man who started babbling geek.

I don't speak geek. There is no try. There is only do.

Cameraman? Grin.

"Oh, bloody *yes*, I think."

SAS? SBS?

Sleepy-eyed stares.

I'll take that for a rousing applause.

Producer?

"This will either make us all bloody famous or out on the street or possibly both . . . I'm in."

They were going for the "it's better to ask forgiveness than permission." I still needed permission.

I had a call.

It was a lieutenant colonel. It was my new battalion commander.

I didn't know him. I pieced some stuff together later.

He wasn't a mech-head. He was light infantry. Airborne and Ranger to be precise.

He'd been transferred to the Corps G-3 shop for his "staff" time. It had to be done, no matter how good you are. They make you do staff. Especially if you're any good at it.

Look, there are probably guys who can only command. I don't know any. Every good commander I've ever met was good to excellent as a staff guy. The reverse is not true. That is, a Fobbit is a REMF is a Fobbit. They may be great at staff, but they cannot lead for squat.

I wish they'd learn to weed them out, better. Last BC? I hear he was great at staff. Lousy at command.

Anyway, this guy was, I found out later, an absolute fucking *genius* at staff.

As a commander?

"So here I sit. With two companies of line trying to play nursemaid the insane and one I can't affect, at all, under a former assistant S-4 with . . . scattered reviews on the other side of the world. What say you?"

"Not much you can do from there, sir."

"For or against?"

"We do *intend* to make it back, sir."

"I've seen your intel analysis. And the analysis of your analysis which wasn't actually bad. And now you're telling me they have Javelins. That is a badness thing."

(I pulled some of these from archive. He *actually said that.* "A badness thing.")

"We will continue the mission, sir."

"Sorry about the scouts. Get me their names and I'll write the letters. If there are any to write the way things are. But you've got enough on your plate. Look, I've got a meeting with the division commander in a bit. New battalion commander and all that. Hail, fellow, well met. Screw that. I don't see why we can't get some sort of air support for you. A damned *news company* flew in reporters. Surely we can get a B-52 or a B-2 or *something* overhead! *Some* damned support! This is just silly."

"Thank you, sir."

"Yeah. Well, I'm not going to joggle your elbow. Good luck and good hunting and all that. Now go dooo that voooodoooo that youuuuu do so welllll!"

Screen blanked.

Holy shit.

Screen came back up.

"Oh. By the way. You just made major. And you've got an okay on the embeds. See ya."

Screen blanked.

Holy shit.

I couldn't figure out if my new battalion commander was a nut or what.

I found out fairly quick.

Graduate of MIT no less. IQ so high he should have had a fucking nose bleed. Spells geek with a capital K. Geeks rarely can command for shit. Infantry don't speak geek, geek don't speak grunt. Me grunt. No speek geek. That worried me when I saw it.

Captain of the MIT football team. I didn't know MIT *had* a football team.

Former Ranger company commander.

Passed Delta Qual and training. Went "over the wall."

Rotated out as LTC for lack of slots. Longest running field grade officer in Delta history. No notations on that but turned out later he'd been a "squadron commander," *Delta's* version of a battalion.

Went to Corp G-3 for operations.

He's already on the colonel's list but the Corps commander has a problem. A battalion so fucked up that you can't even call it mutinous. They're just playing whatever rules they want to play because their commander's having a nervous breakdown and everybody has been watching it in slow time. Know you haven't been here long but you seem like the kind of guy could get this battalion going again. Oh, and one of the companies is the guys over in Iran. What do you say? Help me out, here.

Guy's evals didn't walk on water. He walked on the fucking clouds and angels sang around him. His superiors seemed to be writing that they really didn't *deserve* to be evaluating the messiah.

Nobody was that good.

He was that good.

Was our luck turning?

He couldn't effect diddly except maybe air support. We were facing an unknown but large enemy force ahead and they had anti-tank weapons that were state of the fucking art.

Our luck was turning.

— CHAPTER THIRTEEN —

The Last Centurions

"Welcome to Skynews!

"This evening we have a special report from a team of intrepid reporters embedded with the American and Nepalese unit cut off in the middle east. As many of you know, this unit is attempting to replicate the famous march of the Ten Thousand of storied history. Instead of a dry report, we will be bringing you, weekly, a documentary intended to both entertain and educate. We bring you, now, *The Last Centurions.*"

Call it reality TV. Call it counterpropaganda. Call it, as many *did*, propaganda.

The Last Centurions sort of defies description. Sure, I was the real producer and maybe I shouldn't talk about my show. But I'm not the one to say that, I think it was first said by Murdoch at a stockholder's meeting where people were starting to smile for the first time in a year. And it was repeated on news shows, talk-shows and every other medium of communications over the years.

We didn't send them video and then let them edit to choice. We sent them a complete show and told them to air it as is or else. As time went on, we got support from Skynet. And Fox and even the Beeb at one point. But at first, it was all a few overworked people in a bouncing commo trailer, often under fire.

It always started the same. A shot of some sort of horror that had perhaps become banal in 2019. A dead man Arab in what looked like a looted shop. A man blown apart by heavy machine-gun fire with no apparent weapon. A woman battered to death.

A voice-over giving the impression that some evil had occurred, probably because of the evil Americans.

Then it would back up in time.

Every show was different, but they all had the same theme, the opening lines in that great voice of Graham's:

"This is a picture. All it tells you is what you see. If you don't know the context you know *nothing*."

Sure, it was exciting. Violence sells, as does pathos and sex. *Last Centurions* had it all. It was entertaining as hell. Hell, I lived through it, loved it, hated it, sweated blood. And I still watch some of the segments. Especially the one where Samad is sliding down the hill completely out of control. I laugh my ass off at that every time even though at the time it looked like a tragedy in the making.

And in the middle of it, we'd slip in context. History. Geography. Ethnology. History of propaganda. How news is made and manipulated. Military affairs. Diplomacy. How the two often interact badly.

Putting it together was a nightmare. Not my nightmare, generally, but a nightmare. Oh, I'd input on the basic script and some suggestions on the video we'd gotten. Also some stuff on background.

The scripts were usually, but not always, written by a pimply faced private in Mortars. The kid had . . . oh, a flare for storytelling and he was pretty knowledgeable for being all of nineteen. We'd find a particularly horrible shot and he'd back it up.

We were attempting to, and sort of did, undo decades of propaganda. We'd show the picture at the beginning then do a standard voice-over for the scene. That was usually done by a female announcer at Skynet.

"Stones." That's the one with the picture of the young woman who's obviously been beaten to death.

"American forces in the vicinity of the Iraqi town of Al-Kami were accused today of the rape and murder of Shayida al-Farut, daughter of a local tribal leader. According to local sources (young guy screaming and shaking his fist at the camera) she was seen in the company of American soldiers shortly before her death." Cut.

Back up.

Where in the hell is Al-Kami? Why were American forces there? *Who* was the guy? HOW DID SHE *DIE*?

(Go see the episode. For those of you who've never watched it, remember that thing about "honor rapes"? We tried to stop it, she *chose* to go back. For the honor of her family. That's it in a fucked up nutshell.)

The last shot would always be what happened to create the shot that led in. In that case, a beautiful young woman, dead and battered to a pulp on the ground. Back up and you see the heavy stones scattered around her. Back up further you see the men who had done it, in some cases members of her own family, walking away.

"We are . . . *The Last Centurions.*"

In a way, this whole . . . huge fucking time-waster I've been writing is a written version of *The Last Centurions.*

It was also a living record of our time of suckage.

It spawned a whole fucking industry. *Everybody* tried to copy us. "Realer reality TV" whatever that means. But a story like the Ten Thousand, or *The Last Centurions*, is hard to beat. That's why it's been so popular over the centuries in the first place.

And *everybody* tried to figure out what the picture meant.

Understand, we'd send Skynews the picture and the "false" voice-over as soon as we had the script. And they'd tend to play it over and over. There wasn't much else new in programming at the time. After the first few, it got picked up by Fox News then Fox Network then a couple of minor networks that were holding on and finally it was even on ABC.

And it became, like, *the* standard water-cooler (actually, food line at the time) conversation.

"I think he was a terrorist . . ."

"I think . . ." "I think . . ."

Every week it was a mystery how we were going to fool people. What the "real" story was.

Oh, there was plenty of human interest. We had interviews and clips of just about everyone in the unit pretty quick and kept them up. There was a hard-hearted reason for that. When it involved the death of one of the troops, having file footage helped.

We could never go back and reshoot. The takes that we had were everything there was. Going back was rarely an option.

Of course, we had cameras in the Strykers and helmet cameras and gun-cameras hooked up to both the commander's sight in the Gun Strykers and to the gunner's sight. And both the regular cameraman (for as long as he lasted) and the SAS guy were running around all the time.

We also had the helmet mikes. Those and the gun cameras all could be fed to the commo trailers and recorded. Even if they weren't switched there. So we just continuously recorded everything.

Which was why so much of it was sucky. Reviewers used the term "edgy." I would have preferred better production values, but it wasn't an option.

Oh, and then there was the intro. The "new" intro that was introduced in episode three, "Stones." (The one described above.) I didn't like it. I didn't like the title of the show. I wanted to just call it "*Truths*" and I liked the simple intro. Graham talked me into it.

Centurions were the guardians of Rome. At the height of the Roman Republic there were over five thousand qualified Roman Centurions in the Legions. To be a Centurion required that, in a mostly illiterate society, one be able to read and write clearly, to be able to convey and create orders, to be capable of not only performing every skill of a Roman soldier but teach every skill of a Roman soldier. Becoming a Centurion required intense physical ability, courage beyond the norm, years of sacrifice and a total devotion to the philosophy which was Rome.

When Rome fell to barbarian invaders, there were fewer than five hundred qualified Centurions. Not because Rome had fewer people but because it had fewer willing to make the sacrifices. And the last Centurions left their shields in the heather and took a barbarian bride . . .

We are . . . The Last Centurions.

And this Rome SHALL NOT FALL!

Shot of a Stryker crashing through a house, (trying to avoid Javelin fire, by the way) intro of various characters. (Yeah, that's me on the radio with the mortar round exploding in the background. What we left *out* of the context was the camerman hitting the ground right afterwards. Funny as hell. It wasn't as close as it looked, or I'd have already been down, trust me.) Samad and Fillup and Bouncer (the first sergeant) and whoever was featured in that week's episode.

I didn't like it. I wanted to keep the original intro. Graham talked me around.

I still don't like it. I skip it when I watch the DVDs.

"Lancers," "Stones," "Division" about the battle for Mosul, "Hurrians" about the Kurds, "Loot" about scrounging vs. looting and how we ended up saving centuries' worth of cultural treasures in Turkey and finally, I *thought*, the three-parter "Caliphate" about taking down Istanbul.

My favorite, hands down, is "CAM(P)ing." Now, *at the time* I thought I was going to burst a blood vessel and wanted to kill every damned Nepo in the camp. As I watched one of our precious HERCULES burn because that fucking CAMP(P) was being used by the Nepos to cook food . . . And to see Samad walking up with it in his hands *right after* we'd set off the charges. Oh, *GOD* was I angry.

But I got over it. It was laugh or cry. And it was a very funny episode. The show needed humor and it was usually something between us and the Nepos that provided it.

"Battery" was probably the most poignant. I'm not sure what it was about the death of a minor shopkeeper in a minor town that was so fucked up. But when the batteries turned out to be dead . . . It was just so stupid and so random and so futile. And, yes, after I saw the episode I released some of our precious store of batteries to Goomber for his fucking iPod. Come on, I've got a heart.

Then came "Elephant."

Okay, "Elephant" was a) the only show we did that was pure "activist journalism" and b) the only one that was driven entirely by me. But go back to my point about media and government. The media exists in a democracy so that people can make informed choices about their representatives.

We were going into the first winter of an *ice age* and everyone was still talking about *global warming*!

Picture of a flower with baked mud behind it.

"Despite record cold and snow across the northern climes, global warming continues to be a looming disaster . . ."

By then we had permission to let the Skynet guys do interviews using our commo. And we managed to scrounge up one of the climatologists who had been screaming about the situation, and getting ignored, for months.

Remember, I'd gotten the first word back in *January*. It was *November* and people were still talking about "global warming."

It was insane. We were trekking through road-wheel deep snow in mountains where it usually started to snow in ernest in late December and people were still beating the "global warming" drum.

And we beat them to death with their own drumstick.

The Brit climatologist was almost pathetically glad someone would listen. And he gave us a list of other experts who were trying to get the word out.

We were the first people to break the news that we were entering an ice age and get world-wide notice. We turned the tide. After that episode, even journalists started asking the right questions.

(By the way, I was the "producer" of most of the interviews. What does a producer do? He or she tells the ventriloquist's dummy what questions to ask. I *knew* what questions to ask. Graham, who before the episode had no clue, just asked them.)

I'm probably most proud of anything that I've ever done in my life with that episode. Well, that and my kids.

Were there "issues"? Oh my fucking GOD.

The Bitch was not pleased. She wanted us off the TV. And she hated Murdoch and all his networks. But, on the surface, it was all Skynet. Us? We're just trying to survive, what do you want us to do, censor them?

And from the first episode it was taking the networks by storm. Murdoch, who knew good entertainment when he saw it, had "Lancers" playing on four different time slots on Skynet and two on Fox News. By the time the Bitch reacted to it, we had another episode canned and a third in production. She screamed that she wanted it stopped. The Brass got passive aggressive.

We aired "Stones" and we were suddenly on Fox Network and one of the minor ones. (UPN?) After "Division" episode one, ABC bought the rebroadcast rights and did all three shows as a "miniseries" as a lead in. Then came "Division" episode two and all the guys people had grown to know just suddenly gone...

"Division" was the one that had everyone talking. There was no stopping us after that. She couldn't shut us down because she'd done too many obvious power-grabs and even her closest supporters were glued to the TV every Sunday night at eight.

And Thursday at seven. And various late-night spots and...

Hey, there wasn't much entertainment in those days. We were *it*.

Oh, people ask me, a lot, about "Centurion."

I did *not* produce the last show of the series. I didn't even know it *was* in production. I didn't know much about it until about a week beforehand, when I was kind of busy figuring out how to break the Caliphate. So when I was informed that Graham and Fillup were working on the last show, they had it, it's all good, I just let them do it. I trusted Fillup not to screw it up. Hell, by then I trusted *Graham*. You have good subordinates and you let them do their job. Like I said, I'm lazy.

Fuckers.

And that scene that everybody talks about where we come under fire and I stop telling a story for a second, snap out a string of orders then go back to telling the story?

Look, it's not that hard, okay? I mean, I don't suggest it for nonprofessionals but I'd been doing the job a long time. It wasn't rocket science whatever the episode made it out to be.

(Wife edit: *Now* you see what I mean? He drives me nuts sometimes. Watch the episode. Yeah, it's *that hard* to figure out in your head how to maneuver four different units over several kilometers of terrain while taking artillery fire. And he did it in, what? A half a second? Faster than most people can figure out what coffee to order? Will he ever admit it? Hell, no. Drives me nuts.)

So that's the story of how *The Last Centurions* came about and how things went from bad to good to very very bad. Because we weren't going to be getting many episodes out unless we made it to the filling station. And there *was*, in fact, a *division* in our way.

CHAPTER FOURTEEN

There Has Been A Good Killing

The Sunni Triangle is a bit of a misnomer. But I'll work with it. The "triangle" is elongated north and comprised of Baghdad and Al Ramadi, which are more or less on the same line in the south, and Tikrit, which is a few hundred miles north of that line.

The whole area is fairly built up. Which meant more potential threats and given the population it was unlikely we were going to be greeted with open arms. Yeah, the population had crashed compared to the last time I was in Iraq, but it was still populated.

We were to the east of the Tigris. Looking at the map of village after village we were going to have to pass through, I was less than thrilled. Any of them could have a Javelin team in it. If I'd been the local Sunni commander, whoever he was, I'd have sent out a couple of Jav teams to every one of those villages. Or, at least, scout teams to figure out our route of advance and Jav teams to respond.

I was *not* interested in dodging Javelins all the way to Mosul *then* fighting an armored force.

I looked at our fuel consumption, looked at our available, did some calculations on the back of a napkin then dodged.

Right through the Sunni Triangle.

> It's twenty-five marches to Narbo,
> It's forty-five more up the Rhone,
> And the end may be death in the heather
> Or life on an Emperor's throne.

I didn't want an emperor's throne but I did want to see Blue
Earth some day, even if it *was* going to be freaking cold. And
it was going to be quite a few marches until we'd be free to run
like the wind.

The thing is, to the east of the Tigris it was little fucking villages almost the whole way to Tikrit. To the west they drop off
fast until you hit the Syrian Desert.

I wasn't afraid of desert. I'd have loved a nice open, nobody
around, desert. What I didn't like was little fucking villages and
farms and water courses and all the rest of that shit. It stopped
us continuously making us sitting ducks.

I *needed* to be west of the Tigris.

Only one problem. There were, like, no fucking bridges across
the Tigris. They were only at major cities. Notably, the first one
north of Baghdad was at Zaydan where the villages had already
fallen off. We were past the ones south of Baghdad. And all of
those were in cities that were considered "hostile."

Presumably, Baghdad was where the core of the enemy would
be hanging out.

Keep poking slowly north as the enemy closed in? We'd get
surrounded and then ground to hamburger. We had to speed up.
Speed was life. The quick and the dead.

We hadn't gotten that far north when I ordered an abrupt
change in direction.

"Fillup, tell the Scouts to get on the Baghdad road and hammer west."

"West? Are you nuts?"

We were going downtown.

Commander's intent was what is called a "thunder run."

The commanders in Iraq in the "insertion phase" thought they'd
invented it. They hadn't. Neither had the Black Horse in Vietnam which used it in Cambodia during our brief "intervention."
Probably the first was performed by a Wehrmacht Panzer unit in
Russia. Hell, the very first was probably by the Sarmatians.

Simply put, you put your pedal to the metal, you go balls to
the wall and you fire at everything that even vaguely *looks* like a
target. You don't stop for anything you don't absolutely *have* to.

It required some rearranging. And I did not want anyone running out of gas or ammo on the drive. We did a log on the way
in. Then the Scouts went back out and we thundered.

A thunder run is significantly improved with tanks. Tanks have a psychological effect it's hard to describe. Especially at short range, and urban fighting tends to be *very* short range, they just *look* unstoppable. We didn't have tanks. We were going to have to hope that the gun Strykers were good enough.

We were saved by serendipity. (Which is a term meaning "I fucked up but things came out better than if I hadn't.") Okay, and active stupidness on the part of the local commander.

The local commander had gotten the word that we were out there and it was obvious we were heading for a link-up with the Kurds. He, therefore, did much what I thought he might. He sent out small units to "attrit" us while he gathered his main force to hunt us down.

All smart. Problem being that I "got inside his decision making cycle." What that means is, I wasn't doing what he thought was the obvious thing to do, keep pressing north, and I was reacting faster than he and his forces could react.

We were almost due east of Baghdad, a bit south of the line near Ajrab, when I made the decision.

The first "reaction" force had been sent out pell-mell to attack the drop area. That's the one that got the scout Stryker with the Jav. He was being smart, though, and putting most of his "light" force that he could scramble quick, fedayeen militia some of them organized into Javelin teams, up in the curve of villages I really didn't want to work my way through.

So about half his local supply of Javelins went to the wrong area.

Then he did what any good Middle Eastern commander does. He gathered his regular forces for a harangue. Had them line up with their tanks and trucks and AFVs and told them that they outnumbered the small American unit and that it would be easy to stop. That he knew right where it was going and by the time they caught the "thieves and butchers" that most of us would be smoking wrecks from the Javelins of the fedayeen militia. That there was nothing to worry about.

Scout Team Two-Five had a very specific mission. Barrel down the north side of the Baghdad highway to screen our advance. Don't stop for anything.

Why in the hell they went onto a fucking Iraqi military base I have no fucking clue. They *said* they got turned around and thought it was a parallel road to the Baghdad Highway.

Two-Five consisted of a regular Scout Stryker and the one commanded by the Scout Platoon leader. I happen to know that Boner could read a map better than that. Otherwise, he wouldn't be the Scout Platoon leader. They had fucking GPS and a clear route. How in the *hell* did they take a wrong turn?

What *I* got at the time went like this.

"Fillup, Fillup, Boner. Have encountered a small checkpoint. Area cleared."

"Roger. Fillup out."

"Fillup, Fillup, Two-Five. We are stuck in some sort of army base. Am encountering scattered resistance. Getting a little turned around."

"Roger, Two-Five. Blow through. Only base in the area is Damran Base. Be aware, that is part of the LOG we left behind. Expect resistance by U.S. military grade hardware. Boner, get the hell *out* of there."

Ten minutes later.

"Command, Two-Five! We are in encounter with large force . . . !"

The call cuts off.

"Two-five! Two-Five!"

All the BFT indicators are up on Two-Five. Our little boxes are talking to their little boxes and *their* little boxes are talking back which means the vehicles are not a pillar of smoke. Still not a pillar of smoke. Not responding to radio calls, but not a pillar of smoke. *Still* not a pillar of smoke . . .

"Fillup, Fillup, Two-Five. Happy to report have captured Damran Base and large store of military equipment including approximate equipment for an armored regiment. There has been a good killing."

There has been a good killing.

Picture this.

You're an Iraqi general. You have carefully gathered your armored regiment. The Abrams, Bradleys, Strykers, Paladins and such are lined up in serried rows at the rear. They are an amazing sight, all that armor just waiting to be let free to bring death and destruction to the enemies of Allah.

In front are the users of those vehicles. The drivers, gunners, infantry, techs and their officers. They are in dressed ranks standing at attention listening to you talk. And talk. And talk. Some five *thousand* men.

You have just told your armored regiment, equipped with the

latest U.S. military equipment and capable of taking on any force in the Middle East, that you know where the enemy is going and that they will mostly be destroyed before they are ever encountered. Soon they will engage the small remnant of the enemy in an unstoppable wave which is right and just because Allah is on their side.

As you are delivering your harangue to your freezing troops (it was cold that day), there is distant firing. You ignore it. There is often firing. The Shia continue to resist, militias settle quarrels. People fire off every sort of gun in "happy fire" all the time. When one gets going, others follow. And, anyway, it cuts off abruptly.

As you continue your long-winded speech, there is a bit more firing. It's closer. So what? More people doing "happy fire" for the heck of it.

You may even recognize it as Bushmaster and M240 fire. Again, so what? Your forces are equipped with both.

You might pause as you notice smoke beginning to billow up. But you're well into your speech and others are responsible for fire-fighting. Besides . . . things blow up and burn. Your guys are not exactly experts with their equipment.

Then you see two Strykers enter the (extremely large) parking stand. You have Strykers but they are all supposed to be parked with their crews listening to your harangue. Perhaps they are from another unit, but all the rest of the units are up north fighting the Kurds. Your unit has just been "stood up" on the American equipment that was left and is preparing to head up there and break the Kurds for once and for all.

Perhaps it is from one of those units?

Then you notice the American flag on the lead Stryker's aerial.

By then it is too late.

Picture if you will . . .

Armored vehicles cannot express "body language." Or can they?

The sudden braking as the Scout Strykers, which had been doing a good 40 miles an hour, skid to a stop on the extremely large concrete pad. The concrete pad filled with more armored equipment and enemy troops than they'd ever wanted to see in their lives. The main guns shifting left and right as if wondering just what in the hell they're going to do. Perhaps they begin to back up . . .

So what does our intrepid Iraqi general do?

He shouts into his squealing microphone: "IT IS THE AMERI-CANS! ATTACK!"

Picture if you will, the troops starting to scatter as the general and his staff and commanders try to run. Picture both tracks opening fire.

The nearest cover for the assembled troops are the armored vehicles. The Scout track commanders are not stupid. (Okay, they *were* stupid, but also *very* lucky.) They lay down the majority of their fire in that direction. They know if the crews get those vehicles up and running they're toast.

The next cover is on the other side of the reviewing stand in a set of buildings.

All the way down the five-hundred-meter pad are more buildings associated with a motor pool.

The other direction are the Strykers and *nobody* is running *that* way.

25mm Bushmaster. Coaxial 7.62. Track commander with .50 caliber.

Two sets.

They ran out of 25mm ammo. They ran out of .50 caliber ammo. The track carries thirty-five *thousand* rounds of 7.62.

They ran out of most of that, too.

This I had to see.

It was ugly. You might have seen the shots but it doesn't really convey the ugliness of it. The guys had been fallen out without their personal weapons (probably because the "general" was afraid of getting shot). Not that that would have done much good against Strykers. They definitely didn't have anti-armor weapons. They had nowhere to run and nowhere to hide.

I had seen the word "windrows" in military histories before. "Windrows of bodies." I'd never actually seen what they were talking about but I recognized it immediately. Those guys writing histories back in the Civil War were familiar with agriculture. It wasn't like today when everybody thought their food came from the stores.

When a big wind hits a field of wheat, it lays down the wheat in sort of waves. It forms rows of beaten down wheat that hump up almost as if they'd been plowed by the wind. Neat, regular, long lines of destroyed wheat.

The Iraqis were the wheat.

Massacre? Yes. "Evil!," "illegal!" No. They were enemy combatants.

A few might have tried to surrender. See the whole thing on taking prisoners. Besides, in the gun-camera footage I didn't see many trying until the end and by that time Boner *was* taking prisoners.

All that beautiful *beautiful* equipment and, at first, I could not think of a damned thing to do with it but blow it the fuck up.

Even with all the equipment and bodies there was still room to park Farmer's Freaks. (We didn't call ourselves The Centurions. Ever. In reunions we *still* don't except the techs when they're drunk. We were Farmer's Freaks.)

I climbed out of the commo van, up on the front slope and just sat there looking at what Boner had wrought. I tuned the bodies out pretty quick. I was looking at the vehicles. There were more HERCULES and Hemmitts and Bradleys and Strykers and Paladins. Fuck, there was *everything*. Even Avenger anti-aircraft systems.

Boner came over wagging his tail like a Lab that had just brought back a bird. I let him babble for a bit and then nodded.

"Not bad, Boner, not bad."

He looked like he'd just been handed the Holy Grail with a Medal of Honor in it.

There's a *point* to only praising to the most limited degree.

(Doesn't work with all personality types but the types that it doesn't shouldn't be on a battlefield. They have important things to do in civilian society but if you need people blowing smoke up your ass all the time, don't join the military. I don't work well with that personality type but I tell them I don't and why.)

"I would go so far as saying that I agree this was a good killing."

I thought he would stroke.

All that time I was looking at that gear and wondering what the *hell* I was going to do with it. Nice to not have it as a threat anymore. But . . . damn . . .

Okay, we didn't need any Strykers. Stryke those. I was not going to fuck around with Paladins. I'd loved to have been able to, but I wasn't gonna. Scratch all the Brads, too.

What I wanted was a way to get it all up to the Kurds. No way in hell. Why?

I was looking at over *four hundred* vehicles. Okay, say that we just took the Abrams. There were nearly a hundred of those. I had about a hundred and seventy effectives. But an Abrams requires a crew of four, commander, gunner, loader and driver.

And none of my guys knew diddly about them. A tank doesn't

just run itself. Sure, the Abrams is a sweet vehicle and very easy to use. But maintaining it? Hell, even boresighting the gun we didn't know how to do.

I didn't even want to take the time to fuck everything up, but I knew I had to do it. I couldn't leave this shit in my rear. Somebody was bound to butt-fuck me with it.

But the Nepos were just sitting there . . .

We took twenty Abrams and forty Bradleys.

How? Wait, didn't you just say . . . ?

Ten of the Abrams were fully crewed by guys drawn from the infantry. That left me with very few ground shooters. I'd live.

The other fifty were driven, and driven only, by Nepos, some infantry, the news guys and techs. Why?

Abrams are very hard to destroy. Even with a Javelin if one got hit it was unlikely to hit the driver's compartment. Which was the only way the driver would get killed.

I wasn't taking them to use them, I was taking them to keep them from the enemy. And, hopefully, get them to the Kurds.

They're also very easy to drive.

All of them were fully armed and fueled. We took two trucks of Abrams ammo, a bunch of 25mm and four of parts. They weren't all parts for Abrams and Brads but what the hell.

Then we used five Abrams to shoot up all the rest. Last but not least, we shot those five. They'd fired so many rounds, their barrels were "depleted" and why used "depleted" barrels when you have brand new ones?

I had sort of enjoyed blowing up the LOG base in Iran. I nearly cried at this one. This shit could have really helped out the Kurds. I cursed the bastard that left it here.

I also took two Avenger anti-air systems, fully crewed. They were Stryker Avengers, which I'd left in Iran not thinking I'd need them. And we grabbed four more fuel trucks. We had, essentially, *nobody* riding in the Strykers.

If I'd known about CAM(P)ing I would have taken a HERCULES. I wanted to take everything. We just didn't have the manpower.

Oh, by the way. Fully armed Abrams with their ammunition doors opened? They blow up *really* nice. It was heartening. Sort of. We were now in them.

We rolled out after a bare two hours and continued our thunder run.

Going through Baghdad was . . . unpleasant. There were quite a few fedayeen with RPGs. They got one of the Strykers near the bridge and I think another on the west side. Also one of the fuel trucks. There were, I think, some Javelins. But Baghdad is pretty built up, and I kept as much as possible to the built up areas. The reason I think we took some Javelin fire is that a couple of times buildings had explosions we weren't causing.

We were causing a lot of explosions, though, so I'll take that as a "possible."

A Thunder Run everybody looks out and keeps an eye out for targets. The track commanders were the most exposed and we lost one of them to effects of an RPG. But, mostly, we were laying down so much fire, not much was coming back. We were burning through ammo, but the most important thing was to get to the other side of Baghdad.

We had to slow down, though, for the vehicles that got hit. All the guys weren't dead. We had wounded, now. *Lots* of wounded. Since we didn't have a doctor or any way to evac them, that was going to suck.

We went Abrams (fully crewed) to the front, then a group of gun Strykers, then some trucks, then more gun Strykers, then the rest of the trucks, then all the rest of the shit (nearly empty infantry carriers, mortars, Avengers and the line of uncrewed Abrams and Brads), then some more gun Strykers. The HERCULES were near the rear in case we needed to tow anyone. I wasn't planning on stopping to tow if I could avoid it.

The satellite intel said the bridge was up and engineering intel said it could take all our vehicles.

It was up and it did.

It was also defended by a cluster of fedayeen with RPGs. Which was where we lost one of the gun Strykers. It had an explosion go off on the overhead which I think was a Jav. On the far side we lost a Stryker, again. One of the nearly unmanned infantry carriers. At first I thought it was an RPG. I'm still not sure if it was RPG or Javelin.

Three wounded in the first, one dead one wounded in the second. All my critical infantry troops. Pissed me off.

I do not know, nor do I care, how many we killed on the run. I do know that at one point there was a sort of human wave charge of a few hundred.

What's that line from Patton? We used them to grease our treads.

Did we kill civilians? Possibly. Probably. When an Abrams TC spots a guy with an RPG in a window and orders "fire" and the gunner replies with main cannon . . . Anything in or around the guy with the RPG gets killed. And we weren't just firing at RPG holders. You don't have enough time in combat to say "is that an RPG or a guy with a pipe on his shoulder? Is that person leaning out for a good look or to fire something?" You see anything that looks like a target and you fire.

Getting out of Baghdad actually scared me more than going through. We were back in open country and anyone with a Jav could have lit us up. But we didn't take any.

Oh, prisoners.

While we were "reconfiguring" at the pad and such, I had Hollywood and a couple of other guys who had gotten some "bedroom" instruction in Arabic interrogate the survivors. Which is where I got the narrative about the Iraqi general. Also about him sending most of the Jav teams up and to the east to stop us.

Last bit. We found the main cache of what had been left behind as well. It was in a base on the west side of the Tigris. "Lightly defended." Also had been mostly emptied out. We took some more shit from there (including refueling our fuel trucks and vehicles and ammoing up) and then blew up anything that resembled military hardware.

Take *that*, State Department.

— CHAPTER FIFTEEN —

It's a Good Place to Hallucinate

So where were we going?

Nowhere. We were going nowhere.

As in "Bumfuckistan," "East Bumfuck," "middle of nothing," "beyond the Pale."

We stayed north of the Euphrates out in the salt wastes. There was, operationally, a choke point near Ramadi between it and the Thartar which is a big shallow salt lake kind of like . . . well, Salt Lake. Our dust could easily be seen from Ramadi.

But there wasn't any reaction. It looked as if we were headed for Syria. Our basic path, except for avoiding roads, was the one I'd taken when I did my deployment as Scout Platoon leader. This was the path that the Sunnis had smuggled fighters in throughout the whole Resistance in Iraq, from all over the world to Syria and then down the Al-Ramadi trail.

But there was fuck all in most of that area. If you didn't stay down by the Euphrates there weren't any towns and hardly any roads. It was a big fucking open desert.

We lost some vehicles. I don't know how a group of reasonably intelligent Arabs could fuck up Abrams and Bradleys as fast as they did, but fuck them up they did.

We dropped four Abrams and two Bradleys on the first part of the run. And we were running. There was no ability to switch drivers. We logged and we ran, logged and ran, logged and ran until the guys were obviously becoming too punch drunk to log in movement.

297

It took us two days to get to the "oasis" of Abu Samak. Part of the time we spent on a road that had been laid down, way back when, for the Iraqi military. They used to perform training operations, when they trained at all, out in this area.

Problem was, the area was crossed by wadis. Wadis are gulleys formed in desert terrain by the occasional rainshowers it gets. They flood to their banks at the slightest rain then go down to dry. Arroyos is the term used in the Southwest.

Wadis can really ruin a tank or Stryker's day when they don't notice them. Oh, there were always places to cross. But when you're tired as hell and crusing along at forty knots in the middle of the night, you don't always notice an arroyo. Then you drop four feet through the air and generally slam into the far wall. Even if you climb it, you've just shaken your crew around like peas and somebody is probably injured. Especially the guys in "white daze" or dead asleep.

Taking the road kept us out of wadis. It was a chance and I took it and it never bit me in the ass but I didn't like it.

At Abu Samak we did a full stop.

Abu Samak is where the story "Stones" came from. When we left the guys wanted to just waste the place and be done. But we left it standing.

It had been a fair sized village before the Plague. Did an op there when I was Scout Platoon leader. (Not the one where I got the scars.) Recovery had been centered around three families from two different clans. Only about sixty people left. Which was why killing one of their breeders was stupid. Besides the whole thing being stupid.

But it was their culture and her choice. As long as they don't try to shove that culture down *my* throat, let them have it. Try to do it in my country and . . . Well the muj in Detroit found out exactly how forgiving Bandit Six is about that sort of thing.

(By the way, was she old enough to "consent" to that sort of thing in the U.S., if it had been legal at all? No. But it's their culture . . . In that culture, she was. Fundamentalist Islam is a very fucked up culture IMO, but I couldn't save the world.)

Getting away from "Stones," we did a full stop. We set up jamming, cut the phone lines, told the locals if they tried to leave they'd be shot without mercy, put out security (who tried like hell to stay awake) and got some rest. We stopped for ten hours, rotating so everyone could get some rest other than in a moving vehicle.

Then we fueled, packed and rolled. Leaving the town standing against our better judgement.

We rolled out to the west-northwest until we were way out of sight of anyone and then turned due north. We went nowhere *near* a town for days.

We rolled, hard, dropping vehicles along the way as they just fucking died, for three more days. Days of fighting dust and fatigue that was so bad you shook in pain. Grit in your eyes, grit in your mouth, grit in your clothes. I'd spread the formation so that nobody was in anyone's dust. Didn't matter. It got everywhere.

Two of the wounded died. The rest pulled through. They were as comfortable as we could make them in the supply trucks. The two medics we had worked like hell to keep them alive.

Short of evac, there was nothing else we could do for them.

There were more wadis up north. All over the fucking place. I put the Scouts out front and we lost one of the Scout Strykers to a totally destroyed undercarriage when it hit a fucking wadi doing *well* over what I told them to do speed-wise. I wasn't going to chew the driver out. He had a broken arm. And, no, we didn't know how to set it.

We rolled deep into the desert wastes. It is said that Saddam had sent one of his sons up here, just before we'd entered, with a cache of not only most of his sarin and VX gas but also cash in tractor-trailer load quantities.

If so, nobody has ever found it. We didn't, and trust me I looked. Less for the cash than the poison gas which I was perfectly willing to use.

There were wadis. There were dunes. Not like the Rub Ak Kali or the mojave, but pretty big. There were weird things like this big sort of quicksand area. It was wet. How in the hell the sand/mud/shit that it was in stayed wet I don't know. But we lost a Stryker and an Abrams to it. The Abrams dropped fast. So fast the Nepo driver barely got out.

There were "roads" out there. They were graded desert, mostly, with posts saying "Here's a road. Don't get lost or you'll be absolutely fucked!" Some of them were paved. We ignored them. There was nobody using them. You could see for miles and miles out there, most of the time. Most of what is called "The Syrian Desert" is gobi desert. That's a technical term meaning a desert of flat ground, usually clay, covered in small rocks.

Out in the big desert is a very disorienting experience, even for a guy from the prairie. You keep looking for something to get perspective on and it's never there. We were a line of boats on a flat, hard, dirt ocean. There were mirages.

You rarely see something like an oasis or a harem girl or whatever from a mirage. They're just layers of differential heat that reflect stuff. Like mountains that are hundreds of miles away.

But when you're a bit shy on water and hallucinating from fatigue, you can make up just about anything. Saw a giant rabbit that was running away from silver spears falling out of the sky. And mountains covered in cellophane.

You get the reason that most of the great world religions have been formed in desert when you're out there for a few days. It's a *very* good place to hallucinate. Peyote cults make sense, too. *Everything* makes sense in this big cosmic "Dude, I am soooo stoned . . ." way.

During the day it was hot. The sun just beat down despite a constant thin overcast we were getting used to. At night it was *mother*fucking cold.

We dropped the spare vehicles. Where? I'd have to give you the grid coordinates which are still classified. But we dropped them. We had to, we needed the gas. Those Abrams and Brads were gas hogs.

Day four we stopped. We put out minimum security and we racked out.

Where?

Middle of the fucking desert, that's where. But I knew that we were going to have to do the same sort of thing, under worse conditions, soon.

When we got up, we sent out "Stones" and did a regular "what's happ'nin'?" broadcast indicating we were going to try to head out through Syria.

We were less than six hour's hard drive from Mosul.

CHAPTER SIXTEEN

I Had Them Right Where
I Wanted Them

Mosul was a stalemate.

The Iraqi forces had the outskirts, the refineries and the tank farms. The Kurds held most of the rest of the city. But they were also surrounded. Eventually, they'd be starved out.

There were Kurdish forces trying to break through from the mountains to relieve them. Sort of. The Kurds are fierce fighters but see the thing about "raid" vs. "shock" infantry. They were *not* shock infantry. They were trying in their own way, though, and might have succeeded in time.

Iraqi forces were holding the side towards the mountains, the north and northeast, from bunkers and defense lines. Ditto the northwest and due east. The main push was coming from south and southwest. That was where the bulk of their armor was placed. Every now and again they'd push into the city and try to kill the Kurds. The Kurds had barricaded a lot of the roads, tough enough obstacles that the tanks couldn't just bull through. The tankers and infantry would drive around for a while getting lit up by RPGs and Carl Gustavs (a man portable anti-tank rocket), lose some infantry and maybe a track or two and then pull out.

Stalemate.

We were a short drive southwest of Mosul.

Two problems.

Problem one: There were a bunch of little towns southwest of Mosul. I wasn't worried about them being heavily defended or even a bunch of Javelins. I was worried about them telling the Iraqis we were coming. And there was fuck all I could do about it.

Problem Two: There was at least another full brigade of armor pushing in on Mosul. They weren't great, but it was a brigade of armor. We had, at max, the makings of a company with the Abrams I'd kept. Think outnumbered ten to one.

The Kurds weren't going to be much help. They were raid fighters. Hit hard and run. In fact, the Parthians (Persians) were the guys who gave us the term "Parthian Shot." That is, hit somebody, run away and keep shooting at them as you run away. (Very difficult to do with a bow over your shoulder on a running horse by the way.) Getting the last word in as you leave the room is a *Parthian* Shot *not* a *Parting* Shot. (Yeah, I know, how many pet peeves . . .)

Anyway, the idea being to get them to chase you. Then you flank them and roll them up.

Hmmm . . .

They're going to get word we're coming . . .

People, it is *not* the "Centurion Maneuver." It's not even a "Parthian" maneuver. They got it from the Ugyar (Mongols) and it was probably used way back when by the Scythians. It's been used by every mobile force in history at one time or another. It was used by Native Americans *and* Colonial forces. (Battle of Yorktown.) It's not new.

Doesn't mean I'm not proud of how *we* used it.

The road southwest out of Mosul crosses a tributary of the Tigris near the town of Khuwaitla. Northeast of Khuwaitla, between it and Mosul, is a low ridge.

The tributary was crossable with our bridging equipment, which was still hanging in there.

It started with a thunder run. We got on that road and barreled ass for Mosul. There were some checkpoints set up to control people in the area and some "tax collectors." We fired them up. But I ordered no main guns to be used. I wanted survivors.

Most of us barreled ass down the road. My ten remaining Abrams and four Stryker gun vehicles carrying Javelin teams swung north towards Tall Zallat. They killed anything they saw and drove over the few phone poles to make sure commo was as down as they could make it.

Another Stryker force went south avoiding most of the villages.

That was a good share of my available U.S. infantry and, notably, my bridger.

The group on the main road took its time. We even took a couple of breaks away from the villages. The Nepos got out and set up fires. We were in no hurry.

In Khuwaitla we stopped, again. This time we did a full commo shut-down. And I dropped Jav teams in houses along the northeast side. Those were all Nepos. We'd given them the best training we could on the Javs. Javs are not that hard to use and they took to it like ducks to water. They could see all the way to the ridge and could engage at least half that distance. They had *lots* of Javs, too. I also left my LOG trail.

After Khuwaitla we sped up. Sort of. I got the Scouts well out in advance and we rolled in stately procession down the road.

I had no intel on what was up ahead or what was going to happen until the Kurds called me and said they'd heard from the guys in Mosul that a big tank force was moving out. I wasn't in direct commo with the Mosul guys. I couldn't ask for details even if they could give them. All I got was "many tanks."

Now, I've got about half my Strykers (fully loaded with infantry again) and my bridging equipment to the south. I've got my tanks to the north. It's a fraction of the total unit, mostly Strykers crewed by Nepos and with barely crews for that, rolling down the road. Exept for about half the Scouts who are barrel assing for the ridge.

They get to the ridge. Every fucking tank on the planet is headed their way. The road from Mosul is "packed with armored vehicles as well as a long column of trucks."

They back up and unass some of their dismounts. With Javelins. They fire up the approaching tanks.

Now, a Javelin has a long damned range for an infantry anti-tank rocket. Two klicks by the book, two and a half in normal conditions and sometimes something like three or so. (There's a trick to that.)

An Abrams, which we'd given these fuckers, has *four* klicks of range. And it can fire while in movement.

Which the Iraqis did. Badly. They fired at our Scout vehicles and missed. They fired at the Jav teams, who were up in a pass and moving after each shot, and missed.

But as they got closer, the gunnery improved. The Scout vehicles went behind the pass. The Jav teams continued to fire them up.

We counted four trucks, two Bradleys and *nine* Abrams burning on the road to Mosul east of Centurion Ridge. They did a damned good job, all things considered.

One thing they did was piss them off. The Abrams and Brads could outrun just about anything else. They sped up on the road, getting strung out in a long line. (I found out later that was against orders. Good thing the commander, who was a pretty good guy, didn't have really effective control.)

When they got to within a kilometer, the Scouts pulled out. That was the sucky time.

We were cruising along halfway between Khuwaitla and the ridge when the Scouts pulled out and ran. Right after them came first one Abrams then two then nine then . . .

In all, there were forty Abrams tanks, nine Paladins and sixty-three Bradleys. There was also a convoy of trucks filled with a shit-pot of infantry, many carrying Javelins.

My "main" force was caught on a flat open plain with the enemy on a ridge overlooking us and with superior firepower *and* range.

I had them right where I wanted them.

I put out dismounts and had them open up with Javelins as the Strykers spread out and opened fire. It was a pointless exercise. Except for keeping the Strykers moving. The enemy wasn't unloading to use Javs. And tank rounds do not track. They fired at the Strykers, the Strykers ran around in circles. We lost one Stryker to tank fire. We should have lost them all. To an American unit we *would* have lost them all.

The tanks and whatnot were slowing down as they came across the ridge. That was backing them up. I couldn't have that. If I'd had decent artillery, sure. They'd have been dead-meat. But I needed them to attack.

We turned back around and picked up the infantry dismounts. They'd shot out their Javs anyway. More smoking vehicles.

We ran like hell as the Scouts finally passed us. We'd dropped the dismounts down the road and now weaved to pick them up. They were continuing to take the enemy under fire the whole way.

We ran into Khuwaitla. We ran *through* Khuwaitla. Then we turned back around and drove into buildings, only the 25mm cannons of the Strykers sticking out.

Khuwaitla had a mosque. Just about every little town did. This one had minarets, those towers where the muzzarein call the faithful to prayer.

They make dandy viewing points.

Javelins have huge range but almost no backblast. They are, therefore, one of the very few anti-tank weapons you can fire from inside an enclosed space. Oh, it can't be real enclosed or even their minor blast will hurt like hell or kill. But if you blow out most of the back wall of a hovel, you can fire from a window with a bit of maneuvering.

There was a stand of trees, poplars, running along the northeast edge of Khuwaitla. Also common in the wetter areas. People use them for firewood. The leaves had been stripped by the autumn winds and branches were gray fingers reaching to the sky as if in supplication that spring would someday return.

They affected neither the view nor the angle of fire of the ten Javelin teams, each with eight Javelins, waiting on the outskirts of Khuwaitla.

Most of them were Nepos with a scatter of infantry to lend technical advice. More had emplaced in defense points in case it got down to infanty-infantry fighting. I didn't want it to.

The "Parthian Shot" is only part of the tactic favored by the Ugyars. Everyone thinks of the Mongols as vast hordes, men on light horses that used speed and their incredible numbers to overrun half the known world.

Most of the time, the Mongols were outnumbered. And they weren't just fast little devils, they were very good strategists and tacticians. They also weren't all "little guys on tiny ponies."

Their favorite tactic went like this.

Charge an enemy with "little guys on tiny ponies." Run away shooting.

Behind some sort of visual screen would wait much heavier guys, lancers, (note the name, people) on much bigger horses and wearing much heavier armor.

When the enemy charged the "fleeing" guys on ponies, they'd run into the guys with lances and be stopped.

In the meantime the little guys were swinging around and hitting the enemy in the flank and rear. If there were enough big lancers, *they'd* hit on the other flank. It was a "one, two, three" punch combination that, especially with an enemy unfamiliar with it, was lethal.

The enemy Abrams and Brads rolled down the road, pedal to the metal.

When the lead Abrams reached a klick, I gave the order to open fire.

Fucking Abrams are *mother*fucking tough.

When that SF unit that first proved the worth of Javelins was under attack, they faced four T-55 tanks. Now, T-55s are old stuff. They're, basically, upgraded WWII tech. Just steel armor and very little internal compartmentalization or blow-out doors. But they're tough.

A hit from a Jav took one out every time.

A hit from a Jav took out a Stryker like a tincan. Really fucked up a Bradley.

Fucking Abrams are *mother*fucking tough. On average it took *two* Javelins to get the motherfuckers to stop firing at our ass. Sometimes it was three. Hit the driver's compartment and they stopped but kept firing. Ditto the engine. Hit the ammo storage (side of the turret) and it blew up spectacularly and they were out of main gun ammo but *still* kept firing machine guns!

Best hit was on the turrets. Generally the tank would just turn around and run away very fast. All the guys who were shooting were dead.

Best best turned out to be "hit the turret with the ammo storage compartment open." On Abrams you're supposed to open it, pull a round, close it, load the round.

I don't know for regular tankers but we tended to lock it open in combat. So did the Iraqis. So it wasn't protected when the Jav hit the turret.

We called it "pop-top." Lots and lots of power in those Abrams rounds. When the main ammo storage went off, and the door was open, there'd be an explosion so big and fast you couldn't figure what was happening. Then you'd catch something flying through the air. The turret. Furthest one landed, I shit you not, nearly a hundred yards away from the tank. A *football* field. Fuckers weighed more than a big bulldozer. The explosion was enough to throw a bulldozer far enough to make a goal from the other endzone.

That's how much power.

And when the door was closed?

Fucker would still keep running.

And they weren't just sitting there to be shot. *Oh*, no. They were firing back. So were the Bradleys which were getting smoked at a *very* high rate. Rounds were crashing into and through the whole fucking village.

But Javs have very low signature. Remember, looking at the guys from a klick away, when they were just hiding in a ditch, our Scouts, who were professionals, couldn't spot the Javs firing.

The Abrams and Brads were lighting up the village but they couldn't see, well, where the fire was coming from.

They also had no clue what they were doing.

Tanks are shock weapons. You run them into an enemy, hard. They're the lance cavalry of the modern battlefield. Sure, they've got great range. But the main thing is that they've got shock weight.

The Iraqis were mostly not under effective control. Not surprising given that the group had to have organized since the Plague. And Iraqis are not, by and large, shock infantry guys. They are, mentally, raid attackers just like the Kurds.

They had been barrel assing down the road in more or less a scattered-out line when the lead tanks took fire. They spread out into the fields to fire at the village. More or less randomly. This is the tanks *and* the Brads which were mixed up together in no formation I could figure out.

Then, instead of just pushing forward and crashing into the damned village, they milled around on the fields firing at medium ranges.

If they'd backed way off and fired, that would have been one thing. But the stupid fuckers stayed in our engagement basket the whole time *and* fired from ranges where their accuracy wasn't that great.

Nelson: "Never interrupt an enemy in the process of making a grievous error."

I actually told *my* Abrams to back off.

But they clearly got some sort of order and started to roll towards the village. They weren't rolling fast, which was stupid, but they were rolling.

Then I told my Abrams to come in.

It was Second Platoon and a scattering of Nepos, mostly driving. The guys who had picked up enough English to be able to take commands. They'd never done real tank gunnery before. Oh, we'd fired some rounds at the vehicles in the desert, including while in movement, but they'd never engaged moving targets while moving themselves. And the Nepos? Well, they'd just recently learned to drive trucks. Now they were driving *seventy-three-ton tanks* and taking orders from TCs in English which they *sort of* understood.

To the north of Khuwaitla, at about six klicks, was the town of Tal Zallat. The road they'd taken to the north went up through Tal Zallat in a bend.

There wasn't much to Tal Zallat. Just some houses and a mosque like Khuwaitla. But the houses were big enough to drive Abrams into and disappear.

Hopefully the people got out, first.

As soon as I saw the Iraqi units starting to "consolidate" and get under some control I called the Abrams.

Down from the village they came like ... Boy, I want to get poetic. "Like an avenging north wind" was what I was going to say. Actually, it was more like ten bouncers jumping into a big riot in a bar.

They opened fire at max range and mostly missed. But they just kept coming in a spread-out line, cannons booming from time to time and kicking up a big pall of dust.

The Iraqis were just getting the idea to drive into Khuwaitla. They couldn't drive around it because of the watercourse. But they could drive *into* it. They started rolling forward and all of a sudden they're getting hit from the flank.

A Bradley on the flank was the first vehicle to get hit by one of the tanks. It was the tank of the platoon leader. You could see the "silver bullet" track right in on that fucker on the playback of the gun camera. And it went through the turret and out the other side. Set off all the main gun ammo on the Bradley and apparently killed all the crew and scared the driver enough he bailed out.

By then our Abrams were down to under two klicks and starting to score. The Iraqis suddenly decided that the Javelins in Khuwaitla were less important than the tanks on their flanks and tried to turn to face our Abrams.

And then the Strykers hit from the south.

They'd bridged the watercourse well to the south and moved up through a screen of trees a couple of klicks down. This was my last platoon of U.S. infantry, First Platoon, and they had a dual mission.

As they moved up, they dropped Jav crews into depressions and those guys started lighting up the armored vehicles. But the main purpose of the Strykers was the line of trucks, filled with infantry, which were following the tanks.

The trucks were mostly still on the road and pretty spread out. U.S. ten tons. (Thanks, State Department!) And a bunch of them had .50 calibers in ring mounts, which can do a number on a Stryker.

If there was any effective fire from those trucks, it wasn't evident. The Strykers spread out and took them all under heavy fire with main guns and the TC's gun. They took out one of the lead trucks, first, which backed up all the others. The others tried to escape onto the fields. Some of them bogged down. None of them were as fast as the Strykers off-road.

The Iraqi commander wasn't done, though. He still had about fifteen Bradleys and ten Abrams and he finally got his artillery firing into Khuwaitla. It was random and mostly fell on the back side of the village but it was a nuisance and we took some casualties. Including one of the Strykers in the village when a 155 round fell right on it.

Out in the fields, it was mano y mano as the Abrams and Bradleys charged each other. I couldn't have that.

"Scouts. Roll out and take the Brads in the ass."

Strykers are not supposed to engage Bradleys. Bradleys are much tougher and even have TOW missiles on them.

But when four Strykers are attacking from the rear while ten Abrams are attacking from the front, thirteen Bradleys are in a bit of a pickle.

There were still the remaining Abrams, though. The enemy's that is. One of ours had been taken out and more were about to be charging right at each other. And with them heading north, most of the Jav teams couldn't get an angle of fire.

"Samad. Get the remaining Jav teams out of the houses. Have them engage only the enemy tanks."

Time of flight became an issue. The two groups closed fast. But Javs started launching up. Not as many as I'd hoped. Clearly we'd lost some of the Nepos. But they were outbound.

The two groups closed to within less than a klick when the

Javs started falling on the enemy Abrams. Coming down from the rear, they had a choice (based on their targeting software) of engine, turret or gun.

Most chose engine. Nice big heat source.

It got very fast and furious for a moment. Then six Abrams charged out of the smoke and dust. They ran actually *through* the formation of Strykers, turned around and charged back in.

"All Javelins, cease fire."

I hoped I'd been in time.

Javelins are very smart rounds. And, somehow, the Nepos managed to sort our Abrams from their Abrams. I couldn't.

Out at the trucks, our infantry was accepting the surrender of the surprisingly large number of survivors.

Battle of Khuwaitla bottomline:

Enemy losses.

Destroyed vehicles:

Forty-three Abrams Main Battle Tanks.

Fifty-three Bradley Armored Fighting Vehicles.

One hundred and four trucks.

KIA: 3800 (approx).

WIA: 2500 (approx).

Prisoner: 1586 (exact).

Captured equipment:

Six damaged Abrams MBT.

Twelve damaged Bradley AFV.

Seventeen Ten-Ton Trucks.

Nine Paladin Mobile Artillery Systems.

Friendly losses:

Four Abrams Main Battle Tanks. (Two recoverable.)

Three Stryker Infantry Carriers. (One recoverable.)

Two Stryker Scout Vehicles. (One recoverable.)

One Hemmitt. (Supply truck. No, the wounded weren't on it.)

Nepalese Auxiliary Infantry: Sixteen WIA, four KIA.

U.S. Army Personnel: Seven WIA, nine KIA.

Twenty-three and Thirteen to Twenty-five hundred and Thirty-eight hundred.

That's balling the ace.

CHAPTER SEVENTEEN

Honorable Bastard

We weren't done but we mostly were done.

Wellington had a great quote for the moment the last enemy vehicle was stopped:

"I have never lost a battle. But I cannot but think that the only thing worse than a battle won must be a battle lost."

The fields between the village and the ridge were covered with burning vehicles. Guys were wandering out there chaotically. There were still some shots, especially .50 caliber. A defeated enemy that don't want to be killed had better surrender on a battlefield. Running is the same as fighting under the laws of war.

A lot of my boys, American and Nepalese, were dead. More were injured and that was in a way worse. We didn't have any doctors or medevac.

And we still hadn't taken Mosul or Irbil or the fuel we needed.

I ordered my guys to take prisoners and sort them out. And to use the "special protocols."

Normally, say back in WWII, the way that you take prisoners is this.

You round them up. Any who "show fight" are taken under fire but otherwise you just round them up.

You separate them into three groups: Officers, NCOs, enlisted.

You keep the groups separate.

You ensure the security of the prisoners at all times. Once you capture an enemy fighter, his security is higher than your own security or those of your fellow soldiers.

That's if you're fighting the Germans. Which we don't do anymore.

With Middle Eastern forces, especially any that included or could include "hardcores," that is guys who were fundamentalist nutballs, you used the "special protocols."

There were still three groups: Officers, enlisted and "hardcores."

How to define "hardcores"? It's an art. First, you look for any guy who's got a beard. Military units, even most Middle Eastern units, are down on beards. I'm not talking about stubble, I'm talking about a full-up soup catcher. Fundamentalist Islamics are big on soup-catchers. (Says you're supposed to have one in the Koran. Surah something. Look it up.)

Closer up, you look for the guys who are glaring at you. Look, these guys just took a pasting. Ever been in a fight you lost? I mean, just got the shit kicked out of you? Do you glare at the guy who just kicked your ass? No.

Not unless you firmly believe that Allah or whoever is on your side. Then you keep glaring while he kicks your ass again and again.

Got a beard and glaring? Definite hardcore. Beard and not glaring? Possible. Glaring? Probable. We tended to be conservative. Possibles went into the "hardcore" file.

And you didn't just round guys up. You had them strip down, first. Why? Because hardcores hid grenades and shit in their clothes and would use them on you. And you couldn't be sure you got all the hardcores. Although if a guy had a grenade in his pocket you could figure he was a hardcore. So everybody, from generals to privates, stripped down to underwear. Then the guys searched their clothes. Then a rank tab or other sign of rank, if any, was ripped off the uniform. They were told to hold that in their hand and keep it where it could be seen. *Then* they were separated.

I hadn't brought anywhere *near* enough fast-ties. Those are basically big cable ties that are used for temporary handcuffs. I hadn't planned on fighting a large force much less capturing a good bit of it.

So we had to go to "special special" protocols.

The enlisted non-hardcore were the most numerous. They always are. They're cattle. Middle Eastern units, by and large, are conscription units with low-morale conscriptees. They don't give their captors trouble. We put them out in one field with a couple of Strykers on guard and told them to get their clothes back on. They were given shovels and told to dig latrines and given some rations and water. They were told to stay in a bunch, don't try to wander off and they'd be fine. Best we could do for them at the time.

(Oh, explaining the latrines is always fun with guys like that. They think they're digging their graves. It gets explained.)

The officers, about twenty, were marched down to Khuwaitla. They were run into a barn and told to hold there. Guards were posted including a Stryker. They were given food and water. One tried to escape. He got shot. Must have missed a hardcore.

The hardcores, a fair number (about a hundred including some "officers" and such-like), were marched into a field. They were spread out. They were told to put their clothes on and sit. Do not stand. Do not talk. If you do either, you will be killed.

Some of them didn't believe us. One stood up.

Had Nepos watching them. Why? Nepos are very interesting when it comes to human life. They take it as a dishonor (they got this from Samad and Ghurka stuff) to kill a true noncombatant. That is, a woman or a kid or an old guy. Even an unarmed male who is not a combatant.

They also don't torture. Don't believe in it. Consider it dishonor. Don't rape.

Combatants? You'd better do what they say or you're fucking *dead*. And they sort of enjoy it.

Guy stood up. Two .50 calibers opened up. He was hit. Guys on either side were hit. Guys behind him were hit. Some just wounded.

They screamed and bled out. The Nepos giggled.

U.S. troops might have hesitated. Should have, probably would have, gotten eaten up by it. Sure, they're hardcores, they're the core of the terrorist motherfuckers we've been fighting since the taking of the U.S. embassy in Iran. They're the guys that flew into the Twin Towers. But they're humans.

Nepos don't think that way. There are targets and non-targets and they don't care what happens to a target.

We get along great but we're not exactly alike.

That wasn't all that was going on.

There were still forces in Mosul. I punched the remaining tanks and Scouts up to the pass. They found the Paladins that were still intermittently firing. Captured them. (A Paladin has a .50 caliber on it and their guns can be lowered to direct fire. They're there if a group of infantry hit your unit. If you're a smart Paladin commander, however, when a Main Battle Tank comes calling you surrender. Quick.) More prisoners. Dispatched a couple of trucks with Nepo guards and some guys to drive the Paladins back.

We "consolidated" on Khuwaitla in the meantime. Gathered wounded, redistributed ammo, reammoed. Ran a supply truck up to the guys on the Pass. No movement in the direction of Mosul they could see.

We did what we could for the wounded. I'd brought a plentiful supply of medical stuff with us and picked up more in Baghdad. Most of what was wrong, though, the medics could barely touch. Horrible burns on a couple of guys. One amputation from a tank round. Shrapnel. One of the Nepos, who had been hit on the head so hard a chunk of skull was missing, wanted to go back on duty. We sedated him.

The Kurds in Mosul had a doctor. He was short on medicines. I had lots of medicines. As soon as things were stabilized it was time to link-up.

So I had somebody go get the commander of this ratfuck.

Yes, he'd survived. Got picked up from the "truck" group. Was in a wheeled mobile command post which had stopped and everybody bailed when the Strykers hit. Smartest thing they could do.

He was alive. He'd gotten his clothes back on. He was turning the rank tab over and over in his hands when I walked in.

Decent looking guy. Clean shaven, good haircut. Uniform wasn't tarted up with medals. Smart eyes. Not glaring, just smart.

"Captain Bandit Six," he said very dryly in really clear English. "What a surprise to see *you* up here."

We talked. He didn't do the usual Arab thing of beating around the bush. I got out a bottle of hooch from the Iran LOG base. He didn't turn down a belt or two.

Turns out he was a "real" colonel. Sunni but American trained and hadn't been part of the Resistance. (Not *all* the Sunnis *were.*) Survived the Plague. Kept some people together. Family, some guys from his unit.

Bigger fish took over in most of Baghdad. Not military, a Sunni mujaheddin type. Not even from Iraq, an Egyptian. Grabbed the LOG base. Colonel joined forces with the bigger commander. Fighting would have been stupid.

He was pretty good. Experienced. School trained. (Command and General Staff among others. Guy was better trained than *me*.) Things were quiet in the south. He was dispatched with most of the combat forces around to go up and take the oil fields from the Kurds. Well, beating up on Kurds was just patriotic duty to any Iraqi. Kurds were mountain raiders, ground-mount Vikings, barbarians. Well-known fact. Been that way since time immemorial. The guys on the plains get raided by the Kurds . . . Go back to that bit and read it. Then take it from the POV of the guys in the "empires." "Fucking Kurds."

Couldn't hold fighting the Kurds against him except they were my allies. The Kurds *were* bastards to the Iraqis and vice versa.

"By the way, wiped out the other armored force down in Baghdad."

"Yes, I was told." Very dry again. "Actually, I found out through sources. What I was told was somewhat different. I was *also* told you were on your way to Syria. That I shouldn't worry about you."

"I tried very hard to give that impression," I admitted. "So what do I do with you? You know all the laws and such. And, trust me, I'm down to basic law not regs put on top. Not even basic law to tell truth."

What I was saying was, I no longer felt constrained by the Geneva Convention. Easiest thing was to shoot everybody out of hand.

"Believe it or not, I actually have Kurdish POWs," he replied. "I am keeping them as well as I can."

What he was saying was he felt constrained by the Geneva convention. Fucker.

On the other hand, if he was willing to play by the rules . . .

"Parole?"

Parole, in military terms, means that the officer and his unit agree to no longer engage in combat against a particular enemy. So he couldn't be used to beat up on the Kurds or us. But he could be sent down to watch the Shias or whatever and free up forces from down there. I'd take that.

"If I give my parole Mullah Hamadi will have me killed," he replied, smiling. "And find an officer who is willing to lead this shattered force. I will give it, but you might as well shoot me."

Fuck.

"I don't suppose you can get the forces besieging Mosul to surrender?"

"Probably not and if I could I would not give the order."

Honorable bastard.

"What if you agree to remain under parole *here*," I asked. "Until the local issues are decided?"

"I would go for that. But there are elements of my force which will not."

"The hardcores. What to do with them?"

"Give them to the Kurds for all I care."

Honorable *and* knew who to be honorable about. I was starting to like this guy.

And so it was done.

I called the Kurds. I told them to tell the guys in Mosul that when the tanks came *back* they were *ours*. Don't shoot.

I left most of the prisoners in Khuwaitla with a group of Nepos and, notably, our LOG and wounded. The enlisted prisoners were moved into the shattered houses and given food. They didn't cause problems. The officers did a couple of times. The colonel settled that out. The Nepos were just there to make sure nobody got really stupid. There were a couple of hardcores in the enlisteds. They got stupid. The rest got the hint.

We waited until the next morning then rolled to Mosul.

Don't get me wrong, nobody got any sleep that night. There were hardcores to handle, which is never easy even with blood-thirsty Nepos. Shit had gotten fucked up. It had to be unfucked. I had to spread out units as observation posts and hope they didn't get overrun. There were still some guys moving around that had avoided the sweep. We had to round them up. All the vehicles had to be logged, which since we were spread to fuck and gone took time. I put in a quick call to home. More on that later. There was a probe up towards the pass. It got turned back.

Some of the troops got some sleep, I got none at all and neither did the other officers or most of the NCOs. I'd talk about how tired I was but unless you've been there you just can't know. And if you have, I don't have to explain. But by dawn we were ready to roll.

Creating any sort of "combined action" was impossible. First of all, the Perg Mersha for all their valor were never particularly disciplined. They're great fighters, don't get me wrong, but so were Vikings. Getting them to do anything, though, is like herding cats.

The way to herd cats is to toss treats. The treats were running Iraqi soldiers and Iraqi logistics units that were suddenly unguarded.

Basically, we did what JEB Stuart did at Gettysburg instead of his job. We rolled all the way around the battle. Everywhere we went, the suddenly surrounded Iraqis broke and ran. The guys in the trenches were the least hardcore of any of the units. Getting rolled over by Abrams scared the shit out of them.

As a unit broke, the local Kurds, who kept a close eye on such things and had gotten the rumor that we were in the area, would break out and attack. Raid if you will but when an enemy is running raiders will run just as fast or faster.

Took all day but by the time the sun set the Siege of Mosul was lifted. Link-up was effected with the guys coming down from the mountains. All quiet on the Mosul front.

One tank farm went up. Probably a hardcore. There was still plenty of diesel and gas. Hell, there was enough for us in the trucks supporting the Iraqi forces.

The Kurds did a pretty good job in the aftermath. They'd been civilized, a bit, by dealing with us. They rounded up the Iraqis instead of putting them on stakes or whatever. They used the "special" protocols but that was just sense. They also separated for hardcores. We gave them ours. They still didn't put them on stakes.

We got our wounded under care and the Kurdish doctor (doctors, actually) got medicines from our stores and the Iraqis'. (Which were U.S. medicines, anyway.)

I got with the local Perg Mersha commander. Here's how the Perg Mersha work. They're tribal based. That is, a company, battalion, whatever, will all come from one tribe. When they gather in big groups, one guy is put in charge. There's a lot of arguing about orders at that level. But they all sort of agree as long as the target is clear. Think barbarian hordes. Or, hell, the Confederate Army.

The local guy was the brother-in-law of the president of Kurdistan. (They'd tried a couple of different organizations, politically, and gone with one that is remarkably close to ours. Works for tribes which is what the thirteen colonies really were. And, hell, still are.) Also one of their brighter military lights, by useful coincidence. I looked up his data on the DODnet and DOD agreed. Smart guy, good natural tactician, school trained in the U.S. Fuck, what was it with these guys getting CGSC and *I* couldn't get a damned slot?

The Kurds got under control fast. They rounded up prisoners. They secured equipment and critical installations. They started counting the loot. All under this Kurd guy.

He had things well in hand. Well, fuck me. I'm supposed to have to do *everything*!

We parked in downtown Mosul and just fucking *crashed* while the Kurds had a party.

— CHAPTER EIGHTEEN —

Yeah, Son, We Really Kicked Ass

The next morning I got on the horn. I'd sent in a sort of incoherent report the night before but it was late and I was just
fucking shot.

We'd been in EMCON, electromagnetic something something,
basically not using any of our electronics, for most of the run.
All the way since Abu Samak. We'd told home we were going
EMCON and approximately when we should come back up. But
there was still some "trepidation" on the other end.

Overnight my "staff," Fillup and his XO basically, had done
some work. Fine boys. We had a list of the captured stuff from
the first battle and it turned out the Kurds had a better one. I
called home. BC, being prompted I was going to call, came on.
I opened my mouth:

"Have the honor to report have captured Mosul along with
over seventy enemy cannon . . ."

Had it all written out and the words just flowed "Nepalese
auxiliaries charged forward with great gallantry . . ." "must highly
commend Lieutenant Mongo on his fearless assault into the flank
of the enemy force . . ."

Look, U.S. After Action Reports are as dry as a fucking bone.
If you read the fucking *battle of Thermopylae* as a U.S. After
Actions report you'd be snoozing halfway through. They could
suck the life out of the battle of the Alamo.

In the old days these sorts of things were written by quill,
put into a multi-layer waxed-linen envelope and sent over seas

by way of fighting ships. Who just might have to fight through enemies to bring them home. They were dry and terse but they had a terrible beauty about them. Often they were reprinted, verbatim, in newspapers.

They did not use the term "synergy" anywhere in the report. And they gave fucking credit where credit was due.

The new BC was clearly a history buff. He was grinning after the first sentence and just nodded all the way through. Apparently, despite the wording, he was getting every bit.

"That was a thing of beauty there, Bandit Six."

"Thank you, sir. I practiced."

"I take it you have it written out?"

"Yes, sir. With appendixes."

"Fast work. Send it on. I was copying your verbal. I'm going to send *that* on as well."

"Yes, sir." (Gulp. Let's hope most of the chain of command had a sense of humor.) "Sir, Mosul *and* Irbil have airports. Rupert Murdoch got a plane in here, for God's sake."

"Ready to come home?"

"You're kidding, right, sir?"

"Let me get back to you on that," he said. I could see there was something going on but I couldn't know what.

Lord God I wished I'd known. I would have gone and taken a barbarian bride.

But I'm getting ahead of myself again.

The Kurdish general still had things in hand. My guys had been moved up overnight. The wounded were under care and it was pretty good. I checked up on them and the facilities they were in were at least Vietnam era. Compared to everything we'd seen up to that time, it was like science fiction. Hell, they had a functioning MRI! They'd needed medicines but we'd carried in a lot of those.

The POWs were a handful, there was now a fuckload of them, but there were a lot of Kurds to take care of that. They had pretty much the same approach as the Nepos. Be nice boys and you live. We'll even feed you.

Food turned out to be an issue in the whole region. The harvests were screwed by the weather. Right then I decided if this *Last Centurions* thing worked out I *was* going to discuss the weather.

But there were lots of fields around Mosul. Most of them were fucked up from the weather and plague but some had standing wheat and barley. With the fighting under control the next major operation was to get them harvested. The Kurds really wanted enough food to make it through the winter and next spring.

So I got together with the Kurdish commander and the Iraqi commander and a bottle of hooch.

Thing was, most of the Iraqi commander's troops were Shia not Sunni. Sunni had gotten down to less then ten percent of the Iraqi population by the time the Plague hit and they didn't fare any better than the Shia. Having a Sunni in control in Baghdad was just silly. It was purely a function of State leaving our gear where they did. Oh, and the fact that most of the Sunni left in Iraq were, ahem, "immoderates." (Read "hardcores.") Quite a few of them weren't even Iraqi; they were transplants who had come in for the "great jihad" against the U.S. Most of the long-term Iraqi families left in Iraq were those who just refused to leave and were going to fight the Shia tooth and nail until they were "ethnically cleansed." There were some good guys. The commander of the Mosul brigade was pretty decent as such guys go.

But most weren't.

What now? Lotsoprisoners you can't feed.

Truce with Baghdad. Prisoners. Better operational forces. Your equipment and support . . .

Yeah, on that. Don't bet. Stuff back home.

Still have equipment.

Yeah, on that . . .

Truce with Baghdad.

Mad Mullah.

()

Need a different government in Baghdad.

(Slight wry grin.) Culloden Field.

Now *that* was a reference I was surprised to hear. Go look it up. But clearly this guy realized that taking the Kurds all the way to Baghdad wasn't an option. In which he was smarter than Bonnie Prince Charlie.

I looked over at the Iraqi commander who was quietly sipping my booze and wondering why he was in a high level meeting with two of his enemies.

Need a different government in Baghdad.

There were . . . issues. There always are. And when people started to piece together what I'd done, let's just say that my career got rocky. But that was later.

Here were the issues.

The Iraqis, the non-hardcores, were going to be willing to follow the colonel. He was a pretty good guy all things considered. But they'd just gotten their asses kicked and a shattered unit is rarely cohesive in battle.

But even if the returning "army of conquest" could beat the hardcores working for Mullah Hamadi, and that was an "if," that would leave the colonel in a bit of a pickle. He'd be a Sunni trying to lead a bunch of Shia with absolutely no support from the Sunni around him.

Which had me making calls.

Turned out the mullah I'd left in charge at the LOG base had gotten pretty good relations going with the Shia over in southern Iraq. Basically, the border was a memory. They were getting into good cooperative agreement now that a couple of "issues" had been settled in the area. (HAMB on the Iranian side and the rest of the Mahdi Army over in Iraq.) The "moderates" were in a position that being "moderate" was no longer a survival trait so they'd gotten "immoderate" with the "immoderates" and since the "immoderate moderates" outnumbered the "immoderate immoderates" they'd kicked their ass.

If that makes any sense at all.

There had always been a lot of Iraqis who supported "moderation." Look at their fucking elections for God's sake. But the problem had been large numbers of fuckheads, the Sunni jihadis who were being funneled in and Ba'athist Sunnis who wanted back in power and the Shia who were puppets to the Iranians whether they knew it or not. And their various tribes. And criminals and whatnot.

The "immoderates."

With the Plague the "moderates" had realized that it was fight or die time. And they'd *always* outnumbered the "immoderates."

This pattern, too, was consistent in Islam. There'd been periods of "moderation" and then periods of "fucking nutballs in charge." Causality was pushing in the direction of "moderation."

Didn't mean I would want to be a Sunni in Iraq.

The point being, there was a group in south Iraq which was

already looking at taking Baghdad and tossing the fuckheads out. Freedom and Democracy? Maybe. In time. But they were primarily secularist politically (even the "mullah" I'd left in charge in the LOG base) and that would have to do.

Their problem was, they had pretty good intel on what Mullah Hamadi had in Baghdad. It was way less, now, but it was still a tough nut.

We got everybody in a consult. Hey, I wasn't sure why I'd left the commo vans in the LOG base but I figured they might come in handy. Think the Palantir in the *Lord of the Rings*. (Yes, I've read it. School paper. God that's a fucking snoozer.)

The end point.

Combined assault on Baghdad from the north and south. The colonel would lead his primarily Shia unit on an "invasion of liberation from Sunni oppression." (Yes, he was a Sunni. People could and did ignore that.) They'd have some Kurds to lend esprit de corps and for whatever loot they could get from Baghdad. Forces from the south would come up in support. Food, which was more available in the south, would be sent to the Kurds for their help. Oh, and the Kurds get Mosul, Irbil and all the oil and other stuff up here to the line of . . . figure it out.

Shia?

Yeah, we can go for that. As long as we don't have those fucking Sunni in power anymore.

Guarantees? There's no such thing in the Middle East.

However, that left the colonel in a bit of a pickle. He hadn't been the most popular guy in the world in Iraq *before* the Plague. After it, he was *less* popular except among the Mullah Hamadi crowd who saw a school-trained Sunni. And he was willing to talk a good line to stay alive.

After they took Baghdad, Sunni were *not* going to be popular people.

Sigh. Couldn't have the savior of the country strung up. Which *would* have happened eventually. Life is like that. Or shot by the Shia as a Sunni or the Sunni as a traitor.

He had family in the Sunni Triangle. Hell, bit of the remains of a clan.

"Well, Moses, you know what's got to happen."

"Take my people out of Egypt?"

"Okay, maybe Abraham. Out of Babylon for sure."

So I put in a call to Jordan.

School-trained colonel. Sunni but secular. Nice guy. Probably bringing some weapons, personnel and equipment with him. Got a few things to do first.

Sure, Hussein Jr. would love to have somebody like that. Come on down! We'll bring the couscous.

Did I have authority to do any of that shit? Oh, hell no. And when State got wind of it they damned near wet their short trousers. Especially "justifying" the borders of Kurdistan. Who the hell did I think I was? *Churchill?*

Let me give a little history lesson.

Most of this stuff, prior to WWI, had been owned by the Ottoman Empire. The Ottomans made the mistake of backing the Great Powers, Germany, the Austro-Hungarian Empire, etc, against the Allies, France, U.S., Britain, etc.

The Ottomans had been pretty broken up over the whole thing. Seriously broken up.

So at the end of the War, the Allies broke up the Ottomans. Totally. And created a bunch of "countries" what were just fucking lines on paper. And most of those lines were drawn by none other than Winston Churchill, who was the British Foreign Secretary at the time.

There's a bit of an otherwise straight border between Saudi Arabia and Iraq which dips upwards, giving a bit more completely empty desert to Saudi Arabia and a bit less to Iraq. (At the time, the oil issue was little known.) No fucking reason in the world for it. People call this "Churchill's Burp" because they say he drew the line in after lunch and burped while he was drawing the line.

Most of the lines make no sense. They had nothing to do with terrain and *nothing* to do with indigenous inhabitants. It's one of the reasons that the MidEast has been a continuous battle zone ever since. That and the fact that it's been a battle zone for its entire history. Which is just about *all there is* of history.

Take the Kurds. ("Please!" Just joking.) Here's a pretty homogenous group that has fairly defined borders if you ask them. Nobody asked them. They got broken up into *three different countries*. None of which liked Kurds. And they'd been battling for survival ever since.

Iran and Iraq are, basically, Persia. There's some counter arguments but they're weak. At the very least, if you're going to make an "Iraq" it should go all the way to the Zagros Mountains. But, really, Iran and Iraq could be one really mongo country. (As they are today.) Breaking them up was basically so that a particular Arab clan which had helped out the Brits could have "Babylonia." (Churchill was a romantic. Romantic Babylon and all that. I've been all across Iraq. Ain't romantic.) And to cut down on the power of the Persians.

In time it led to the Iran-Iraq War which left over a million dead on one of Churchill's little lines.

The First Gulf War happened on another.

Most of northern Saudi Arabia was inhabited by Shia. Who were under Sunni control and never really liked it.

And the family that Churchill liked so much?

The only one left in power of the Hashemites was Hussein, Jr. Who was barely holding on. The Sauds had killed the last Hashemite in Saudi Arabia and Saddam's predecessor killed the one in Iraq.

All I was suggesting was that we get the lines to look a bit more like the people involved.

Hey, they'd lasted a hundred years. That's a long time for a border to last in the Middle East.

Assuming everyone won their battles, we ended up hashing out some new lines. Until something could be worked out with the various "Fars" city states (the guys running bits and pieces of Iran), the line of demarcation for "Babylonia" would be to the Zagros. *Both* sides of the Shat Al Arab. Border with Jordan stayed more or less the same. In the north, the Kurds got all of their previous Iraqi territory. They were in de facto control of all their "Turkish" territory and "Iranian" territory anyway. They even were in control of a good bit of "Syrian" territory.

Assuming Mullah Hamadi and his goons could be kicked out of power, most of the Sunni who were willing to leave would go to Jordan along with not only everything they could carry but a bit of a goodwill offering. And some who weren't willing to leave.

There were three or four guys in charge in Syria. None of them were fucking with Iraq at the moment and most were Shia. (One was a Ba'athist Alawite fuck, which was the group in power before the Plague.) That area of "diplomacy" would have to wait.

This sort of negotiation should have taken months. How long did it take?

Three hours. And *that* was with a break for lunch.

(The mullah at the LOG base actually *could* answer a direct question when four angry people were staring at him over satellite video. He's actually a great guy and much better at MidEast normal negotiations than I could ever be. Hell, he's got a fucking Nobel Prize. *I* don't.)

It wouldn't be fast. Things were going to have to be "consolidated." Both the Iraqi colonel and the Kurd guy realized there was going to need to be an OpPlan.

I left them to it. They were using one of my commo vans. The other was in use cutting "Divisions" and keeping an ear out for The World. Nothing on redeployment or even evac. I went and checked on the wounded. They were way more upbeat than they should have been. There was the Nepo missing a chunk of his skull. He'd held out to be operated on. He thought it was great. The Kurd surgeons had put in a chunk of metal so "Now my head is even harder, sahib!"

Burns, shrapnel. Most of the guys who weren't sedated were in great spirits. "We really kicked ass, didn't we, sir!" This from a guy waving the stump of an arm.

There were a couple that just weren't going to make it. They were out in a bliss of morphine. One of them was less out, sort of one long quiet moan. Unconscious and still moaning.

Yeah, son, we really kicked ass.

Centurions one and all.

— CHAPTER NINETEEN —

There Was an Issue

The guys were resting up after their travails. I was getting some rest, starting to pine for Shadi and considering the beauty of Kurdish women, but mostly waiting for the other shoe to drop.

We could get out via the local airports. It would be "logistically difficult" given that most of the airbases that the U.S. depended upon for "global dominance" weren't available. But you can refuel a C-17 in-flight. Hell, there were planes that could fly in non-stop from Britain, which had some functioning airports. There was fuel here. Irbil was well on the way to becoming the best place to land between Britain and India.

The other shoe dropped.

I got called to come over to the commo van. Everybody was "taking a break" from cutting the next episode. They'd been tossed out. The BC was on the video conferenced in with the brigade commander and a couple of other people I didn't know. One of them was a suit. Another was a lieutenant general, Air Force no less.

Uh, oh.

The good news.

C-17s configured for medical evac were on the way. Ask the Kurds if they have any casualties that would respond better to top-flight treatment. Everybody's coming to Walter Reed.

Thank fucking God. I'll get right on that, sir. What about . . . ?

There was an issue.

We'd finally picked sides in Turkey. The side we'd picked had, according to them, most of the territory that used to be Turkey. And it was kinda, sorta, stabilized. (Yeah. Right. More on that later.) They had Ankara, the Turkish capital. They had most of the Anatolian Plain. (Arguable as we'll see.) They were leaving the Kurds alone. The Kurds had their area stabilized and that was good enough for now. (And they're going to *keep* it, suckers.)

They were mostly Turkish military which meant secular. They wanted to restore freedom and democracy and all good things to Turkey.

But there was an "issue."

A fundamentalist group had some territory. Notably, they had most of the territory around Istanbul and the Bosporus. The big problem being Istanbul.

History again.

Byzantium, Constantinople, Istanbul. Hell, I think there's a name before Byzantium.

The Bosporus is actually a big fucking river if you think of the Black Sea as being a *big* fucking lake. It consists of the Bosporus which is a narrow bit exiting from the Black Sea that Istanbul straddles, the Mamara Denizi which is a big lake, then the Dardanelles, which is another narrow bit by the Med (okay, Aegean, same diff). Rivers from Eastern Europe to the Stans dump to the Black Sea and the water, in turn, dumps through the Bosporus (I use it as a general name for the whole thing) into the Mediterranean. (In fact, there's a *continuous* outward current. It really *is* a river.)

Rivers have always meant trade. So the choke point, from back *before* there was history, for all that trade is the Bosporus. And people have been plying their trade on the Bosporus since they were moving better flints down from the Volga region. (Seriously. They've found sunken boats that had cargoes of *flints*. Like for making chipped stone knives and stuff. *Way* before history.)

Remember Troy? Forget all that shit about it being about Helen. Troy was one of the first major cities to control Bosporus trade. It got really rich on it, and the Hellenes decided they wanted the money. Simple as that. It's over at the entrance to the Dardanelles on the Aegean/Med side. Guy named Schliemann found it in the late 1800s using mostly *The Illiad* as a guide. Well, he found *one* of the cities that was, sort of, Troy. There were layers and layers he never got to.

Anyway, The Big City for controlling Bosporus trade pretty much since history had been written was Istanbul. And it had a special significance to the Turks.

The faction that had taken most of Turkey was never going to be able to really control things until they controlled Istanbul.

And whether they had the forces to take Istanbul or not, they didn't have the moxie. They needed stiffening up. They needed a little Viagra in the old pencil.

We were the Viagra.

The Air Force general burbled. Airbase in Incirlik was available as soon as they took Istanbul. How the two were linked I had no idea; they were about seven hundred miles apart.

The State Department guy babbled. Improved relations with the Turkish government. Stabilization of the whole region. Opening trade through the Bosporus links.

Nobody was doing much "trade" back then. Most shipping lines weren't operative. An opening up the Bosporus was no big deal. If we really wanted to help this guy, we could send a MEU over and take Istanbul. Trust me, we wouldn't make the mistakes that the Brits made at Gallipoli.

But for some reason it had to be "Farmer's Freaks." They wanted me to cross the Tauric range, in what was starting up to be a fucking iceage of a winter, and on the far side link up with notionally friendly forces and take a city that was a fucking fortress?

I let them burble. The brigade commander and my BC watched me nod in agreement.

When the two idiots wound down I nodded again.

"No," I said and cut the connection.

I walked out of the commo vehicle and looked at the on-duty RTO, who was looking worried for good reason.

"When they call back, tell them I'm unavailable."

And I made myself unavailable.

The Kurds had some running Humvees we'd left behind. About the only thing we'd left them. I found a Kurd who knew who I was, and wanted to know if I was married because he had a cute female cousin . . . and he was talking marriage mind you . . . and rode out of town.

I drove up to Centurion Ridge. I parked where from the marks a Javelin had been fired. I looked down at those pretty good fields covered in the wrecked trucks, tanks, Bradleys, in all the mess we'd made.

They were pretty good fields. Not as good as Minnesota. But with the right equipment and knowledge, they could be made to really produce. And, hell, just because all that shit was fucked up now, didn't mean it had to stay fucked up. Some of the engines down there were in pretty good shape. Find a busted up tractor, put one of those truck engines in it and you'd be stylin'. Pimp my tractor, baby. Hell, I could put a fucking Abrams engine in it. Burn up the wheat as I was harvesting but, hell, that would keep down all but the grassy weeds . . .

Might be some unexploded ordnance. French farmers dealt with that all the time.

I wonder how cute that cousin is? And it wasn't the first such offer I'd gotten. The Kurd general, who was related to the Kurdish president, had mentioned introducing me to his sister . . .

What was there for me in the States? What was there for most of my boys in the States? Families were dead. The government was screwed to the max. The cities were a nightmare and the Army wasn't being *allowed* to do anything about it.

Things would get pretty peaceful in this region pretty soon. Especially if we helped out in Baghdad. The Kurds were mostly Hurrians but they had all sorts of tribes in truth. Maybe it was time for a tribe of Americans.

They'd called me pretty late in their day. It was noon local when I said no. I sat there all afternoon. Watched the sun set. Watched the fields turn to silver as it got really fucking cold. I pulled out my poncho liner and wrapped up. I watched the fields get more silver as a thin moon rose over my shoulder. I slept. I dreamed and they were ragged dreams. Dreams of empire. Hell, the whole Middle East was ripe for the taking for somebody who had the right force and mentality. I saw myself on a throne. And I saw disaster and Mom calling me in from the fields and Dad's big hands working on a tractor. I dreamed of battles I'd been in and battles I'd never seen. I'd never held a shield or sword in my life and I saw those as well as if I'd lived it. I saw cohorts and just big groups of guys with bows and ragged cavalry charges. And I woke to the birds singing outside the room of my house and knowing I was late for school. That there was something I had to do and it was nagging at me.

Till a voice, as bad as Conscience, rang interminable
    changes
    On one everlasting Whisper day and night repeated—so:
"Something hidden. Go and find it. Go and look behind
    the Ranges—
    "Something lost behind the Ranges. Lost and waiting
    for you. Go!"

They were the wrong birds. Magpies squawking in the pass. Ravens croaking their harsh cries.

Could those green hills of Kurdistan have ever been home? I don't know. Maybe. If they pushed me, they were going to be.

There was a radio in the Humvee. I'd had it turned off. I turned it back on, punched in the right frequency and called the commo van. I was coming back. Call the BC. I'll call back when I was ready, give me an hour or so.

I had a leisurely breakfast. I'd taken some pogie bait with me, every soldier carries some food with him, but not much else. I was going to need the blood sugar.

I tossed everybody out of the van again. I called back. I got put on hold, which I'd expected.

Took about fifteen minutes for the conference to come back up. Different group. Still the BC and the Brigade. And the Army Chief of Staff. And the Air Force Chief of Staff. And a different State weenie. This one looked less Weenieish. Sharper.

Chief of Staff, Army, opened.

"Bandit," and he *called* me Bandit, "we know what we're asking. We know. We can send replacements for your casualties. We can send you gear if necessary. Supplies. Whatever. But we need this done. And you're the guy who can do it."

"*I* was laying odds you were going to take a barbarian bride," the BC said. There were glares all around. Water. Duck.

"I get that, sir. The you-want-this-done part. Note, that you *want* it done, not you *need* it done. Turkey means exactly *dick* to the U.S. strategically right now. The Middle East means *dick* right now. In five years, ten years, maybe. Right now? Diddly. So you *want* it done not *need* it done."

"That is actually a fair assessment," the State guy said. "But there's a high probability that the Anatolian League can help with stabilization. There's an oil shortage building in the U.S. Less use but we're heading into a cold winter and we're going to need oil. We're mostly looking for the oil platform in the Black Sea. If the Kurds can get their act together and the Anatolian League can get their act together we could be shipping by January. And we're going to *need* it in January."

"Uh, huh. I've done some stuff... Well, I've done quite a lot of stuff to stabilize the situation down in the Northern Gulf. Shia will sell you oil."

"Bandits in the Straits of Hormuz," the Air Force Chief of Staff said, shrugging. "Maybe we could escort with Navy ships but we're still pretty tasked out. The Med is clear. Italians are sort of back up, ditto the Greeks. And the Brits took back Gibraltar so the Spanish don't matter. They're *not* back up."

"The Kurds are becoming a linchpin," the State Department guy said. "They are stable. Especially after your actions at Mosul. Mullah Hamadi cannot, in the near future, take back northern Iraq. And the pipeline to the Black Sea is up. Venezuela and Brazil aren't pumping. Gulf of Mexico isn't entirely back up but it's keeping us alive. By January we're really going to need oil. So are the Europeans. So we need the Bosporus."

"Uh, huh. MEU?"

"That's not the only thing we're working on," ACOS said. "Screwed up as we are, we're still the World's Policeman. The Marines are *way* overtasked with that. This is part of being the World's Policeman. If you want a traffic whistle I'll send you one."

"Oh, I do," I said. "To be precise, I'm going to give you my needs, wants and desires. The needs are nonnegotiable. If I don't get them, we're going to become Kurds and I wish you luck in you Bosporus adventures. The boys are getting pretty tired of being handed the shit end of the stick."

"People?" the Chief of Staff asked.

"No," I replied. Although, truthfully, I should have gotten more troops. But I trusted the guys I had. New troops would be an unknown quantity. And I was seeing glimmerings of ideas. "Maybe some..."

See, here's the fucked up thing. Give me a problem, one that's damned near insoluble, and I start solving it. I *hate* that trait. Especially since the ideas are *never* straightforward and always have a huge number of consequences. They solve the problem but they make more problems. And then there's the whole "the reward for a job well done is a harder job."

And you know, no matter what you do in the Army, you get paid *exactly* the same as some same-rank Pentagon weenie who takes a two-hour lunch?

There's a list of staff officer sayings. One of them came to mind at that moment:

"The secret to this shop is to find the one or two guys who are not complete incompetents and work them to death."

Military leadership in a nutshell.

"First, I'm going to need something like a designation as ambassador plenipotentiary to these Turkish guys."

What the fuck does that mean?

Back in the days when communication to a foreign country took *forever*, see the thing about waxed linen envelopes, the ambassador to a foreign country would be "plenipotentiary." That is, he (and it was always a he) spoke with "full power" (plenipotentiary) of the government he represented.

All ambassadors these days are, technically, plenipotentiary. The reality is, State does whatever it damned well pleases with or without the ambassador's say-so. Probably a better system, but I wasn't having it.

"If I'm going to do this, I'm going to need concessions and support from a lot of local groups. I have to be able to negotiate with full powers to get it. And I'm going to be negotiating with the Turkish guys, not some State suit. State doesn't joggle my elbow. State doesn't back-channel. State doesn't back *stab*. State stays the fuck out of the way and you get what you get when I'm done. The same goes for anyone above State."

The only person above State is the President.

"I am notionally accepting of you being an ambassador," the State guy said. "Although that is rarely a military post it has precedents. I cannot guarantee it being done. I also cannot guarantee lack of *any* interference. But if you detect interference from State we should be able to work that pretty hard. We also should be able to . . . handle interference above State. May I ask, in general, what you are going to be negotiating?"

"No."

"What else do you require?" the ACOS asked.

"Really, that's it, General," I replied, shrugging. "I would *like* a bunch of other stuff. But that's the only requirement. Fly my wounded out. Be ready to do that again when it becomes necessary. I'd *like* air support. I don't see why we can't get a wing of *something* over to Irbil and have them work out of there. We've got plenty of fuel here. Might have some parts needs, but last time I checked we're good on that. But I *need* serious room to negotiate and I don't know for what. I won't put the U.S. in any binding treaties and you can be sure I won't promise anything I can't deliver myself. Given that I've gotten nothing delivered to *me* this whole time, like, you know, redeployment to the *States* or some fucking *air support*, promising anything to the *Turks* would be silly. Although the way that things have been going, why would it surprise me if *they* got more support than *we* have."

"Major," the ACOS said, sternly, "I have been, I think, very accepting of your attitude in this discussion. But I will remind you that things are tough all over."

I looked at the cut-off button for ten seconds then looked back up, right at the Chief of Staff of the Army.

"You want 'tough,' General? General, I'm sure that you still have access to satellite imagery. I invite you to task one of those satellites on the fields outside of Khuwaitla. General, a company of *Stryker infantry*, some of them in tanks that State O so kindly gave to the enemies of the United States and that we took *away* from those enemies and that they had *never* before driven or fired along with a group of *Nepalese tribesman* who had not worn *shoes* a year ago and were asked to use *practically every weapon in the U.S. infantry inventory* took on an *armored brigade* in *more* U.S. inventory that State gave to our enemies and *crushed them*."

I grabbed my somewhat too long hair and screamed.

"I KNOW THE PENALTY FOR A JOB WELL DONE IS A TOUGHER JOB BUT THAT WAS A *PRETTY FUCKING TOUGH*, GENERAL!"

Short answer? I got what I wanted. Every bit. Surprised the hell out of me.

Oh, I asked for and received other stuff. I got a C-17 loaded with Javelins and another with ammo. I didn't, then, ask for food. I knew it was in short supply in the U.S. But I told them I was going to need quite a bit at some point. At least a freighter's worth of grains and suchlike. They sent me some MREs which was nice of them.

I said I might need heavy duty air support at some point. I'd give them time, but there might be a point where B-52s would be a good thing. The Air Force COS said he'd get working on it.

And one of the C-17s that got blocked for us carried a courier with a piece of paper signed by The Bitch calling me "envoy" and giving me "all the authorities of ambassador plenipotentiary of and for the United States to the nation of Turkey and the Anatolian League."

When I had that in hand and the sat-phone number to the military leader of "The Anatolian League" I got on the phone and started negotiating.

The problem was somewhat similar to Iraq. The mullahs in Istanbul had grabbed a bunch of hardware. And there were some Turkish officers who were less secular than the Turkish military liked. And some of them had survived the Plague and now worked for the mullahs.

The Anatolian League, according to this Turk, controlled the Anatolian Plains and the high ground over the Bosporus Plains. But their lines stopped at Adapazari and it was another stalemate. The Islamic Caliphate held the whole narrow tongue all the way over chunks of what had been Greece and Bulgaria. The Greeks were still consolidating and not willing to get in a row with the Islamics as long as they didn't try moving more in that direction.

The problem was, Istanbul. The city frankly sprawled. I mean, it was continuous city from the "Europe" side of the Bosporus most of the way to Izmit. Then there were high ridges, Izmit (a port city on the Marmar or whatever), then more ridges then Adapazari where the main bulk of the Anatolian range reared up.

There was a big reservoir called the Sapanca Golu which anchored the corner of the Islamic League lines then it ran along the river from there to the Black Sea. Going back towards Istanbul and Izmit it followed high ridges.

The Islamic League, clearly, had quite a few troops. And breaking something like that was going to require lots of street fighting. I didn't see where one unit of Strykers was going to be more than spit in a bucket.

One unit of Strykers wouldn't be more than spit in a bucket. But I wasn't planning on just bringing Strykers. And I wasn't planning on fighting them head on.

It would all depend on the Turks. Our Turks that is.

Turkish troops could be very very good. Oh, not as good as American troops, not in that day and age. But very good. Disciplined, certainly. It was rumored pre-Plague that a Turkish officer didn't have to file paperwork if he only shot one soldier, below the rank of sergeant, a year. I saw one beat the shit out of a private one time.

Didn't mean the officers were good. They were a mixed lot. Some of them were excellent, some got off on the power and not enough on the suffering if you know what I mean.

But, generally, Turkish troops were good.

What I didn't know was how good they were *now* and how good the *Islamics* were. They were Turkish troops, too, and presumably had a pretty serious hardcore element.

A lot was going to depend on this Turkish general. I'd have to play it by ear when I got there. So far, though, things seemed on the up and up.

A couple of things were bothering me, though. I was getting some strange vibes from the States. Oh, not, "as soon as you come back you're going to be hung" vibes. Once I made it clear I'd do my best to complete the mission everything was smiles and roses and "what little temper tantrum?" And the smiles and roses weren't "the long kiss goodnight." I was getting what I needed in the way of equipment and supplies. (And personnel. Get to that in a minute.)

It was little things like the State guy saying "We also should be able to . . . handle interference above State." And who was the State guy? He was never introduced. And why did he say that he notionally could consider me for ambassador. He wasn't the Secretary of State or the President. I looked around and couldn't find him as even a deputy secretary of State. Yet, here I had the document in my hand.

Very odd.

And here was the answer. It wasn't "a military coup" as later historians have suggested. It was more "a coup of the adults."

It was sort of like what the oil companies did. (And more on *them* later.) The Bitch was being . . . innnsuuulated. Yeah, that's a nice term. Insulated. She was under a lot of pressure. Everyone knew it. It was obvious every day. She didn't need a lot of shocks. We're . . . *helping* her.

By basically telling her what she wanted to hear and doing whatever the fuck adults saw needed doing.

It had started with the military units, ordered to deliver food to areas that were completely out of civil control but also ordered to not fire even if under attack, "using initiative in the field to complete the commander's mission concept." IOW, since they were getting arrested for defending themselves they started "breaking down" in areas where they *didn't* have to defend themselves. And delivering the relief supplies there.

As time went on and the Bitch's orders got weirder and randomer higher and higher authorities started ignoring them and implementing real-world solutions. In the meantime, they were simply lying to higher about what was happening.

Occasionally this became evident on what news the Bitch was watching. Sometimes she freaked out and called for heads. (Apparently at one point she was *actually* screaming "cut off their heads." I knew she was the Queen of the Reds but I never realized that meant The Red Queen.) Other times she apparently was able to rest in a comfortable state of denial.

Why was she still in office? It was a clear-cut case where a President needed to be impeached for her own good if nothing else.

Democrat Congress, Democrat Senate. After she started the Big Grab several impeachment bills were started up and all of them were killed. None even got to the floor. All on party line votes in committee.

I'm not going to flay the Democrats entirely. There were Democrats amongst the "adults" who were performing a de facto if not de jure coup. But what should have been done was impeach her and get someone in office who could handle the, crushing, pressure. I don't think her running mate would have been a good choice, either. But, Jesus, somebody who wasn't going totally fruitloop.

Instead they let her fiddle while America . . . well . . . froze.

She was even running for *reelection*.

It was the adults who saw we needed oil, desperately. And if they could free up Istanbul (actually, we just needed Ismali but the Turks were bargaining for the whole shooting match or at least the south side of the Bosporus) we could start getting tankers moving with Kurd sweet-light crude. Pumped over the Anatolian plain to Ismali then on to the good Ole USA.

What we were going to *pay* for it was an interesting question. But the Kurds knew we were good for it and we still had stuff to offer. Like, well . . .

I was a bargaining chip. Hell, soldiers often were. I could live with that.

On actual "stuff" I asked for there were two notes.

I'd said I didn't need troops. That wasn't *quite* true. With this op in the works, I started backpedaling and negotiating all over again. What I needed was tanks. And tankers.

My guys were having a lot of fun driving those Abrams. But they really didn't know what they were doing. I was going to need at least the six I had left, preferably ten or more, to do this op. I had a notion what I was going to do and I was going to *need* tanks. And guys who actually knew how to shoot, drive and fix them.

So that was one thing I got. What I asked for was:

"I need a tanker unit. Enough for ten tanks and all the support they're going to need to keep them running in the field under *awful* conditions. And I need guys who can, no shit, no question, no ifs ands or buts, go wherever I tell them to go however I tell them to and can fight like motherfuckers when they get there. I need the best tank platoon in the Army and a couple of extras for spice."

I don't know if the Mongrels was the *best* tank platoon in the Army. I do know they were very good.

Second Platoon had liked their tanks and didn't like giving them up. They felt they'd proven their worth.

I had the Mongrels take them out and show them something about the systems they'd been using.

Technically, an M-1 has 4000 meters of range.

One of the Mongrel crews went over the pass and, with intent, went off a small cliff on the south side. Fired in air, gun pointed sideways. Hit one of the, admittedly stationary, Abrams that was out on the plain from nearly *5000* meters.

Before it hit the ground. Then it fired four more shots in about ten seconds as it headed down the, very bumpy, ridge. Three of the four hit other targets. Most at very near max range.

Second Platoon stopped bitching and went back to their Strykers.

The Mongrels were a "reinforced" platoon under a first lieutenant. He quickly learned about "coffee."

— CHAPTER TWENTY —

Adana, Van, Christ It Sounds the Same with a Turkish Accent

Meanwhile I was shucking and jiving.

I offered all the Brads and the Abrams I'd left in the desert to the Kurds. Almost all. I needed to rebuild my losses. I also needed other things.

Most of the Kurds in the Mosul area came from that general area of Kurdistan. The tribes in the immediate "Iraqi" area.

I asked for, and got, Perg Mersha to "assist me in actions in the Anatolian region." But.

This is where I needed negotiation room.

I pointed out to the Turkish general that I was going to need some things if I was going to do this op. And he'd been informed that if I didn't get what I wanted, I had the final say-so on conducting my operation. Basically, he'd better geek or I'd pack up and go home.

Which is why the Kurdish areas of what was once Turkey are now "Kurdistan." (The Iranian areas came later.)

Also why Istanbul is named, again, Byzantium. (I wanted to go for Constantinople but my own guys talked me out of that one.) That one was kind of silly, but it had bugged me for years.

I didn't ask for the statue. I didn't know about the statue until it was practically done. That Turk general had my number. If he'd asked me I'd have screamed blue blazes. Fucking thing is a nightmare. Every damned ship, including cruise ships, that goes through the Bosporus can see the damned thing. I mean you *can't fucking miss it.* As an engineering work, it's pretty fucking impressive. Pissed me off, though.

339

I also didn't ask for the sword. Still got it over the mantelpiece, though. Heirloom and all that.

And I'm actually sort of surprised at the statue. When we left, the Turks were a little pissed at us.

But that's for later.

The Kurds were, basically, attacking in two directions with damned little in the way of logistics. Very Kurdish in that.

It took two weeks to get everything in place. Including plane loads of gear. I'd said I didn't need it then got pack-rattish. But, fuck, I needed it.

Then we set off to waves and yells from the Kurds. Somewhere they'd found flowers and all that stuff. The troops were getting kissed by girls and it was a grand send off.

It was snowing like a bitch. Nice of them to turn out in all that snow.

It snowed harder. And more and snowed and fucking *snowed*.

The first part was easy-peasy. The Kurds controlled all the territory up the Tigris well into what used to be Turkey. And the Tigris went *way* into Turkey. Since it cut through the mountains down that way, the roads and railroads kinda followed the same line.

Yeah, there was a railroad. I'd thought about loading the Abrams on it but things were kinda messed up and I was only a company. I couldn't get a railroad running. So we drove.

We'd gotten tank-carriers, though, for the Abrams. The Iraqis had them. We had to unload sometimes when shit got bad. The Abrams made dandy snow plows.

The shit got very bad. The Taurus mountains are not exactly Alpine but they are very rugged. And they're very volcanically active. We ran across the hot-spring we based "Elephants" around up in the Taurus and decided it was a good place to lay up for a couple of days. The guys camped (not CAM(P)ed, that was later) and warmed up in the water. "Battery" was later, too. But that was in Turkey. When it got worse.

There was actually a border post when we passed out of the Kurdish region. By then we not only had the "task force" of Bravo and the Mongrels and the Nepalese, we'd picked up a fair trail of Kurds. About a battalion of infantry under a tough old guy from the Turkish regions. The Turks *really* didn't like it when we turned up with *him*. Turns out he was wanted as a terrorist. Looked like one. But we were all friends now. I invited him to "coffee" and he brought a couple of lieutenants and the commo trailer was getting really overloaded. Since we were having to stop to log these days, we just scheduled a log-stop for "coffee" time and did it then. I missed the old "Bravo Company . . . arriving" thing but if they ever build a commo van large enough to hold an officers' call for a short brigade I don't want to be in it.

Once we passed out of the Kurdish region, though, things got tougher. The Kurds had been keeping some of the roads open. None of these were. And although the Turks said that this region was "under their control" there were, to say the least, areas where control was spotty. We got ambushed about every other day. Mostly it was the equivalent of bandits, guys trying to steal our shit. But getting hit by bandits isn't much different than getting hit by muj. And quite often you can't tell the difference in places like that.

Hell, there was a reason to hit us. We had food. Most of the region was starving already. What they were going to do in the spring and summer I had no idea. Assuming there *was* a spring and summer.

There was a main road running from Van to Ankara, where the Turk general's capital was. I *thought* he said they had it all under control and that it was open. Problem was, there was no good way to get to it.

Last Kurd control was the edge of Diyarbakar province. We were on little fucking hairpin roads trying to get to Mus, where the "highway" was. Passed the Kurd outpost in the pass above Mus. Fucking bunker with a stove going for all it was worth and the pass was already under six feet of snow. The Abrams were off their carriers and towing *them*.

Then they were trying to keep them from sliding off the mountain on the other side. I'd thought we'd hit some mountains in the Kurd region, got a new appreciation for the term in the fucking Taurus.

The Nepos, of course, loved it. Oh, they called them "hills" and said they weren't "real" mountains. But they were running around at every stop, and there were a lot of them, like little kids. We hit places where you had to sort of gasp for air. They said it was still too thick but getting better.

Runty Himalayan fuckers.

We finally made it to Mus. Not much to see. It was just another

Plague-ridden city with a crashed population and, at that point, a serious weather problem. And, as it turned out, a group of hard-cores that were more of a gang than anything. See "Battery."

We rolled out of Mus with less of a security problem and food eating problem, for them, than when we arrived. There is little good that soldiers can do but we can, occasionally, reduce the bad.

So much for the Turks having "control" of the whole road. Also so much for the road being open. It was just as choked as the little ass ones we'd crossed. Just a bit wider which was nice.

We still lost two Abrams and a carrier trying to get to Ankara. And the HERCULES of course, but that wasn't really anyone's fault but the Nepos.

I forgave them two days later.

We were just out of Erzincan near the town of Goyne. This, by the way, was, like, the headwaters of the Euphrates. There had been a route up that but it looked worse. Probably was.

Anyway, lots of little valleys and pretty major rivers. All frozen solid. Ish. The road we were on had good bridges, thank God. Turned out the Turkish military had a big mountain-training base not too far away, pre-Plague.

And apparently a depot or something in the area. Because as we came up to the pass, lo and behold it was defended.

Our first inkling of this was the Scouts yelling like hell and backing up. And then, over the yells, we heard the echo of a big gun firing.

Up in the pass were a couple of tanks. Dug in. Getting up to it was a long damned switchback. They had it covered.

We tried Javelins. They couldn't get a lock. The tanks were in revetments looking down at us. The Javs needed more of a view.

The Abrams guys looked at the situation and shook their heads. They'd go. But they figured they were going to get whacked and whacked hard. Most of the way to where they could get a good firing position they'd be driving with their flank to the enemy. And if those were Turkish tanks, which was the only thing that made sense, they were Leopards. And Leopards are just about as good as Abrams. (Just about. Not *as* good. I don't care *what* the Krauts say.)

Get some infantry up on the pass? Brother, those mountains

were steep! And high. It would take a couple of *days*. And my guys weren't trained mountain troops they were . . .

Wait.

It took me, seriously, about ten minutes to slap my forehead. Sometimes, most of the times, a solution that easy comes to me fast. Then other times I'm pretty damned dense.

"Samad!"

Assault the pass? Tanks? Possible infantry? Carry Javelins up there where eagles dare? Of course, Sahib. I will arrange.

Ever seen a goat trail? I mean one in a mountain?

They're switchbacks, too. And about two inches wide. Back and forth, back and forth, occasionally punctuated by spots that the goats jump lightly from the path to a small rock and then on to the path again. There being no other way to make their way across a sheer cliff.

Ever seen guys *trot* up a goat path. For *hours*? Carrying, like, more than their body weight of gear? I mean, the Nepos were carrying not only personal weapons but Javelins, which are heavy motherfuckers, and medium machine guns and ammo and even some light mortars. It was a *motherfucker* of a load.

I began to understand Sherpas. Even the Kurds, who looked a bit pissed at first to be left out, were getting impressed quick. They were "mountain" fighters, they thought. The Nepos were still referring to these as "hills."

There was an area to the north that it looked like the guys up on the pass couldn't observe. Goat path up to the ridge. Ridge up to the cliff overlooking the path. Presumably Javelin into the pass. Trot, trot, trot . . . Who is that I hear trotting on my ridge?

Wait, hope they're not Turkish military. That would be embarassing.

I called ahead.

No, they are not ours.

I thought you said this road was a) *clear*. Which it is not. And b) *under control*. Which it is not.

I thought you were going up the *Adana* road. Why are you in *Erzincan* province? We haven't even *tried* to get control in that area. All the roads are blocked by the snows!

Mus looked closer and I thought you said the *Van* road was open and . . .

Fuck me.

We're going to be a while.

Did I fuck up? I don't know. I do know that there wasn't Kurd control over to Adana and from what I gleaned later the "control" of the Adana road was spotty. But . . .

And I *swear* he'd said the Van road. I didn't keep a copy of the conversation, though, so it's his word against mine.

Clearing the pass.

We parleyed while the Nepos climbed.

The Avesi Alliance now owned this patch of ground. You will pay a toll of all your vehicles, those are nice tanks by the way, and equipment. We'll let you leave with a couple of trucks and fuel and enough food to get you back to those heathen Kurds. Oh, you have some heathen Kurds with you? Well, take them back where they came from. These are *our* lands!

I appreciate your sentiment. However, my orders are to proceed through this region on the way to complete a mission of some importance. Move or I'll move you.

How?

I have great and wonderful powers you cannot begin to understand. And if worse comes to worse I *can* get airstrikes. Move.

Fuck off and die.

Okay, Burger King, you *can* have it your way.

The Avesi are not really the most violent people in the world. Most encyclopedias talk primarily about their contribution to Turkish music. (By the way, that sort of *makes* them violent in my opinion. I'm *not* a fan of Turkish music.) They're a branch of Shia that are related to Sufiism and . . .

Ah, Christ. Go look it up.

"After Action Analysis" indicated that a former infantry captain (hey, look at me!) took the name as a way to build local support. He'd established a little feudalism in Sivas province. I don't think he was actually doing *bad* things, unlike some of the bandits and others we cleared out. At the time I didn't really care. And the Turks did reestablish order in the region after we passed through. Having someone clear out all your troublemakers makes that easy. When we got done the Van Road was pacified with a capital P.

The Nepos got up on the ridge about nightfall. They made it to a good firing point around 2100. Yes, they had night vision gear.

I called up the local commander.

Yo, dude. You've got two Leopard tanks and three trucks up there.

Wait, how did you know about the trucks?

I have *mysteeerious* powers. Look, surrender, now, and I'll leave you the use of your legs.

Hah, hah, you are very funny . . .

Then one of the trucks blew the fuck up.

What have you *done*?

Blew up one of your trucks. Don't try to move the rest of the shit. Just lay down your guns and surrender. I have wondrous and mysterious powers. Don't make me kill you all.

So they pointed the tank guns to the rear and we drove up and accepted their surrender.

We left some Kurds to guard them and the pass while we sorted things out. They promised not to kill and eat anyone. We picked up the Nepos down the road so they never knew what my "mysterious powers" were. (Javelins. Low signature.) It was less of a walk for the Nepos. But that's where Samad slipped on his way down, something of the ultimate insult to a Nepo along the lines of drowning in his fucking bathtub to a SEAL, and turned into a human snowball. Very scary at the time, very funny in retrospect. Made for great cinema.

"Sorting things out" took a couple of days and one or two skirmishes. We also had to leave a bunch of Kurds behind. And they didn't interact great with the locals but we pointed out that they were just there to guard the prisoners and we'd get Turks over to straighten things out shortly.

Bandits by day, sneak thieves by night, occasional feudal lords. Some we could negotiate with, they were trying to decide which way to hop on the whole "who's in charge" thing. Some we had to fight. They lost. We took almost no casualties because a) I never fight fair and b) when the Nepos couldn't flank someone the Kurds could. In retrospect, it was good training for what was to come.

Turned out we didn't hit the first outpost of "order" until we got to Kirkkale. Actually *west* of Kirkkale. Ankara was near the *back* side of what the Turkish general controlled.

But I rolled in with seven more Leopards than I'd had at the beginning. Also down two Abrams, a HERCULES and a carrier. Five WIA, two KIA. Two cases of frostbite. One guy lost toes.

Maybe I *should* have taken the Adana Road. But I *swear* he said Van.

— CHAPTER TWENTY-ONE —

Of Course We Fucking Looted

So there we were ready to perform our heroic . . . What do you *mean* you *can't fight in this weather?*

Okay, the weather *was* rather bad. We'd explained that to the world. Well, not all of it. We only *had* an hour.

Go back to the Global Warming thing. One of the things that was raised about why Global Warming was going to Destroy Civilization was that Storms Got Stronger.

Uh, huh.

Maybe, *maybe* an argument for hurricanes. (I can argue ag'in it. And so would most paleoclimatologists and even hurricane experts.) But hurricanes don't affect most regions of the world. Very few, actually. Oh, they're big news in the U.S., but they don't hit most parts of the world, period.

Cold fronts do, though. And warm fronts. And they can be pretty fucking powerful. See "Storm of the Century." Well, it might have been for the 20th Century, but in the 21st we've learned a whole new definition.

Why?

Meteorology 101. "Storms are governed by differences in temperature between the polar regions and the tropics."

Global Warming would have meant warmer temperatures in the polar regions and pretty much the same in tropical regions.

Global Cooling meant *much* colder temperatures in the polar regions and pretty much the same in the tropical regions.

Oops.

And, yes, that meant the weather was a bitch. Especially since weather is always worse when there's a big change going on. All those thunderstorms you get with a cold front are because the air temperature is suddenly changing. It gets colder, air condenses, storms build up, ice movement makes static electric-icity, water falls, lightning strikes.

The air temperature all over the *world* was suddenly changing. We'd gone through some motherfuckers of thunder *snow* storms in the Taurus. Those are *not* regular occurences. I'd run across, maybe, two the whole time I lived in Minnesota.

The weather was a bitch.

And bitchy weather favors defenders. And for the plan I had in mind to work, it was going to take our friendly Anatolian Alliance fighters climbing out of their trenches and bunkers and assaulting.

Which was going to suck. No question.

It also was the only way to get the oil flowing by the end of December. Which was the "drop dead" date for the U.S. Somewhat literally.

Things had never gotten anywhere near pre-Plague normal in the U.S. and now we were going into "the Mother of All Winters." It had taken a fucking Brit news crew and a bunch of infantry stuck in the middle of nowhere to get people to stand up and notice but it was finally happening. And now everyone was going ape-shit because they realized we didn't have the fuel *or* food to carry us through.

We eventually realized that was bunk, but in November of 2019 it really looked like total Disaster. This is the Big One. End of Civilzation As We Know It. Here come the glacial sheets! Fuck you, buddy, I'm heading for the hills!

(It *did* suck if you lived in Canada. But, hey, Canoeheads are tough. They tell us that all the time.)

I hadn't traveled all this way through those fucking mountains, okay, okay, maybe you *did* say the Adan road, just to sit on my ass and let my country freeze to death. We were here to open up the spigots. And we can't do it on our own. Get off your ass or I'm going over to the Dardanelles and catching a ship for Greece. And, no, I won't be leaving useable equipment. I'll send it back with the Kurds. Don't try to stop them.

I didn't need a full-court press. All I needed was for the Caliphate to be using a lot of supplies and concentrated on Adapazari.

The E80, in that area a full-up interstate, ran from Istanbul through Izmit and to Adapazari where the bulk of the fighting was centered. The main log base for the fighting, though, was at Izmit.

On the south it was well protected by a range of high ridges that were strongly held by Caliphate forces. South of those ridges was Alliance territory.

What I proposed was to take Izmit. If we could cut the E80, Adapazari would become untenable to hold. The Caliphate forces would have to fall back and either retake Izmit or, if it worked properly, be forced back beyond.

The general pointed out that trying to take the ridges would signal the Caliphate that I was coming and then we'd have to fight heavy forces all the way.

I pointed out that a B-52 strike would clear the way long enough for us to dart down to Izmit. All *he* had to do was reinforce us. Fast. Please. Don't dawdle.

It was a Japanese technique called the roadblock. It wasn't the cavalry raid of old. The idea was to get a force across your enemy's resupply and *hold* there. Don't let anyone past. There were ways for the Caliphate to resupply around Izmit. But the intel said the bulk of their military stores were *in* Izmit. And getting around it was difficult. Think "Ruffles have ridges." And all that snow.

Just east of Izmit the E80 and the E100 crossed. Between them was the Izmit airport which was where the main log depot for the Caliphate forces had been established.

That was our target. We were going to blow a hole through the Caliphate forces on the ridges, dash down to the Izmit depot and take and hold it against all comers.

Sounds easy, right?

God, it fucking sucked.

It took a week to arrange. B-52s had to be flown back to England; closest bases that could take them. The Alliance had to get their guys ready to charge. Build up artillery supplies.

The good news was that the bases the B-52s were returning to were the same ones they'd used pre-Plague. And the Brits never really lost control of them. So there was plenty of ordnance on site. If we'd had to move ordnance it would have been impossible.

I also arranged for resupply drops. We were going to be using a lot of ammo. We might be able to use some of the shit in the depot but I wasn't going to count on that. We hoped we wouldn't have to blow it all up again. The Alliance *could* use it.

So we got into position and we struck. Easy, right?

Fucking ridges south of Izmit are motherfuckers. I mean moth-er*fuckers*. We could barely get the Abrams up them.

And the Caliphate was dug in hard. We hit them with an arclight strike that should have blasted them to the stone age. They were *still* fighting.

What saved us was the Nepos, the Kurds and the Mongrels. The Caliphate, thank God, did not have good anti-tank weapons. And the Nepos had worked with tanks quite a bit at this point. And, okay, I threw in something I'd learned in a book.

If you're very careful, you can fire an anti-tank round right past infantry. It's not as easy with these new tanks; silver bullets have a tremendous sonic backlash. But you can fire close. The Caliphate was dug in, deep, in bunkers with interlocking fire. They were Turks and the Turks know how to fight.

The way to take out bunkers with interlocking fires is to have your troops get as close as they can get without getting killed then hit the bunkers with *tank* fire. The tanks have to fire right past the infantry but they can suppress a bunker like nobody's business.

We had to get up the ridges fast. We started off fast, with the Scout Strykers tearing up the hairpin roads.

They got hammered halfway up the ridge. Most of the crews bailed out before they brewed up, but they got hammered.

In go the Nepos. They're going up sheer cliffs, it looked to me, like it's a walk in the park. They're still taking fire, though. The Caliphate was dug in hard all along the ridges.

Enter the Mongrels. They rolled up the road in the teeth of the Caliphate fire. By then there was artillery but they're still not letting go. And as the Nepos started pointing out bunkers, they'd take them under direct fire with anti-tank rounds.

A bunker may be strong. But a sabot from a 120mm Rhein-metal tank gun will ruin *everyone's* day inside.

We started from the Alliance held town of Turgutlu. And up we went. It took time. It took more time than I thought we could possibly have. It took three days to fight our way down onto the plains south of Izmit.

I don't know why the Caliphate didn't reinforce. Possibly they thought it was a feint. And the local forces *did* close the road behind us, for a time. Maybe they thought they could cut us off to die on the vine.

Maybe they thought the tank battalion that was camped south of Izmit as a strategic reserve would stop us.

Oops.

The battle of Rahmiye is ... Well, let's just say when I *did* finally get to CGSC it was fucking humorous to have *two* battles I, ahem, had "participated" in be ones that were refought in class. Rahmiye, though, wasn't really special. We just let them come into an ambush and lit 'em up. Okay, so I got a *little* deceptive on them again. In the Koran it says that it's completely okay, indeed a good thing, to lie to an unbeliever. If so, the reverse is obviously true, right?

And, yeah, Rahmiye is the place where they got that shot of me snapping orders then going right back to what I was saying. Like I said, it wasn't really hard. You know? I mean it was like muscle memory at that point.

We took casualties, though. Both going over the mountains and at Rahmiye. Lost six Strykers and two Abrams. The Abrams really hurt but, hell, that was for nearly sixteen Leopards and a bunch of AFVs. Captured more and dragged them along with us. Then we got to the base. That was easy-peasy. Sure, it had defenses but nothing to stop *us* or even slow us down.

I expected the Caliphate to put in a heavy assault. And they did. That. Sucked.

The Caliphate and the Alliance had been trading blows for nearly four months solid. They'd gotten over the Plague pretty quick to do that but they'd been steadily building up on both sides. Originally there'd been several other factions on the Alliance side. Therefore "Alliance." The Caliphate was about three which had united under Caliph Omar something something something. (Look it up.)

But the point was, they'd gotten okay at what they did by then. And what they did was WWI style assaults. Okay, maybe even WWII. It went like this.

Shell the hell out of you for hours. Just rain down metal. Then send in a line of infantry and tanks, generally behind a curtain barrage. Sometimes they used AFVs to carry the infantry.

They had some planes. They'd bomb and strafe.

We dug in. Then we dug in deeper. We lost Strykers, quite a few, to the artillery. We lost an *Abrams* to artillery. We lost guys to artillery.

We held the position.

They tried to filter supplies past us. They were in range of our Abrams, which would shoot the trucks carrying the supplies. Eventually they took the long roads.

What saves us was a few things.

We got more B-52 strikes. We could generally tell when they were getting ready for a big push. We were getting intel from the Alliance among other things and occasionally Predators and Global Hawks. We'd call the B-52 and ask them to stop by around when we thought we'd be getting assaulted.

Sometimes we timed it right. Other times we didn't. Then they'd fly over the main area of the Caliphate and just sort of bomb at will. But when we did it would really fuck the Caliphate forces up big-time.

We hadn't thought about defending the B-52s. Fortunately, the AF chief was no idiot. There was no way, at the ranges they were flying, to establish "air superiority." But they could send F-15s and F-22s as escorts. It was real old-fashioned stuff. But they could generally slam the Caliphate fighters long before they could threaten the Buffs.

There were anti-aircraft missiles. There were anti-aircraft missile site anti-missiles.

I think we lost two Buffs. I'm sorry as hell for their crews but they did a hell of a job.

The second thing that saved us was the airdrops. We had brought in a lot of supplies. We shot through much of it in the first couple of days. C-17s and C-130s dropped supplies. Again, they had to be escorted and were more vulnerable to anti-aircraft. But they managed to drop the supplies without being shot down. By the end of the battle, they were landing on the airstrip, dropping the shit fast then taking back off. Very ballsy.

The third was that the Caliphate commander was an idiot. He should have massed a force and overrun us. Instead we'd get hit by whatever he gathered at any particular time.

So we'd get hit by three Leopards, some IFVs and a bunch of infantry on foot. We'd wax the Leopards and IFVs with Javelins then the infantry with machine-gun fire.

Then we'd get hit by a shit-pot of infantry. Machine-gun fire.

Then a bunch of tanks, no infantry. Javelins.

Then some IFVs. Javelins.

We got hit from the east and west. But we never got hit from the east and west *at the same time.*

The artillery sucked. Other than that, "they came at us in the same old way and we beat them in the same old way."

Casualties? Nasty. And at first no way to evac. Then a C-130 landed and picked them all up, American, Nepo and Kurd. Thank you, Air Force. I take back every evil thing I've said about you.

Meantime, the Alliance was trying to cross the damned Sapanca River and failing miserably. That is until one of their battalion commanders, and the guy deserved and got a medal, noticed that *his* section had frozen solid. He wrapped a bunch of his guys up in bedsheets of all things for camouflage and infiltrated them across.

Turks are bastards with bayonets, I'll give them that.

The Alliance got a foothold on the far bank and held on for dear life. Then they expanded it. Then they got a bridge. It was blown, but they could repair it.

It took them five days to really get serious forces across the river but at that point it was Katy Bar the Door.

The Caliphate forces broke and ran. They had to go around us. Roads got choked. Control disintegrated.

We got relieved on day six of taking the base. A bunch of stuff on the base was fucked up. But we had an airstrip and logistic materials for the Alliance forces.

Then we moved out. We'd barely gotten over getting hammered and we moved.

Straight to Istanbul, right?

Give me credit for sense. The Caliphate was hurt, its main force was retreating, but it wasn't licked. And it had most of its functional forces defending the E80 and E100 to Istanbul.

We went for the side roads.

The Alliance forces ground forward towards Istanbul. The main line of resistance was on the hills near Hereke with the main supply and control base at Gebze.

Guess what we went for?

Up through more fucking mountains. And they were defended. A lot of the Caliphate forces were in full-out retreat but there were enough hardcores, and hardcore formations, to make our life miserable. And the weather still sucked.

On the other hand, we were in mountains and we had Nepos and Kurds.

Hit a defense point in a pass. Lay in intermittent fire. Send the Nepos up the hills on one side and the Kurds on the other. Tell them whoever got the pass cleared got priority on the trucks to ride. The other formation got to walk.

They'd *race* each other to clear the pass.

Move on.

It was at one of those passes that we had "coffee" while under artillery fire. Was dick all we could do about it. The Nepos and the Kurds were flanking and our job was to be targets and smile. "Would you care for a (FUCKING WHAM! as an artillery round landed) finger cake?" Veddy British.

We took Gebze. Bit of a battle with some remaining Leopards near Pelitli. But the Mongrels, those who were left, were *very* much their betters. Like "Who's your Daddy?" their betters. Which is what the Mongrels painted on their tanks after Pelitli.

This time we didn't hold it. We hit the Caliphate defenders in Hereke from behind. Lots of surrenders.

By then we were getting into serious urbanization but we kept doing the same thing. Hit a defense point? Swing short, swing long, whatever. Hit them from behind or in the flank. Move on. Alliance forces pushed straight in since they had a harder time with command and control. We'd swing wide and low sweet chariot.

Push 'em back, push 'em back, waaaay BACK.

There was a whole nother Caliphate "Army," more like about a division, up by the Black Sea. They got cornered and surrounded by Alliance forces at Bali Bey and surrendered en masse.

We hooked and we flanked and they fell back. They were dealing with desertion en masse and we occasionally routed forces and "had a good killing."

The Caliph blew the Abdullah Aga bridge leaving a shitload of forces on the "Asia" side of the Bosporus. They surrendered. We hooked up to the E80 bridge and, lo and behold, it was still up.

Hooked back down.

We were outrunning most of the Alliance forces at this point. Okay, I was going a bit hog-wild. But, hell, how often do you *get* a chance to take a major historical city?

Fuckers tried to blow up the Hagia Sophia. Man, that pissed me off. I sent in the Nepos with orders to prevent it with extreme prejudice. There went a bunch of their remaining hardcores.

The Caliph made his final stand, with a core of about a battalion of hardcore Sunni fundamentalist motherfuckers, in the Topkapi Palace. It was mostly a museum before the Plague but it had been the palace of the Ottoman emperors for four hundred years.

The motherfucker was big. And there were about a billion fucking rooms. Turned out the Caliph had turned the harem back into a harem. That was *really* damned interesting when we hit it but we were just passing through, alas.

(Me? Running around in the Topkapi? When I should have been carefully controlling my elements? They all knew what to do and I had a good commo guy. Used to work for a satellite company.)

Found the Caliph, finally, in a throne room. Called the Hunkar Sofasi, which apparently means "Throne Room." I'm afraid to say that it took a certain amount of damage. That's what plaster masons are for. And, okay, you're going to need some lapis lazuli to patch the murals. Sue me.

It took most of the night to run down the last holdouts. Most of them weren't asking for quarter and we weren't giving it.

Okay, let me say a little something on the subject of "looting." Yes, there *did seem to be some trinkets missing* from the Palace when the Turks, finally, showed up the next day. I performed *a very thorough shake-down* of my Nepo, U.S. *and* Kurdish troops. None of those trinkets were found. Given that the Caliph had the palace for months, I suggest you ask *him*. Except you can't, he's dead.

As to the various shopkeepers along the way that accused my Kurds and Nepos of looting, fuck 'em. We hadn't been paid in months. And I never saw looted item one. I've so stated in various reports on my honor as a U.S. Army officer.

WE TOOK *ISTANBUL* YOU IDIOTS.

OF *COURSE* WE FUCKING LOOTED.

Jesus.

CHAPTER TWENTY-TWO

Been Down So Long Looks Like Up to Me

Can we go home now?

The Turks couldn't get rid of us fast *enough*.

Here's a very nice gold-encrusted sword that was carried by Pasha (I'd have to look it up) in his great battles against the (I'd have to look it up, it was Europeans is all I remember; I think there was a subtle insult there) to go along with all the *other shit that's missing* now get the hell out.

The Air Force, again, came in and picked up all the Kurds. Food was going to be delivered as soon as a couple of passes got cleared. There was already a ship in the harbor. They dropped off technical specialists in oil pumping to help get the pipelines back up. They took the Kurds home. Wounded were flown to England for treatment then U.S. and Nepos went to the States. (Oh, clearance for the Nepos to immigrate had been granted. Thank you INS or whatever. The acronyms keep changing.)

Incirlik was back up. It started getting more back up.

There was a very nice ceremony where they gave me the sword. All the other officers got similar stuff except Samad who they barely deigned to recognize. It was okay. I believe he'd picked up a couple of souvenirs. Sentimental value only, of course.

The ceremony was somewhat marred by the fact that the Mongrels, who had somewhere found some *huge* fucking concert speakers, were playing Manowar so loud you could, literally, hear it on the other side of the fucking Bosporus. The tanks were lagered about a klick away but it didn't matter. I rather liked their taste in music but "Swords in the Wind" clashes, badly, with the Turkish national anthem.

However, I do think just about everyone in the formation got tears in their eyes when they started playing "The Fight for Freedom" over and over. The Turkish general trying to be heard seemed somewhat pissed. Especially when we started singing along to the chorus.

Where The Eagles Fly I Will Soon Be There
If You Want To Come Along With Me My Friend
Say The Words And You'll Be Free
From The Mountains To The Sea
We'll Fight For Freedom Again!

God knows we'd been from the mountains to the sea. More like from sea to sea and over the mountains and... Just work with me here. We were *very happy to be going home*.

The day the C-17s landed to fly us home, I really had a hard time believing it. I mean, sure, I'd worked on cutting the orders, had done the arrangements, had "integrated" with the Air Force. But "The World"? Going *Home*?

Well, it wasn't the home we'd left. But, yeah. We were going home.

We landed at a base outside of London. They drove us by bus to Heathrow. There were food lines. It was snowing. I mean like a bitch. London's weather was never great but it ran to rain, not snow. Not in early December, 2019. Still doesn't run to rain. Might not for a couple of centuries. But before the chill, the Brits were famous for umbrellas not those fur hats they all wear now.

The Skynet guys were already home. They promised that they'd get the last episode of *Centurions* right. Actually, there were *two* last episodes. "Crusade" about taking Istanbul and "Centurion" about me. Murdoch, I found out later, told his senior producers that he would "break their fingers" if they thought about touching the "creative control" of the guys who had been producing *Centurions* all along. The same kid from Bravo had written both scripts. He's now working for ABC. And they don't get why he wears a Sith t-shirt all the time.

There was a ceremony at Heathrow. People turned out, despite the depression and despite the fucking snow. They cheered. It was weird. I hoped it was over after that. We got on a 747 where we rattled around like peas. The stewardesses (sorry, flight attendants) treated us like they wanted to have our fucking babies. I think a couple of the guys got "relieved" on the flight home. It was weird.

There was a ticker-tape parade in New York. Okay, from what we were getting from the Skynews guys we *intellectually* understood that we were celebrities. Emotionally, it took a while to kick in. We were a group of worn-out grunts who were just looking forward to a real fucking barracks and quarters. Someplace with working heat and a mess hall. Maybe some chow that resembled real food and not MREs or goat fucking stew. For those of us who still had family and someplace to go, maybe a little leave. We knew that even those of us who were "over time" were going to be staying in. We were in "for the duration" according to our current orders.

We were just grunts.

Oh. My. Fucking. God.

A fucking ticker-tape parade. In what amounted to a blizzard. You could barely sort out the confetti and shit from the snow. We had to march. It was worse than the fucking Taurus. And people were *lining the God damned street* in that fucking blizzard *cheering us.*

We were hooked up with "Public Information Officers." I now know where they put the guys who cannot survive in Protocol Office which is where they send the guys who are fuck-ups in line units. There is no greater Fobbit than a PIO asshole.

I had essentially been overseeing a damned docu-drama every week, more or less, and now I had some shit for brains telling me how we were going to "present the Army in the best possible light."

Eat. Me.

Things were more or less under control from NYC to DC. They put us on a train that stopped at every stop along the way. We had to make speeches. The troops were paraded in the fucking snow. Guys gave interviews. There were contests to meet people's "favorite Centurion."

It had not been my intention. I swear to fucking God. I wish I'd never thought of that stupid fucking idea.

I got put on talk shows. I tried to stay terse. I'm Minnesotan.

It's our job. I got angry at some of the lame-brain questions though and ate a few assholes.

People fucking Ate It Up with a *spoon*.

People called me Centurion.

Look, my name is Bandit Six. You can call me Bandit if you *really* outrank me or I *really* like you. Otherwise it's Bandit Six. Whatever my rank Bandit Six if we're being formal. Mr. Bandit Six when I finally took off the uniform.

Do. Not. Call. Me. *Centurion*.

And I don't like Cincinnatus much, either.

It went on and on and fucking on. They put us on tour. We had to kiss babies.

I couldn't tell if we were rock-stars or politicians or fucking what.

All we wanted to do was grab a fucking snack and get back to fucking work. Maybe some *leave* for fuck's sake.

But the worst part was, we were back in commo.

Hell, I could have picked up the phone any time and called Bob. But if I did it, then the troops should get to do it. Before I did. Rank has certain privileges but it doesn't work that way. And there was only so much commo. So we were sort of in information black-out from home.

So I didn't find out until I borrowed the PIO asshole's cell phone that I didn't really have a home to go to.

The farms, all of them, had been "nationalized."

Bob was still, sort of, running two. He had some dipshit in DC telling him what he was supposed to do. The guy was an "agronomy expert" from the USDA. Actually, he was an "environmental agronomy" expert from the USDA.

The guy was in DC trying to tell a farmer in Minnesota, who has twenty times his experience and a *hundred* times his savvy, what to do in the middle of the worst natural disaster in history. Especially for farmers.

Like a lot of people, Bob was tuning as much as he could out. But he had to go through that guy to get supplies. Seeds, basically, since, you know, herbicides and pesticides and all those other 'cides were icky.

And plowing has to be this way and planting has to be that way and none of it was anything resembling what was actually going on. The guy was getting his "forecasts" from hand-picked "climatologists" in the department of the USGS that was the leading study farm for "global warming" and they were still using *the same fucking models.*

Bob was only directly running two of the farms. The other seven had been turned over to "hand-picked" experts in "environmental agronomy." Tofu-eaters. They gave *my* farms to *tofu-eaters.* It was Lamoille County all over again. It was the Zimbabwe Plan, the Cambodia Option. It was nationwide famine in the making.

It was going to make 2020 *and* 2021 suck like a gigantic vacuum. Even *without* an ice age.

I went back to shucking and jiving.

I was an officer of the United States Military. Legally *and* ethically I could *not* say *anything* contrary to the policies, military or domestic, of the Commander in Bitch. Said so right on the package. I know that there have been officers and enlisted who have ignored this doctrine. The officers should be stripped of rank and thrown out. The enlisted should be made privates and sent to somewhere like, oh, Minot. Or Iran.

I slipped up *one* time. I'd just gotten some particularly bad news from Bob about the state of one of my farms. (The Hanska property, as it happens, where the dipshits had let the fucking well-pump not only freeze but just about self-destruct. And then called *Bob* to come over and "get their water running.")

So right after that I'm talking to some reporters about stories I've already had to tell a dozen times and clearly not as "up" as Bandit Six normally is and one of them asks me why and I lay out something like "bad news at home."

Well, by then my bio was so public record it practically was platinum. They all knew Dad was dead. So what's the bad news? So some reporter started sniffing around.

Before I knew it, I was *only* being asked what I thought of the Bitch's farm policies!

Oh, Christ. I didn't like *any* of her policies. Taking *my farms* was just icing on the cake. (And, yes, they were *my* farms. Dad was dead. I was his legal heir. My. Farms.)

That was into late December of 2019. Much had already been made of the fact that "Centurion" and his forces had been the ones responsible for opening up the Kurdish oil fields to start supplying Western Europe and the U.S. Quite a bit had been made, now that reporters could get in and interview others in the area, of that fact that Bandit Six had:

1. Established a new nation called Kurdistan with which the U.S. now had formal relations and which hadn't existed prior to the plague and only existed (so the story went) because of the Centurions and especially *The* "Centurion."
2. Had participated in diplomacy to essentially rewrite a good bit of the Middle East and had groups talking together and working together amicably who had been enemies for thousands of years.
3. Was held up as *the* major reason that there was a new republic forming around Iraq and the area that was *very* friendly with the U.S. It was expanding slowly but might soon have all of Iran and Iraq back to some semblance of civilization. And The Centurion was the primary cause.

Look, all I did was talk on the phone. It was the rest of those guys who were doing the hard work. But it's very hard to stop a meme once it gets started. I Was The Shit.

Because:

Heating oil, which was at a premium and rationed anyway, was only available because of "the heroic actions of these Last Centurions" who had somehow saved the world while doing nothing but running out of the Middle East with our tails between our legs. (Okay, not quite, but there were nights when that was what was going through my head.)

Ditto gasoline, natural gas, etc.

And politicians were already "declaring" their run for president.

And suddenly the fact that "*The* Centurion" had had his farms seized (months ago) by the U.S. government was a political hot potato. People were trotting out, I shit you not, that old story about Maximus that Russell Crowe did a pretty good job with in *The Gladiator*.

I was off the news so fast it was incredible.

I was "unavailable for comment." I was "on operations." I was "working hard for the nation."

I was in the fucking Pentagon.

— BOOK THREE —

The New Centurions

CHAPTER ONE

Ruminations on Durance Vile

It's said, justifiably, that in the Pentagon, light birds are the coffee bitches.

I was a fucking major. A very junior one. On temporary duty no less. I carried the piss-pot.

It didn't matter that I was "Centurion." The REMFs were just jealous and pissy. The warriors who were stuck in durance vile knew it was all a crock, anyway.

I thought they were just hiding me out. Oh, no. They were putting me to work.

I got stuck in "The Department of Emergency Supply Methodology."

Okay, an "oxymoron" is when two words don't go together. Jumbo shrimp. Happy marriage. (Wife edit: HEY!)

What is it when *three* words don't go together?

In an emergency, plans always leave out the emergency. So no matter what method you'd planned on using, you always end up finding out it don't work. "No plan survives contact with the enemy" or the disaster as the case may be.

And supply is always short.

Troxymoron?

So what *was* the "Department of Emergency Supply Methodology"?

It was the Army's Department of the Agriculture and FEMA combined.

USDA was just about the largest department in the government.

It had, I shit you not, more county farm agents than there were total *counties* in the U.S. The one thing that is eternal, forget the stars—they burn out in a few million to billion years—is a government program. The USDA had programs that went back to the horse and buggy days. It had programs that were designed to "ensure critical military supplies of . . ." stuff that the military hadn't used in decades. Like, say, mohair wool. (I think that one actually finally got cut in the '90s.)

Were farmers at least in part to blame. Oh, *hell* yeah. We'd been major lobbyists since it referred to some hotel in DC where guys would hang out in the lobby to snag the arm of visiting congressmen. Back then, nobody stayed in DC if they could possibly avoid it (it was listed as a "hardship post" by the State Department) and most of Congress stayed in various hotels. The most powerful stayed in one in particular (damned if I can remember the name. The Lafayette?) and guys hired by various interest groups would hang out in the lobby hoping to snag them. And Farmers were one of the interest groups.

Am I gonna justify it? I could try. People that lived through 2020 and 2021, though, can probably justify it better by the results of farming "special interests" NOT getting their way in 2019 and 2020.

The point is the links between the USDA and the Army went waaay back. Back before the Civil War when it was the Agriculture Bureau of the Department of the Interior.

Here's a thing for you. Army veterinarians and vet techs (yes, the Army has both) were *also* the Army's food safety inspectors. Why?

Because the Army used to buy most of its meat on the hoof. And then slaughter same. You didn't used to be able to store beef and pork for very long. If you wanted meat, you slaughtered a steer and ate it. Vets made sure the beef wasn't ridden with diseases. Ergo: Food inspectors.

When storage methods improved big companies started supplying in big ways. ("Uncle Sam" actually came from the Civil War. One of the main suppliers of Union Forces was owned by a guy named Sam. The stuff was stamped "US." "We got another food delivery from Uncle Sam.") But the food still had to be inspected. Companies did then and do now occasionally cut corners a little too close.

Thus vets were the food inspectors. End of history lesson.

But, generally, the Army kept out of agriculture and the USDA didn't tell us how to fight wars. As long as USDA kept up the supply of food for the troops and we kept people from invading, nobody tread on each other's turf.

Problem was, in 2019 the USDA wasn't keeping people fed.

Don't get me wrong. The USDA can't feed a damned person. They're not farmers or distributors or processors. But they can, and their mission was, to "create a favorable environment for American agricultural production."

The problem being . . . the Bitch. And all the thousand of appointees she'd brought in.

Look, the Bitch wasn't, essentially, an environmentalist. I don't think so anyway, not beyond the "I won't throw stuff out my window cause that's littering" level of environmentalist. She contributed to some environmental groups, sure, but that's just feel good stuff unless you give all your money to them and live in a hut and a ragged shift.

But she had had to make a lot of political deals to get elected. And more notably to get the nomination because she was not what the hard left considered "a true believer." And while she'd packed important posts like Justice and Commerce and Defense and State with her more core supporters, mostly lawyers, she'd had to give stuff to the wackoes to keep them on her side.

Where did they go? All those departments they'd been feuding with for decades. Interior, USDA, Met Service (where there was too much support of "global warming deniers"), EPA of course. Anything that had to do with keeping the "environment" in that pristine state of pre-Columbian U.S. You know, where the Indians wiped out the mammoths and horses and used to run giant herds of buffalo off cliffs to get a few cuts of meat and a really cool blanket.

Logging had gotten to the point of "well *we're* shut down," CO2, which is produced by every living thing on earth *and* the oceans *and* volcanoes, was a "pollutant" and under strict regulation. Taxes had been imposed for "excess carbon generation" and things were already starting to get hard in industrial farming *before* the Emergency Powers Act.

But before the Act there was only so much they could do. Congress knew that the farmers were a massive lobby and huge income, tax and jobs generator. Hell, about the only major export you could put your hands on from the U.S. anymore was food.

They hadn't thought the Bitch would use the Act to screw up the one thing that was sort of working post-Plague. But she did.

USDA cannot produce food. What it's *supposed* to do is create a *favorable environment* to produce food.

What it *can* do, easily, is create an *un*favorable environment to produce food. It had detailed knowledge of the American farming industry. It knew where all the levers were.

The long-service people in USDA fought back, passive aggressively, as hard as they could. They, I'm told, tried like hell to keep the damage to a minimum. But they couldn't stop it.

And USDA had been being infiltrated, if you will, for years by the tofu-eaters. Why?

Most things that county agents *used* to be used for were pretty much gone by the 1980s. Back in the 1930s, say, county agents conducted classes in things like proper tillage to reduce soil erosion, better crops for the local soils, how to use modern fertilizers, soil chemistry, etc.

By the 1980s, you'd better have had classes on those and lots of experience before you were making decisions on a real productive farm. Or you were going to go out of business.

But you *couldn't* get rid of county agents. They were *county agents!* Besides, they were the eyes and ears of the USDA. They were the guys who compiled all the local crop reports.

But as the need for county agents to be expert in *real* farming decreased, there was an upswing in their need as "alternative farming" experts. Tofu-eaters were moving away from the cities because their "little brown brothers" were making them harder and harder to live in. Rich tofu-eaters would move out to the country, buy a small farm that was going under anyway and then not know what to do with it. (See *Green Acres* and multiply by hundreds of thousands and *both* members Eva Gabor. But crossed with Karen Carpenter and take away *all shreds* of common sense.)

Well, the tofu-eaters wanted to grow grapes or broccoli or whatever, but not using those icky and "should be illegal" methods. They wanted to be "all natural."

My dad didn't talk much but when he did get to talking he could tell a hell of a story. I recall one time he'd come back from a convention (yes, farmers have conventions) and was talking about a group of "old time" county agents, old guys who were actual experts in mass production of huge quantities of food using every method that was currently available, talking about the "Green" invaders they were encountering more and more. Very heavy along both coasts, less so in the Midwest but still some. But the tofu-eaters invading in Virginia were a particular source of amusement. And the old guys were just shaking their heads. Whatever. "They're not *real* farmers."

But they were, increasingly, the county agent's main customers.

So the old guys got out as fast as possible. They didn't want to deal with the airheads who couldn't understand why their corn was getting eaten by grasshoppers and worms and fields that had been pretty clear when they got them were cropping up with weeds.

Enter the new generation of county agents. Their mainstay was helping out the tofu-eaters. The "urban immigrants." They'd conduct seminars on organic methods and quite happily explain "alternative methods" that were "fully organic." Didn't stop the pests and weeds but it made the tofu-eaters happy that someone from the government, which was Good, was there treating them like adults. Actually, they were being treated like children but they had been their whole lives and didn't know the difference.

Treating like an adult: You're fucking up. Here's how to fix it. Now fix it.

Treating like a child: You're trying *really hard*! Good job! It's not the *result* that matters, it's just that you *try*!

(That's actually a functional way to deal with children up to a point. In most cases they can't do a real job. But when they get to the point they can, when they're ready to learn to be adults with adult responsibilities, "it's a good try" should *never* cut it.)

The old guys treated them like adults and it "hurt their feelings." The new guys treated them like children and they were happy little tofu-eaters.

So by the time of the Big Freeze, the stage was set. Most county agents couldn't explain industrial farming methods or modern farming tech if they were held over a fire and interrogated. That's the ground troop level. The "generals" and "colonels" were people so dead set against modern farming techniques they'd rather the country starve to death than support them. And the guys in the middle were just getting squeezed out. If they opened their mouths, well, there were the bread lines. Go get in them.

Farming depends on weather. The Met Service, which should have been beating the drum and sounding the alarm about the upcoming weather cycles, was also in a bind. Lower level employees had grown up on a constant drumbeat of "global warming, global warming." One of the big environmentalists sounding the drumbeat had actually said once: "Global warming, global cooling, it's all the same thing." And it was all caused by man.

Various bad hypotheses had been advanced over the years about what drove long-term fluctuations. They'd all been debunked, one by one, but the New Breed of meteorologists knew that they were True and they were Right no matter *what* the science said.

Look up (during the daytime). See that big burning ball in the sky?

That's what drives temperature. Always has, always will. Eventually it will cool down then expand and we'll be absorbed into its arms and the Earth will become more iron in its dying furnace. It won't be as hot then, but it will be very big. And then it will either explode, not too violently all things considered, or die down to go to a long slow bake until it's not much more than a big, fairly hot, metal planet.

Guys and gals further up the chain knew better. They knew that things were cooling off, fast, and that it was old Sol driving it and that things were going to a very hell in cold handbasket.

But their bosses knew better than *they* did. They knew it was all "global warming." This was just a temporary fluctuation then things will get hotter and hotter again until we all burn up! Seas will rise! Dogs and cats will be living together!

So the forecasts for weather conditions, which were based on "climate models" that ignored solar activity, were all for a long-term warming trend. It's cold right now, but it will be *hot* next spring. Expect droughts and hurricanes and terrible tornadoes! (Well, we had those but for all the wrong reasons.)

Real farmers knew there were more prediction groups than the U.S. Meteorological Service. Most of them had gone down in the Plague but a few were still up. And their forecasts were dismal. But even in dismal weather, good farmers can react, adapt and overcome. They'd started to.

Then came the Big Grab. Most major farms, including those run by massive farming corporations like Arthur Daniels Midland and Con-Agra, were seized. The tofu-eaters in the USDA had lists and lists of fellow-travellers, many of whom were standing in bread lines, who were ready to "assist in this time of need."

Out they went to the farms. Taking the place of experts with decades of experience.

In Zimbabwe it had been "veterans." Most of them weren't; they were just violent psycopathic supporters of the president. They had gone out, thrown out the (experienced, professional) owners and been settled on high function farms then run them into the ground.

In the U.S. it was reluctant sheriffs going to farms and telling the managers-owners that this is the new boss. You obey his/her orders, now.

I don't have much charity in my heart for those tofu-eaters but there is some. They'd been going to soup kitchens and lining up for their bowl of gruel in the snow. Suddenly, they're plucked up and whisked out to a fucking farm and told to run it.

These were people who had written pamphlets on the proper care and storage of your organically grown vegetables. How to run an organic garden. Some of them not even that, just people who *subscribed* to those journals in the hopes that someday they, too, could be expert organic farmers.

They're dropped off on a massive farm in the beginnings of a killer winter and told: You're in charge.

Ever seen a combine harvester? Even the small ones are fucking huge. They look like a cross between a dump truck and an insect.

Most of the managers had already been told their services were no longer required. They'd stuck around long enough for the "government nationalization management personnel" to turn up then waved goodbye. Most of them didn't live on the farms. The ones who did had family they were going to. There were houses, with small acreage, up for grabs. Might be some trace of the dead residents but that's okay. They'll understand.

They were planning on setting up for the winter as well as they could and using their long experience to provide enough food for their family to survive. Most of them were thinking greenhouses, most efficient production method thereof. Where can I get a whole bunch of plastic sheeting and some iron tubes?

Ranches. Here's how the majority of the beef in the U.S. is produced.

Cattle produce males (bulls) and females (cows) at the same rate as humans, pretty much 50/50. Cows have a long-term economic benefit; they provide more cattle. In the dairy industry, well, you don't get milk from a bull or a steer.

The majority of males, 90%, do not. They are useless for providing more cattle. One bull and ten cows is a decent ratio. You can go with one in fifteen or so.

The rest are deballed at six months, generally, and spend the next few years, three normally, eating grass on big spreads. (These are steers. Males without balls. Also what farmers call male tofu-eaters.) People think they're all in Texas. They're not. *Florida* had more beef cattle than Texas. More rain equals more grass equals more steers you can run on an acre. Average in Florida was three head of cattle per acre.

Out west, Wyoming and such, there were areas where it was *three acres per head.* But they had lots of room. And there wasn't anything *else* you could do with the land. (Unless you were a tofu-eater and then you just left it "pristine." And killing cattle is murder. Fine. You eat your tofu. I'm going to be over here with a nice juicy steak.)

They get up to a certain age and they're then moved to feed lots. Cattle that eat nothing but grass are a) very very tough meat and b) taste "gamey." (I don't really mind gamey meat but most Americans were pansies about their eating. I *do* mind tough.) There they sat on "feed lots" with piles of corn and mixed foods (to give them that perfect taste) and fed up. Also various additives to speed up the fattening process.

Last they were moved to slaughter houses and turned into steaks, hamburger and all the rest. Bits that American humans wouldn't eat became pet-food.

Comes the Big Chill. Professional ranchers are looking at the real weather forecasts and going "oh, my God."

See, even in good winters the grass falls off. You've got, say, one head per acre. That works in spring and summer and into fall. But come winter you've got to lay out hay (cut grass) for the cattle so they can make it through the winter. Harsher environments you have to lay out more than nicer environments. But in both you've got to lay out some.

Hay harvests had gotten massively fucked up by the weather. Storms were coming in all through the summer, what there was of it. To get hay, you have to cut it, let it dry and then harvest.

If it gets rained on after it's cut, or if it's still wet from the rain when you cut it, it "sours" and gets fungal infections. Even cows can get sick from it. (Horses will die.) Ever heard the term "hay-making weather." Hot, dry and stays that way?

We didn't have much of that in the summer of 2019.

Hay was short. And they were looking at the most fucked up winter in recent history.

Way up north, cattle will *die* if it gets too cold. And it was predicted, by everyone except the Met service, to get *really* fucking cold. That meant the only cattle they could run were those they had shelter for. Which meant nothing but "base stock." Those ten cows and one bull.

Ranchers were calling feed lots all over the place, trying to get their cattle sold. Nobody was buying. There wasn't food to feed them. The slaughter houses were overrun and *everyone* was trying to recover from the Plague.

The USDA probably couldn't have been any help. But even if it could, the bosses didn't see the issue.

"The forecast for the winter is not that severe. And killing cattle is murder, anyway. Let them graze in happy peacefulness. It's good that they can't be industrially slaughtered."

Are you grabbing your hair in fury? You should be. The famines of 2020 and 2021 weren't because of the farmers or the evil farm corporations. Hell, they weren't *in charge* of food production. The "rationalizers" were in charge. When the farmers got back in charge, they proved they could react, adapt and overcome. 2022 wasn't a bumper crop year, but it fed not only the U.S. but various other nations.

Ranchers, too, were getting pushed out. Nationalization of the farming industry was the Hero Project of the latter Warrick administration. People could sign up at the soup kitchens. A lot of people figured that being on a farm was going to be a better place than in a city come winter. And how hard could it be?

The county agents were overwhelmed. They were supposed to be "organizing" the local "farming cooperative groupings" to "produce maximal output for the upcoming season" and they *knew* they were in deep shit. They might *like* organic methods but they *knew* that industrial was more efficient. And most of them were smart enough to know that the shit coming from the Met Service was so much baloney.

Enter the U.S. Army.

We'd gotten, in most areas, the food distribution, what there was of it, under control. We'd gotten local groups, "voluntary associators" and even companies to handle it. We couldn't turn it over to corporations because they were "bad." (Bechtel, by the way, handled something like 90% of the recovery from Hurricane Katrina. It was defunct but another would have started up, from pretty much the same people, if we'd put out bids. We couldn't let bids. Neither could FEMA.)

But the point was, we were distributing what we could and turning most of it over to local control. However, we also knew we were going to be fucked come winter. Because *our* meteorologists were going "holy FUCK."

USDA was acting like a tofu-chicken. "Nationalization" was hammering what production there was. Something had to be done or the nation we were sworn to protect and serve was going to starve to death. Not just over the winter, but the projections were for widespread famine by next May.

"Emergency Supply Methodology" was a department that had gotten formed when the U.S. Army had to try to supply food to a famine in Somalia. What was absolutely evident to anyone who was there was that there was no reason for the famine. Yes, there was a drought. All a drought means is that you get less food from an acre. There were enough acres and enough acres that could be irrigated, that Somalia should have been able to feed itself.

It couldn't because of the security conditions. Farmers were being killed and driven off their lands because of the militias. *That* was what caused the famine. And in many areas it was intentional. See also Darfur, the Kulak famine and the Great Leap Forward. Starvation is a good way to enact "ethnic cleansing." Starving people is easier and cheaper than shooting them.

It got started as a think-tank to figure out how to do the best job you could in a fucked up situation. Most food distribution was done by Non-Governmental Organizations. (By the way, "random associators" are NGOs. Just very small ones.) One thing that was noted was that some NGOs were "better" at distribution than others. There were a huge number of *apparent* factors but it really came down to which were the most functionally pragmatic. That is, if the mission was to feed a population that was enemies with the local strongman, turning the food over to the strongman was non-functional for the mission. It would feed him and his henchmen and the people they liked. It would not feed the populace he was starving on purpose.

The way to avoid this was to use some of your precious NGO funds to hire enough "security" that the local strongman left you alone. And you could feed whoever you wanted. If you could also get some of the farmers farming again, that was a benefit.

If your personal opinion of violence was "nothing is ever settled by violence" then you lost your food to the strongman and therefore failed in your mission. It didn't matter how "actualized" you felt as you flew back to your hippie commune in California. You'd failed in your mission.

It was an unfortunate fact that the most "functionally pragmatic" groups tended to be Christian missionaries. Tended. Some of them were not "functionally pragmatic" and some of the secular NGOs were. But it was a general trend. It was a conclusion that was very quietly distributed, though. The Army had too often been accused of being friendly with Christian Fundamentalist groups.

They also looked at factors like "throughput." That is, if a group was given ten tons of relief supplies, how much of that actually got to the refugees or whatever. Again, Christian groups tended to have the highest throughput.

Here's an example of throughput in money. It involves charities pre-Plague. One of the richest charities in the U.S. pre-Plague was the March of Dimes. Every March people all over the country would walk around raising money for "childhood diseases." The March of Dimes would collect the money and then send it on to "worthy researchers."

MoD would never release its records to anyone but the IRS, but outside analysis indicated that only about *30%* of the money collected actually went to "researchers." The other *70%* went to "support" of . . . The March of Dimes. For every ten bucks some poor "marcher" collected, *seven* went to the MoD and only *three* went to researchers. The leadership was not volunteers. Indeed, above the "street" level there were *no* volunteers. Salaries for the upper management were astronomical. The president of the MoD had a *private* 737!

By the same token, one of the largest Christian charities in the world, Christian Children's Fund, *would* release its records. (As did many others, secular and religious.) They had an average throughput, every year, of over 90%. Nine bucks out of every ten reached the children it served.

Ninety percent throughput vs. *thirty* percent throughput. If you're going to contribute to a charity, do the math.

The U.S. Army did the math. They couldn't always pick and choose what NGOs they supported, but when they could they looked at the functionality of the NGOs and chose them on that basis. Yes, that tended to be Christian groups but the reality was they didn't care. They just wanted the stuff they were distributing to get to the people who needed it.

ESM was the first department to look at that methodically and come up with "key factors" for commanders to consider when choosing which NGO to support in their areas. They also expanded into producing pamphlets for commanders and staff on "key secondary response methods" in emergency and humanitarian relief missions. That is, how to get a country back on its feet. Especially agriculture in a famine.

But with first the Plague then the Chill, ESM became big doings. That had caused some problems as the minor little department suddenly became a focus and every fucking Fobbit wanted to jump on the bandwagon. For a while in the summer, I was told, "ESM" bumped out "transformational" as the big buzzword. Somebody pitching a new weapons system had to throw "ESM" in on the PowerPoint presentation to get it even looked at.

"This new super-duper artillery system is the killer app for ESM. ESM cluster systems can provide wide-spread terminal coverage of ESM priority materials..."

In other words, we can shoot the food out of the cannon at a high rate of fire and hope it doesn't knock anyone out when it gets there.

And, yes, that's from an *actual* presentation.

When I got to the department some of the hoo-hroo had settled down. Yes, it was a bigger department with a general in charge instead of a colonel. But some of the vampiric Fobbits that had grafted to it over the summer had been sent back to wherever they came from (PIO, Morale and Welfare, Systems Procurement) and the core guys were back in charge.

Its mission had changed, though. Use *actual* ESM to look at what was happening in the U.S. and "react, adapt and overcome" wherever the Army could be a benefit.

Bunch of smaller departments in the department, now. I was in the "Agricultural Emergency Response" department. I was a farmer. I had a degree in agronomy. I don't know what fairy godmother thought I could *do* anything there, but there I was.

And at first I *couldn't* do anything. I was a major. I carried the piss bucket. Meetings on "agricultural emergency response" involved colonels and generals. (None of whom, as far as I know, had agronomy degrees. But they were doing their best.)

My particular piss bucket was to be put in charge of the "Mid-watch Phone Response Center."

That was not some sort of switchboard. It was a call center. It was a call center that commanders in the field could call for help when they were dealing with "agriculture emergency issues."

Okay, here's the thing about an agricultural emergency. Most of the time, by the time you realize you have an emergency, you're already fucked. Farmers have huge lead times. Go back to my dad telling me he was investing in triticale because the forecast for *six months later* was for "cooling regimes."

The decisions that were being made in 2019 were going to affect 2020 *and* 2021.

2020's a no brainer. By November of 2019 farmers would have been planning what they were going to do in 2020. No brainer.

But 2021? Why 2021?

Hello! Seeds!

The *seeds* for 2021 crop cycle were *produced* in 2020. And they were based on really long-range forecasts by the major seed companies. They'd have to guess what the major crops were going to be two years in advance and lay on the right seed stockpiles.

But most of those companies had been "nationalized." The seeds they were considering were *not* being based on the long, long-range forecasts. Not the right forecasts, anyway. And genetic modification? I don't *think* so. Genmod was bad. Evil. Wicked.

But the emergency that was going on right then was cattle. There were too many. And no way to feed them through the winter. Most of the tofu-eaters who had taken over as ranchers didn't even realize that. And you couldn't tell them.

Some of the people moved out to ranches, though, weren't idiots. They asked the locals what the hell they were supposed to be doing. Mostly the locals told them to push off. But occasionally they'd get a bit of "you're going to lose them all come winter."

Everybody "culled" in the fall. It was the whole point of Thanksgiving and all the other harvest festivals in history. You fed up certain animals during the summer and culled them in the fall. That way you didn't have to feed them over winter. Pigs especially but also cattle. See *Charlotte's Web*.

Oh, yeah, pigs. Most pigs were raised on factory-farms. Ever seen the movie *Babe*? That big warehouse looking thing where all the piglets are? That's where most pork comes from. You don't turn out pigs to feed. (Not since the Middle Ages when they used to be herded through oak forests for acorns.) They have to be fed continuously. And there wasn't any feed.

So we'd get calls from local commanders. They were out there doing whatever mission and as one of their "corollary missions" they were supposed to provide "support" for "emergency agricultural situations."

So, you're a sergeant in charge of delivering a "packet" of emergency supplies. Let's say that it's to Lamoille County since we've talked about that before.

You go to the "random associator" which is the NGO you're favoring at the time. Say the Lutheran Church. And you drop your packet. But there's this guy trying to get your attention.

He's in a quandary.

"I'm an accountant. I worked for Smith Barney. They went under in the Plague. I signed up for this 'agricultural nationalization' program cause it had to be better than eating soup on the lines. I thought I'd be sent out to *work* on a farm not *run* it. My wife and I got put in charge of a dairy farm. I figured out how to hook the cows up to the milking machine and even found a guy who's still collecting the milk. But he tells me that I don't have enough feed for the cows for the winter and the feed I *do* have is running out and I can't find any more for love or money. The county agent's never answered my calls. I know you're Army but do you have a *clue* what I'm supposed to do?"

You had to be, at first, pretty desperate to ask an *Army sergeant* a question like that. After a while, though, people started doing it all the time.

So the sergeant says he has no clue but he'll ask around. And he asks his platoon sergeant. And the platoon sergeant remembers something about a department that is supposed to be handling shit like that. And because he's devoted to his job he dips into institutional memory and finds a number to call.

And, late, he calls the Emergency Supply Methodology, Agricultural Emergency Supply Methodology help-line.

And he gets a private.

"ESMAESM help-desk, Private Smedlap speaking. How can I help you sir or ma'am?"

Milk cows. Feed.

"Where is this? Vermont? Hang on ... I'm waiting for my system ... Oh, right. Okay. Vermont is anticipated to experience extreme climatic conditions in the upcoming winter ... Waiting ... Cattle will require long-term shelter for survival. Will require feed equalling x pounds of feed per head per day. Grazing will be a minimal option of no significant note to survival. Feed stores are at an all-time low. Current feed prices indicate minimal availability and are anticipated to increase over-winter. Absent large stores of on-site feed, recommendation is culling to breeding stock. Does that cover it? Yeah, that means they have to kill them all, and hopefully keep the meat and stuff, because ain't no food for them and they're not going to be able to graze. Hell, if they're outdoors most of the time they're going to freeze. I dunno if you've seen the internal forecasts but I hope you've packed your EWCS. I can e-mail you this shit if you've ... okay ... Platoon. Sergeant@us.army.mil. Right. On its way. Thanks for calling the ... Okay he hung up."

As time went on, the number got passed out to civilians. At first the help desk wasn't supposed to answer questions outside the military but by the time I got there that was old history. AESM had been up and handling for nine months or so. So we often had to deal with tofu-eaters. Which was always frustrating but occasionally really funny.

I ran the help-desk. It wasn't exactly rocket science most of the time. I had about sixty guys on my shift. "Guys." Okay, I had about forty guys on my shift and twenty females. Two female lieutenants, even. It was strange. I was infantry. Having women working for me was an adjustment.

Generally, the response stuff was set up. Sometimes, though, there'd be a call that needed actual, you know, farming expertise. There was a progression for that. But we didn't get many calls on my shift and I was bored so I generally got on at Phase Two calls.

"Major Bandit Six. Hang on, waiting for the data to transfer."

(Note, my actual last name was fairly common. I don't think any of the people calling knew they were talking to "The Centurion" and I *never* let on.)

"Okay, I see that first line said you need to cull all but breeding stock. Frankly, I don't know if you can even keep the breeding stock. Pigs eat a lot and there's not much sw... Ma'am, they're there to be *turned into* food. You gotta kill 'em to do that. I know they're cute, but that's the answer... Yes, that's a lot of pigs to kill. I suggest a .22 in the back of the head... Hello?"

Yeah, I got some complaints. Screw 'em.

And then I'd occasionally get some guy who was really fucking trying and needed an expert to tell him what to really do. When I got those I treated them like fucking *gold*.

"The good news is you're in a zone where the climate's actually better for most farming under current conditions than before. This shit that's going on actually helps some regions. Okay, give me your e-mail address... Damn. Okay, gimme an address. I'll send you everything I can get on what should work there. I can't give you a degree in agronomy but as long as I'm sitting in this chair I'll hold your hand as much as possible. There are stores of seeds, pesticides and herbicides that you can use. We can release them... Don't go *organic* on me... Oh, okay. Right, here's the deal. You can still get winter wheat in the ground if you're quick. You're going to need hands to pick rocks... I'll explain..."

The problem being with livestock that had to be culled, well, we're back to everything getting backed up.

"Yes, I know the slaughterhouses are overloaded. Look, you're in *Wisconsin*. You're not going to warm up for *months*. Just slaughter them on site. Should have been done months ago. Store the carcasses anywhere you can keep them away from scavengers... Yes, I know it's a gruesome business. I *grew up* on a farm. Yes, I'm a real farmer, thank you. I've got a degree in this stuff... Actually, I can send you a pamphlet on the proper method of slaughtering cattle. But just remember, if you've got anything like feed for them, keep some breeding stock. That's the bull, he's the one with balls, and a few cows. You'll need x pounds of stock feed or x rolls of hay per animal per week. And with the temps they're predicting for your area, you're going to have to barn them every night ... Yes, it *is* a lot of work. No, I don't know where you can get more help. There's a lot of people standing in soup lines. Go to one of those and ask ... Sorry if you found that offensive, sir. Perhaps you could find some Mexicans. But the last time a soldier saw enough Mexicans to help was at the Alamo and we all know how that turned out ... Hello?"

Okay, *a lot* of complaints.

California started getting "unseasonable" rains. That would have helped, a lot, in Imperial Valley if most of the people there had any *clue* what they were doing. But the *real* farmers were on soup lines (okay, most of them weren't) and the idiots from soup lines were trying to farm.

And the farms didn't have a lot of food on them. The ones that had actual houses (many didn't) had been stripped by the departing owners or managers. They weren't going to leave their food for the grasshoppers.

So some of the "experts" sent out to "rebuild the farming industry" decided that they were better off in soup lines.

ADM, when it got "nationalized," sent out along with its pink-slips a way for their various managers and "associated farmers" to keep in touch. Basically, it was a "forwarding address" database. Some of them didn't do it. But farmers are planners. And if they had any chance of getting back onto the farms, they were going to take it. It took a while and Con-Agra just basically went tits up. But in 2021 when the new administration went into reverse on all this, ADM was waiting. Which is why it *really* dominates the industry now.

But that's then.

A disaster? It was more of a nightmare. And at the call center we were the acoustic engineers getting *every last nuance* of the sound of the train wreck.

I was *still* there as spring came around. And the nightmare really got in motion.

But I'm getting ahead of myself again.

I think I only contributed one useful item the whole damned time I was stuck in the call center and *that* was by accident.

I was just coming off shift. I looked and felt like shit. I knew I was going to get a few more complaints added to the stack. It had been one of those nights.

I have no clue why the general in charge of ESM decided to

stop by the field grade officer's can. But there he was, taking a whiz, when I flipped out my pecker in the next urinal and had to, as usual, back waaay up.

(Wife Edit: Be nice!)

I knew who he was. I didn't say anything. He did.

"You're Bandit Six."

"Yes, sir."

"What the *hell* are you doing in *here*? Get lost in the Puzzle Palace?"

"I work for you, sir."

"You do?"

"ESMAESM call center night shift supervisor."

"How in the hell . . . ? Lieutenant" To his aide. "You know who Bandit Six is, right?"

"Yes, sir!"

"Sorry, Bandit. I had no clue you worked in my shop. But you were a farmer, right?"

"Yes, sir." (Zipping up.)

"Any suggestions?"

"Gotta get the livestock slaughtered, sir. That's all you *can* do this time of year. Should have been done months ago. And plan for next but we can't do that. All *we* can do is react."

"Slaughterhouses are full, so is cold storage. I had a brief on that yesterday . . ."

"Sir, we're looking at the coldest winter on record. Zones one through three, maybe four, you can slaughter them and hang them from trees and they'll keep all winter. Hell, we'll have eaten it all out by spring."

"Most of the farmers that are part of the . . ."

"Are idiots. Yes, sir. I run the call center, sir. And even then, the ranchers don't have the hands and the ones that are . . . transportees don't have the experience. Or in most cases the guts or will or willingness to do the work. But we, the Army, are going to need that food, sir. And we, the Army, *do* have hands. Sir. And guts. And willingness to work hard for survival. Sir."

"Interesting point. Lieutenant, block out some time for Bandit Six to stop by. I used to be a tanker before I got stuck on this crap detail. I'd like to talk to you about Khuwaitla."

"Yes, sir."

I went back to my quarters and forgot about the incident.

However, a week later the order went out to start "Emergency Slaughter Teams."

It wasn't just soldiers. Groups would go to the soup lines and pick up any people who a) looked fit enough and b) were willing to "do some hard work for better food." There was no pay. The pay was fresh meat, which was rare for most people in those days.

Some of the "farmers" didn't want to slaughter their pets. Most, however, had seen their feed almost totally depleted. In "Zones One through Three," the northern border down to North Carolina, dipping down to southern Oklahoma and then back up to northern California, snow was already on the ground to stay. Pigs, especially, were out of food. Pigs will eat anything. So will people. There wasn't any food for the *people*.

Well, there was. Rye bread from farmers who had seen that the summer of 2019 was going to be screwed and soup made up of anything that was available. Spices were a rare commodity.

Meat quickly became a *common* commodity for a while. There was quite a bit in those soups during the winter of early 2020. Might have kept the death rate down a touch.

Lost *a lot* of livestock unnecessarily. By the time the ESTs were really getting in gear most of the livestock, including breeding stock, had died of malnutrition or exposure. But we got some of the food. That was something. Not that it helped in the long-run but few things do.

By February all the livestock was either slaughtered down to breeding groups or dead. People were dying, too. Lots of people. Despite my "heroic efforts" fuel for power and heat was at a premium. There was a, in my opinion, good government program to make sure people could get what they needed. Ration cards and such. But there was *never* enough. And people died in blizzards when their meager stocks of food and fuel ran out. And cities lost power and people froze.

Everything froze. The sugar cane in south Florida froze. Old people in retirement in Phoenix and Miami *froze*.

And people died on soup lines because they were already malnourished (one small chunk of rye bread and a cup of soup is not enough to keep most humans going forever) and it was bloody cold and *nobody* had the right clothing and China wasn't making Gortex parkas anymore.

People got frostbite and hypothermia. They dropped like flies.

And it wasn't even the really *bad* winter.

Farmers are planners. They sit on their tractors and in their dens and peer into the future though cloudy crystal balls, trying to discern what wheat and soy is going to be worth a year in advance. They look at the long-range weather reports. They watch the flight of the wild geese.

I'd been trained to do that since I was a baby as a form of osmosis picked up from the few words my dad would say at the dinner table. The hands would be talking a bit and my mom would be chattering and one of the hands would say something and my dad would grunt.

"Soy isn't going to be worth the price of sand next year."

And when I got older I'd try to figure out why he knew that. And he was usually right.

There's going to be a glut in the soy market next year. Why?

Long-term weather looked right for soy. China was projected to do a big buy. Monsanto had just come out with a new seed strain that was going to increase yields, on average, by two percent. (Which, right there, was enough to cause a glut, believe it or not.)

Big corporations were shifting towards soy. Managers were talking about it over coffee in the corner greasy spoon, around the counter in the feed store. Bio-diesel from soy. Soy was the word. "Soy's going to be big next year."

And it was. Bumper crop. Perfect weather, great seeds . . .

China wasn't buying as much as predicted. Bio-diesel wasn't really taking off. Overall sales were about the same or down.

Supply and demand. High supply, low to normal demand. It was worth the price of sand.

This, by the way, is what "commodity markets" are all about. Dad didn't buy his seed in cash. He bought it, everyone bought it, on "futures." That is, credit. But the seed had to be paid for by something. So commodity markets gambled on what was going to be big in next year's crop. Or even this year's crop. People put money into the market, the market created the "margin" for the seed and pesticides and everything else. And at the end of the year you found out if you'd made money or not.

Hell, you could "day trade" on the commodity market. Going "long" on wheat, selling "short" on sow-belly (bacon). But it was always, truly, about going long. It was reading the crystal ball.

By December all the money was counted and all the bills were paid or you'd lost the bet. You'd gotten the wrong answer from the crystal ball.

My dad was the fucking prophet Elijah, every single year. Which was why we stayed in business. Hell, I always wondered why he didn't just give up farming and trade in commodities. He would have made a killing.

I wasn't a prophet but you only had to be reasonably keyed in to see where we were heading. You only had to have the sort of head that could put five or ten variables, not complicated ones, together, plug in the known constants and get an answer.

The "model" in my head said that we were looking at a famine in 2020 and 2021. Could be marginal, looked to be major. But there simply *wasn't going to be enough food* for all our remaining mouths. And the winter was going to be another killer.

And the internal ESM models said the same about both production and weather.

Then I'd look at what the USDA and the Met office was saying and shake my head. That, by the way, was one of the variables. The fact that the people who should have been making *accurate* predictions were making predictions based purely on politics and fantasy.

Commodity markets were back up by spring of 2020. USDA was saying one thing. Independent research firms were saying the exact opposite. (Army data was secret but leaked.) Trading was all over the board. Long on wheat? Short on wheat? Hell, was there going to *be* any wheat?

Generally, the trading was very "stagnant." Which meant less money available for supplies. But just about anyone who got into the commodities market in 2020 got their balls handed to them.

It was supposed to be pre-planting. Met office was saying temps were going to be coming up, fast. USDA was predicting soil temperatures that were on with 2018 or *earlier*. Like they were totally ignoring the fact that we were entering an ice age.

But it was so clear, by then, that all but the most "government uber alles" tofu-heads were tuning them out. They'd constantly predicted better temperature regimes. Because of "global warming." Which everyone was starting to realize was so much bunk. They'd stood in food lines in below zero, Farenheit, temperatures. They knew it wasn't getting warmer. Not that year, by God.

And the Bitch was starting to campaign for office. She still had supporters. Some. The core of the news media, for sure. The "limousine liberals" who had managed to sail through the Plague and the Chill because, of course they got immunized and of course they got paid and had access to all their usual foods. But even that was starting to crumble.

Her opponents were beating her with a *stick* every time they got a second of airtime. Polls showed her numbers to be in the low twenties. And going *down*.

So then she started . . . reacting.

— CHAPTER TWO —

We Are TOO Going to Have an Election!

In March of 2020 the Bitch "nationalized" a major radio network. It had always been fairly right wing. It broadcast not only on local stations but on satellite. And it had hung in there, barely, through the whole Plague and the depression that followed. Lots of marginal stations just shut down, but it was still hanging in there.

Then it was announced, on all the stations, that they had been seized by the federal government for "violation of Fair Use laws." Essentially, their commentators had been saying Bad Things about the Bitch and thus she shut them down.

The FCC was ordered to ensure "Fair Use" of airtime in all radio and broadcast TV stations.

Short of simply turning off all the radio stations, she couldn't get rid of every person working for the company. And most of the "talent" were not exactly Friends of Warrick. But they knew the score. Toe the Party Line or toe the soup line.

But, hell, they were experts in playing with words. I got sent an MP3 in an e-mail from a guy who was still on his talk show down in Georgia. Very right wing. But he was "toeing the party line." The opening:

"We have another pronouncement of better things for tomorrow from our glorious leader President Warrick!" All in a tone of utter sincerity.

Subtle propaganda works for Americans. It was the stock in trade of the MSM. *Over the top* propaganda they spot in a heartbeat. And laugh their asses off.

But they weren't being "unfair." They were giving Warrick almost all their airtime. And when they spoke of her opponents it was ...

"Today, the evil Senator from Tennessee, Fred Carson, who has the *audacity* to think he can best our glorious leader in November, suggested to a paltry group of scum-sucking supporters that perhaps some of her actions were *uncalled for* or perhaps *wrongly judged.* How dare he! The evil of the man suggesting that the vaccine distribution was, and I quote as the words cause bile in my mouth, 'less than optimal.' He should be shot and then hanged and then torn to pieces for suggesting our glorious leader is not perfect in every way!"

Yeah, they were "fair." Don't you think?

(Actually, there were people who *complained* about the presentation of Warrick's opponents as being "unfair" and "destructive." Some people just *cannot* get a joke.)

But we were getting into normal planting time in Minnesota. And snow was barely melting in *Virginia.* USDA estimates of "optimum soil temperature regimes" for various foods passed and were updated, passed and were updated. Based on those estimates, the tofu-eaters following the directions on the packet (that packet being the pamphlets they'd gotten from the county agents who were passing them from USDA headquarters) had laid in seeds, where available, for planting that were designed for a normal season.

It wasn't a normal season.

And a lot of the tofu-eaters had died on those farms in the middle of winter when they didn't ration their heating oil well enough and were stuck in the middle of nowhere in a blizzard and they couldn't even walk to their local emergency shelter for food and a place to sleep out of the killer cold.

Nine farms, recall. Two, Bob had managed through finagling to hold onto. I won't give the list of destruction that those tofu-eaters did to my farms. What I *will* say is that three of the seven died over the winter. Two of the other four only survived because they made it to Bob and he kept the grasshoppers alive.

The other two weren't bad folk. They're *still* my farm managers.

In Zone One, that is the great-white-north, that was about the rate. Three in seven of those "government cooperative farmers" died. So did all their livestock. It ripped the guts out of one of the most productive agricultural areas of our nation.

Going further south they survived in higher numbers. In a way that was worse. They were there to fuck things up.

Okay, let's return to Blackjack since we've used that before.

They manage to pull a good bit of their population through the Plague. The farmers in the community (and it's a heavy farming area) are looking at the forecasts. Cotton is a dead letter for the time being. People aren't buying new clothes. Food is the key for 2020 and although it's still summer of 2019, they're looking in their crystal balls. They've also looked at 2019 and have laid in their crops. Corn, wheat because the temperature regimes are going to be good for wheat in Georgia. (Wheat was not a major crop in Georgia prior to the Freeze. It's now one of our big wheat producers.) Potatoes. Soy because there's all sorts of things you can do with soy.

Some of them are seed farmers. They only produce seed. They get the base stock seeds from a seed company and plant those. The "harvest" is actually different from the base stock and *that's* what gets planted to make food and the harvest from *that* is different than what you get when you plant the seeds. (Trust me. It's complicated. I've given enough classes, I'm not going to give one in transform genetics. I'll just say it's not fucked up, it's how plants work. Period.) I don't mean it's a different species. It's just you wouldn't want to try to make bread from the stuff the seed companies send them to plant to make next year's seeds. You don't even want to make bread from the seeds. (Gluten content is wrong.)

So, they've got the seed in the ground. They've found sources for pesticides. They're ready to rock in what farmers do best; watching money grow out of the ground.

They first hear from the seed company. It's been nationalized. Not sure what that's going to mean except we've been told no genmod. We pointed out that the seed for next year is already in the ground and it's all genmod. They're in meetings. I have my pink slip. See ya.

Then the sheriff comes around looking pissed.

Farm's been nationalized. You gotta get out.

This has been in my family for generations. The hell you say.

I don't like it. Don't get stupid. Too many dead already.

Where go?

Parrish family died. House is in county hands. No buyers. Move there. Ten acres. Best I can do. Take personal stuff. Furniture even. No farm equipment.

So they move over to the Parrish house. And they look around at the belongings of people they knew through their kids going to school together. There are pictures on the walls. All the people are dead.

They take the pictures down. They move the Parrish furniture out into the storage shed. They put in theirs. They put the cans of food they've brought from home up on the shelves. They figure out how to get a new house going.

They walk five miles to town. They go to the feed store. There's a lot of other farmers in there, bitching. There's talk of revolting but it's just talk. There's a lot of "The South Shall Rise again" but the world's already a fucked up enough place and they know it. They're ants. If the South *is* going to Rise Again it's gonna have to be fed, first.

There's seed in the feed store. It's not much but there's seed. Most of the good stuff is getting stripped, fast. The feed store owner is pretty damned tight and he's not tied into the whole "futures" thing. But he gets another loan from the bank, which is only holding on from the government propping it up, and he buys more seed. He gets orders in advance and he lets people he knows buy on credit. Long-term credit.

There's a shortage of seed but what the hell.

There's a program that people who are farming can get gas for their tractors and combines. If you're a registered farmer. If you're a registered farmer and not tied into the "nationalization program" you're likely to be out on your ass.

People pool their gas rations. There's barely enough. There's a certain amount of "scrounging" and some finagling by local gas providers. But tractors get filled. Horses become a primary means of transportation.

Ten acres ain't much, unless you're a very smart farmer. Then you can do a lot with ten acres. There's land that hasn't been tilled in a long time. It's not great, but you're a pretty decent farmer. You get more credit for herbicides to kill the grass. You do soil samples. You have to get them tested through the county agent but you're not a registered farmer so you're waiting a while. In the meantime, you're planning.

Also in the meantime the "government cooperative farmer"

has arrived at the farm. This is a "grade A" farm on the list the USDA keeps. It's gone to well-connected tofu-heads. Call it a former female marketing executive who specialized in promoting organic farming and her husband the lawyer, also an "agricultural expert." They've both been on the soup line a couple of times but mostly they've been able to get along. They don't have children because "they never found the time." As part of their "resettlement package" they've been given extra gas rations to drive to their "resettlement farm" and start a new life as happy farmers in the big wide open.

They arrive to find nothing in the house. Not a damned thing. Some scraps of paper. Everything else is gone. They drive to town to complain to the sheriff. He's to say the least uncaring.

They drive to the county agent's office. He's out and his secretary is less than helpful. They're handed a bunch of pamphlets.

They're low on gas to get to the farm. But they make it. They have, as part of the resettlement package, a bunch of instructions. They attempt to decypher them. "What is soil chemistry?"

They attempt to call the listed, USDA, help center. Their phone has been disconnected. They'll have to drive into town to get it connected. They run out of gas. They are out of gas rations for the time being. (As far as they know. Actually, farmers had plenty of gas but farmers needed it.)

They walk to town. On the surface people are very nice. They find the phone company. They get the phone and electric connected. The gas for heat and cooking is rationed. There's some in the tank. Don't use it up quick.

There is an "emergency food distribution center" at the Baptist Church. They don't like churches but they go there to get food. They explain who they are and that there's no food in the house and that it's a long walk. Reactions are mixed. A few people are hostile. Most smile and say "Bless your heart" a lot. (Southrons never ever say what is truly on their mind. They're very Japanese that way. In this case, "Bless your heart" means "So you're the poltically connected assholes that took over the Beauford farm . . .") A very young lady gives them enough simple foods to last for a few days. They leave. They try to hitch a ride back to the farm. Finally a guy in a pickup truck picks them up and drops them closish. They walk the rest of the way.

There is a truck garden the farmer's wife put in before they were thrown out. They pick some beans. There's a pig. They don't know what to do about the pig or the cows. They read the instructions. They try to figure out the instructions. They call the help center. It's a busy signal (because there are thousands like them in the same predicament).

The lawyer actually sits down and reads all the documents. The main thing he extracts is that they are entitled to "supplementary emergency fuel" allocations on the basis of being farmers. Okay! Styling. They can get gas!

They have driven down a Mercedes SUV from Atlanta. A gas turbo. The "fuel" they can get, by special delivery to the tanks at the farm, is diesel. Their car sits on the side of the road for a *long* time.

There are no diesel vehicles at the farm except a tractor. The diesel F-350 is at the Parrish farm, up on blocks until the "real" farmer can find fuel.

There are crops growing in the field. They look at them. There's not much else to do. The cable is out and the only channel they can get on the TV is CBS and that's snow-filled and nearly impossible to understand. There are no books in the house.

The wife runs out of birth control pills. They don't have any money to buy some from the small-town pharmacy that's still struggling along. It's not going to sell them birth control pills on credit. They are extremely polite but firm. The wife makes a scene.

At this point, some of them get fed up and find some way to get back to being real grasshoppers. The soup lines are better than this.

But we'll say they hang in there.

At some point an officious woman turns up at their house. The officious woman is the new rep for the seed company. It is pointed out that all of their crop is owned by the government. But it's genmod seed. So it can't be used. They need to till it under and plant new seed. That will be provided by the government, as well. And when it's harvested, it will be turned over to the government.

And we get paid . . . ?

In seed.

That's the next point where people said "blow this for a game of soldiers" and found *any* way back to civilization.

There are lots of such points. I'll skip most of them.

The husband finds out that driving a tractor over a plowed field is not easy. But he does it. The wife does not. She is attempting to learn how to cook. He also learns that:

Hooking up a plow is a bitch.

So is plowing. And it's very fucking boring. And it takes forever, especially if you're in a fucking little 35-horse tractor that the farmer only ever used for minor stuff. But he'd taken one look at the big combine and gone "oh, no *fucking* way."

The seed is delivered. He plants it. Despite being an intelligent person he is confused by the concept that the seed he's growing is going to be *seed*. But if that's what he's doing for a living . . . I wonder if the town needs a lawyer?

No, as a matter of fact. Ours survived, alas.

He then finds out.

Seed bags are very fucking heavy.

So is a spreader and if you don't know how to hook one up you can kill yourself. Or hook it up wrong and then bad things happen.

A standard grass spreader is a lousy way to spread wheat seed. He doesn't know that there's a seed planter sitting there. He doesn't know what a seed planter is. And, besides, it's designed for the big tractor he's avoiding.

And he has to keep filling the spreader with those heavy fucking bags of seed.

Things break. They always do. Some things you just have to get a repair guy for. Most, farmers can fix. He can't. The tractor stops. He doesn't know why.

He goes down the road to the next farm. That's no help, that's a young couple who look like they just stepped out of a rock concert and they haven't even bothered to figure out the tractor. They've got a nice crop of ganja out back, though. The crop's like, whoa! It's beans and shit! I think! Dude you have got to try some of this shit! Hey, Stacey's pregnant, man, 'cause we're like out of birth control pills . . .

His wife has cut him off because she's not going to have a baby, the tractor is stuck in the field because the spreader is on backwards and it's jammed the transmission and he really needs a drink, not a toke.

Leave point.

Instead, he goes into town looking for help. There are choices as to what to do.

There were those who said: "I'm a bigshot and you farmers had better fix this or I'll get the gub'mint on your ass!" Or just were hostile and in people's face.

In which case they got exactly dick for help. And the crops never got as far as planted. Seed sat in bags until it got rained on and rotted and was lost. This, alas, was common and contributed to the famines of 2020 and 2021.

We'll give this guy a more optimum situation. He's a dick normally but he also knows when he has to crawl. He's just not sure where to.

Sometimes he runs into the county agent who is running around like mad and gets some help. Enough to get the crop in the ground.

Sometimes he ends up on the phone with me. If he's not a dick, I'll do what I can long distance. Because I can see the train wreck on the way. If he's a dick, I figure he's not worth the time.

Sometimes he walks into the feed store.

There are a bunch of guys sitting around not doing much. There are rocking chairs. None of them are available. Some other guys are standing up.

He doesn't know it, but there's a defined pecking order to those chairs. If a guy gets up and leaves, a *specific guy* is going to get his chair.

The hayseeds in the feedstore kind of nod and go back to talking about the weather. He waits around for someone to walk up and ask him what he needs. No one does. He's not sure who works there and who is just hanging around. Everyone is in the same clothes.

He is, more or less, ignored.

One of the guys makes mention that it's gonna be a cold winter. The woolies are already getting wooly already. (And the old farmer knows where to look for real long-term predictions.)

The lawyer contends that predictions are for a mild winter. Yeah, it's been a cold spring but it's warming up and what with global warming . . .

They look at him as if he's a Martian. One of them finally says:

"Can I help you?"

He pours out his tale of woe. Little does he know that the guy he displaced, whose truck garden he is eating off of, is sitting in one of the rocking chairs. Everybody knows who the newcomer is. Everyone knows his "tale of woe." Everyone knows that the harvest is going to be fucked and famine is on the way. What they're discussing in quiet voices is how to survive.

"Put the spreader on backwards," one of the hayseeds contends. "Reverse and take it off. Put it on right ways round. That'll do ya."

"Why you usin' the spreader? There's a perfectly good planter."

"What's a planter?"

If, at this point, he just says "Look, I know this is fucked up. I didn't think we'd be *taking someone's farm.* I thought I'd be *working* on one. Helping out or something. I don't have the slightest clue what I'm doing. The only thing I know about farming is from watching reruns of *Green Acres.* But I've got to get this right or . . . it's going to be bad . . ."

Well, then sometimes they'd help out.

We'll continue this in two directions.

The first is the optimal result. It wasn't common, but it happened enough that it's probably why *any* of us survived 2020. And, remember, we're back in summer of 2019 when I was over in Iran.

The guy whose farm he took, the guy with the Browning ballcap on his head and the Winston dangling from his lip (in violation of the universal smoking ban in indoor public areas) pushes the ball cap up.

"Got a deal fer ya."

The guy in the Browning ballcap will teach him how to farm. The lawyer and his wife now work for him. The lawyer does what he tells him to do and he's not going to enjoy it. But the guy even knows where there's some furniture up for grabs and he knows there ain't none in the house. Do what I tell you to do and we'll make it through.

"Why? I mean, why would you do that?"

"I get a cut of the pay. An' cause that's *mah* John Deere you done fucked up. An' ah don't want it fucked up again."

There was, thank God, a lot of that. The two "good" farmers on my farms. They found out about Bob quick and told him they had *no clue* what they were doing. Teaching people who have no clue what they're doing, and are mentally and physically unsuited to farming, how to farm is ten times the trouble of professionals.

And it was a *very fucked up* planting season. But Bob did it. And they didn't totally screw up.

The other five? They were . . . suboptimal results in various ways. I had to replace a lot of equipment over time. But the government paid for it eventually. Why not? It was the Bitch's fuck up in the first place. And the Congress let her get away with it.

But we'll go to the less optimal result. The farmers and store owner tell him the minimum he needs to know and suggest he call the USDA help-line. He points out it's overwelmed. The feed store owner finds a number for another help line. It's Army. See if they can help you.

So now we're back to the seed farmer.

He was not, in fact, in Blackjack. I won't say where he was except that it was "southern" and in prime farm country.

I never would have noticed if I hadn't been bored and listening to the techs answering questions. I always kept half an ear on that in case things were getting out of hand, as they frequently did.

This wasn't out of hand, it was the tone of confusion. That was nearly as good. So I hooked into the circuit.

". . . don't have *any* information on how to fix equipment, sir. We can give advice on crops and weather and pests but we don't have anything on equipment, I'm sorry. Have you tried contacting the manufacturer?"

"Major Bandit Six, cutting in. I've got it, Smedlap. Say problem again, over. Start at the beginning, go to the end and I'll see if I can help."

Tractor broken. Information I got doesn't work. Lawyer. Didn't know I was *taking over* someone's farm. Out of my depth. Army knows about farming?

Army knows everything. What kind of tractor?

I don't know.

What kind of spreader?

I don't know.

Get pen and paper. Go find out. Here's a number you can get through to me.

While he was gone, I considered the voice. The guy was clearly over his head and just a touch angry.

But it was also the middle of the damned night. And he was still working the problem. If he could get over the anger, there might be some worth to him.

He called me back.

"Bandit Six, if you've got the time, I've got the dime."

He had all sorts of information about the tractor and the spreader. All I needed was the model numbers.

"Oh, hell, yeah you've got the spreader on backwards. When they said 'reverse it' what they meant was just pop it in reverse then back out. You can't *back it up*. I hope you didn't break the spay arm. Okay, get ready to write this down. Memorize it. You won't be able to read it in the dark and do it at the same time. Do you have the lifting tines hooked up? Okay, I'll walk you through how to bring it back with the lifting tines, too. Get ready to write..."

It took about two hours to get through a fifteen-minute evolution. The guy wasn't getting much sleep that night. But we got the spreader back to the equipment shed.

"What were you using it for? It's not time to spread grass seed. Wheat? Why were you using a *spreader* to lay down *wheat*? Don't you have a planter...?

. . .

. . . . . .

. . . .

. . .

. . . .

"Okay, calm down." Grin. "You're what I class as a C. That means there's some promise. You can get your back up and wroth and decide you're the expert here and then you're going to go to D and you'll be talking to my call center guys until you get tired of it and go back to the soup lines as an F. Or you might work your way up to A. But I'll give you the chance. It's late and it's about time for you to actually go to work. If you're willing, though, I'll walk you through a lot of shit and you might make a barely functional farmer... Yes, I grew up on a farm and I've got a degree in the shit. I'm about the only guy working this place who *does* so for anything farming beyond C-A-T equals cat, you're going to have to talk to *me*... I work nights. But that's not a problem. Because you're going to be getting up around... an hour ago. And you'll be going to bed around sunset... Yes, there's a reason. Are you listening? Is this actually sinking in? Because I'm not going to waste my time if it's not... You're welcome."

He'd been a lawyer in Memphis specializing in "environmental agricultural issues." He was, in fact, every farmer's worst nightmare. The kind of guy who environmental groups hired to sue farmers for drying out a plot of land that they considered "wetlands."

His wife started out the complete bitch.

We'd gotten beyond C-A-T equals cat by then. We were talking as he was getting ready for another hard day's work. He was fixing what he could find for breakfast. I asked him where his wife was. Asleep.

"Farming is team work. *You're* supposed to still be asleep. *She's* supposed to be cooking breakfast. Who's cleaning? Who's taking care of the garden?"

Getting his wife to sit down and talk to me was, I take it, not easy. But it happened.

"Bandit Six, this number is permanently connected to a nuclear tipped missile aimed at *you*, keep that in mind . . . Oh, Hi Roger. Mrs. Roger? Oh, that would be Miz Roger. Miss Roger-Not-Roger? We're going to have such a nice time. Hello, ma'am. My name is Bandit Six. Here is the deal . . ."

You and your husband are in deep cacky.

This winter things are going to be a nightmare.

The nightmare will continue into next year.

I don't care what the President and her ministers say, trust in me, I'm with the High Command.

You are an expert in whatever your field used to be.

You know nothing about farming or being a farm wife.

If you do not listen to me, you and your husband are going to *die*.

Did you hear me? Do you believe me? D-I-E.

Okay, here is lesson one. There will be many more. And you'll like them less.

"'A man he works from sun to sun but a woman's work is never done.' That's not a complaint. That's reality. Your husband, in case you hadn't noticed, is now going out all day just about every day working his tail off. It's hard, brutal, necessary work. He's probably losing weight. He'll gain it back as he gets better at things and if there's food. But he will always be expending more calories in a day than you do. He will be working *harder* physically. You will be working *constantly* physically but at a lower level.

"Farm work is team work. You are part of the team. The part

you *have* to do, not sort of have to do, not can ignore, is vitally important. You're going to think it's demeaning. It's not. You are a *critical member of the team*. Your job, accept it or not, is support for you husband and hands . . . Well, you're going to need them eventually. If you stick this. Here's your job list . . ."

Fix heartiest breakfast you can fix before your husband is awake. Cereal, if available, is insufficient. Carbo-load but add any available protein. There's a reason that bacon, eggs, hash browns and toast is called "A Farmer's Breakfast" on menus.

Wash kitchen thoroughly after each meal. Foodstuffs available to you have no preservatives. Flies carry bacteria. Flies are endemic to farms. The combination means any foodstuffs left out become bacteria magnets. You *will* suffer from food poisoning, sooner rather than later, if you don't keep the kitchen area spotless . . . If you don't have soap make it or trade for it in town.

Next chore is pick eggs. Get your kids to help you . . . Then I'm sorry. Hands are hands. Kids learn, early, they've got chores on farms . . . Go see if there are any orphans available . . . No, I'm not joking. If we chat some time I'll tell you about how my great-grandpappy started in the farming business. Short answer: he was an orphan from Baltimore who was sent out as slave labor. No, I'm not joking.

Then you're working in the garden . . .

Lunch for you, husband, family and hands. Heavy carbo load again.

Clean house. More garden work.

Dinner. Make it light. He'll be asleep in an hour.

Clean from dinner. Make sure everything is locked down and correct. Go to bed. Get up before husband and do again and again and again.

Canning.

Household maintenance.

Laundry.

Clothing maintenance. What do you mean, you don't know how to sew . . . ?

"There's a hole in the bucket dear Liza dear Liza there's a hole in the bucket dear Liza a hole . . ."

She eventually made a decent farmer's wife. She's a lobbyist for farmers now. Leopard can't change its spots, much.

There were about fifteen like that. "A"s that is. People who were out of their depth but willing to admit it and somehow got on the line with me.

There were way more that I tried to help and fell by the wayside. Farming is not easy.

One of the "A"s, sort of, that I tried to help was funny. I say "sort of" because there wasn't *anything* I needed to tell the guy about farming.

He'd been a farmer. He'd moved to Arizona when he retired. Sold the farm (big *farms* plural) to ADM. Didn't want to live in a retirement community. "Liked some space around him." Didn't like people much, that's for sure. Crotchety didn't cover it. Talked to his wife, once. Nice old lady. Didn't have to tell her about being a farmer's wife, either. She was glad he was back working since "he'd been a handful" retired. Given what he was like when *I* dealt with him, I cannot *imagine* what he was like retired.

Anyway, he'd bought a pretty big spread of fuckall. Think that desert I went through in Iraq. He wanted land around him, but he didn't want to actually have to *work* it.

Come spring of 2020, he's looking at what his internal computer is saying is prime farmland.

Huh?

Cli-*mate* Was *Chang*-ing. And not *always* for the *worse*.

Back in pre-Columbian days there was this race of "Native Americans" called the Anasazi. Had something sort of approaching civilization in the Southwest. Up and disappeared. Some indication of violence. Pueblo builders are thought to have been Anastazi "in retreat." But in retreat from what?

Probably each other. And surrounding tribes. See, in the mini-ice age back in the Middle Ages, the rains shifted. The "desert southwest" was about like, oh, Kansas. Prime farming country. As things started to warm up, it slowly dried out to the desert we know and love today.

Same thing was happening. The arid belt around the world was shifting south and contracting. *Positive* effect of global cooling. Thank God there was at least that.

Point is, this guy walks out one cold morning. Food around the nation is rationed. He's still keeping his ear to the ground about farming. Things are looking like fucking nightmare.

And here he is looking at what is quickly becoming some of the most arable land in the U.S. Rainfalls have been, for the southwest, nightmarish. The "arroyos" are rivers. Standing ones. He's not a climatologist but he's thinking they're going to stay that way. Sort of what the long-range forecasts, the good ones not U.S. Met, are pointing to.

Now, if he only had . . .

A big tractor.

Plows.

Planter.

Fertilizer.

Herbicide (still a bunch of that pesky sage around).

Pesticides . . .

Hell, it's a long list. If he only had everything he'd left up in North Dakota. And some weather numbers he could count on.

Oh, seed . . . that would be helpful.

So I'm leaning back in my chair, trying to stay awake and wondering how in the hell I'm going to get out of durance vile. There has to be a way. Marry a general's daughter? Nah, he'd think I did it to *stay* in the Pentagon . . . And I couldn't come right out and say "I married your daughter so I could get some career progression again, sir. Not that she's not a nice piece of ass but could you maybe call branch and get me the *fuck out the Pentagon*?"

"Yes, sir . . . I understand that, sir . . . Sir, we're not here . . . I don't think we have any actual *equipment* available, sir . . ."

I figure it's a tofu-eater. Let Smedlap take the heat. That's what enlisted guys are for, to take the fire.

"Sir, let me transfer you to my supervisor . . . No, sir, I'm not 'passing the buck.' *He's* a farmer, he might have *some idea what you're talking about!*"

Fuck.

"Major Bandit Six. What?"

"Do you know what time it is? I've been on this damned phone *all night* looking for *somebody* in the U.S. government who has a *brain*! I doubt it's you but maybe I'll find somebody sometime and I'll *stay* on this phone all night if I have to! I didn't pay taxes my whole adult life to get the run around!"

"All of which told me nothing about why you've called. So if that's all you've got . . ."

"My name is Farmer Bill. I've been retired for five years. I moved to Arizona and bought a spread. It was desert. It's not, anymore.

I don't know what your *bosses* are saying, but as a professional I can tell you, *sonny*, that we're going to be short on food as a nation next year. So I don't see why a bunch of *prime farmland* should just go to waste. Can you understand that or are you as dumb as a box of rocks?"

"Hang on . . . No, seriously, I'm looking at the damned climate plat, okay . . . ? Yeah, Arizona's forecast for long-range increased precipitation. Gimme a township plat or your GPS location or, hell, your address . . . Okay." Tap, tap . . . "Yeah, you're right. But we both knew that. I see your plat. You're now the proud owner of four thousand acres of prime wheat, corn or soy farmland. Congratulations. And, yeah, Department of the Interior and the USDA *both* still have it marked as desert, the dumbasses . . . I'm not using their climatology models is why . . . Because I'm not as dumb as a box of rocks . . ."

Farmer Bill was a character. Called me every week or so just to chew me out. Reminded me of my dad if Dad had been a motor-mouth. It was heartening. I got to looking forward to his calls for the comfort zone.

Took me a while to find what he needed but the Army had "stood-up" a "military farming support network." And eventually I found *everything*.

Look, an army travels on its stomach. Soldiers are always the last people to go hungry.

In most societies, that's because we've got the guns. But the U.S. Army tries, very hard, not to steal all its food. (Sherman's March to the Sea being a notable exception.)

But our models were forecasting "chronic, serious and endemic nutrition shortages" in the U.S. That's a fancy way of saying "famine." It was classified Top Secret because the Policy Makers were saying everything was coming up roses. *I* saw the actual reports. And as the growing season of 2020 went on, the reports were getting worse and worse.

So the Army had set out to rectify that as well as it could. It was stepping all over USDA at that point, but it didn't care. Soldiers were going to eat. If for no other reason than so that they'd have the strength to stop the food riots that were coming. *Without* killing the rioters.

"Stuff" for farming was available. Dealerships had gone into receivership. Stocks weren't getting distributed. Seed that was "genmod" was just sitting in warehouses and getting ready to go bad.

The Army was handpicking some farms to make sure soldiers ate. It might not be perfect, but soldiers would have something to eat.

I really think it was mid 2020 when the coup was closest. (Other than at the election and I'm getting ahead of myself again.) The Joint Chiefs were looking at the fucking country *starving* and the President and her advisors leading the charge into famine. But they didn't revolt. They held firm to the concept of The Society of Cincinnatus. Civilian leadership control never truly broke. But they did whatever they could under the table.

Farmer Bill became one of those "under the table" deals. He got what he needed from "seized" stocks that were just sitting around. He sold his food to the Army when it came in. Quite a few soldiers ate actual wheat bread during the winter of 2020–2021 because of Farmer Bill.

Enough of Farmer Bill. This is about me.

It took several months for the general's schedule to open up enough for some chit-chat time. And it was late when we started and I had duty that night. He had my predecessor sit in for part of my shift. We talked late.

He really was interested in Khuwaitla. He wanted out of this rat-fuck, too. But we both agreed we were doing useful work even if we hated it. So I talked about Khuwaitla. And he agreed that Abrams were tough and thought it was funny that I was so ambivalent about them. I pointed out he'd never had to *fight* them. He laughed.

We talked about getting them over the Taurus and the Anatolians and he thought it was funny that I'd gotten the routes mixed up. He told a story about when he was commanding a brigade in the Entry Phase in Iraq and despite GPS getting on the wrong road and running into a hell of a firefight. I told him about swinging wide on Mosul, which I'd *gotten* from that op. And some reading over the years. We talked about Slim and he'd read "Unofficial History" and he recommended a couple of others that turned out to be excellent. Slim was big on logistics. We segued from that.

He asked me if I'd seen the classified reports on food production.

I admitted I had.

He asked me if I had any suggestions. Beyond expanding the "food for soldiers" program which was already as big as we could do and get away with under the table.

I said I'd had a lot of time to think on night shift.

And?

What? You want the full PowerPoint presentation?

That's how I got into Plans and Ops of ESM.

Not that that was a lot better. Every answer came down to the same equation: H.R. Puffinstuff. We could do a little, but we *weren't* going to be able to do enough.

Things were totally and completely screwed. Factor after factor was building up. The Plague. The bad weather. The false forecasts. The utter stupidity of the Zimbabwe Plan. USDA being forced to give all the wrong suggestions. "Organic" uber alles. Remember my rant about "Organic." Three times the tilled land for the *same amount of food*. We had *less* tilled land and mostly organic and all natural farming. "Farmers" breaking stuff for which the parts were becoming scarcer and scarcer and scarcer because the factories that used to make them were abandoned and the *rate* of breakage was beyond belief. And the "farmers" didn't know how to fix anything. (Okay, by 2020 the worst of them were gone. Most died in the winter of 2019. But then they got *replaced* by a *new* crop of idiots.)

Any single one would have been bad.

The combination had things totally and completely FUBARed. Fucked Up Beyond Any Recovery.

And we knew deep in our bones that as soldiers we were going to be left holding the bag. We'd be the ones that people threw stones at when there wasn't even the food for the soup lines. Or shot at.

The economy was *still* not coming back. Stocks were trading, commodities were trading, banks were sort of getting their feet under them again. But the damned "nationalizations" had people running scared. Say you bought stock in a company then the next day it got "nationalized." Know what you got? Nada. Nichts. Nothing. *Nobody* wanted to invest under those conditions.

And in the meantime anyone who was paying any attention to the news could see that the coterie around Damen Warrick was getting fatter and fatter and fatter.

Hell, if people had had the energy there would have been a flat-out revolt.

And, yes, that did break out in places in 2020. And as soldiers . . . we were left holding the bag. We were the ones that had to kick down doors and round up "insurgents." Our stock was starting to fall. We were going from saviors to "oppressors."

People, *we* didn't vote for Warrick. Nor for the Dems that gave her absolute power.

We just got left holding the bag.

It was July of 2020 and I pulled an idea out of my ass. It was shit. I knew it was shit. And soon enough everyone in the U.S. and in several other countries ate my shit.

I invented the Kula Bar.

Yes, that's right, people. You can blame that abortion purely on *me*. I am at fault. Mea culpa, mea culpa, mea culpa.

The Kula Bar. The most reviled and despised food on earth, with the possible exception of Spam.

The Kula Bar in all four revolting flavors: Piss yellow, leprous green, horrible horrible blue and that truly stomach-turning red. I cannot to this day get the taste out of my mouth. I refer to them as their colors because there is no way to explain to those who have not experienced them the taste.

The sole redeeming quality? It kept the death rate down. Not gone, but down.

Here are the factors that led to that monstrosity.

Food was going to be short. Not "soup lines" short but "nothing" short.

Fuel was going to be short. Not "perhaps we should use the hybrid" short but "we can't even boil a cup of water" short.

It was going to be cold. Not "it's cool in here" cold but "if we don't get five or six people under this blanket we're going to be corpsicles in the morning" cold.

With enough food energy and some common sense and shelter you can stave off the cold. But we were going to be low on food. And you can't just hand out a bunch of semolina to somebody and tell them to come back in a week to get more when they can't *cook it*.

We needed emergency distribution rations that:

A. Would keep for a long time.
B. Contained a tremendous amount of energy so that people could use body energy to stave off the cold.

    C. Were nutritionally complete. Preferably one "packet" was enough for one person for an entire 24-hour period.

    D. Could be easily stored and transported.

    E. Were in a smaller packet than MREs. Preferably "energy bar" sized.

    F. Were as easy to produce from readily available materials (what there were of them) as possible.

Oh. And here's the kicker.

    G. Tasted Bad.

We didn't actually *want* people to eat them. We wanted them to be *starving to death* before they'd eat them. They were "the food of last resort."

We were planning on passing them out in job lots. But we wanted people to eat *anything* before they'd eat the "Emergency Ration Bars." Because they were for even worse emergencies. Like, we're cut off in a blizzard and out of power and, fuck, all we have left is those fucking Kula Bars!

They tasted horrible *on purpose.*

We *might* have gone a little overboard on that one. I never saw any certified reports on it, but it was widely held allegory that people were found as emaciated skeletons with a pile of Kula Bars right in front of them.

Ever have a Bandit Bar?

It's a Kula bar with a different suite of artificial flavors.

Gotcha.

Do not mess with the Bandit.

When we got the harvests in from the "farmers for soldiers" program we looked at projected needs for the next year, compared the total input from the program and saw that we had a surplus. A sizeable one. The FFS program used *only* trained farmers and *every trick in the book*. The FFS program proved that the famines of 2020 and 2021 could be laid squarely at Warrick's feet. Also classified at the time. It's been released since under FOIA.

We poured that "excess" into Kula Bars.

That was starting in September of 2020. By then it was Warrick vs. Carson.

And then . . .

I mean how *stupid* could she be? Yes, it was clear she was going to lose barring some miracle. That the Dems were, across the board, about to take a shellacking.

But having her opponent *arrested*?

Power corrupts, absolute power corrupts absolutely?

I don't think so. I think she truly believed that She was Right and that The Way She Showed The Nation Was Just and . . .

I think she was thinking in capital letters. And the advisors she had around her were so insulated from reality that they weren't going to tell her different.

There had been a lot of quieter arrests. Commentators, reporters, minor political figures, even Congressional staff. Hell, members of the Army for that matter who hadn't obeyed her edicts and had been caught out. They weren't making the news because the MSM was still in her corner, I think horrified but horrified more of what would come out if she didn't get another term. They'd been covering for her and a change of administration was going to make that patently obvious.

She arrested Carson and about a dozen other senators, all from states with Democrat governors, and shut down Fox News and a bunch of radio stations all at once. For "conspiracy."

Yep, it was a conspiracy. It was a group of people coming together to enact political action. It's called a *Political Party,* you moronic *Bitch*!

But, man, can you imagine being on the *Secret Service detail*?

They'd already taken over security for Carson. He was the Republican candidate for President. They take over when a person gets *close* to that position. He's starting to be briefed in on peripheral matters, just in case he wins. (It's as clear as glass he's going to.)

And they get orders to take him into custody. Total incommunicado. Disappear him.

And they do it. Why?

Because you obey orders. You obey the law. The *Congress* had passed a *law* saying that this *bitch* can do *whatever the fuck she wants.* The Supreme Court had not overriden it. They let the son of a bitch stand. (5–4 vote. The dissents are scathing. Read 'em some time. Scalia has a way with words. You can practically *feel* the spittle.)

There's one other thing. One other reason to go along with the Bitch.

Because on November 2nd, or maybe January 20th, it's not going to matter.

Those are the drop-dead dates. Those are the dates when things are going to come apart.

What if she fucks with the elections?

I wasn't in on the "privy councils." They didn't even take place at the Joint Chiefs level. The JCS knew that if wind got to Warrick about any "special political operations planning proposals" that they'd be the first to disappear. It was going on at a much lower level.

But Warrick was serene in her belief that the People Would Do Right And Choose The New And Fresh Voice for the 21st Century. That she had Conducted A Conversation With The People And The People Would Make The Right Choice.

And she figured she'd assured it by sticking her political opponent in the Federal Prison in Marion, Ill. Right next to Manuel Noriega.

Things exploded. The military knew all it had to do was hold on until the election. If she didn't fuck with that, we were golden.

There were more than a few people who were tired of waiting for things to get better. And figured that if they couldn't kill Warrick they'd kill whatever representatives they could find.

Quite a few of the tofu-eater farmers were "made examples of." Democratic representatives, a few journalists.

"Right-wing death squads?" Try people who are fed up with being in a tyranny.

And the SCOTUS upheld the damned Act *again*!

"Interference in Executive powers during a National Emergency . . ."

Another scathing dissent. Thomas's was great, too. The "plantations" metaphor had a bunch of levels.

There's a song that has a line in it: "Everything exploded and the blood began to spill." That was the autumn of 2020. We were damned short on food. Harvests were in all over and they were scanty. Distribution was still fucked. Fuel was short.

The only thing that the U.S. seemed to have in abundance was anger and weapons and bullshit from 1600 Pennsylvania Avenue.

The Chairman of the Joint Chiefs finally had had enough. On October 5, he called for a press conference under emergency broadcast rules. He worded the order as if there was some new huge emergency and it was presented by the news media that way. So lots of people tuned in and turned on. Also simulcast over the Internet for those who had access and "Psy-Ops" units set up bullhorns near food lines.

"This is General Gordon. I'm Chairman of the Joint Chiefs of Staff of the United States Department of Defense. I'm not here to declare martial law. I'm not here to say that an asteroid is about to hit the Earth, which is about the only disaster we *haven't* had. I'm just here to say this.

"There are a lot of people who are very angry right now at the situation in the United States. I can understand that anger. But would you *please* quit throwing things and shooting at my soldiers? In less than a month you can feel free to express your opinion in a normal setting. It's called a polling booth. This is *America*. It is *not* some Third World dictatorship. Quit acting like it is and wait for your chance to be heard. Make the decision in the polling booths. And *whatever* the outcome, face it like *Americans. Not terrorists.* Thank you for listening."

Things calmed down. The Bitch asked for Gordon's resignation. He told her to stick it. And a bunch of the brass sent word through their contacts that if Gordon left, the Society of Cincinnatus was going into abeyment for "the duration of the current emergency."

On October 29, the last working day before the week of the election, Executive Order 5196 was issued ordering a "suspension of all Federal elections for the duration of the current emergency." At the same time, the news media released "secret testimony" indicating that Carson had been involved in "redirection of essential disaster relief material." It was on every remaining network and front page news in every major newspaper.

On Tuesday morning, November 2, 2020, people started lining up, early, at the polls. Most places it was snowing or freezingly cold. Right down to the bottom of "Sector Three." It didn't matter. People lined up in droves. Soup kitchens shifted over to polling places.

Almost every polling place in the U.S. opened on time. And the areas that did not? Well, they were the ones that were controlled by very hard-core factions of the Democratic party. Das (feminine) Fuhrer had said that there were to be no more elections and so there vere no more elections! Alles in ordnung!

The census of 2020 had never been completed. Nobody was absolutely sure what the population of the U.S. was. There were some areas where there were questions about voting. People had moved around, a lot. Documentation was sketchy. There were a lot of "questionable" ballots that had to be set aside for determination. A lot.

Things were not as efficient and fast as they'd been before the Plague. Ballots were primarily paper. Returns were slow coming in.

Warrick ordered the military to shut down polling places. She also ordered local police to do so. She went on television under the Emergency Broadcast rules and ordered it.

Flash Order CJCS Number 2187-20, OpPlan Open Polls, ordered local Regular and National Guard troops, by unit down to platoons (it had been written months before), to move to polling places and "ensure security and continued function of same." In any area where polling was not open they were to "find local polling officers and escort them and any necessary materials for polling to the designated polling office and ensure function of same until the normal close of polling."

Mutiny? Oh, *hell*, yeah.

Coup? No. That would have been what was contemplated for November 3 if the vote *didn't* go off.

Flawless? Not hardly. Nothing had been close to flawless since 2018 and that was a pretty fucked up year all things considered.

Good? Good enough, anyway?

Yeah.

The news media held its ground as long as it could. It was still declaring for Warrick when Army numbers showed *California* had gone to Carson. So had every other state in the nation except Vermont, Massachusetts and Connecticut.

Carson was still unavailable to comment. He was in jail.

Warrick refused to concede. The vote was "illegal." The person elected a "criminal."

(Warrick, by the way, was one of the people to first castigate against "the politics of personal destruction.")

Not even the SCOTUS could take that one. November 23, when all the states had certified their results, they declared the vote valid and binding. 8–1. They ordered the release of the President-Elect on a 5–4 vote for.

Warrick said that nothing was going to change. She ordered the arrest of the CJCS and the members of SCOTUS, all eight, that had certified the vote.

The Capitol Police ordered to arrest the CJCS went to the Pentagon, took one look at the troops guarding the doors, and went away.

So did the ones that went to the Supreme Court building.

So did the ones ordered to arrest more Republican congressmen and senators.

We'd turned over most of the emergency resupply duties. The troops were just sitting there. Might as well camp out on the doorsteps of various "distinguished persons." Hell, we even had teams around the Democrats. Fair and balanced and all that.

The Secret Service brought Carson to his home in DC. He gave a very nice acceptance speech. Finally. He also mentioned that he'd been well treated during his "unfortunate stay in federal custody" and was pretty humorous about it. You got the impression he'd been at a resort.

Warrick threw the Secret Service out of the White House. She brought in a private security firm to protect her. She also never left from before the vote until January 20th.

Food was getting very scarce. Nobody was talking about it in the news.

The Carson "transition team" got underway. The word was out that as soon as Carson was in place and things were relatively stable, the Joint Chiefs were all going to resign. Carson wasn't having any of it. But they were pretty adamant. They'd performed a sort of de facto coup. And they weren't going to continue with power under those conditions. It couldn't be seen as a good thing. They were not only going to resign, they were going to forego any government service for the rest of their lives. They were going to disappear and live off their meager (for the job they do, anyway) pensions.

I felt really sorry for Carson in a way. He had a lot of picking up to do and there wasn't any good news in the near future. Projections for 2021 and 2022 were for colder and colder temperatures. Ice age here we come.

December we started distributing Kula Bars and the public view of the Army hit an all-time low. Everybody knew we'd saved the election but . . . *Kula Bars*? Fuck 'em. It kept people alive.

We were still in the "taking care of everybody" business and starting to get sick of it. We wanted things to start getting back to any semblance of normal so we could get back to learning how to kill people and break things. That didn't look to be happening any time soon.

India sent us grain shipments. India. My grandmother used to say "Eat all your food. There are starving children in India." By then there *weren't* starving children in India. But there had been in her memory and Grandma was a little besotted by then. Back when she was no more than middle aged, we'd been sending grain to India to help out with *their* famine.

Now they were sending *us* grain. We made it into Kula Bars. When they found out, they got a little testy. Till we explained the rationale.

Oh, India was an interesting case. But this isn't the time for that. Maybe later.

January 20th. Inauguration Day. Cold as a witch's fucking tit. I was part of the security. I know.

Carson stood up, raised his right hand and then let loose one hell of a speech. He didn't even use old catchphrases that were perfect for the conditions. The closest he got was his "continued hard times that will require great sacrifice. We will face them together as Americans and *triumph* over all that stands against us."

The guy had been an actor for a long time. He *knew* how to deliver a speech. He made even the weakest phrases ring with conviction that was so solid you could cut it and serve it as food. Better than Kula Bars, anyway. Could barely break *those* with your *teeth*. (Another "feature," not a bug.)

Warrick was not present. Her VP was and gave a short speech praising the new Prez and wishing him good luck.

Warrick had to be removed from the White House more or less with force. Actually, her personal physician sedated her and she walked out under her own power. She just thought she was taking a moonwalk or something.

— CHAPTER THREE —

Gosh, Here's a Thought . . .

A new Congress was in. The House of Representatives looked . . . somewhat different than before. It was incredibly white-bread. It was even short on females comparatively and it had never been a really heavy girl group. The Senate, of course, had less turnover. One election in six years. All the arrested Congresscritters who were up for reelection got reelected in a landslide and just about every Democratic senator got trounced. The new crop was also less than "collegial" with their Democratic colleagues seeing them as, essentially, lame ducks. The majority leader was not elected from the Old Guard. He was a former Congressman but he didn't play by the old rules.

Carson asked for six months of continuation of the Emergency Powers Act. He went to Congress and asked for it, doing a speech on the floor. He explained that he simply needed the same powers to undo the damage.

At the same time, the Joint Chiefs stood up and gave their retirement speeches. They explained that, as they saw it for the good of the country they had violated the honor of their offices. Gordon was great.

"Were I a Japanese General in World War II I would now cut open my belly to expiate the shame. There has been enough death. We ask to simply fade into history."

None of them have ever, that I know, written a memoir. I wish they had. I'm reasonably certain there was a group planning the coup and I'd love to have the inside scoop on it. The most I ever got from a pretty good source was "Task Force 629."

So far, nobody has ever geeked. Cowards. I admitted to creating the Kula Bar. How bad could it be to admit you were getting ready to take Warrick down? Hell, they should have given out medals for doing the tasking paperwork!

Carson got his six months. And my God was he a busy little beaver. Or, rather, his staff already had been.

They'd gotten the full list of seized farms from the USDA along with data on farm output relative to 2018. They also had a list of when farms were "family owned cooperatives" (we actually fell into that category, it was an actual line item under USDA rules) vs. really big farm corporations. And another list of farms that had been "moribund" due to the family or managers being killed by the Plague. And then there were the ones abandoned by "government cooperative associates" not to mention dead folk in them.

Hey, presto! Add a few good database geeks and you had . . .

A list of farms that were to be turned back over to farming corporations.

A priority list of farms to be turned back over to owners.

A list of farms that had been seized and turned over to new farmers but which were a) performing well and b) the owners were dead anyway.

The problem in many cases was finding the original owners and/or managers of the farms. That might have bit us in the ass but, well, there were fewer people to feed. And we had some time since what with the weather, ground breaking was going to take a while yet for most of the major crops.

People were dying, though, while he was giving his speech. And he knew it. Wasn't much he could do. Everybody who had a clue was already on the job trying to keep the death rate down.

Businesses were "denationalized." Money, at this point more or less fiat money based on our really junky bond rating, was made available to get them back on their feet. Warrick's coterie was out on their ass faster than you can say "tofu." Most of them couldn't be prosecuted for what they'd done because, hell, it was a valid executive order. Fucked up as hell, but that's what happens when that many factors come together.

The ag situation was still badly screwed. Everything was in short supply. India came to the rescue, again, with seed and pesticides. We actually ended up producing enough of the latter and herbicides by the time planting season came around. But they sent a couple of tankers full which were quite useful.

They'd also opened up the Persian Gulf. My buddy the mullah down in Abadan had "expanded his sphere of influence." Mostly through negotiation and occasionally with a bit of fighting he and the south Iraqi "moderates" had taken over most of the Gulf areas of former Iran. But the "pirates" in the Straits of Hormuz (the ones on the Iranian side of the strait) were armed with the weapons left over from the Iranian military and *liked* owning the Straits.

He didn't have a problem working with the "heathen" Indian military in straightening them out.

And, okay, we punched some Marines over there to help, too. As the general had said to me on the phone, we were still playing world's policeman to an extent.

Then my mullah friend said, effectively, "We've got oil *and* food. Y'all come on down!"

The "Fertile Crescent" was getting *extremely* fertile. The same change that was going on in Arizona was happening in the Middle East. Which is why the PU has become a net exporter of food. And, hell, everything else. I'm wearing a jacket right now says "Made in Persia."

And most of the minor little crap in the house says "Made in India."

India. Okay, time for the digression.

The Plague hit India hard. Real hard. Lots of vaccine distribution but it was Type One. Total death toll was right at fifty percent, which is a bit off the sixty but given their vaccine, spread should have been better.

Anyway, the thing was "where'd it hit?"

Well, everywhere equally. Right? Plague doesn't care if you're a king or a criminal.

Sort of.

Airborne spread flus have a harder time in hot environments. They don't last as long on surfaces, not even hands.

But there were large segments of India, especially the very poor, who were in very crowded conditions. And they didn't, by and large, get vaccinated. It hit those segments at a rate of about 60% with secondary effects adding another 10% or so.

Not to be coldhearted but what I'm saying is that it hit the least productive segment of their population the hardest.

India, since it climbed out of socialism and got with the mainstream, had two problems. One, it was *over*populated and *under*educated. They were working hard on the second problem even before the Plague but the first was making the conversion hard. Too many new babies being born to poor people who couldn't help either through taxes or direct payments to get them educated meant more babies that weren't educated and couldn't get modern jobs . . .

It had a huge middle class, don't get me wrong. And they were functional and productive to their country and the world. Its middle class outnumbered the U.S. total *population*. But everything they did was against the inertia of this huge population of the poor. And other inertia.

Despite all the surface changes of modernity ("India is the largest democracy in the world!") there were still huge and very definite class differentiations. And if you weren't from a certain "class" there was little or no chance of you getting beyond a certain point. It was glass ceiling after glass ceiling after glass ceiling.

Don't get me wrong, most of the underclass wasn't going to produce Einsteins or Reagans. But it was going to produce *some*. But it wasn't going to happen as long as caste still ruled. And it did.

Come the Plague.

Most of the "upper class" no longer lived in daily constant heat. The heat that Kipling spoke of so luridly about India. India had discovered air conditioning in the 1990s and taken to it with abandon. At least if you could afford the enormous electric bills.

But.

Nice cool air-conditioned offices meant nice places for H5N1 to hang out for a bit longer. Yes, the "upper class" had gotten vaccinated. Most of the strains that hit India were mutated binding sites.

The upper class of Indian society got hit nearly as hard as the very poor. It wiped out whole families that were proud of the fact they could trace their ancestors back five thousand years.

It also took out about 30% of India's college graduates. Which was bad. But it tended to take out the ones with degrees in "English" and "Literature" and "Marketing" and "Social Finance."

The less well paid "Engineers" and "Mathematicians" and such like had a much lower death rate since they tended to spend less time in air-conditioned environments.

Before the Plague, despite all the changes, India was a fairly sharp financial and social pyramid. That is never good for a society.

After the Plague the tip had gotten sliced and a big chunk of the base had gotten sliced. That made it a much more functional country than before.

Oh, it was a maelstrom at first. Everywhere was. But it recovered faster than most of the rest of the world (including us). Well, there were still "issues" even when they were shipping us grain. "Restive local populations." (Read Moslems.) A nutball in Pakistan had seized that country's nukes. Various other "issues." (Including an abortive invasion by a Chinese general that never really amounted to much.)

But India was, and is, a comer. Are they ever going to be a "super-power" to rival the age of Pax Americana? Well, when they do send "blue water" task forces over to play with the Navy, they still end up towing some ships home and often cancelling part way through. Nor can they field a supercarrier to save their ass. They still can't get what is called in the military "systemology."

But they're a comer. And, hell, we're not exactly out of the play-pen.

But I'm getting ahead of myself again.

Thing is, India was doing better than the U.S. in 2021. Part of that was they didn't have an idiot like The Bitch in charge. Part was environmental. But they were definitely doing better than us.

However, they were also friends. It's not only okay, it's a good thing, when friends are strong. They were strong friends in our hour of need and I'm glad we're on such good relations. Hell, I helped to make some of them, I've got a vested interest. But I digress, again.

I'm basically avoiding talking about Detroit.

The economy hadn't started booming by any stretch, but people were "cautiously optimistic." Coming out of the Great Depression had required WWII. Coming out of the effects of the Plague only required a stable business environment. People wanted to get back to work and there was work to be done. It's just that nobody wanted to invest in anything when they couldn't be sure the government wouldn't seize it.

But there was another problem. The cities.

Many of the cities, especially in "red" states, were back up and functioning at some moderate level. They were, at least, as secure as they'd been pre-Plague. (Some more so since people were less forgiving of criminals. A lot of the stupid had been beaten out of the surviving tofu-eaters. And unless it was a religious thing, they were *all* willing to eat meat if it was available.) Red states had eventually sent in their own "security forces" to reestablish order.

However, there were some cities that remained free-fire zones. Where gangs or even whole small organized "governments" held power that refused to recognize the authority of the feds *or* the states. Generally, those hadn't voted. You had to be under state and federal authority to vote. If you weren't, you didn't vote. Most of them were functional dictatorships, or de jure dictatorships, anyway.

The list of cities that were definitely functional city-states is small. Chicago, Boston, Hartford, Newark and most especially Detroit. There was a list of others where order had broken down and never been reestablished. But that's different from "we have order, and we *are* the order."

Detroit was a very special case. It was . . . touchy. It shouldn't have been but it had a number of "political correctness" factors associated with it.

The group that had taken over Detroit was the "Islamic Caliphate of the 9/11 Martyrs." Now, right there most people like me were thinking "There's no better group to take out."

Problem was . . . Warrick and the MSM had treated the IC9M with kid gloves. Why?

The leader of the IC9M was Mullah Ali . . . sigh, here goes, don't get pissed if I screw it up . . .

Mullah Ali Al-Kirbi Aqal ibn abu Meiri Al-Haj Amani El-Haddi abu Saleh Al-Ahad ibn Mohammed Al-Rashid Al-Kuwukji abu Kahdra Al-Wohoush Akim ibn Tamud ibn Bakdash Abu Saeb.

I had, as part of a lot of briefings, an explanation in detail of his name. I cannot for the life of me recall any of it.

Call him Mullah Ali or Caliph Ali as he styled himself. I don't give a shit. I called him "burrhead."

Okay, yes, that's a racist comment. Caliph Ali would make *Martin Luther King* racist.

Somehow Kuwazi Jones, aka half a dozen names ending in

Mullah Ali, former drug dealer, armed robber and rapist, had become the darling of the media and what was left of the tofu-eater set. He had "established order" in Detroit and was "working for the poor and oppressed peoples of color of the degenerate and oppressing" United States by bringing a "new order" of "equality and enlightenment."

He was, I'll admit, photogenic and charismatic. He was very good on camera. He was well-spoken and could deliver a good line. He knew all the liberal mantras to spout.

But somehow the refugees that made it out of Detroit with tales of horror never got as much air-time.

And Warrick had treated him like fucking God. He could do no wrong. Getting food shipments to the "established government" in Detroit had been a high priority. Whenever the Army tried to balk, somebody got canned.

Since Caliph Ali was very good about not shooting at the troops, as long as they dropped off the shipments at the *edge* of his territory, the Army geeked. They didn't like it, but they geeked.

Problem being, we also saw the intelligence coming out of Detroit. We knew that life in the "Caliphate" was, well, life in a Caliphate. Which meant hell for values of hell. Worse than most Caliphates, really, because Mullah Ali was one fucked up psychopath.

Right-wing radio had long had Detroit as one of its underlying themes of how fucked up Warrick was. Carson knew about the conditions, he thought, from that. When he saw the *real* conditions in intel reports, he was said to have nearly thrown up.

The problem being, well, the story that everyone had gotten for going on two years was that Detroit was a "model of modern good governance in a multicultural environment."

Just rolling into Detroit and hanging every fucking hardcore would have thrown everyone for a loop. Sure, he had overthrown established order and governance. But for most people in 2021, *that wasn't good enough*. Here was an African-American spokesperson who had "saved the people of Detroit."

The other cities that were "city-states" all had similar "image issues." To cover for Warrick, the news media had had to avoid finding anything wrong with dictators holding American cities. Since they'd practiced for years finding nothing wrong with Fidel Castro, they were very good at it. They'd made people look as if they *enjoyed* the chains. Hell, there were people who *wanted* to go to Detroit. It *sounded* like paradise.

The only thing that would work would be showing people the truth of the situation in such a way as they couldn't ignore it. The Army was going to have to counter the propaganda. Hard.

"Gosh, here's a thought . . ."

CHAPTER FOUR

The Penalty for a Job Well Done Is . . .

Look, you don't get on the short list for promotion to lieutenant colonel after a year and a half as a major. You don't. It doesn't matter if you walk on clouds and suck every general in the Pentagon. You don't.

Suddenly, I was up before a promotion board. And on the promotion list for lieutenant colonel.

You don't *go* to boards, by the way. Officers sit on the board and consider a whole bunch of personnel packets. Based on the personnel packets they pick a group of officers and give them a score. Depending on the number of officers the Army needs for that rank, if your score is high enough they promote you.

(When I got "selected" for major, that is the promotion board said I was a possible, the "promotion" rate was 93%. So all but the absolute *lamest* captains got major that board.)

I'd been on the short list each time. Okay, I'm pretty good at what I do. And I'm a handsome devil and charming. (And, yes, unfortunately that matters.)

But promotion boards are supposed to be "lacking in influence." A general isn't supposed to stop by, toss a packet on the table and go, "We really like this guy and if he doesn't get promoted you all might as well figure on staying at your current rank for the rest of your lives."

Promotion boards are supposed to consider only what is presented in front of them. It's like a jury. Even if they've seen TV stuff about the guy they're judging, they aren't supposed to consider it. And they're also not supposed to consider if somebody calls them at home and says "he walks or your child goes through life blind."

I didn't like the way it got handled from all appearances. If they'd said "you're a light bird" and given me the oak leaves, that would be one thing. There's paperwork and precedent for that. But it *appeared* that someone had fucked with the promotion board in my favor. That sort of thing, down the road, can really bite you in the ass. Besides . . . it's dishonorable.

(So later I went digging. There is "standard minimum time in grade" for all positions. There is also "nonstandard minimum time in grade" for all positions. When promotion boards sit, they can, at their discretion, consider "nonstandard minimum time in grade" officers. The promotion board had looked over the list of all majors in "standard minimum time in grade" and found some that deserved the next rank. Then, since they'd done their jobs efficiently, they had some extra time and considered "nonstandard minimum time in grade officers" for light bird. And ran across Bandit Six in the bunch. And, well . . . People who are on the board are *not* supposed to talk about the board. What happens on the board, stays on the board. But a guy told me about when they ran across the "Centurion" packet as they put it. And passed it around. And talked about shit they're not *supposed* to talk about like "I fucking *die* every time I watch 'CAM(P)ing'!" And moved it to the top of the stack and recommended the packet be "selected under waiver of time in grade." Still kind of pisses me off. There was some guy my grandstanding fucked for that go-round. To whoever it is, I apologize.)

So I was now a major promotable. Big whoop. I was still in the Pentagon and still shoveling horse-shit. Nice bump in pay, though, when the promotion finally came through.

So one day I get word I need to report to a different department for "consultation on Emergency Methodology." I've got an office. And the name of a major.

I go to said office and meet a nice major. The major is wearing the tabs for aide to a full general. The nice major asks me questions. I answer them politely. Some of them are on the borderline of "wrong." They were a touch . . . political.

The Army has to play politics all the time. That is, they have to find the Congresscritters who will support funding and all that. But within the Army, it's a written rule that you don't discuss or argue politics. You don't ask someone what their politics are. Yes, it gets done all the time, but *not* in an official setting. It was the equivalent of asking me "Are you now or have you ever been a homosexual?" It's Just Not Done.

At the end of the "interview" I was told "thank you very much, we may be talking again."

And I got orders. To my old unit. As Battalion Commander.

Wait. *WRONG!*

First of all, I can't think of a time when a guy who has been a commander in a unit has been brought back as a BC. There are too many battalions in the Army. Just luck of the draw says you're not going to get your old unit. At the level of major, you've scooted off somewhere else. If you spend the normal time as a major, you've done staff time at various levels and some in a battalion to get the feel. You probably have been an XO. But not of your old unit. Doesn't work that way.

Second, it was like taking over the Company. Normally, the "career progression" was that I'd get promoted to light bird and take a staff position for my rank. If I was a *very* good boy I *might* get a battalion. But not until I've gotten some experience under colonel's silver.

And I *still* wasn't on the books as a light bird. Majors hadn't commanded battalions since WWII.

Oh, wow, look. I'm a light bird. Fancy that.

Promotion came in the day *after* my orders.

My skids were being greased. And greased hard. "Selected" *way* out of zone. Command time when I should have still been shuffling papers. And now promotion out of zone.

Once is happenstance, twice is coincidence, three times is enemy action.

Note, this sounds crazy. But there are two things about promotion in the Army. If you get promoted at one rank too fast, you're bound to get fucked over later. I, eventually, wanted to be a general. Despite the number of generals around, getting to general is *very hard*. Having my skids greased *now* would probably fuck that up *then*. (Absent, like, a World War.) The other is, if someone is hand-selecting you, and that is pretty much verboten in the Army, it's rarely for something you're going to enjoy. It means somebody wants you to do something fucked up.

I didn't know at the time *how* fucked up.

I drove down to Stewart, which I hadn't seen in a while but it hadn't changed much either, and found quarters. I reported in to the Division. I got the usual smoke blown up my ass but not as much as usual. I was an old Division hand. The Army's "Third Herd." (The actual motto is *"Nous Resterons Là"* "We Shall Remain." Don't ask.) I got the standard incoming battalion commander "in-brief."

With FEMA actually starting to be left to do its job, the Army was coming more and more off of "disaster relief" duties and getting trained back in on "kill people and break things." The Brigades (which were the actual deployment units) weren't by any stretch back to their glory days of being able to break your hearts and your armies any where, any time, but they were getting back in shape.

My battalion was the next one slotted up for "combat retraining." I got some frowns but they weren't explained even when I asked. But I did notice that my *Brigade* wasn't up for combat retrain, yet. We were getting bumped up the queue.

Combat retrain means starting from the ground up. Soldiers train on individual tasks while officers try to remember how to conduct operations. The latter is mostly "TEWTs," Tactical Exercises Without Troops, and can range from sitting at a table working over a problem to sand table exercises to going out in the field and considering how to take terrain to full up computerized battle with independent scorers.

Later on the officers and troops are "mated up" for field exercises and then finally go through a test to see if it's taken. Generally, after the test (called an ARTEP) there's a stand-down for maintenance to fix all the shit that broke in training then the unit, if it passes the test and the inspection of its equipment, is considered "combat certified." It's ready to go to war.

Normally, "combat retraining" is a six-month process.

We were scheduled for three.

I looked at the, very tight, schedule, kissed sleep goodbye then looked again.

We were scheduled, if everything went well, to be "combat certified" one month before the end of Carson's requested "six months."

We weren't going to be the *first* "combat certified" battalion available while Carson still had "Emergency Powers" authority, suspending habeas corpus and posse comitatus (the law that said you couldn't use federal troops in United States territory for police forces) but we were going to be *one* of the first.

Okay, once is happenstance, twice is coincidence, three times is enemy action. What is four?

It's a puckering feeling in the rectum.

I still didn't have the word "Detroit" in my head. But I did have the word "pacification actions." Okay, it's a phrase.

I *also* didn't have the word, phrase, whatever, "Centurions" in my head.

We started training. Part of the training was learning to be a battalion commander without:

A. Being an S-3 (operations officer).
B. Being an XO (second in command of a battalion).
C. Ever having been to or even taken the correspondence course for Command and General Staff College, which was normally a "must have" for battalion command.

I'd had experience with "large force" command. Don't get me wrong. Hell, by Istanbul I was commanding the forces of a light brigade. Or a heavy battalion "team."

But that was there under make-it-up-as-you-go-along rules. Now I had to learn to play by Army rules and there were a lot of them.

But I had very good help. All the staff officers were excellent. They'd been trained in by my previous commander and for the first month or so I just let them keep doing what they were doing. Hell, I never really made a lot of changes.

And my company commanders were also "hold-overs." They'd all been doing their jobs a bit over time for when they should have rotated out. They knew them well.

The only fly in the ointment, at first, was me. But I'm a quick learner. I didn't make the mistakes I'd made as a company commander because, among other things, I'd sort of done this job before. I just had to figure out the details.

We trained up, hard. We had a pretty decent budget for it, thank God. And I knew some tricks to get more. Budget was a "use it or lose it" proposition. You had to use up all your budget by the end of the year.

Unfortunately, we weren't near the end of the year but there were still some units that were looking at their projected training and going "I'm not going to use all this budget." Normally, it's the other way around. But there were some. I found them and got more budget for stuff like ammo for live-fire training.

(Hell, there was a lot of ammo sitting around. We hadn't been using much for the last couple of years and we'd stopped very abruptly in the middle of a war. There was plenty of ammo. Less fuel but that just meant the troops learned to walk.)

We were getting ready for ARTEP, not up to that point but close, when I got orders cut for TDY to the Pentagon. What the Fuck? I'm a *commander*! You don't send battalion commanders TDY (temporary duty) to the Pentagon for fuck's sake! Not when there's an ARTEP scheduled in *two weeks*!

I got on a plane and flew up to the Puzzle Palace, again, cursing under my breath.

And got "briefed in."

The mission of my battalion, like it or not, was to "pacify" the city of Detroit and return it to "normal order" under the laws and customs of the United States of America and the State of Michigan.

But that wasn't all.

I was asked, not ordered, asked if it would be possible to reactivate the *Centurions* stories for the mission.

Some of those meetings were totally fucked. The PIO assholes had somehow become involved. They had lots of "recommendations" on ways to improve *Centurions*.

Look, I'd made it up as I went along but it was *still* the highest rated show in reruns in the U.S. and maybe the world. A lot of people were just starting to get back TV, especially cable. And they'd *heard* about *Centurions* but had never seen it. DVDs were selling like hotcakes. (I swear, Murdoch owes me, big-time. The bastard.) It was about the only thing that *was* selling, consistently.

I didn't need PIO shit-for-brains giving me recommendations on how to improve *Centurions*. Especially recommendations that amounted to turn it into a steer. It was a bull. That was its horror and glory. If they couldn't figure that out, they could kiss my ass.

Oh, and they wanted it more "family friendly" and "gender friendly" and "culturally friendly" and . . .

I wasn't just meeting with them, though. I was meeting with serious colonels and generals who were laying out the problem. Detroit had to be taken down while we still had posse comitatus. The President was smart but he hadn't realized how long it was going to take to get units back in shape for combat. And it was going to be combat. The caliph had seized NG military hardware early on, both convoys that were under orders not to defend themselves and stuff that was already in the Detroit area. An entire company had been "suborned" and turned over military grade weapons and hardware. He might have all the shit I'd faced before. Low ammo for most of it, maybe none. But he had the gear and some ammo was very much missing.

And with the caliph being held up as a shining light by the news media, it was going to be a shit-storm. The MSM wasn't going to just take us taking down the caliph. They were going to spin for all they were worth. And they were going to be all over the mission. No way to keep them out, practically. If we did, it would look like "censorship" and that was the last thing we needed.

We had to get the word out about what was really going on in Detroit. And we needed to get the word out fast. And *hopefully* show what the media was spinning.

And the one thing the generals agreed on, but weren't going to shove down my throat, was that the name needed to change.

Thus was born *The* New *Centurions* mini-series.

I started getting balky. I was getting dozens of "briefings" on every conceivable subject. Some of them were useful, much of it was crap (especially any that involved PIO). I was digesting all of it, sure. But I was on short time. My battalion was getting ready for its final exam and I was having to be thinking way past it to a mission that still wasn't clear and was going to be very very complicated. And very secret. That we were going into Detroit was Top Secret. That we were planning a *Centurions* broadcast about Detroit was Top Secret and compartmentalized.

And, thus far, nobody was asking me anything. I was given information and "suggestions" but nobody was asking me what I thought or how I thought it should be done or, critically, what I was going to need. It was like they thought I could just pull one out of my ass.

I was in a meeting on "potential taskers" that had one of the

main generals sitting in it and at one point when they were discussing "communication strategy taskers" I just stood up.

"This is bullshit. And it's got to stop."

"You have a problem with the mission, Bandit Six?" the general
asked. He was sort of stern but I could see he was also alarmed.
Everyone assumed I was totally going along with "information
management." If I wasn't willing to, the whole plan was in the
shitter.

"No, sir. I'm up with the mission. My problem is that for the
last three critical days I've been getting briefings more or less at
random, most of which have been useless and a waste of everyone's
time. It's like every department in the Army got a secret message
there was going to be a *Centurions* broadcast and wants to get
its two cents in. And, thus far, none of the meetings have been
about what I suggest much less what I'm going to need. And those
meetings are going to take a long time and there are going to
have to be decisions made. And not by committee, General. And
may I remind everyone that in less than two weeks my battalion,
which is going to be somewhat necessary to this whole jug-fuck,
is up for ARTEP. And if it fails said ARTEP, because for example
its commander has been sitting in meetings for two weeks, it's
not going to be combat certified, rendering all of this moot."

"It's not going to fail the ARTEP," the general said.

"We've been working hard, sir, but..."

"No," the general said. "Listen to me. It Will Not Fail The
ARTEP. If I have to personally pencil in all the results. Besides,
it's a good unit. It will do fine. On that you're just suffering
from pre-ARTEP jitters, which is normal. You're a new battalion
commander. Had them myself. Your unit is good and will pass
ARTEP. If it doesn't, It Will Pass ARTEP. That's been decided at
a much higher level than this. Okay, who or what do you need
for these meetings?"

"I need..." I said then paused. "I'm going to need someone
senior from PIO. Someone with a brain and preferably real media
experience if that exists. Pretty quickly I'm going to need geeks.
Since I don't talk geek, I'm going to need translators from my
unit, two sergeants from Bravo. They're still there. I stopped by
and said hello already. I'm going to need overhead specialists.
I'm going to need Graham and the crew if I can get them. They
can come in late. I have an op-plan for this. It's not the op-plan

that's been presented. The op-plan presented, especially the 'suggestions' from PIO, will not work. *My* op-plan will work. Oh, and I need someone senior enough in each of the meetings that require coordination with other departments that when I say 'this is what I need' the person can say 'do it' and it gets done. And eventually I'm going to need a lot of savvy and devoted-to-the-concept eyeballs. Those can't come from my unit and should probably all be geeks. Intel geeks might work. Say an intel battalion. Maybe a DIA unit."

"How short can you make an operational outline?" the general asked.

"Depends on if people are going to joggle my elbow."

"1700. My office. Verbal only. Meeting, and all meetings on this matter for the rest of the day, adjourned."

My op-plan was simple in concept and *really* complicated in detail. A simple *Centurions* broadcast would not work. The media was going to be all over the op like shit on stink. We were going to have to not only do a normal *Centurions* show but on top of it, woven into it, deconstruct most or all incidents of "spin."

Which meant we were going to have to cover the *media* like stink.

Every photograph from every stringer was going to have to be caught by an Army team who would find the context the stringer was, intentionally or unintentionally, missing. Every broadcast of every news network was going to have to have another camera on it, showing what the cameras were not reporting. When it was impossible to really show that, we were going to have to "craft" imagery that got into the details.

And we were going to have to turn a one-hour show out in nearly real time. Preferably every evening the op was going on. Graphic imagery, script, the thematic elements and step *all over* the news media's reporting. Since most people still got their news between 5PM and 7PM, and that was when all the really spun news was going to hit the airwaves, we were going to have to do a show *while they were spinning*. Then show the counter spin. Show the reality they were missing or essentially falsifying.

Waiting until the next day, waiting until the next week, wasn't going to cut it. We had to hit people when they were still gathering their opinions about what they'd seen on the news.

"That's impossible," were the first words out of the mouth of the PIO general in the meeting.

"No, sir," I replied. "Taking Istanbul with a Stryker company was impossible. This will just be very very difficult."

And it was.

So while I was working on all the shit involved in getting combat certified, I was *also* working on getting *that* operation ready. And it was a massive fucking exercise. Worse, really, than getting through the ARTEP which, the general was right, was not as hard as I'd expected. I had very good subordinates. Thank God. And the previous commander.

After our inspection by the IG, another hair tearer while I'm simultaneously juggling the "secret" side of what we're going to do, we got our, secret again, orders for our upcoming operation. Finally, I could get the battalion staff working on that op, but I still didn't have them in the loop on the *Centurions* side.

But it was obvious I was working something else. Most battalion commanders don't go through pre-ARTEP and then ARTEP and ORSE without contributing much but "Uh, huh. Sounds good. Great job. Keep up the good work." Delegation was one thing, this was crazy. They input *something*. I just didn't have the *time*.

I finally got the go-ahead to bring the battalion staff in on "Operation New Centurions." And they looked at me like I had two heads. I gave them background. Then I gave them more background. Then I tried to explain what a massive fucking headache it was going to be. And I also explained that while the operation was going on, I was going to be juggling both sides.

We were still waiting for our "combat certification" when the PIO guys started filtering in. They were gathering "background" on people. It quickly became evident that the *Centurions* thing was starting up again. Sergeants pointed out that talking about it was a bad thing.

The last remaining problem was, we didn't have an outlet. We could release it on the Web but that would only hit a fraction of the available households.

The Army cut a deal with the networks. One broadcast network would get a new *Centurions* show for free. Each night, 8PM Central, guaranteed broadcast was all that was required. Resale rights would be minimal for cable networks and one cable TV news company could get it for free. But it had to air, guaranteed, without editing. That was the only proviso.

The networks *knew* they were looking at something radioactive.

They also knew that *Centurions* meant vast numbers of viewers glued to the TV.

In the end the network execs went for the money. They couldn't pass up new *Centurions* shows.

Fox got the cable news rights. ABC, again, got the broadcast rights. Four or five other minor networks picked it up as well.

The news hit the Internet before we were even starting to move out. Actually, while negotiations were still going on with the networks. From the way it was sounding, it was coming from our side. Hit the conservative blogs first. I figured it was someone in the battalion. I didn't care. It was creating "buzz."

But what the operation was was still secret. When we moved out, we moved out at night and spread out our units so we could be going anywhere.

Three days later, all the units were assembling in a state park near Lansing.

— CHAPTER FIVE —

I Am Your Centurion

"Rubble" was our first episode.

We moved out from our assembly areas at dawn. It had been determined that for reasons of "reduction of collateral damage" we should do most of our fighting during the day. Also, because that way we were able to "craft the image."

There were reporters on scene by the time we hit the edge of Detroit. They'd been told we were coming and punched out crews immediately. The command track I was using had, besides all the usual shit, four TVs in it tuned to every major network. We had the "regular" networks split and one for Fox and one for CNN. Graham had done one bit for us then faded out. He was actually on the "other side" of this war.

There were actually reporters "embedded" with the Caliphate forces to show the "truth" of this "unconscionable use of force" against "peaceful Muslims" who were being "oppressed" for "voluntarily choosing" an "alternative lifestyle" to the "Fundamentalist Christian orthodoxy." Graham wasn't with *those* idiots, but he was still on the other side of the propaganda war.

I didn't spot the shot. But one of our "savvy eyes" did. CNN had broadcast a touching piece while we were still on the outskirts of Detroit about the "horrific collateral damage" of our "military assault." As far as I knew, nobody had fired a shot, yet, and there was a female CNN reporter standing in front of a pile of rubble we had presumably made.

And right behind it came the "alternative view" from an Army

433

videography team. The guys on the team had the right idea. They stayed on the reporter though most of her bit then zoomed in, so you could still see the reporter's shoulder out of focus, on some rebar sticking out of this rubble we had, presumably, made that day. It was rusted.

"Get me all the information we can about that building," I snapped. "I need to know when it fell down and why."

Sure enough, it was a lead-in shot for most of the evening news shows. And they were all over us like stink. We were barely fighting and they already wanted us to surrender.

Hell, no. I haven't yet begun to fight. *Either* war.

"Rubble" talked about how "Caliph Ali" had been tearing down buildings to build a mosque. The "Martyrs of the Great Jihad of September 11th Mosque." We had overhead of "people" still working on it (more on that later) even as we did our approach. Also dated satellite imagery showing that particular building standing, then being pulled down. Nearly a year before.

We discussed the basis of Islam and, notably, the way that the Koran talked about slaves. Because we already knew where we were going with the overall story.

We took the outskirts of the area "Caliph Ali" held with fairly light fighting and about *no* casualties. We put out sniper teams to counter their sniper teams. And we bunked down for the night.

Normally, the U.S. Army fights at night. We've learned to own it. But we wanted the news media to get good video. So we could hammer them with it.

Two-front war. The main front was taking down Ali. The second front was showing the media we could fight *that* war, too. I'm not even sure they shouldn't be reversed.

Second day was "Collateral."

The main shot for that was a shot of one of the Mongrels' Abrams taking out a building. And the line of dead bodies, females and kids, that were outside the building. Clearly dead because of those evil U.S. Forces since nobody else was shooting, right?

Another shot from CNN, broadcast all over the place as we expected. It was the most newsworthy shot of the day and we were pretty good at figuring out which would be the lead-in story for the news at that point.

We showed the heavy weapons emplacement in the building. And had Predator video of the women and children being shot, by Caliphate forces, as they tried to get out of the way of the battle.

The Caliphate was using human shields all over the place. We showed just how very hard it was to avoid collateral damage. We had video of soldiers taking fire and casualties and not returning it until they could target the actual fighters. Also of kids being used as spotters.

Body slammed them again.

The third was "Tangled."

The shot for that day was an Abrams with a plow ripping down a building. Urban renewal indeed.

The Caliphate had laced their penultimate defenses with IEDs. Most of them anti-personnel.

We had one, unfortunate, shot of a civilian trying to escape who ran into one and got blown to rags. Sniper overwatch and we were gathering everything in realtime.

We had graphics of how they were laid out and how we took them out, mostly by going through buildings.

Of course, we were also showing the Caliphate how we were coming, but I didn't really care.

We were picking up lots of video of some horrific stuff that we weren't showing. That was for the last segment.

The last day we did start out before dawn. I took the Bandits, the Scouts and the Mongrels on a sweep to the east.

While the main force of the battalion, and most of the media, were concentrating on the main fighting, we swept around in our standard flanking maneuver. There were defenders in that area but they weren't numerous. Also IEDs but we had those licked.

We breached their final defenses and shoved, hard, for the central command post.

Why?

Hostages.

The "Caliph" had gathered many of the "dhimi" (cover that in a bit) as well as *all* of his slaves around him. Well, most of them were packed into the roads that the battalion was slowly and with much noise and commotion grinding forward on.

They were forced to stay in place with chains on their legs as well as guards behind them with machine guns.

We swept in behind them. And we got the guys with machine guns, mostly, before they could open fire. At which point I told the battalion to speed the fuck up and watch out for civilians. And handle casualties.

The "Caliph" had taken refuge in a former library that was, for the time being, the most palacious building he could find. It was, he considered, heavily defended. And he, again, had hostages.

I had the Mongrels take out the forward defenses and then the Bandits unloaded and started raising all kinds of hell.

Our intel was that his "throne room" was in an upper lobby. I had Third Herd assault the front while the rest of us went around the side and up the fire stairs.

The "Caliph" was on his "throne" (a canopy bed) surrounded by his harem, not one of which was over sixteen. He had his "martyr guards" oriented to take Third under fire.

When we came out of the stacks, everybody was looking towards the main stairs.

Second Platoon lit them up. They want their 72 virgins, we'll make that easy for them.

Which left the caliph surrounded by terrified teenage girls and holding a naked ten-year-old up as a human shield.

I was a commander. I didn't shoot people if I could avoid it. That's what snipers are for.

I had Second's sniper shoot him in the elbow. It was nice and exposed.

Then I shot him.

And, yes, he appeared unarmed. But I couldn't be sure. He was still moving and thus "a potential threat to myself and non-combatants."

So I shot him *several* times. Some of the shots at point blank range.

Sue me.

That night we broadcast "Chains."

Two hours, by previous negotiation, it laid out what had really been happening in the "kindly" Islamic Caliphate of the 9/11 Martyrs.

Mullah Ali had established true Shariah. There were three classes of people. The Muslims, "dhimi" and slaves. Dhimi were any people who refused to renounce Christianity or Judaism but were able to successfully contribute to the Caliphate's brutal "tax regime."

If you could not contribute, you were made into a slave. Sometimes. Actually, what usually happened was that you sold a member of your family. Usually a pretty daughter; they brought the most money. Or you'd lose your business and eventually become a slave.

It was, in fact, very much on the normal lines of a caliphate.

The only added fillip is that each week every dhimi household was paraded before the "faithful" and forced to undergo a ritual auto de fe in which they were at first threatened with death and then "reprieved" if they paid their taxes.

Dhimi females were, by law, not to be veiled. They had to wear the "hijab," the headscarf, which is a sign of ownership by the way, but they could not wear veils.

At the weekly auto de fe, females ranging as young as ten were pulled out of the dhimi households and "used" for the pleasure of the caliph and his "generals."

Sometimes they were used publicly while the parents and husbands were forced to watch.

Rape is a method of control. It is an exercise in naked power. It was used as such to ensure that things in the Caliphate were "peaceful" and "ordered."

Then there were the slaves. The slaves were dhimi who could not pay their taxes. They did the majority of the labor on building the mosque, as well as the combat emplacements. Chained in long lines, the shackles on their legs were muffler clamps mostly, they were as ragged and emaciated as death camp survivors.

Given all that, you'd think that anyone would want to become a Muslim, right?

Only "persons of color" were permitted to "submit to Allah."

Like I said, he'd have made MLK a racist.

The news media, by the day of the final assault, was trying to change its tune. Why?

People had stopped watching anything but *The New Centurions*. They knew they would get their news as facts, not spin. Not a picture of something and a whining bitch talking about how soldiers, who were incredibly well regarded by then, had been killing innocent women and children but what was *actually* happening.

There's no point in watching a 24-hour news cycle if all the "news" is wrong.

People were turning off TVs until *Centurions* came on.

By day four, the news media was getting the hint. It was taking a clue-bat, but they knew that whatever they showed that night, we were going to deconstruct and destroy them with.

"Chains," we actually had a hard time. But CNN could be counted on to toe the party line and they had a shot of dead women and children lying in a roadway.

They'd been chained up to stop our advance. They couldn't run and they couldn't hide. They were shot in the back by "soldiers" of the Caliphate when Farmer's Freaks breached the perimeter. And the "soldiers" died seconds later, courtesy of two fast acting TCs and the World War One era Ma Deuce, thereby saving hundreds of lives.

CNN showed the bodies, from the hips up.

They didn't show the *chains*.

They didn't show the sobbing men, women and children being released from them by soldiers of the United States Army.

They didn't show the women screaming at us, "WHAT *TOOK* YOU SO LONG?"

(Actually, they showed the angry mob, they just did a voice-over that cut out what they were angry about. We deconstructed *that* one, too.)

We deconstructed piece after piece that showed the Army and the Carson administration in the worst possible light. We talked about what the Koran really said, how it could be interpreted and how the "Caliph" had perverted even *that* perverse document. (Don't like my take? Go read Surahs Eight and Nine. Skip One. It's superceded by Mohammed's own directives in Surah Six.)

We found "moderate" Islamics, real ones that were immigrants and had been good Islamics their whole lives, and got interviews about their anger at what had been done. The one imam from Iraq who was crying and apologizing over and over again was particularly good, I thought.

By the next day, the news media was effectively broken. They were interviewing survivors and even CBS and CNN reporters were getting a bit testy at what had been allowed to happen.

"That this travesty could be permitted in America at even the worst of times says something about the previous administration. And the news media has to share a portion of the blame."

CBS evening news, President of CBS News, Day Five.

By then, units were going into all the "contested" cities and finding similar horror stories. None as bad as the "Caliphate" that had been held up as "enlightened" but very fucking bad in their own way.

Then came "Trust."

That was all me. I'd actually built most of it from footage going back to the very beginning of the Plague. It was, in parts, very dry. It's not anyone's favorite and perhaps I should have quit on a high note. But I wanted my swan-song to be *my* song.

I talked about trust. I talked about societal trust, when it worked and when it didn't. I talked about assimilation, the "melting pot" concept vs. "multiculturalism," the "salad" concept. I talked about studies of societal trust. I pulled in shots from *The Gangs of New York,* talking about how "multicultural" it had once been when Italians and Irish and "American" Americans couldn't talk to each other and didn't trust each other and therefore killed each other in such droves that the Army had, way back then, had to do a "Detroit" on New York City itself. And now one group had great food and the other great beer and it was otherwise hard to tell them apart.

I talked about how Swedes and Norwegians, two cultures as white-bread as you can find, had once battled even here in the U.S. over differences brought to our shores.

"If we sunder ourselves internally, if we accept the false divisions, then we bring with those false divisions all their ills, all their blood of centuries. Where then, can we find trust? If we cannot see the difference between the evil that stands here before us with blood-soaked hands and what we are told is the evil we do in bringing peace and plenty to foreign shores, where then is the trust? If we cannot remember who we are, if we cannot comprehend what it means to be this shining light on the hill, this country of wonder and riches, this . . . America, then we shall surely slip into the long dark night that the enemies of our freedoms so richly desire.

"We are told, always, that there is no black and white. That there are only shades of gray. This is a picture that is held up to us. But it is only a picture and it is false. Each day, each of us makes countless choices, and each of these choices is black and white. If we choose, over and over again, as we have for so long, to choose the black choices because they are easier, to choose 'me' over 'us,' to choose division and strife over assimilation and trust, then we slowly slip into that black night.

"I do not so choose. I am your Centurion. This America Shall Not Fall!"